Also by Peter Caulfield (as Peter Facer)
Available from Amazon worldwide.

LEGITIMATE TARGETS
Pc Jake Sullivan's world just got turned upside-down

ASCENSION DAY
Pc Sullivan's world just got darker

THE TROJAN CODE
Pc Sullivan's world just took a deadly turn.

~~~~~~~~~~~~~~~~~~

Cover Design by Peter Caulfield.

Flame effect graphic created by macrovector at www.freepik.com

The back cover graphic of Catherine on horseback is adapted
From "Warrior" graphic, courtesy of freeimages.com

Sword and dagger graphics courtesy of Dreamstime.com

ISBN: 9798798865949

Catherine

Blood & Fire

Peter Caulfield

With thanks to Mary Jackson, for her input,
to my wife, Jan and all my family and friends
who supported me during the writing of this novel

Peter Caulfield has been writing novels for around fifteen years. As Peter Facer, he has published a trilogy of adrenalin-fueled crime thrillers, known collectively as the Jake Sullivan Novels in which an ordinary village 'Bobby' is thrown into high-octane, rollercoaster adventures. As one reviewer said, "Think of them as Dixon of Dock Green crossed with Jack Reacher."

This new historical time-slip novel is a clear departure from his Jake Sullivan stories, hence writing under his own name. Peter explains, "Quite often, fans of a writer won't accept a change of genre, so I want to keep Peter Facer's novel completely separate."

Peter is married with three children and five grandchildren. He lives with his wife in north Essex

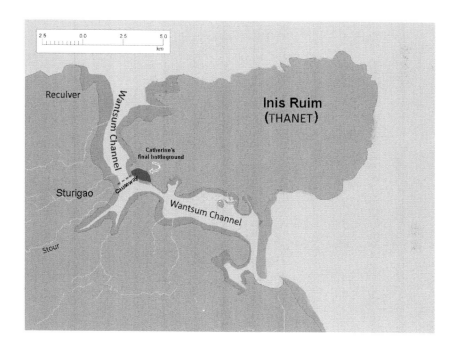

CHAPTER 1 – 452 AD
Meitheamh (June)

The point of the dagger hovered a hair's breadth above the artery pulsing in her neck. She pushed up with all her might against the hand of the man straddling her but the blade didn't budge.

"No, no, NO!" she spat through gritted teeth as she writhed and twisted to get away from the lethal shard of steel.

He leered down at her again, exposing his broken yellow teeth. "You – are – going - to – die." he panted as he pressed down, determined to end her life.

"NO!" she spat again and her eyes flared the brightest blue.

The man quickly looked away. "No magic can save you now," he grunted as he leaned on the dagger as hard as he could. Her strength was ebbing fast. She saw visions of her mother, she saw her father too and her beloved Vortiger, and then, as the man fell upon her with all his weight, her strength finally gave out.

"Yessss," he hissed as he felt the blade pierce her skin.

She felt the sting of the cold steel as it sliced deeply into her neck and as the blade sank through her flesh it severed a thin leather cord around her throat and a silver Celtic knot fell into the river mud which swallowed it greedily. Her eyes opened wide in terror, "Hengist... no…"

A wide arc of blood spurted from a severed artery and quickly pooled across the slimy brown mud that covered them both.

He leered again, his face now inches from hers; she could taste his foul breath. "Yes Catherine," he snarled, "Yes… at last."

Catherine tried to speak again but the knife had severed her

1

windpipe. She could feel her life drifting away as her vision faded. She had to offer a prayer to her gods before it was too late. She had to ease her passage to the afterlife; she had to. She…just…had…to…

Hengist rolled off and pulled himself onto all fours. He was panting hard; it had been quite a battle. She was a fierce fighter and there had been times when he truly feared he wouldn't survive this final encounter.

A nervous whinny came from the riverbank. Until now his horse had been standing dolefully grazing on sparse clumps of samphire. Now it pawed the ground; its head up, ears back and its eyes staring wildly as the metallic stench of freshly spilled blood assailed its nostrils.

Hengist pulled his dagger from Catherine's neck and then prised her dagger from her dead fingers. It was beautifully made with an intricately carved hilt and finely honed blade. "So this is Fire-Sting."

He climbed unsteadily to his feet and stood waveringly as he weighed the two daggers in his hands. He managed a weak smile and threw his own into the mud before he looked back at the body lying at his feet.

The greatest priestess that the tribes of the Southlands had ever known now lay dead and drained of blood in the stinking river mud. Without her strength and rallying cry, there would be no more resistance from her loyal tribes. He dragged her ornate sword, Blood-Taker from the mud. Now it was time for him and his brother Horsa to turn their attention to those that had harboured and aided her over the past few months. Hers would not be the last blood spilled before this week was done.

CHAPTER 2 - The present day.
Isle of Thanet, Kent.

Antoinette Deselle clambered out of the water-filled trench in the back field of the Riverside Primary School in Kent.

"What now, Walter?"

A short podgy man was hailing her. Antoinette smiled at the sight of him; his trousers were too short and his belt was cinched so tightly that his large belly wobbled fluidly over the top. A mop of unruly ginger hair flopped up and down as he trotted across the field towards her. He thrust a newspaper into the Frenchwoman's hand. "It's made the press."

"Oh you're joking!" She unfolded the paper with a snap and glared at the headline. *HENGIST AND HORSA LIVED! New archaeological dig suggests our most notorious Saxon warriors really existed.* "That's just great!" Her French accent, normally soft and lyrical, was much sharper than usual. If there was one thing this renowned 50 year-old professor of archaeology hated above all else, it was publicity about her work. Worse than that, the school had put a strict embargo on any publicity, in exchange for permission to excavate the site during the school holidays. The governors feared it might attract hordes of treasure hunters who would continue digging up their precious sports field long after the archaeologists had left.

She stood and read the article in full, her brows knitted above her angry green eyes. Her grey hair, devoid of most of its blonde rinse, was scrunched up into a hairband. Several rogue wisps had pulled free and were annoyingly blowing in her eyes. Every time she pulled them away, her fingers left fresh muddy smudges on her face. Typically though, no matter how dirty and dishevelled she got, Antoinette's Parisian elegance and vivaciousness shone through, much to the envy of the other women on the dig. She finished reading and turned back to the trench, "Charley!"

Kneeling in thick, sticky sludge, Charlotte Chandler-Price had just sliced another thin wafer of mud from the side of the trench wall. "Coming."

She withdrew her trowel and stepped out of the ditch. For a second or two, the slice clung determinedly to the edge before it succumbed to gravity and slowly peeled itself away and plopped into the brown mud below. Something protruded from the face by the tiniest fraction and glinted in the muted early morning sunlight - something that had been waiting fifteen hundred years to be discovered.

Charley nodded at Walter and took the paper that Antoinette held out to her. At 28 years old she was considered to be a mature student, which rankled with her, especially as she looked a lot younger than her years. Even the chipped and peeling mirror in the dormitory tent couldn't help but reflect her flawless skin, strong cheekbones and mass of tousled dark brown hair. At 5'9" and nicely proportioned, even Walter Smith, who was generally unappreciative about everything, had to admit to himself that she looked good, even in mud-soaked overalls.

Charley was one of a number of students at the site who regularly volunteered for field-work to improve and sharpen their skills and she had proven herself to be an exceptional archaeologist, something that had not gone unnoticed by her professors and Mlle. Deselle in particular. Unofficially, Charlotte was there as her protégé.

She read the headline. "Oh what? Oh this is terrible. We're going get all sorts of rubber-neckers now. Where on earth did they get this information?"

Walter Smith scowled angrily at Antoinette. "You have archaeologists and several students working this dig, not to mention two technicians, a digger driver, a local historian and an archivist. It's hardly surprising it's got out."

Antoinette stepped forward and poked his big flabby stomach with her finger, "I can vouch for my students just as I can for the rest of the team. Most of these people have worked with me on many, many excavations and I trust them completely. In fact, Walter, the only people I do not trust, are you and your fellows from the British Museum, so drop that accusatory tone."

Walter looked aghast and stepped back, out of poking range, "What? I... how dare you."

Antoinette's Deselle's demeanour relaxed instantly and she laughed, "Oh come on mon cher ami, I have no doubt you have been wanting us to go public about this dig from the outset. You are desperate to appease the NAS Grant Committee and let the world see how they made our wonderful discoveries possible, yes?"

"It's true that the National Archaeological Society is watching this dig with particular interest Ms Deselle, but as far as I'm aware you've not actually made any wonderful discoveries.

Antoinette laughed again, "All in good time, Walter, all in good time. C'mon, let's discuss this over le petit déjeuner"

"What?"

"Breakfast, Walter. Come on."

She turned towards a tatty-looking marquee and beckoned Charley to follow but Walter caught her sleeve. "I am not discussing anything in front of your students, Miss Deselle."

Antoinette's vivid green eyes flashed angrily as she peeled his fingers from her fleece, "Charley isn't just one of my students, Walter. You know her background, yes? She completed her Bachelor's degree with the highest of plaudits from her professors, myself included; she is now working on her masters *and*, if you remember, it is predicted she will achieve a doctorate in record time. I - *we*, are very lucky to have her on this dig. Now come on." She set off across the field, her arm linked with Charley's. Walter Smith sighed and trotted after them and when he caught up he couldn't resist trying to start another argument.

"I still say it was a mistake to hire you, Miss Chandler-Price," he panted, "fresh out of university, little or no field experience. What were you studying before this, languages wasn't it? It strikes me you don't stay grounded for very long before you lose interest."

Charlotte glanced back at him, "I'll ground *you* in a moment you old twat," she muttered

"Shh!" scolded Antoinette.

"What was that," Walter cried indignantly, "I didn't quite catch…?"

"I said, I've had plenty of field experience thank you Mr Smith. I doubt Professor Deselle would have invited me along if she thought I'd be a liability."

They passed-by the two dormitory tents and entered the big marquee. Smith stopped and looked about him. He was tempted to head straight to the rest area and plonk himself in one of the camping chairs, but the smell of coffee from the kitchen/dining area was just too appealing. He looked over at the section of the marquee used as the dig's HQ; where artefacts were collated and the daily excavation plans were drawn-up. "How much is all this costing I wonder?" he grumped.

Antoinette rolled her eyes. "A lot less than staying in hotels, Walter,"

In the dining area one of the students was on breakfast duty. In front of him was a not-so-healthy supply of fried food. Charlotte grabbed a freshly washed tray from the stack and helped herself to a plateful of fried egg, bacon, beans and toast and sat herself down at the nearest table. Antoinette took the seat next to her, and Walter shuffled over and flopped down opposite. Charlotte stared at his tray in astonishment.

"Are not feeling well, Mr Smith? I thought a man like you would be eating double rations. Are you sure that mug of coffee will see you though to lunchtime?"

"A man like me? Are you suggesting I'm fat?"

Antoinette kicked Charley's ankle, "I'm sure she meant nothing of the sort, Walter."

Smith looked thoughtful. "Hmm. Well as it happens, I've got no appetite; not today."

The women chose to ignore the man's overt invitation to ask what was wrong. They knew that once you opened that particular sluice gate, you would be quickly drowning in a torrent of self-pity and depression. No doubt his boss, Rosemary Forrester, had been giving him a hard time again.

Charley filled her fork with bacon and was about to put it to her mouth, when she stopped and turned to her Professor. "Are you worried about that local rag?"

Antoinette nodded, "It will reach the Nationals." She looked pained. "It's bound to. We've only got these few weeks of school holidays to complete the dig and any disruption to our routine will be disastrous."

"I would have loved to have seen the faces of the children when they were digging that hole for their time capsule and unearthed a Saxon dagger." Her bright green eyes flashed mischievously, "I wonder what it would fetch on the open market." She stuffed the forkful of breakfast in her mouth and tried not to laugh.

Smith spluttered, spraying coffee onto his lap. "You cannot be serious…." The promised tirade died quickly when he realised she was teasing him. "Very funny."

"I thought so."

Smith tapped the table, "All joking aside, you don't seem to be getting very much done."

Charley glared at him. "We haven't done as well as we'd hoped, for sure. Trench one, where the Professor and I are working, has only given-up the original dagger but…'

'But, Walter, we have found a few artefacts in trenches three and four," offered Antoinette, soothingly.

Smith stared glumly into his coffee, "Such as?"

"Such as weapon fragments, some clothing toggles made from horn and some pottery; all of it, as far as we can tell, Saxon."

He continued to look miserably at his coffee mug. "But why do you think this dig will prove that Hengist and Horsa really

7

existed?"

"Hengist and Horsa are not the point!" jumped in Charley. "The Saxons landing here in Thanet is stuff of legends. Until those children found that dagger, there had been no finds anywhere in the county to suggest any early Saxon occupation..."

"Charlotte's quite right," interrupted Antoinette. "East Anglia or Northumbria had always seemed much more probable as landing sites and we know that Maldon in Essex has quite an enviable Viking history; but now, for the first time, we have possible proof that Saxons were here in Kent from the start of their occupation."

Smith looked up. "So how do you account for Kentish towns having names that derived from Anglo-Saxon?"

"Walter, I'm not saying the Saxons never occupied Kent, of course they did, but Anglo-Saxons came later; the product of inter-racial unions between Britons and Saxons, Jutes and Angles." Antoinette looked over to the artefacts table. "That dagger is Saxon, but it predates the Anglo-Saxon period."

Walter sat back in the cheap plastic chair, which complained by creaking loudly, "So by virtue of that, Hengist and Horsa could have existed."

Antoinette raised her eyes to the heavens. "Let's not get ahead of ourselves Walter. We're not here to hunt-down proof of those two brothers; we're simply trying to establish whether that dagger and the other artefacts are part of a Saxon settlement."

"But if they are definitely Saxon, what else could it mean?" he protested.

Charley shook her head. "Mr Smith, it's possible that artefacts were actually in the hands of ancient Britons, maybe the spoils of some plunder or other; they could simply have been discarded or dropped in the river."

Smith looked incredulous, "You mean that small river beyond the school grounds?"

"Yes," Charlotte replied. "It's a tributary of the River Stour."

"Yes I know that but it's a good hundred yards away!"

Antoinette reached into her bag and pulled out an Ordinance Survey map which she spread on the table.

"In the fifth Century, the Isle of Thanet was an actual island. There was a wide estuary where the Stour curved inland. It was known as the Wantsum Channel. Over the centuries it silted-up until it was impassable by ships and Thanet effectively merged with the mainland. That little stream, and many like it, is probably all that is left." She traced the route of the stream with her finger. "I think this is part of the old channel and trenches one and two are in the old river estuary."

Smith studied the map and then looked at the coconut matting on the floor, "So you're suggesting this whole area could have been under water? How can you tell?"

"The type of mud, animal remains, vegetation remains, silt deposits etc. Trench one is totally different to trenches three and four. They all indicate that this was a water course."

"So what are you hoping to find, a big boat?" Smith guffawed and stole a slice of Charlotte's toast.

She shot him a look, "Do that again Mr Smith and I'll stab your hand with my fork."

Antoinette winked, "She means it; you can't steal a girl's toast and get away with it."

Smith took a bite and tossed the slice back onto Charley's plate. "Here, you can have it, if it's that important to you." He scraped back his chair and hauled himself to his feet, "I'm returning to London to see if I can keep the Press at bay. I suggest you step-up the pace a bit and start finding something to justify this charade."

As he shambled-off, Charley removed the slice of toast from her plate with a grimace and glared at him, "Go fuck yourself."

He stopped instantly and spun around, "What did you say?"

Antoinette grinned back at him, "She said good luck, Mr Smith."

He knew exactly what she'd said, but he wasn't about to make a scene. Instead he just glared at her and left without another word.

Antoinette waited for him to leave the marquee before

remonstrating with her protégé. "You must learn to hold your tongue Charley. We cannot afford to upset him, however odious he is. If the NAS pulls our funding, the dig will stop."

Charlotte mopped-up the last of her beans, "I'm sorry, he just..."

It wasn't necessary for her to finish the sentence; Antoinette Deselle felt exactly the same.

CHAPTER 3

"Oh bugger"

"You have a problem?" Antoinette looked into Charley's trench.

"A whole wodge of the trench wall has just fallen into the mud. Would you pass me that spade please?"

Antoinette handed her a stubby spade. "Be careful. It will be very easy to lose small artefacts in that mud."

She nodded, "I've got my sieve."

Satisfied, Antoinette set off to monitor the work in the other trenches, leaving Charley scooping mud into the sieve. She decided to abandon the spade and get her hands dirty instead. She pushed her fingers into the cloying sludge and her fingertips fleetingly touched something cold and hard. "What's this?" Her fingers probed deeper into the mud and briefly touched the object again before it slipped away. She felt about again and this time her fingers closed around it. "Got you!"

Charley pulled the object clear and wiped it on her overalls. "It's a brooch!" She clambered from the trench and crawled on all fours to a nearby bucket and dropped the artefact into the clear, purified water. She gave it a swirl and pulled it out again.

"Holy shit, it's perfect." Charlotte's hand started to tremble as she looked down at the shiny, intricate Celtic brooch in her open hand. It was possibly the finest example of ancient Brittonic silverwork, she'd ever seen. It was circular - about two inches in diameter and consisted of two distinct parts: a beautiful raised centerpiece, probably an inch across, consisting of a solid silver ring containing an intricate pattern of intertwined knots, set upon a larger, flatter pattern of knots.

Charley was suddenly aware that her hand was tingling. The sensation quickly became full-blown pins and needles and she dropped the brooch onto the grass. "Ow, ow, ow." She shook her hand to ease the sensation and it dissipated almost immediately.

Her mind was racing; she knew she should call Antoinette over to see it. She knew it, but somehow, she couldn't bring herself to attract her attention… not just yet anyway. Charley wanted to be up-close-and-personal with the brooch a little longer, before it was taken away and bagged-up.

With a quick glance at Antoinette, who was still at another trench, Charley removed her neck chain and poked an end through one of the knots and then fastened it around her neck again. With one more glance over at Antoinette, she tucked the brooch out of sight, into her shirt.

The moment the pendant touched her skin she felt a fierce attack of pins and needles spread across her chest, "What the hell…?" She reached inside her shirt to pull it out, but before her fingers could close around it she felt a massive jolt. It felt like being hit with a sandbag. The force of the impact bent her double where she knelt. She clutched her chest; it felt as if it were being crushed. Wild thoughts careered around her brain, "What's happening? Is this a heart attack?"

She tried to get to her knees, she had to call for help but another jolt toppled her back into the trench. She tried again to stand but was hit by a third jolt and that time, everything went black and she fell into the mud, face-first and unconscious

oOo

As Charley came round she was aware that she was still lying in the mud, but now there was a chill breeze blowing across her back. She felt cold, wet and extremely uncomfortable. Her memory was hazy; had she been taken ill or maybe been in an accident? She lay still and kept her eyes tightly closed, in case anything hurt.

"Shit, I can't breathe properly." Her hand flew to her nose and mouth and found a thick layer of mud had covered her face and clogged her nostrils; She scooped the mud clear and then slowly lifted her head - just enough to aid her breathing. She relaxed a fraction. "OK, so I'm not hurt; that's good." She turned her head to one side, opened her eyes…. and screamed!

CHAPTER 4 - 452AD
Eanáir (January)

Charley was lying in the mud, face-to-face with another woman and staring straight into her bright blue pleading eyes. She screamed again and pushed herself away. There was a ragged slit in the woman's neck and the mud all around was grotesquely mixed with the blood that still gently pumped from the wound.

"Holy shit, what's happened to you?" She looked around for help and to her astonishment, she saw that they weren't laying in her trench, but on the mud flats of a river. She slid around in the mud to get her bearings. Behind her was the furthest river bank, about twenty yards away. She scanned it, looking for something – anything that was familiar – the school buildings maybe - but it was all open fields and woodlands.

"What the hell's going on? Where's the school?" A noise made her spin around to look at the nearer riverbank. There was a man clambering out of the mud and struggling through the reeds towards a horse.

"Hey!" she shouted, but the man didn't seem to hear. "Hey, I need some help here!" *Why is he ignoring me?* She was just about to shout again when she realised he must have been the person who had attacked the woman.

Instinctively she pressed herself back into the mud, fearful that if he saw her, he would come back and kill her too; he wouldn't want any witnesses who could alert the police. *Police.* She pulled her phone from her back pocket. No signal. She was trapped. What to do now? She couldn't just let this woman die, but if that man saw her moving about, she could be as good as dead herself. Her

13

teeth were chattering. "Jesus I'm so cold."

Charley looked at the woman. She was still alive – just, and mouthing something. "What are you trying to say? Why did he do this?" she whispered.

The woman was all but dead. The blood flow was weakening by the second and Charlotte knew that she couldn't be saved; not without an immediate blood transfusion... and still the woman mouthed something...

She steeled herself and slowly crawled back through the blood-red mud to the woman's side, praying that the man on the bank wouldn't see the movement.

"What is it? What are you trying to say?" With an involuntary shudder of revulsion, she put her ear close to the dying woman's lips. Whatever she was saying, it was virtually inaudible. She had no breath left to speak, but still the mouth moved. Charlotte plugged her other ear with a finger and moved so closely that her free ear actually touched the woman's mouth. "What are you saying to me?" she pleaded.

This time when the lips shaped the word, her last breath completed the task, "Hengist," she whispered.

"What?" Charlotte snapped her head up to look at her. "Did you say Hengist?"

The woman said nothing more. Her mouth had now stopped moving, her lungs were as empty of air, as her veins were of blood. Her lifeless blue eyes now stared fixedly ahead.

Charley glanced up at the river bank again and saw the man was now on his horse. Now she could see him more clearly and she was determined to get a good description for the police, but she frowned. He was wearing a knee-length cloak held with a brooch. Beneath the cloak was a bright red tunic of linen and on his legs he wore leggings, bound with strips of cloth. He reached behind and produced a conical helmet from a saddle pack. "Jesus Christ, he's dressed as a friggin' Saxon."

As he pulled his horse away from the river, his long, dank hair flowed out from beneath the steel helmet and Charley let out a

14

gasp - About twenty yards inland, a bank of early morning mist slowly rolled away from the river, and through the haze she could see glimpses of more riders. Within seconds the mist had revealed an army of several hundred men on horseback and all dressed as Saxons.

The man raised an ornate dagger to the sky and let out a chilling scream of victory as he kicked his horse into a canter towards his men. A huge cheer went up and as he reached them they all turned and disappeared into what was left of the mist. Charley only just managed to stifle another scream before she blacked-out again.

CHAPTER 5

When Charley opened her eyes, she found herself lying on her camp bed in the dormitory tent. Antoinette was sitting quietly next to her.

"Ahh ma cher, you are awake. How do you feel?"

She sat up slowly. "Erm, I'm ok I think. What happened?"

"We don't really know. We found you unconscious in the trench about fifteen minutes ago. Richard carried you in. We are waiting for the local doctor to arrive."

"Really? I don't think I need a doctor. I feel fine; a bit disorientated, but I'm fine, honestly."

"I'm not so sure. Have you seen the state you're in?"

Charley looked down at her clothes, soaking wet and muddy, "That's another trip I'll have to take to the launderette."

Antoinette frowned, "You are a muddy mess for sure, but there's something wrong with the mud; it's too red."

"Too red? What do you mean?"

The professor pointed at Charley's arm, caked in dried red mud "Red soil is one that's rich in iron oxide…"

"Yes, and deficient in nitrogen and lime."

Antoinette looked through the tent window. "There's no iron oxide in the soil around here."

Charley squinted at her arm. "Nor should there be; it's normally found in warm, temperate, wet climates. It doesn't make sense."

"It is bizarre. You were working in a normal trench, oozing good old-fashioned British mud and now here you are, caked in mud that couldn't have come from that trench. It looks almost like mud mixed with blood…" She broke-off suddenly, a look of

16

intense concern on her face, "you're not injured are you?"

Charley began to laugh, "No, I'm fine, honestly." But then something spiked her memory - something to do with the Saxons. She tried to pull it forward, but the detail was just out of her grasp. "I think I had a dream of some sort."

Antoinette raised a finely-shaped eyebrow, "Really? You can remember that?"

She nodded and tried to pull the memory into focus, "Something about the Saxons, but it's all so hazy."

"It's hardly surprising that you should dream about Saxons, given our project here." She saw a look of bewilderment across Charley's face and decided to change the subject. "Look, don't worry about it now, you've obviously had some sort of episode and need to be medically checked-out; I'm sure the doctor will be here soon, perhaps I should go and check."

Charley shook her head. "No, I think what I want most is to get out of these cold, wet clothes and into a nice hot steaming shower. Did you say Richard was on site?"

Antoinette looked at her reproachfully, "Yes he is, but we have a perfectly adequate camping shower."

Charley shuddered, "A cold trickle in a cold tent? I don't think so. I need something a bit more than that."

"Charley, you know Richard quite likes you; don't take advantage of him."

"How can I be taking advantage? Look at the state of me; I'm hardly dressed for seduction." She giggled mischievously as Antoinette shook her head disapprovingly. "Anyway, Antoinette, I think that under the circumstances, asking the school caretaker for the use of his bathroom is quite acceptable, don't you?"

"Ok, ok, "Just don't lead him on."

As Charley swung her legs down to the floor, Antoinette suddenly leant forward. "What is this?" She pulled Charlotte's matted hair away from her face. "Bon Dieu, What's happened here?"

"What?"

"You *are* injured. When you've had your shower we must take care of that wound; you have blood all over your ear and down your cheek."

oOo

Charley stood under the hot spray. Her hair was clean and all traces of mud had been washed from her body, but instead of feeling refreshed, she felt lost. Mingled with the clean water that cascaded down her face, were tears that started when she looked into the mirror and which hadn't stopped since.

Before she had stepped into the cubicle, Charley had hung the chain and brooch on the towel rail and then looked in Richard's shaving mirror to examine her injured ear. She wiped the blood way with a wet flannel and was immediately puzzled. There was no injury. Whatever had left its bloody mark was not a cut or graze. "It's not my blood." The realisation was as shocking as it was puzzling. She stepped back from the mirror. "If not my blood, then whose?"

Then she remembered. She remembered a dying woman in the mud – She saw herself pressing her ear to the woman's bloodied mouth, and then came the name - whispered so quietly, it could have been the ghost of a memory; so light that it could have been blown away by the faintest breath of air:

"Hengist."

The images in her mind rushed and swirled and she felt dizzy and sick. She grabbed hold of the wash basin to steady herself and shook her head to shake the visions from her mind. She stood, swaying; her breathing heavy and laboured. Her heart raced, her temples pounded and tears filled her eyes. "Ok girl," she said aloud, "calm down. It was all a dream right?" She choked-back a sob, "How can it have been a dream? I was covered in that woman's blood. I had blood on me, but I wasn't injured."

Dream or not, Charley was convinced she'd seen Hengist riding off and it was Hengist who killed the woman.

Something was nagging at her memory though; she'd missed something, some vital fact so she closed her eyes and tried to

18

visualise the scene…and there it was. "Oh my Lord," she gasped. She could see the river again; she could see the woman lying there, dying; she could see the Saxon warrior riding away with his army and, for the first time, she could see a dagger lying in the mud, just a few feet from the woman's body – A dagger about nine inches long with a short handle and a stubby finger guard; a dagger that appeared to be similar to the one a class of 6 year old children had found under their school playing field.

She could see a half inch nick in the blade, about four inches from the tip. "It's not just similar," she whispered to herself, "It's the same one. It's the dagger of Hengist, legendary leader of the fabled Saxon hordes." She blinked back her tears and opened the shower door and stepped into the hot spray.

CHAPTER 6

Richard was making two mugs of tea but stopped mid-pour as Charley entered the kitchen. There was bewilderment in her eyes.

"What on earth have you been up to?" He replaced the teapot on its heat mat and pulled a chair from under his old rickety melamine table. "Here, sit down. Are you alright?"

Charley sat down and dropped her carrier bag of muddy clothing on the floor. She felt refreshed after her shower and change of clothes, but she also felt a little frightened and confused. Richard would want to know what had happened, but she just wasn't sure how much she should tell him. "I'm fine."

Richard finished pouring the tea and plonked a mug in front of her. She looked up gratefully and smiled. She had only known him a couple of weeks, but felt comfortable around him. She studied him appreciatively. He was taller than her by about four inches and nicely proportioned and muscular. She liked that. Dark brown, wavy hair and hazel eyes completed a very nice package that Charley would be happy to look at for hours, given the chance.

He returned the smile, "You're clearly not fine; what happened to you out there?" He scraped-out a chair from the end of the table and sat down with his tea. "I find you unconscious in your trench and then you turn up at my door, tears in your eyes, caked in mud and blood, asking to use my shower. You still look distressed."

Charley didn't know how to respond. She wasn't sure she was ready to share about the brooch and she hated the thought of him taking the piss if she tried to explain what had happened. Come to think of it, she wasn't even sure she knew what happened – not properly. Was it a time-jump? Was it a dream? Was it a vision?

20

Richard saw the look of confusion that flickered across Charley's eyes as her brows knitted, "Tell me. Maybe I can help in some way; even if it's just by listening."

She glanced up at him and wondered if she could trust him. "It sounds so stupid, Richard."

He reached out and took her hand. She tensed; it was the first time there had been any physical contact between them. Richard sensed her body stiffen and pulled his hand away. "I'm sorry, I didn't mean anything untoward."

She smiled disarmingly and reached out for his hand again, "It's ok. It's nice that you care." She pulled his hand onto the table and interlocked her fingers with his. "What happened to me today was probably just some sort of seizure that caused a hallucination or something."

"Seizure?" Concern flashed across his face. "Have you been checked-out by a doctor?"

"Like I said, Richard, I'm fine. I've got no physical injuries and just a slight headache as a reminder."

He squeezed her hand, "So what was this hallucination?"

And there it was; the question she had dreaded. The problem now was how much to tell him? She decided she needed to know more about this man before she confided in him. "Remember when we first arrived at the school you opened-up the gates for our cavalcade of vehicles?"

"Yes, of course. I noticed you right away."

Charley blushed slightly. "And I noticed you too. I thought you had a disarming smile."

He laughed. "Well it's never been described like that before; more of a leer."

Charley grinned at that. She remembered their first proper conversation, when she noticed him leaning on the metal five bar gate that blocked access between the playground and the field.

A frisson of excitement fluttered through her as she drew near.

"Hello," he'd said with that disarming smile. "I've never seen an archaeological dig before. How's it going?"

Charley remembered the banter. As she stepped lightly onto the bottom rail she said, "Will this take my weight?"

Richard had looked her up and down and snorted derisively, "I expect so; there's nothing of you."

She feigned hurt feelings. "Are you suggesting I'm too skinny? I thought I had a decent figure, thank you very much." As if to emphasise the point, she pulled down the hem of her T-shirt which stretched the fabric tightly over her pert breasts.

Just as she'd planned, Richard was clearly embarrassed, "Oh, I'm sorry, I didn't mean... Er, you look fine... more than fine actually."

Charley giggled, "I'm just teasing. So what is there to do for fun in this one-horse town?"

He hadn't responded immediately, mesmerised by this lively, spirited woman. His previous relationships had all ended badly and he had told himself was 'off women for good.' Unfortunately, he hadn't bargained with Charley's arrival. "Well," he'd said thoughtfully, "there's a pub down the road – The Barleymow. It serves decent cask ale and good food."

"Thanks I accept."

He blinked, nonplussed, "What?"

"I accept your invitation for drinks, and if you're especially nice to me, I'll let you buy me dinner too."

Richard laughed, "Ok, drinks it is, but a meal would make it a date and as we've only just met that would be too presumptuous. Meet you back here at eight."

Before Charley could engage in further banter, he had turned on his heels and headed off to his house near the main gate.

Charley remembered how Antoinette had remonstrated with her. "I hope you've not found a distraction before we've even started."

Charley smiled and her blue eyes twinkled in the sunshine "I think I might have."

oOo

Richard stirred his tea. "Earth to Charley."

22

She dropped her spoon on the table. "I'm sorry. I was miles away."

"Thinking about what?"

"Our 'date' at the Barleymow. I've just realised we know hardly anything about each other."

"Well let's remedy that now. One question each. Your last two dates. Who were they with and what were they like?"

"Blimey, straight for the jugular eh?" She paused. "Ok, the last one was Hamish, a caber-tossing Scot who I met online."

Richard winced. "Please don't tell me you use those dreadful dating sites."

"For my last two dates actually, but never again. As soon as Hamish opened his mouth I found myself totally bewildered. His accent was so thick I couldn't understand a word he said." She looked into her coffee mug. "I'm ashamed to say I made an excuse to visit the toilets and never went back."

Richard laughed. "I can't really blame you; must've been a bit of a one-sided conversation that night."

"Yeah, it was. Then there was Peter Ruskin who claimed to work for MI5. Well that date lasted of all ten minutes. I mean what a prick; as if a woman would fall for that sort of flannel."

Richard raised an eyebrow. "You could have been dating James Bond."

"I sincerely doubt that. Ok, your turn." At that moment, Charley realised she didn't actually want to know about his past girlfriends. "Tell me something else instead. Tell me about *you*."

Richard shrugged, "Not a lot to tell really. I'm not academic like you."

Charley snorted, "Like me? You think I'm academic? Jeez, I'm as thick at two short planks."

"Oh come on. I bet you've got a university education. You're in a highly specialised field after all."

"This is about you, not me. Come on then Mr. Armitage, I'll fire some quick questions at you. No time to think, just answer, OK?"

Richard's eyes narrowed. "OK."

Charley heard caution in his voice and wondered how truthful his answers might be. "How long have you been a caretaker?"

"Just under a year."

"What did you do before?"

This time Richard paused before answering. He could never talk about his past career without seeing images of broken people, both civilian and military, of smouldering homesteads and roadside craters. They would jump into his mind and tumble over and over, each one pushing to the front, competing for attention. The worst image was that of his best friend, shot in the head by a Taliban sniper.

Charley saw the fleeting look of pain, "Are you alright. I'm sorry, I didn't mean to intrude. We were only talking about work."

Richard suddenly smiled and grabbed his empty coffee mug "Refill?" Charley shook her head. He reached for a jar by the kettle and dropped a spoonful of instant coffee into his mug. "The truth is I was in the Royal Marines."

Charley's eyes widened, "Wow. Were you a commando?"

"I was part of 3 Commando Brigade. It was mainly Marines but we also had Royal Engineers and Royal Artillery from the Army, the good old Fleet Air Arm and some RAF flyboys. Good times." He returned to his seat and put his mug on the table. "Mostly."

"Did you go to war? I mean were you in Iraq?"

"And Afghanistan, but if you don't mind, I'd rather not go into detail." He sat quietly for a moment, deep in thought, running his finger around the top of the mug.

"Charley leant across the table and touched his arm, "I understand. We'll keep it loose. So how long were you a commando?"

He laughed. "God, you don't give up do you? I served fifteen years altogether. I joined at nineteen and left about two years ago."

"Do you miss it?"

"I miss the people, but I don't really miss the soldiering."

Charley looked puzzled, "You had to learn how to make electronics too?"

It took a second for Richard to make the connection, "No, you numpty, I said 'soldiering,' not 'soldering.'"

Charley doubled-up with laughter. "Got ya."

"Oh very funny."

Although Charley had resolved not to tell him too much about her background, over the next hour, she found herself drawn into the conversation by his warmth and charm. After the fright she'd had earlier, it was good to feel safe and comfortable.

Richard learned that Charley's father was a Head teacher at a private boarding school and her mother was the Mayoress of Portsmouth; that her favourite colour was blue and that she hates the colour pink. She even told him about her very first boyfriend. All in all, Charley had laid herself open and probably told Richard far too much.

He obviously felt very comfortable in her company too because he also shared something that he normally kept to himself. "I should probably tell you that I suffered quite badly from PTSD after my final return from active service."

"Oh, you poor thing. May I ask how it affected you?"

Richard mulled over his answer for a few seconds. "I'm sorry to say that it left me with a very short fuse. I felt rejected because they wouldn't take me back."

Charley looked concerned. "You would have gone back again, after seeing the horrors of war?"

"Like I said, I miss the people. They were my family, really. I felt very alone and I struggle with rejection now. Like a say, I've a bit of short fuse."

"Did you get any counselling?"

He smiled. "Yes some. I had a fling with my counsellor. Not my best move. It got her suspended."

Charley's face must have been a picture because Richard suddenly burst out laughing. "Got you…again. My counsellor was a lovely old gent called William. Not really my type."

"You bastard. You really had me worried there."

Despite the fact she quite liked him, she had decided there

would be no romance; the revelations about his PTSD worried her a little. Also she was only there short-term and had a career that required total commitment. He was a lovely distraction, but she couldn't allow herself to think beyond that. However, she had decided to trust him with one thing more... her experience earlier that day.

"Richard, I want to tell you what happened to me earlier..." She allowed one of her intertwined fingers to caress his. "...but I'm not sure if I can."

"Try."

"You mustn't repeat it Richard, any of it. Do you understand?"

"Yes Ok."

"Promise me. Promise you won't breathe a word." Her words were urgent, jerky and full of emotion,

A worried frown creased his tanned forehead. "Ok, Charley I promise, just tell me."

"I found an artefact; a beautiful, intricate brooch in perfect condition."

Richard's eyes widened, "Wow, that's good. What did your boss say?"

"I haven't told her."

His brows narrowed, "Oh. Why not?"

Charley ignored the question, "I hung it around my neck, and the next thing I knew I felt a massive thud on my chest, where the brooch was touching me, and I blacked out. When I came round I was face to face with a dying woman." She looked up at him, expecting to see disbelief or derision in his face, but was relieved to see nothing but concern.

"When you say, 'face to face...'"

"I mean I was lying in the mud of the river that used to flow through these grounds, face to face with a woman who was killed by the dagger the kids found here."

"You saw it?"

"I did. And then, *wham,* I was back in my trench, covered in river mud and her blood."

Richard said nothing for a moment or two and Charley gripped his hand tightly, "Say something. Say I'm mad, say I imagined it, but say something." A tear tipped over the edge of her right eye and trickled down her cheek; Richard caught it with his finger.

"Well you're not mad, and you didn't imagine it," he said at last.

Charley looked to see if he was making fun of her, but his face was set and serious, "Why do you say that?"

"I happened, Charley, it must have. How else can you account for the blood? I don't think this was a dream or a vision or hallucination."

"Then what?"

"Sounds like good old fashioned time travel to me."

"Are you taking the piss out of me?"

"No, I'm serious. Something happened. It sounds as if you were really there."

"Then why couldn't Hengist see or hear me?"

Richard frowned, "Who? There was someone else there?"

She nodded, "Yes, I'm sorry I forgot to mention it. The man who killed that woman was Hengist, the Saxon warlord. I watched him clamber out of the river and climb on his horse. I was calling out to him for help before I realised who he was. He didn't hear me, or couldn't hear me. I swear he looked right at me though, but he didn't react."

Richard let go of her hand and took a sip of his coffee. "Well I never professed to be an expert on time travel. You should tell Mademoiselle Deselle."

Charley paused, trying to frame her answer so that Richard would understand her motive for keeping quiet. "It's not about keeping the brooch a secret, I will tell her everything soon, but…" Fresh tears brimmed in her eyes, "I can't tell her yet."

Richard looked disapproving, "I'm no archaeologist, but I watch Time Team. Don't all finds have to be declared and recorded? How can you justify not telling her? What if it goes missing or gets damaged?"

27

"I'm *not* telling her yet," Charley's eyes flashed angrily.

"Give me one good reason why not."

Against her will, she could feel her temper rising. "I think it was the brooch that took me back and I intend to go back again."

He sat back in his chair, dumbfounded. "Are you mad?"

"I need to know more."

"But you can't possibly know where you will end up. The woman is obviously dead, so what do you hope to gain?"

Charley fixed his gaze with hers, "Knowledge. The Dark Ages, Saxon England, they're shrouded in mystery. Few people back then could write, and records are scarce. Maybe I have a chance to go back and see it all first-hand. I need to try, at least." She irritably scratched her left forearm.

"Problem?"

"No just a little eczema. It flares up from time to time. Anyway, don't change the subject."

"I'm not, but if I didn't think you were mad before, I do now. This could be extremely dangerous, Charley – life-threatening even."

"I don't think so. They can't see me, remember. I reckon I'll just be an observer." She was becoming animated and excited, but the look on Richard's face stopped her in her tracks and she glared at him. "You're not thinking of telling Antoinette I hope. You promised not to breathe a word."

"I know I did, but really, Charley, if something like time travel happened to you, then what you're planning is so dangerous."

Charley could feel her temper start to spike. This was *her* adventure and he was trying to discourage her. She didn't want that. She wanted support. She stood up and banged her fist on the old table, "Don't you dare break your word to me. If you do, I'll never speak to you again."

"Then don't do it," he replied quietly.

Charley glared at him and walked angrily to his back door, "I mean it, Richard." She attempted to wrench open the door, but it wouldn't budge.

"It's locked." He allowed himself the briefest of smirks as Charley turned on her heel and strode off to the front door instead. "Charley, I'm only the school caretaker; I'm not getting involved in your dig, but please, don't leave like this; come back and talk."

"Fuck off," was the only response she could think of and she slammed the door behind her.

CHAPTER 7

"Expand the trench Charley, why?" Antoinette Deselle did not look impressed.

"We have to," she pleaded and pointed at the muddy ditch where she had blacked-out. "Just widen it from the point where the dagger was found. If you'll just allow me to widen it by about thirty centimetres…"

"No. We made an undertaking to keep the dig site as small as possible. We have to make this all good again before the next term starts and you haven't given me a reason yet. I say again, why?"

"I… I can't explain, but I know we'll find something."

"Not good enough," the Professor chided. "You must have a reason."

Charley frantically tried to remember the placement of the woman's body in relation to where the dagger was found. "We don't even have to go as deep. I reckon about fifteen inches; that's the depth that the dagger was found."

"Why are you being so insistent Charley? What are you not telling me?"

Charlotte flopped down and sat cross-legged by the trench. "You'll only laugh."

"Try me," Antoinette remained standing, her arms folded and an expression of mild amusement on her face.

"It was my... er... dream; you know, the one I told you about? I saw something and I need to satisfy my curiosity. Please don't ask me explain further, you'll think I've completely lost my marbles. Come on, Professor, please. There is a precedent isn't there? Whenever we find something, evidence of a dwelling for example,

30

we always expand the search area to uncover the shape and size of the building, so why can't I widen this trench?"

"Because you've not found anything, Charley. If I am to sanction this, I need evidence of a find."

Charlotte thought of the brooch, now tucked away in her field rucksack, "But we *do* have a find; a fantastic find."

"You mean the dagger?"

Charlotte was about to correct her and tell her about the brooch after all, but something made her stop. The brooch felt like it was hers and she couldn't bear the thought of being parted from it. The brooch had been the catalyst that had taken her back.

Antoinette looked at Charlotte with concern; her protégé seemed to be suddenly lost in thought, "Charley, is it the dagger, yes?"

Charlotte snapped her thoughts back to the conversation, "Oh, I'm sorry, yes, it's the dagger and I know that if we expand the search area we'll find something else, something amazing."

Antoinette shook her head despairingly. "You know? Ahh yes of course, your dream."

Charlotte looked away. "It was more of a vision and it was just so... real."

Antoinette hunkered down and studied the trench. "You had a vision whilst you were unconscious mon cher ami? I thought you had to be awake to receive a vision."

Charlotte sat on the damp grass next to her mentor and swung her legs into the trench. "I can remember fragments of my dream and they are just so real. If everything I've seen is correct, we should find something within a foot or so of where the dagger was found, but not where we're digging now. We need to widen the trench."

"So what did you see in this dream, or vision?"

Charley faltered. She wasn't ready to share that information yet. It felt personal, private even. "It frightened me, Antoinette, I don't want to go into detail, but I'll explain once I've worked it all out."

Antoinette nodded, "Ok, That's fair enough. I can wait until you're ready.

"Thank you."

"I should tell you that I am a believer of the paranormal and the unexplainable. Did you know that?"

Charley shook her head, "No, you've never mentioned it."

Antoinette scraped a handful of mud from the side of the trench, "I always try to get a spiritual or psychic connection with my digs. I like to feel the lives that passed through the area, so I understand your feeling of connection, but don't get carried away by it; it's not science and it's unreliable.

"But my vision..."

"Who knows? I've never had a vision in my life so I can't comment. I find it suspicious however."

"Suspicious? You think I'm lying?"

"Of course not, but confused maybe?" Antoinette thought for a moment and then came to a decision. "I'm going to give you some latitude."

Charley shielded her eyes from the sun and squinted at her mentor, "So what are you saying?"

"I'm saying, ok. You can widen the trench by thirty centimetres, but just for a one metre length, no more. Keep the depth to thirty centimetres too. In fact I will come and help you later."

Charlotte jumped up, "Thank you Antoinette, I just know it'll be worth it."

"We'll see," she replied as she walked away.

oOo

A strip thirty centimetres wide was marked-out next to the trench and four hours later Charlotte was just about at the level where the dagger was found. It had been painstaking work. The first twenty centimetres were dug out with spades fairly quickly and sifted, but Charlotte insisted in resorting to trowels for the next part.

"Stop, look there Charley, what's that?" Antoinette quickly stepped into the trench and grabbed Charlotte's wrist to stop her taking another scrape with the trowel. Something had displaced and was now lying under a small clod of mud. Charlotte put her trowel down and carefully lifted the mud away to reveal what appeared to be a small grey pebble. It was about an inch long and a quarter of an inch in diameter. Carefully she picked it up and placed it in the professor's open palm.

"It's a bone fragment, Charley," chirped Antoinette, "A phalange I'd say, probably a fingertip."

"Charlotte slumped down and started to tremble. "It... it's a woman."

Antoinette looked at her student with an edge of scorn tinging her eyes. "Pah, how do you know it's a woman?"

Charlotte looked up at her mentor, tears streaming down her face again and her chin trembling, "Because I was with her when she died...."

CHAPTER 8

They had been sitting in silence for several minutes. Charlotte couldn't bring herself to say anything, so she just had to wait whilst Antoinette finished reconciling the fantastical story she'd just heard.

Eventually Antoinette clambered back into the shallow trench and knelt down in the mud. She contemplated the sidewall where the bone fragment had been found. She looked back at Charlotte, "And you can't explain the catalyst that transported you back in time? You didn't touch anything? You didn't mutter some sort of Celtic incantation?"

Charlotte's eyes flickered in the direction of her backpack. She had told Antoinette everything, except about the brooch. "I was kneeling in the trench, just as you are now when wham! That's all I can tell you." She looked away, not wishing to make eye contact. She hated lying, but she desperately wanted to try on the brooch one more time and see if it would happen again. Whatever the outcome, she would tell her after.

Antoinette smiled and pulled herself out of the ditch, "Ok. Dig away. See what you can find."

"Really? Oh thank you. I promise you won't regret it."

"Somehow, I think I might," said the Frenchwoman as she wiped her muddy hands on her towel, "I believe that there are things in the Universe that we cannot comprehend, so I'm going to give you your head, but just for today. If you find nothing more, then we go back to the original dig plans, ok?"

Charlotte stood up, stiffly and embraced her. "Thank you. I'd better crack on then." With one last smile, she dropped back into the trench and resumed filtering the mud.

It wasn't long before she uncovered more bone fragments but her excitement suddenly squealed to a halt. "I can't do this. I can't disturb her final resting place, it feels like sacrilege." She looked at the fragments in her sieve, all from a hand or foot and then, with a furtive glance around to make sure no one was watching, She pushed them all back into the sidewall.

oOo

It was getting dark. Charley looked at her watch, 21:30hrs. The site was deserted; most of the dig staff were at The Barleymow, the rest were in the mess tent watching television.

She grabbed her field back pack and slipped from the dormitory tent into the warm night air. She made sure the coast was clear and then headed over to her trench which was now covered by a large tarpaulin sheet. She dropped her backpack alongside it and pulled out a dark blue overall which she tugged over her clothes.

She had told Antoinette that there had been no more bones found and the phalange she discovered earlier must have been a one-off, a fluke. She had asked to fill in the trench, much to Antoinette's annoyance. "You begged and pleaded with me to let you expand that trench, and now, just a few hours later, you say there is nothing to find and you want to fill it in? That will not do at all, Charley. No, you found a bone, we will continue the dig tomorrow… together and that's an end to it."

Charley delved into her backpack and pulled out the brooch. As she gazed upon its exquisite beauty, a thought struck her, "If I go back in time from this same location, will I just end up in the river again? Should I move to the landside, trenches and go back from there?" There were too many questions and she didn't know the answers to any of them. She dropped the chain over her head, tucked the brooch inside her shirt and felt it touch her skin. Again she felt an intense sensation of pins and needles; it almost burned. And then the jolt came. It smashed into her chest so hard that she screamed out and was propelled backwards across the grass, where she fell, unconscious.

35

CHAPTER 9 - 431AD
Eanáir (January)

Brid stepped back and nearly slipped in the blood that soaked the mud floor. She held up a new-born baby, squirming in her hands.

A large bear-like man stepped forward into the flickering light of the open fire. His long black hair almost seemed to blend into his big bushy beard. Across his shoulders he wore a mantle trimmed with a thick covering of rabbit fur, dyed black from oak galls, under which was a leather over-tunic. His under-jerkin and trousers were made of rough grey linen and he wore thick leather and fur boots. "Give her to me."

"Let me clean her first and get some cloth about her."

Madron nodded. His eyes shone like dark granite as they reflected the flames. 'Yes very well, do so."

He looked over at two young women, standing in the shadows of the large round wattle hut, tears flooding their cheeks, "Maybn, Nessa tend to my wife."

As the girls moved to the lifeless body in the straw-filled cot, Brid looked down at her and tears filled her eyes too.

Madron followed her gaze. "We survived the Romans, we've survived those cursed Pictish raiding parties, we've survived starvation and disease and yet Ailla has perished in giving me the one thing she knew I wanted most."

Brid glanced up at Madron's large bearded face, strangely distorted though her tears, "She loved you. It was a union blessed by the gods."

Charley watched from her hiding place behind a large ornate wooden trunk. She watched with a mixture of enthrallment and fear; enthrallment in seeing history first-hand and fear that she

36

would be discovered.

"Madron," said a silky voice from the shadows, "you cannot be thinking of allowing the child to live, surely?"

Brid clutched the baby tightly to her breast and looked desperately at her chieftain. With pained eyes, Madron turned towards the voice, "I know that the gods demand the sacrifice of a baby that kills its mother, but I have no other children. Four times we lost our babies before they could be born."

"I know, but…"

"Timancius, I will not lose both my wife *and* my new-born daughter, and that's an end to it."

Timancius, high priest of the Avertci tribe, moved out of the shadows. Tall and thin, he lowered the hood of his black robe, revealing a shiny bald head, a crooked hooked nose and thin lips, red with the juice of the berries he furtively produced from a pocket, as if they were contraband.

His hawk-like eyes darted about, taking in the Madron's dead wife and the baby, still in Brid's protective arms. "If she had borne you a son then maybe the gods would forgive you, but with a daughter, you have no choice; if you do not sacrifice her, the gods will find another way to be appeased. Either way, she will not survive."

"Then I will make other sacrifices instead, Timancius. Shall I start with you?"

Timancius recoiled, "*Me?*"

"Yes, you. As the voice of the gods, your death would make a bold statement to them. It would say I am prepared to sacrifice my own priest to protect my daughter."

"You cannot!" He took another pace back, but even at a distance, his fetid breath assailed the chieftain's nostrils.

"You have no stomach for that solution, Timancius? Very well, choose five children from the village and slaughter them to appease your gods."

Again Timancius looked shocked. "*My* gods? They are your gods too and you will pay a heavy price if you abandon them."

With a cry of rage, Madron grabbed Timancius by the throat and pushed him against the wall of the hut. "*My* gods would not hurt a new-born or any child for that matter. *My* gods bestow life as a precious gift, not one to be traded away for their amusement. I suggest you look away from your tyrant gods Timancius and towards mine."

He released his grip on the priest's throat and shoved him away. "You forget your place, Timancius; I am Madron, chieftain of the Avertci and if any harm befalls my daughter, I promise you will pay with your life."

The high priest, seething with anger and clutching his bruised throat, backed silently to the doorway and drew aside the animal skin curtain. He stepped outside into the freezing night air and pulled up his hood. His eyes narrowed and his nostrils flared. That child would die. It had to.

oOo

Charley watched in fascinated horror as the argument between Madron and Timancius reached its climax. She felt intense pity for the tribe's chief as he looked upon his dead wife.

Brid finished wrapping the baby in clean linen and handed her to Madron who took his daughter from the nurse and held her aloft, "I shall call her Catherine and I promise that she will have the strength and guile of a hundred men." He paused and lowered her down to his chest and gazed lovingly at her, "And she shall have the wisdom and compassion of her mother." He faltered for a second before adding, "And I pray to the gods that they bestow upon her, the same powers that blessed her mother, and her mother before her."

The old nurse reached up and took the baby back, "There is a young woman in the village who gave birth to a dead son a few days ago. Her name is Elowen. I will take Catherine to her for suckling. She has plenty of milk."

Madron put his hand out, "No. Catherine does not leave here, not yet; it is too dangerous, especially now Timancius has made his feelings clear."

"But my Lord, the baby needs milk," Brid protested.

"She does." He beckoned to Nessa, "You will go and fetch this Elowen. Tell her she is to live here until Catherine is weened."

Brid touched his arm, "Forgive me, my Lord, but she has a husband, he will surely not allow…"

"Not allow??" Madron bellowed.

Brid recoiled. She knew that Elowen's husband had no choice. She nodded at Nessa, "Find Elowen and tell her to come at once."

Madron looked at his dead wife once more and a sudden thought struck him, "Maybn, pass me her brooch."

The other young girl stopped washing Ailla's body and fetched a silver brooch from the table. The King held it up to the light. "Is it not beautiful? Bring the baby here, Brid." Gently he fixed the brooch to her wraps. "She will wear this all her life and even after death. It will be the bond between her and her mother."

From her hiding place, Charley gasped and clutched at the brooch hanging around her neck, "That's the brooch; my brooch. What am I seeing here? The birth of the woman I've just seen die?"

Madron's words echoed in her mind… *"Even after death."* A shard of ice seemed to stab her. "Even after death he said, except now I've got it." Charley closed her eyes. "What if I've evoked some kind of curse by taking it from her?"

Maybn stepped over to Charley's hiding place and placed a pile of dirty wooden bowls and plates on top of the trunk. As she turned back, three of the plates slid off and crashed to the floor next to Charley. With a gasp she pushed herself back against the wall as Maybn turned back and grovelled on the floor to retrieve them.

"I'm a goner," she thought. "She's going to see me."

Maybn reached for the plates and at one point was virtually nose-to-nose with Charley, and yet the young women didn't see her. With the plates in her grasp, Maybn shuffled back to the other side of the trunk.

"How's that possible?"

Madron sensed something though, and lifted his nose to sniff the air like a dog sensing its first prey of the day. He snapped his head round to look into the corner where Charley was hiding, stared right at her, but saw nothing. He shivered involuntarily, "Brid, take extra care with Catherine tonight; I fear I might have woken Timancius's gods.

oOo

At the time of Catherine's birth, Taraghlan, Madron's closest confidant and advisor, was climbing the last few rungs to the top of the wooden gate tower, from where he could look across the sodden fields. As the commander of Madron's small army and guard, it was his responsibility to ensure the village was safely bedded-down each night, but tonight Taraghlan sensed trouble.

The high palisade wall around the village was just over a mile long and for no tangible reason, he had doubled the guard. Most of the dwellings were huddled close to the walls for protection but there was no logical layout to the village. Houses were timber-built with conical roofs. Some were built in the old style where the roof virtually reached the ground, whilst most had side walls around five feet high. Madron's hut was the largest, situated to the left of the main gates. In the centre of the village was the great hall, solidly built from the trunks of oak and ash and with a heavy thatched roof that stopped about three feet from the ground.

Taraghlan reflected that many Britons were abandoning their traditional ways of building. Many tribes were using materials scavenged from abandoned brick built Roman dwellings. The Avertci however, stuck to the old ways; familiar, safe but very inefficient in weather like this.

The rain had been relentless for weeks. Valuable crops had been washed away, the byres and pens were deep in mud and heavy streams of rainwater cascaded through the village. The muddy torrents had even flooded through the conical wooden huts turning living spaces into filthy, slippery, quagmires - seas of mud that got splashed everywhere.

The land of the Avertci was small by comparison to their neighbours. The village was the tribe's focal point, but there were

40

many unfortified settlements within the domain.

At times like this, Taraghlan envied the higher class Romans who had lived in the now derelict brick-built villas that dotted the countryside; wondrous feats of engineering with stone walls and marble cladding, intricate mosaics on walls and floors. Few were lived in by Britons for they believed them to be filled with bad omens, a view shared by Taraghlan.

He looked up at the black clouds that lumbered across the darkening sky. He was used to discomfort, but life in the village was becoming unbearable. Clothing and bedding were constantly wet and there had been some deaths amongst the very young and the very old. He shivered and pulled his fur cloak tightly around his shoulders.

The sound of chattering women, leaving the village through the gateway beneath him, snapped his mind back from thoughts of the weather, to the more pressing issue of security. They were headed for the nearby woods to make offerings to the gods where the swollen stream had carved a deep cut across the forest floor.

"Do not be long; it's getting dark."

The sound of his stern voice momentarily startled the women, who giggled loudly when they realised who had called to them. Taraghlan was somewhat of an attraction to the tribe's women and even the fact that he was married to a fearsome woman who would gouge out the eyes of any woman who gazed upon her man, did not detract them from admiring his muscular and handsome physique when the opportunity arose.

The night was closing in and the temperature was dropping. He pulled his cloak around him but folded it above the hilt of his sword and rested his left hand on the pommel. His short beard itched and he knew it was about time he de-loused himself. The lice had probably worked their way down from his black wavy hair, which he kept short too, to make de-lousing easier.

He made his way back to the ladder, but a cry from Madron's hut stopped him in his tracks. It was the cry of a baby. "Ahh." He smiled broadly. "Ailla has given birth." There would be much rejoicing and celebration for the next few days. Goodness knows the village needed a happy distraction at a time like this.

The baby's cry was followed by a wail of despair and Taraghlan's smile vanished. He saw Timancius storm out of Madron's hut and stride angrily across the sodden village. "Timancius, what has happened?" The priest turned and glared at him, but did not reply and did not stop.

Other villagers paused in their activities to look towards the chief's hut and murmur to each other. Nessa appeared and hurried through the mud towards the far side of the village.

Taraghlan could still hear the baby crying, so no harm had befallen it, so why the anguished cry? Unless.... Ailla! He dropped down the ladder and ran through the mud to Madron's hut. He burst in to find Madron standing by his dead wife's body, with the baby cradled in his arms. He looked up sadly, "Ailla is dead."

Taraghlan wasn't sure how to respond, but Madron took the initiative. He held out baby Catherine to him, "Taraghlan, my dear friend, this child is the future of the Avertci. You will protect her with your life. You will ensure she learns how to survive, by every means you can teach her."

"But of course. I would have it no other way."

Madron handed the baby to Taraghlan and looked mournfully at his dead wife, "We must help her on her journey as soon as it can be arranged."

Taraghlan cradled the baby in his arms and gazed down at her, "She is beautiful, my Lord." Catherine opened her eyes. "Oh, what blue eyes; just like her mother's." Catherine's eyes suddenly flared an even brighter blue and Taraghlan took a step back in surprise. He had seen that flare before, at times when Ailla was about to create great magic. He knew immediately that this baby was very special. He also felt a sudden and strong connection to her; she knew him, she trusted him and she expected him to be loyal. He smiled down at her, "You don't need to command me, little one," he whispered, "I will protect you until the day I die." He kissed her on the forehead and handed her back to Madron, "As for Ailla, let me organise the pyre."

Madron's eye's narrowed. "No Taraghlan, that is for Timancius to do; he is the priest, let him earn the name for once."

Taraghlan smiled, "Has he upset you again?"

"He always upsets me, but this time he has gone too far. He threatened Catherine's life."

Taraghlan nodded sagely, "Ahh, do you mean that old god who demands the sacrifice of a baby who kills its mother during birth? I thought he had been banished by Maponos the god of youth?"

"Yes, with the help of the god Lovantucarus, the protector of youth. But everyone knows Timancius is firmly embedded in the old ways and to him many of the old Gaulish gods still reign supreme."

"Then Catherine will be in danger until he is gone."

Madron put the baby into its crib, "Yes, or until she comes of age as a woman, but if we harm Timancius, we will bear the wrath of his gods and I cannot put us in such danger. We will just have to stay vigilant."

Taraghlan gripped Madron's shoulder, "Always, my friend, always."

CHAPTER 10

"It happened again," Charley blurted out, the moment Richard opened the front door.

"You'd better come in. Are you ok?" He stepped aside and ushered Charley though to the kitchen.

"I'm fine. No injuries."

There was a bottle of Cabinet Sauvignon on the table, next to a nearly-full glass. Richard fetched clean glass and gestured to Charley. She nodded and he poured her a large measure and pushed it towards her. She sat down and took a long sip. "The woman I saw murdered was called Catherine. Her father was Madron, King of the Avertci and her mother was Ailla. She died giving birth to her."

Richard picked up his glass and plonked himself down in a nearby armchair. He stretched out his legs and crossed his feet, "Well you have been a busy girl." He took a sip of his wine and stared sourly at the glass.

Charley frowned, "Are you ok?"

"You mean apart from being told to fuck off?"

"Ahh, that…" Charley put her glass back on the table and swivelled herself round in the chair, so that she was directly facing him, "I'm sorry. Really."

Richard continued to stare into his wine and said nothing.

"I was confused, I was excited, I was frightened. There were so many emotions running around and I was terrified you'd tell Antoinette before I could get back there again." She left the table and hunkered down next Richard's armchair. "I *am* sorry for being such a bitch. Honestly."

Richard leaned over the edge of the chair and put his wine glass on the floor out of harm's way and then he looked directly at her. "I was challenging you, because I… I care about you."

"I understand."

He smiled, "I'm not sure you do." Before she knew what was happening, he leaned forward and kissed her lightly on the lips.

She pulled away, a look of puzzlement on her face, "Richard?" He pulled her gently towards him and kissed her again. This time she responded and kissed him back.

It was a long and tender kiss. There was no urgency; none of the frantic desire that she experienced with most men who kissed her. This kiss seemed to have depth and meaning.

"Well I didn't expect that," she said when their lips eventually parted.

"Neither did I; it was an impulse, sorry."

"Don't be sorry; it was lovely." She shuffled to her feet, smoothed out her clothing and sat on his lap. She snuggled up to him and put her arms around his neck.

Richard pulled away a strand of hair that was tickling his cheek, "So tell me about your latest trip back in time."

"Well, the brooch is definitely the catalyst for it. The moment it touched my chest, I was knocked out again. I came round in Madron's hut just after Catherine was born. One thing that's been confirmed is that they definitely can't see me. I had someone within inches and staring right at me, and they didn't react at all."

"Well that's a blessing. If they can't see you, I guess they can't harm you."

"There's more. The brooch used to belong to her mother who I gather was some sort of sorceress or priestess maybe; she apparently had powers of some sort."

Richard laughed, "Are you about to go all 'Game of Thrones' on me? Were there any baby dragons about?"

Charley thumped him on the chest, "Don't take the piss. No, Madron referred to Ailla's powers and hoped they would be passed on to Catherine."

Richard chuckled, "I guess they were very superstitious. I wouldn't read too much into that. I suppose you'll be going back again?"

Charley looked into his brown eyes, "Yes, of course. I hope you're not going to try and stop me."

He shook his head, "Right at this moment, I'm more interested in kissing you again."

Charley smiled. "And I would like you to." She paused for a second.

"But?"

"But, Anoinette warned you'd be a distraction for me and she's right. I like you, very much, but I'm only here for a few weeks and then I'll be off back to London.

"We'll call it a holiday romance then," said Richard with a twinkle in his eye.

She kissed him on the cheek and stood up. "I'd rather stay friends if that's ok with you."

Richard frowned. "I'm not sure that it is."

"Well you know where I stand, so I guess the ball's in your court now, chum." Charley smiled disarmingly.

oOo

Timancius paced angrily around his hut. Ailla had been a powerful priestess. She had made it clear she despised him and she had challenged him at every turn. She had been the tribe's priestess long before he arrived in the village, but it was the Avertci's custom not to allow their Priests or Priestesses to marry, Ailla had a decision to make when she fell in love with Madron: become the chief's wife or remain as the tribe's spiritual guide.

Timancius, on the other hand, was a fraud; he had no spiritual abilities. He valued only position, wealth and power and he recognised that the role of tribal priest brought all three.

He desperately wanted to be recognised as a powerful priest so he invented a host of stories about himself and a history of working miracles and of communion with the gods. By the time he arrived at the Avertci settlement this fearsome, albeit invented reputation

46

was known throughout the Southlands, as was his ability to wreak havoc and revenge on those who crossed him. He put himself forward as Ailla's successor and took on the mantle, unopposed.

Timancius believed only in the gods who suited his purpose, and he kept them on his side with frequent sacrifices and blood-letting. Only Ailla saw through his lies, but despite frequent pleas to Madron to banish Timancius, the odious priest remained in power.

Timancius was fearful of her; he recognised that she was a true priestess, imbued with genuine powers and because of that, he knew that he must destroy her if the opportunity arose. It never did, but today the gods accomplished what he had failed to do and took her life.

His quiet rejoicing was cut short when he discovered she had given birth to a daughter; a daughter who would no doubt, inherit her mother's powers and grow up to be another real threat. Somehow he had to remove that threat once and for all, but without raising suspicion of his true motive, or invoking Madron's wrath. So far that had proven to be difficult, to say the least.

Had Timancius been a real priest, Madron would be of no concern to him; he would be able to silence him with a wave of his hand; but he wasn't a real priest. His powers were about as strong as dandelion seeds clinging to its host until the slightest puff of wind wrenched them away and into the air.

He pulled a small chest from under his cot and from within, he pulled out a small pouch of coins. He gathered his cloak around his thin body, pulled up the hood and left the hut.

He hurried through the mud to the far side of the village where he turned toward the sturdy palisade that protected the inhabitants. Halfway between two of the defensive towers that Taraghlan had insisted were built, was one of the village's few rectangular houses. The light of the fire and torches within flickered through the open doorway, but it was the pitch black area behind the house that was of interest to the priest.

He groped his way through the darkness until he reached the palisade; thick trunks of oak about eight feet tall with sharpened tops. "Ceud mìle fàilte," he whispered.

"Ciamar a tha sibh," came the reply from the other side of the wall.

"Yes, I am well," Timancius replied. He pulled away a thick clump of brambles to reveal a man-sized gap. In that moment the moon broke free of the cloud and bathed the area with its cold muted light. He gulped at the sight of the man standing in front of him; he was large and wearing heavy furs. His hair was long, his face was bearded and covered in intricate tattoos, as were his arms. Around his waist he wore three heavy belts, each one supporting a different weapon - a sword, a club and an axe.

The man held out his hand and Timancius passed the pouch of coins through the gap. He weighed the pouch in his hand.

"When will you attack?"

"At dawn."

"Madron's house is close to the gates. It's the largest in the village. He has a new-born daughter. Kill the child and kill Madron."

The man tucked the pouch into his belt. "There will be *no* survivors. We are not selective. If you do not want to die then hide in the woods like the turd you are."

Timancius glared, "Uvan, you have done very well from the information I've given to you over these past few months. If you want more then you must ensure I am *not* killed."

"I really don't care whether you die or not." The man put one leg through the gap and pulled out his axe. "In fact, I might as well finish you here."

Timancius recoiled and let out a whispered shriek. "No, I will go." He turned and fled back toward the centre of the village. He detested the Picts but by befriending their raiding parties, he had set up a profitable trading system that provided him with a lot of treasure - much of it looted from neighbouring villages. As he got closer to his hut, he slowed his pace and allowed himself a smile. By the time the morning light arrived Madron and his daughter would be dead.

CHAPTER 11

Rosemary Forrester slammed down the receiver and spun angrily in her very expensive executive chair. "Walter, what the sodding hell is going on down there? According to the Press Office, only that local rag bothered to print the story. What's the point in leaking a headline if it's not picked-up by the Nationals? You really are a waste of space."

Walter Smith winced. "Please, Rosemary, don't speak to me like that; it's hardly becoming." He tried unsuccessfully to cross his fat little legs.

Forrester's dark eyes narrowed, "Don't you dare lecture me on decorum."

Smith glared back at his boss. "I'm not going to apologise; I resent your constant demeaning comments and bullying. If you continue I will make a complaint to the Board of Trustees."

Forrester sat back in her chair and smiled broadly, "That's better Walter. I was wondering when you'd grow a pair; it looks like you found them. I consider myself well and truly ticked-off. "

"Good. Well I…"

"So now, before you waddle off to make your complaint, answer my question. Why didn't the nationals pick it up?"

Smith's ego deflated again like a pricked balloon. He hated these audiences with the Chairwoman of the National Archaeological Society. With her elegant suits and immaculate hair and make-up, she looked every inch the professional career woman, but Walter knew to his cost that she was actually a foul-mouthed bitch of the first order. As far as he knew, it was a side she only showed to him. Maybe she sensed his weakness. Her

49

other minions wouldn't stand for it. Perhaps she knew that and used him to vent her spleen, which was often. To her peers, politicians and the Media, she was the consummate professional, but with Walter, her favourite sport was to drop the F-bomb and watch him squirm.

She glared over the top of the spectacles that perched on her hooked nose. "For fuck's sake Walter, well?" Her pinched face hardened and her narrow eyes glared meanly across the desk at him.

Smith winced and shook his head. "I'm not responsible for the editorial decisions of the national newspapers."

Forrester pointed at him with her pen. "Unless the Nationals run the story, I can't get the dig shut down."

Something was driving her to sabotage that particular dig, but she didn't know what. When she first heard about the discovery of a Saxon dagger, she felt a cold chill riffle across her flesh and she hugged herself and shivered. The more she heard about the find, the more worried she became and when she saw photographs of the dagger itself, every fibre of her being screamed out that the dig must stop. Whatever was concealed in that thousand year-old mud should stay concealed. Forrester inexplicably knew that if the archaeologists were allowed to continue, they would be unearthing a lot more than just artefacts.

She had hated Antoinette Deselle for many years. They had been colleagues on several digs but had fallen-out when they each began to produce papers for archaeological academia. The French woman's assertion that Forrester had plagiarised some of her papers and claimed the ground-breaking content as her own, had nearly crushed her career. It was true of course, but in her typically bullish manner Forrester had ridden out the storm by launching counter-claims and accusations that muddied the waters so much, no one in the society wanted to take any action. In short, she intimidated them into backing-off.

But in Forrester's mind it wasn't Antoinette who was the threat to her on this particular dig, it was Charley. She didn't know why;

she had never even met the girl, but she just knew she had to get rid of her. Charley was the real threat, even though she didn't know what that threat was.

She tossed the pen onto her blotter and reached behind her head to gather up her long hair and pull it into a tight ponytail which she fixed in place with a hairband..

Walter inwardly grimaced as her pinched-up face was pulled even tighter. *"She looks like a vulture,"* He tentatively raised his hand. "No publicity was the number one condition given by the school for allowing the dig; they don't want Nighthawkers and other idiots digging up their playing field…"

"And because and there are child protection issues too." She interrupted. "They were very clear about that."

"So would our Trustees pull the funding?"

Forrester rolled her eyes. "If the national papers get hold of it, it's the school that will shut us down."

"But their local paper ran with it; isn't that enough?"

"You'd have thought so, but I spoke to the Chairwoman of the school's Governors half an hour ago and offered to close the dig, but the stupid woman decided we could continue as it was only a local paper. It's so frustrating."

"I'm still not sure why you want to stop this dig."

Forrester raised her eyes to the ceiling, "I thought I made it clear. I want that French bitch and her protégé to fail."

"Yes I know that, but why?"

"It's personal. We have a past history."

"Tautology."

Forrester glared at him, "What?"

"I could be wrong but I think that 'past history' is tautology."

She retrieved her pen and threw it at him. "You'll be history if you correct me again. If you think I'm going to share my reasons with you, you're mistaken."

Smith heaved himself from his chair and shuffled to the door, "So what now?"

Forrester's eyes narrowed again, "If the Nationals won't pick it

51

up, then find another way to stop the dig. Find someone on the inside who can be bought. I want that dig sabotaged and quickly."

Smith raised his eyebrows. "Sabotaged? How?"

"I don't know. Work it out for yourself and let me know what you come up with."

Smith thought for a moment. "As it happens, Rosemary, I might have just the chap and he's already on-site."

"Well don't just stand there like a simpering schoolboy, get it sorted!"

CHAPTER 12

Charley stepped from Richard's house just before 6am and hurried back to the mess tent. Work on the dig would be starting at 6:30 and she needed to freshen-up first. She and Richard had sat-up all night talking. In Charley's mind she was simply cementing their friendship, but for Richard, it was more than that. He still carried the hope that he could win her over, and into his bed.

"And where have you been, little lady; gallivanting about all night eh?"

Charley jumped in surprise and spun around to find Greg Collier sauntering across the dew-soaked grass, towards her. "Who's the lucky fella then?"

Charley's heart sank. Greg was a large muscle-bound oaf and the fact he had a plethora of first-class honours degrees coming out of his backside, didn't make him any less of an oaf.

Charley hadn't seen him for at least a year and had forgotten all about him, but now the memories of his chauvinistic attitude towards women and his constant corny chat-up lines came flooding back, as she remembered their time on an excavation at Colchester. For a while he had become a serious irritant. Charley had tried to ignore him and she made sure that nothing was done to encourage him, but he spectacularly failed to get the message and Charley was forced to ask Antoinette to warn him off. As a result, Greg had apologised but Charley wasn't really interested; she just wanted him to leave her alone.

"Shit, really? You're here? I didn't know. Antoinette should have warned me."

"I arrived late last night. As you know, Saxon history is my forte and she wanted me here. Didn't she tell you?"

"No she didn't," she said coldly and turned back towards the mess tent but Greg grabbed her elbow. "Let go of me!" she snapped and wrenched her arm out of his grasp.

Greg held up both hands in surrender. "I'm sorry. No offence meant Charley; I just wanted to talk to you." His blue eyes sparkled under his unruly mop of fair hair. His jaw seemed squarer and more set than she'd seen before.

"What do you want?"

I just wanted to reassure you that I'm not here to cause you any trouble and I don't want you making trouble for me either."

Charley was incredulous, "What planet are you on? Why should I make trouble for you?"

Greg's eyes narrowed and his light brows frowned, "For what happened at Colchester? As far as I was concerned it was a simple 'Boy Meets Girl' situation. I liked you and I paid you lots of compliments, which unfortunately you took the wrong way. That was hardly my fault was it?"

Charley bristled. "Antoinette agreed your behaviour was out of order."

Greg looked sourly at her and his demeanour hardened, "Well OK. I get the message. I guess I'm wasting my time trying to be nice to you. I'd hoped we could start anew." He untucked his red and blue checked shirt from his jeans, "I must go; I need a shit." He turned on his heels and set off in the direction of the toilets.

"Fuck you Collier!" Charley shouted after him.

Without looking back, he held both hands above his head. "Whatever."

oOo

Antoinette Deselle peered into Charley's trench, "That's coming along well."

Charley carefully brushed some dried mud from more of the bones, "I've got some remains of leatherwork here too."

Antoinette beamed, "Excellent." Charley climbed out and handed her a small fragment of leather strap with a highly corroded

54

buckle still attached. Antoinette turned it over in her hand and studied it, "Iron Age for sure. Celtic in origin I suspect, not Saxon."

Charley looked at her trench. Her plan to leave the remains untouched was thwarted when Antoinette took it upon herself to have a poke around and uncovered some more bones. Now, she had no choice but to disturb Catherine's final resting place.

About two-thirds of the skeleton was now above the bed of the trench; a noisy little pump kept it clear of water. Although the bones were largely lying flat, it was clear that the body had been lying on its right-hand side, knees slightly drawn up. Her right arm had been beneath her, but her left had separated and fallen in pieces next to her, as had her left leg.

"I wonder who she was, this murder victim of yours." Antoinette looked sadly into the trench.

Charley replied without hesitation. "Her name was Catherine. She was either the Queen or Priestess of the Avertci tribe."

Antoinette frowned, "No mon cher ami, you have that pronunciation confused. You mean the Averni tribe from Gaul."

"The Avertci is the name I heard."

Antoinette's frown deepened, "I've never heard of the Avertci. Atrebates, yes; they inhabited Hampshire, West Sussex and Berkshire."

Charley looked exasperated, "I've studied all the British tribes too, as well you know." She stepped carefully back into her trench, "I'll research the Avertci when I get the chance."

Antoinette tutted, "You are wrong, Charley, but I will leave you to it for now." she smiled sadly at her misguided protégé and strolled-off to check on progress elsewhere.

Charley crouched by her skeleton and lightly brushed away more dirt from the base of the skull and neck. She fished in her overall's pocket for a magnifying glass and peered closely at the vertebrae. "Jeezus!" She moved closed and adjusted the glass until she got a sharper image of the bones. There was a deep nick in the third cervical vertebra. "The knife wound." She looked up for

Antoinette, who was now engrossed in another trench. As she weighed-up what to do, she wondered if the dagger would fit the nick. "I should have been a crime scene investigator." She shuffled around and sat next to the bones. It felt strange sitting there next to the woman she'd seen in 'real life.' She needed to go back again - and soon."

CHAPTER 13

"You want me to do what?" The voice at the other end of the phone sounded perplexed.

"Sabotage the dig. It's quite simple." Walter Smith was sitting in a cubicle in one of the gent's toilets at Carnarvon House, headquarters of the National Archaeological Society in London.

"Who is this?"

Smith tutted. "Don't worry about who I am. I just want the dig stopped."

The voice now had an edge of anger. "I think you've got the wrong man. There's no way I'd interfere with the dig."

"Oh you will, trust me."

"No I won't, but I'll tell you what I *am* going to do. As soon as I've hung up, I'm going to tell Ms Deselle about this conversation."

Smith could feel his frustration rising. "I saw you recently."

"What do you mean?"

"At that casino in Ramsgate."

"What the hell?"

"How much did you lose? The management looked pretty pissed with you."

"Sod off; this call ends now."

"Then you won't see a penny."

"What do you mean?"

"You'll be paid of course - for sabotaging the dig."

"I don't need your money."

Smith chuckled. "Yeah, I think perhaps you do. How long did they give you to pay your debts?"

"Casinos don't let you run up debts."

"The legit ones don't but The Piccadilly is hardly legit is it? I imagine you've only got a couple of weeks to find the money or they'll come knocking at your door. Or should I say, come crashing through it."

There was silence at the other end of the line.

"I'm prepared to pay you well. Enough to sort out your cash flow problems and have some left over. There's another bonus for stopping the dig, well for me at any rate - it'll get rid of that little madam."

"You mean Charley?"

"No respect for authority, rude and has Deselle totally wrapped around her little finger."

"Ahh," realisation dawned. "You're Mr Smith aren't you." It was a statement, not a question. "Well I like Charley as it happens. I'm not sure I want to be involved."

"Not even for five thousand pounds?" Smith inwardly winced as he said the words. There was no monitory value to the dig, budgets were on a shoestring and yet that stupid woman had given him carte blanche to spend her own money.

The line went quiet again for a few seconds. "Did you say five thousand?"

"I did. You just have to find a way to sabotage the dig, discredit it or whatever, and ensure that you keep that girl and the Frenchie on-side so that they don't suspect you."

The man laughed derisively. "Is that all?"

"It shouldn't be hard for a man with your charm."

"Double it. Ten thousand pounds."

"Seven, and that's my final offer. Do we have a deal?"

The man weighed up his options and then smiled. "Absolutely."

oOo

Charley waited until the camp was settling down for the evening before she returned to her trench. She was just about to pull the brooch from her bag when Greg Collier wandered over.

"Hey," he said, with an apologetic grin.

Oh great. "What do you want?"

"I thought I'd have another stab at making peace with you. Can we start again. I'm really not the villain you think I am."

Charley's mood softened a little. She still thought he was a complete idiot, but she had to admit seemed to be genuinely contrite. "We'll have to see. Now sod-off, I'm busy."

Collier looked under the tarp at the partially exposed skeleton. "It's coming on well. Any idea who it is?"

Charley smiled. "I do actually. I've already told Ms Deselle, but until I can verify it, I'd rather not say anything more."

He shrugged. "Ok, well I'm off for a cuppa. I'll be in the mess tent if you want me."

"I won't." She watched him make his way across the field and out of sight before she slipped under the tarpaulin and popped the brooch around her neck...

CHAPTER 14
Feabhra (February) 431AD

Charley found herself lying in the shadows of a round hut. "Not the same one as before," she thought as she looked about. These walls too were made from wattle and daub and the roof was a thick, well-made thatch. A fire burned in the centre, its blue smoke curled up to the hole at the tip of the conical roof. In all respects it was the same as Madron's, only smaller. On the side of the hut furthest from the doorway, was a low wooden bed filled with straw and covered with a rough woollen blanket. Next to it was an ornate chest upon which some items of clothing had been strewn. "Probably dirty laundry." She chuckled to herself.

She suddenly froze; there was a man sitting at a large wooden table near the fire. How had she not noticed him before? He had hawk-like eyes and a hooked nose. His cowl was lowered and his bald head reflected the light from the flaming torches that lit the interior.

Timancius! Charley's first instinct was to drop further back into the shadows but then she remembered no one could see her, in theory at least. She decided to give it a little test and carefully rose to her feet and took a couple of tentative steps toward the centre of the hut. The priest stopped what he was doing and looked up. Charley froze again, rooted to the spot. She was breathing so hard, she was sure he'd hear her.

Timancius shivered and carried on with his writing so Charley moved right into his field of view and slowly negotiated her way around the table and stood behind him. He shivered again and then started muttering to himself.

Charley looked over his shoulder and studied the papers. They were map-like diagrams and notes. "I wonder where this is."

Timancius's muttering became a full-blown conversation with himself. "If those Picts fail me, Madron will kill me for certain." He glowered at the drawings, "If they succeed they will kill me too unless I can hide."

Charley's eyes grew wider and wider as she began to realise that Timancius was planning an attack on the village. She looked at the drawings again and saw that he had indicated a breach in the circular outer wall. Charley also noticed a crudely drawn figure of a man with a wide hat and long flowing hair at the location of Madron's hut.

She immediately recognised the image; it was Ankou, a Celtic representation of the last person in a community to die. After the run-in she'd witnessed between him and Timancius it was obvious there was no love lost between the two men, but did the hostility between them warrant his death?

Then the truth hit her like a brick. It's Catherine he's after. She's the target. After all, he wanted her dead, didn't he?

Charley's mind was racing. She had already seen Catherine as a grown woman lying in the river, so she must have survived the attack on the village. "But how? Did the attack even take place? Did Madron protect her and fight off the assailants?" Then another thought stuck her. "Did I intervene?" That made no sense: she couldn't interact with this world. No one could see or hear her. Charley searched her brain for some inspiration because she just didn't know what to do for the best. If she didn't try to intervene, would Catherine be killed tonight? Would her lack of action change the course of history?

oOo

Charley stood outside Madron's hut. She had found the breach in the wall and now she felt obligated to warn him… but how? It was raining steadily and her long hair was soaking wet and straggly. The icy water trickled down her neck and her teeth started to chatter as the cold began to cut through her clothing.

61

She looked up at the rain and felt it hit her face like sharp little needles. "This isn't right." She looked down at her heavily soaked, quilted anorak. "How is this possible?" The conundrum was clear, but the answer wasn't. How was it that she couldn't interact with the people, yet she was standing there interacting with the weather? She could feel the weather, could be soaked by the weather and be frozen stiff by the bloody weather. Then she remembered the river mud and Catherine's blood on her face.

"What else can I interact with?" she wondered and reached out. The door to the King's hut was just inches from her hand. Charley could feel her terrified heart thumping steadily in her chest as she reached out to the huge animal skin that hung across the doorway. She stopped, her fingers almost touching it, and took a deep breath. She could smell the leathery odour of the skin mingled with wood smoke from the fire within the hut. She steeled her nerves and with one positive, decisive movement, she swept the fur aside and stepped into the hut.

Madron looked up from his place by the fire and glared toward the doorway but did not react to Charley's presence. Brid and Elowen, who had Catherine to her breast, sat opposite him. The two women talked quietly whilst Taraghlan and half a dozen of the village men, talked animatedly with their leader.

Charley stood rooted to the spot as water dripped from her sodden clothing and pooled on the floor. No one seemed to notice. "How long has passed since my last visit?" she wondered. "Hours, days, minutes?" She carefully made her way across the hut towards Elowen and the baby. Every couple of steps she would pause, just to make sure no one was reacting to her presence. None of them did.

At last she was in a position where she could gaze down on the child. The moment her eyes settled on her, Catherine detached herself from Elowen's teat and looked up straight into Charley's eyes and met her gaze. Her eyes suddenly flared bright blue and Charley staggered back in shock and surprise. It was as if Catherine could see her. Not only see her, but look into her very soul. In that instant, a connection had been made and Charley knew it could never be broken.

"We *do* need an army," Taraghlan insisted

Madron's response was curt, "You have the men of the village,"

"And I have trained all the fit and able-bodied men we have."

"So they can fight if needed."

"But they are not battle-trained. They can wield a sword or an axe, they can fend with a shield, but they are not warriors. They are farmers not fighters."

"And they only number about five hundred," offered another man. "Only about a hundred live within the palisade. The others are spread across our territory."

Taraghlan agreed. "Caderyn speaks true, Lord. We've lost so many men to slaughter by the Picts in recent months, we cannot retaliate. We need to find more. We need an army to respond to the attacks and to protect you." He smiled briefly at Caderyn, his close friend since childhood. The two men had grown up together and shared the same fortunes and misfortunes. Their fathers were both killed fighting the Catuvellauni for the Avertci's rights to settle, and their mothers died within days of each other.

Caderyn was taller than Taraghlan with fairer hair. He wore it tied back, knotted with a leather thong. Both men were muscled and ferocious fighters and each commanded the Avertci's small army.

Madron stared into the fire and said nothing for a moment. Yellow flames danced among the logs and reflected off the faces of the people gathered around him. "Hmm." He looked up at Taraghlan. "Train fifty of the hundred who reside in this village and train them to be battle ready…"

"*Fifty?*" Taraghlan was incredulous.

"Do not interrupt me!" Madron bellowed. "You will train fifty and they will become my guards. They will man the walls day and night. They will be our first line of defence."

"We need an army," Taraghlan persisted.

Caderyn pointed towards the hut wall. "We could ride north,

maybe to the lands of the Corieltauvi. We can raid smaller villages and take prisoners. They can become our army."

Madron snorted derisively. "You speak like a child. If we do not have enough warriors, how do we raid and take prisoners?"

"My point exactly." Taraghlan was becoming increasingly frustrated. "The Corieltauvi in the North are a good example of what we should do. We are not a big tribe. We are pressed between the Dobunni and the Catuvellauni. The Corieltauvi have joined with other small tribes to make an alliance. They have one leader to govern them and peoples from each tribe to counsel him."

"I will not dilute my kingdom!" roared Madron.

"I mean no disrespect, but your kingdom is not really a kingdom at all. You are not a king; you are a tribal chief; you rule about three thousand people."

Madron roared again and leapt to his feet, sword drawn and spittle flying from his mouth as he shouted at Taraghlan. "You do disrespect me, you worm." He slashed the sword at Taraghlan's throat but stopped the blade the instant it touched his skin. Madron drew it back slightly and a small gash appeared on the side of Taraghlan's neck. "Tell me why I should not slice your head from your maggot infested body."

Taraghlan ignored the blood that trickled down the collar of his jerkin, and slowly stood up, Madron's blade still at his throat. He appeared to be unmoved by Madron's display of disapproval and the imminent threat of death. He was Madron's most trusted ally and he did not believe his chief would take his life. He knew that Madron saw him more as a brother than a servant and he hoped that was enough to protect him. "Lord, the Dobunni and Catuvellauni territories are big beyond imagination and either one could crush us with ease. If we make alliances with other tribes then, there's our army. You would still rule the Avertci and might even rule the alliance. Nothing changes there, but, we draw warriors from all the tribes in the alliance."

Madron grunted and sheathed his sword. "Hmm." Taraghlan's words seemed to have resonated with him at last and he reconsidered his position. Eventually he nodded. "Very well. Send your most trusted men to the other tribes. See if there is interest." He threw a cloth to Taraghlan. "Clean yourself. You speak well my friend, but you always do." Taraghlan wiped his neck and Madron sat again. "See Brid, She will heal your wound."

oOo

Charley had watched in fascinated horror at the argument between the two men, but it had confirmed her fear that the village would be unable to defend itself against the forthcoming attack by the Picts. If she could only alert them somehow then maybe, without the element of surprise, the Picts might not be successful. Maybe the village menfolk could fend them off.

She looked at the fire and slowly, the germ of an idea began to grow. "I wonder if I can interact with fire?" She visualised herself setting fire to the house next to the breach in the palisade but shook that idea from her head; there would be people living in there, maybe children. Certainly fire seemed to be the obvious way to raise the alarm. She had noticed several fires burning in the open. Maybe she could take some embers or burning sticks.

"That's what I'll do," she thought and peered over Elwyn's shoulder at the baby. "If only I could tell you about the danger you're in." The baby made eye contact again and it steeled Charley's resolve to help. "Now I must go and play with fire, if I can." Her mind was made up, but just as she turned towards the door, she began to feel faint. "No, no, no, no, not yet. I'm not ready." She clutched at the pendant, "Please, don't take me back. I have to try and save them."

Her head started to swim and her vision became distorted. "NO!" she cried out and then collapsed to the floor and everything went black.

CHAPTER 15
Feabhra (February) 431AD

Catherine stirred in Elowen's arms so she looked down and gently smoothed the baby's wispy blonde hair. Catherine turned her head and stared straight up at her wet-nurse and her eyes flared blue. Elowyn recoiled, unsure what had just happened, but the feeling of foreboding that washed over her was overwhelming. She looked for Brid who had just finished tending Taraghlan's wound.

The old woman shuffled back and sat wearily on the bench. "Men!" she said tartly. "It's always the same. Someone always ends the night bruised or bleeding." She looked sideways at Elowen. "What's the matter girl, you look quite ill." Elowen's chin was wobbling as she fought to keep her tears at bay, but said nothing. Brid glared at her. "Speak child. Whatever is the matter?"

Elowen looked about, frightened that her words might be overheard. "We are in great danger."

"Pah! What do you mean."

"We are in great danger," she repeated.

"What sort of danger? How do you know this?"

Elowen looked down fearfully at the baby in her arms. "She told me," she whispered. "Catherine told me."

Brid slowly shifted her gaze from Elowen to Catherine and back again. "Has this happened before?"

"No. I don't know what to do."

"Come with me." Brid stood and pulled the girl to her feet.

Madron broke off from his discussions and glared across at the two women. "Silence. If you cannot be quiet then leave. Go back to my hut."

Brid pulled Elowen and the baby across the hall to her Chief and knelt before him. "Your daughter has indeed inherited her mother's powers, just as you prayed she would."

Madron frowned. "How do you know this?"

Brid pointed to Elowen. "She has spoken to the girl. Lord we are in grave danger."

Madron impatiently waved Brid to her feet. "Get up woman." He pointed at Elowen. "Explain yourself."

Elowen was too frightened to speak to her chief, for all he had ever done to her was to bark instructions and chide her about almost everything she did. She looked pleadingly at Brid, who replied for her.

"Elowen cannot explain what happened, Lord, except that she claims your daughter spoke to her. Not words, but thoughts, just as Ailla used to do."

"Ailla? What trickery is this?"

Elowen was shaking. "No trickery," she whispered.

"She spoke to you?" The frightened girl nodded. "Then find your voice, girl and tell me what she said."

Elowen swallowed hard. "Lord, there were no words. She looked at me and I sensed a powerful warning of danger."

"What sort of danger?"

"I have no idea. I am sorry."

Taraghlan stepped up to Madron and whispered in his ear. "Ailla was a powerful priestess, you know this. She could control men with just the power of her thoughts. She could also pass on warnings. We have both witnessed that before. You know it to be true."

Madron stepped forward, picked his daughter from Elowen's arms and held her out to Taraghlan. "And you think this small baby has her mother's skills?"

"I *know* she has." Taraghlan insisted.

Madron handed Catherine back to Elowen. "A warning you say. For when?"

Elowen gulped. "Soon, my Lord, very soon."

Madron whirled around to face Taraghlan and Caderyn. "Arm the village men. Rouse your best warriors. Put bowmen on the towers and take everyone else to the gate."

"No!" Elowen shouted in panic. "Forgive me, but the danger comes from over there." she pointed towards the back of the village.

Madron hesitated. He had always trusted Ailla's prophecies, but his daughter? This tiny baby, just a few weeks old? Could he afford to ignore what seemed to be Ailla's legacy? "Taraghlan. Fifty men to the gate, the rest go with Caderyn to patrol the village perimeter."

"For how long?" someone shouted.

"Day and night?" someone else called out.

"Until I tell you to stop." Madron pulled Taraghlan by the sleeve. "If this truly is a warning, then we might stand a chance."

"By taking away the element of surprise."

Madron smiled. He was trying to look and sound positive, but at the back of his mind ran the possibility that the danger might not be an attack. "I wonder if we have been told true."

Taraghlan frowned. "How so?"

"Maybe it comes from another direction; another flood maybe, or an illness."

"Or a fire." Taraghlan added thoughtfully. "Maybe we should cater for all events? I'll get the women to raise the food stocks to higher ground in the morning, and I'll post a guard on fire watch too."

Madron grasped Taraghlan's shoulder. "Thank you."

Taraghlan smiled and left Madron's hut. As he led his men through the village to the gates and prepared for an enemy that he couldn't identify, he wished he could see what was in that baby's mind.

oOo

The rain had started to ease, but the night was dark and the ground so sodden and muddy that it was hard to walk without slipping. Streams of brown, murky water ran through the palisade and downhill from the village towards the swollen River Gade.

Uvan stepped cautiously through the gap in the strong palisade and then waited as a hundred more dark shadowy figures scrambled through behind him. They were all heavily armed with long swords, axes and shields. A dozen also carried flaming torches and Uvan directed them to set fire to the dwelling adjacent to the opening. Once the torches were buried deep into the thatch, he quickly led his army towards the centre of the village, leaving three men behind to slaughter anyone who ran from the burning house.

Caderyn watched from the shadows. He knew they were outnumbered but it was he who now had the element of surprise. As soon as he saw the Picts breach the palisade he pulled his men into the shadows and sent a messenger to Taraghlan.

He waited until the Picts had passed his position and were moving silently along the track towards the village centre, then screamed, "Now!" and his small force charged roaring and screaming, across the sodden earth to attack the Picts from behind.

Uvan's men were caught completely off-guard and those at the rear didn't even have time to turn, before they were cut down. The rest however, recovered and ran at Caderyn's men.

"Let them come to us," shouted Caderyn, pulling some of his men back.

The track was about ten feet wide with circular huts flanking both sides. His plan was simple enough; to reach them, the Picts would have to get past or over, the bodies of their fallen men. They were a natural obstacle and hopefully he and his men would be able to butcher many of the invaders before they found solid footing.

The first few stumbled and fell, to be set upon by Caderyn's men. Swords sliced through the air, limbs were severed and heads were separated from their bodies. The remaining Picts realised what was happening and divided into two screaming groups that charged around both sides of the dead and dying. Caderyn parried and lunged at the nearest. His sword met bone and gristle and the

kill was sealed with a scream from his victim. He parried and
lunged again. This time his sword was met by a shield and his arm
jarred painfully.

His small band was now surrounded by screaming Picts. Blades
flashed, shields clashed and his men were falling. He met a blade
with his shield which he rammed into his attacker's face. The
round metal boss in the centre, split his face in two and he fell into
the stinking blood-soaked mud. Caderyn felt a blow to his shoulder
from behind and wheeled around to see a young boy, his face full
of terror, about to strike him for a second time. Caderyn hesitated;
the youngster looked so young, but then his childlike face
contorted with rage and he stabbed his blade at Caderyn's stomach.
Caderyn side-stepped the lunge and thrust his sword into the boy's
throat. For a split second the lad's eyes showed confusion, the
next, they showed nothing at all as he fell at Caderyn's feet.

He looked about desperately. He must have lost half of his men
and in a few moments he will have lost them all. He ran and
barged a Pict who was just about to eviscerate one of his soldiers.
He hit him hard from the side and both men tumbled across the
sodden ground. Caderyn picked up a rock and killed him with a
single blow to the head. He knelt up, readying himself to stand, but
was pushed hard from behind. He fell forward into the mire and
rolled quickly onto his back, sword ready to parry. Standing over
him was Uvan, his tattooed face and bare arms covered in the
blood of his victims.

He raised his axe high but stopped before he could strike. He
looked down in confusion and saw the tip of a sword's blade
sticking out of his stomach.

Taraghlan pulled his sword from Uvan's back and kicked him
hard behind his knees. The big man fell just missing Caderyn,
and Taraghlan finished him off with a stab to the throat.

"Quickly. No time to sleep, Caderyn," Taraghlan yelled as he
turned back to help his reinforcements finish off the remaining
Picts.

Caderyn laughed. At last the numbers were now more even and

it shouldn't take very long to finish the job. "Leave some alive," Caderyn shouted, but by the time the blood-letting had stopped, none of the Picts had survived.

oOo

"A hole in the wall?" roared Madron when Taraghlan told him how the Picts had entered the village. "How is that possible?"

"It would have taken many hours to make that breach and I'm sure the sentries would have seen such activity outside the walls."

"Then what? They had help from inside in the village?"

Taraghlan and Caderyn both nodded.

"Who?" Madron's eyes flashed with fury.

Taraghlan shrugged. "I cannot think of a single soul within our tribe who would wish us such harm – except for one man."

Madron glowered towards the door. "Me too."

CHAPTER 16

Charley looked over at Richard. "I think I have to tell her."

"Who, Antoinette?"

"Yes."

He frowned. "How come?"

"Tonight I discovered that the Avertci's priest was plotting with a band of Picts to attack the village. I think the plan was to murder Catherine, but before I could intervene and warn them, the brooch brought me back." She pulled a blanket around her shoulders and shivered; after the high daytime temperatures, the marquee felt very cold. She hauled herself wearily from the camping chair and ambled over to the kitchen area and flipped on the kettle. "I don't know what to do for the best."

Richard frowned again. "But I thought you said you can't interact with them. No one can see you. How could you possibly warn them?"

Charley turned back excitedly. "That's true; they can't see or hear me but I've discovered I can interact with the environment. It was raining and I got wet, I brushed through some furs that covered a doorway. I figured that I could maybe set a fire next the hole in their palisade and that would have brought them running…"

"But you never got the chance."

Charley's face tightened. "But I never got the chance."

"Well you can't go back again tonight. The brooch must have brought you back for a reason. Maybe you were not destined to intervene; what's done is done."

"I know. You're right and it's because of that, that I want to come clean to Antoinette."

"And what if she confiscates the brooch and forbids you to return?"

"Then I'll just have to get it back again," she said mischievously. "Whatever she decides, I've got to go back and find out what happened."

oOo

Greg Collier edged quietly out of the marquee; he couldn't quite believe what he'd just heard. It had to be nonsense, surely. Maybe she'd just been relating a dream, but then why would she have to come clean to Antoinette about a dream? And what was she saying about a brooch? Apparently it had 'brought her back,' but brought her back from where? *"I need to find that brooch."* Quietly, he made his way to the women's dormitory tent.

The ten beds in the dorm were positioned along the right-hand wall. Between each was a modesty screen and each bed space had a privacy curtain fixed to rails that ran from screen to screen. Each space also had a small camping table. In the communal area were clothes rails where the girls could hang muddy outer garments and waterproofs. There were no mod-cons or homely touches for the dig team; no lockers or lights; they were expected to live out of their suitcases and use torches at night.

Greg peered through the door at the end of the tent and was greeted by the sound of gentle snores. He crept past the first two beds and noted that the third was empty. Charley's. He quickly ducked into the space and pulled out his torch. He filtered the light through his fingers and began to search her bed-space. He grasped the bedding for balance as he hunkered down and checked under the bed. As expected, her suitcase was there and he gently pulled it clear and unzipped it. He rummaged through her bras, knickers, shirts and jeans, but found no brooch. He pushed it back and ran his hand under her mattress. His fingers touched something – something metallic and cold.

"Night Richard."

The suddenness of the voice made him jump and he jerked his

hand from under the mattress. *Dammit.* Charley had just stepped into the tent and there was no time to grab the brooch.

Charley entered her bed-space and froze. "Who's there?" She peered into the darkness but could see nothing. "Who's there?" she said again as she pulled out her torch and switched it on. The space was empty. *"Phew. You're jumping at shadows."* She mentally told herself off for being so jumpy and switched on her battery-operated lantern that hung from the modesty screen.

She turned back to face her bed, and froze. She could see her suitcase underneath it. *"I'm sure I left that out of sight."* Then she noticed a ruck in the bedding. Her bed was always made with military precision and creases and rucks were just not acceptable. "Someone *has* been here." As she bent to smooth back the covers, a cold breeze wafted against her legs and she glanced toward the tent wall.

The bottom edge should have been turned inwards with the groundsheet over the top, but the groundsheet and had been folded back and the tent wall had been pulled up, giving enough room for someone to crawl underneath.

"Shit! The brooch." Charley stooped and thrust her hand under the mattress. The brooch was still there. "Thank God for that." She stuffed it into her pillowcase and looked about again. An involuntary shiver rippled down her spine. She felt confused and scared. Why would anyone invade her private space? Were they looking for the brooch? Unlikely; Richard was the only person who knew about it. Cash? No, she trusted her co-workers up to a point but... Her thoughts trailed off and she fingered the brooch through the pillowcase. Could someone other than Richard know about her find? She had told no one else, but maybe he'd let it slip? Her mind was in turmoil, but one thing was now clear, she wasn't ready to hand over the brooch just yet.

oOo

"She has what?"

"A brooch, Rosemary." Walter Smith felt more at ease talking to Forrester at the end of a telephone; she was so intimidating face-to-face that he always found himself stumbling over his words or blushing brightly. On the phone, he felt more assertive, more confident. Maybe it was because he didn't have to look into those dark malevolent eyes. "That Chandler-Price woman has stolen it from the dig and is keeping it for herself."

Forrester frowned. "What sort of brooch?"

Smith felt exasperated. He had just given her the ammunition she needed to get rid of the girl and bring the whole dig into disrepute, yet she only seemed interested in the brooch. "I don't have a clue, Rosemary; it's just a brooch, but the point is, you can close down the project now."

Forrester glared. "Go and find out more about this brooch – what it looks like, how big it is and what it's made from." Her glasses had slipped from the bridge of her hooked nose and she pushed them back again. "And don't call me until you know more about it."

She slammed down the receiver. The mention of the brooch stirred something inside her, but she couldn't put her finger on it. She looked at the clock – 9am – and wondered if she should visit the dig and see for herself.

oOo

Antoinette glared at her protégé. "Show me!"

Charley reluctantly produced the brooch from her rucksack and handed it to her. "Careful. If you feel any pins and needles, put it down straight away."

"If I feel what? Pah, you are not making any sense." Antoinette turned it over in her hand and her eyes widened in wonder. "C'est magnifique," she breathed, "It is exquisite."

"It is. Antoinette I need to explain why I…"

"You do indeed," Antoinette interrupted, her anger returning once more. "You have just admitted to me that you found this brooch days ago and yet you said nothing? Why, were you planning to keep it for yourself?"

"No!" Charley was shocked by the suggestion and hurt that her mentor could think that of her.

75

"Did your conscience get the better of you?"

"No, Antoinette, it's not like that."

"Then tell me what it's like, because right at this moment I'm inclined to remove you from the dig." She turned the brooch around in her hands again and marvelled at its condition and intricacy.

"It's beautiful isn't it?"

Antoinette's demeanour mellowed for a moment. "It is. I think it's the finest I've ever seen." She glared at Charley again and the sharp edge returned to her voice. "Is that why you were going to steal it?"

"No, Antoinette, I promise you. I was never going to keep it, I just…" This was the moment she was dreading even more that making her admission. Now she had to find a way reveal what she'd been doing and she just knew that Antoinette would not believe her.

Antoinette tilted her head. "You just…what?"

Charley moved quickly to the doorway and checked that there was no one outside within hearing distance.

"Charley, sit down and tell me what's going on."

Charley sat opposite and took Antoinette's free hand in hers. "Please, please keep an open mind about what I'm about to say. I really fear you'll think I've gone mad or that I'm fantasising, but I promise, everything I'm about to tell you is true."

Antoinette pulled her hand away and reached for an artefact bag. "This needs to be sealed first; do you want to do the honours?" She held out the brooch and the bag.

"No. I can't. I daren't touch it."

Antoinette rolled her eyes and sealed the brooch in the bag. "So tell me, why the melodrama?"

Charley inwardly winced. If Antoinette's turn of phrase was an indicator, she was going to be in for a hard ride. "You remember our discussion about my vision and the supernatural?"

"Yes. I said it seemed more like time travel and I asked if there'd been a catalyst that took you ba…" Her mouth dropped open. "The brooch?"

Charley nodded. "The moment I touched it, I had pins and needles and then I felt as if I'd been kicked by a mule. When I woke up, I was lying in the river, face-to-face with Catherine."

"Incredible."

"I've been back twice more since then."

A look of anger crossed Antoinette's face as she picked up the artefact bag and tipped the brooch back into her hand. "You are a stupid girl, meddling in things you do not understand. You must tell me everything, Charley, everything; don't leave out the slightest detail."

CHAPTER 17
Feabhra (February) 431AD

As the first streaks of daylight appeared in the grey, depressing sky, Taraghlan and Caderyn found Madron at the top of the gate tower gazing sadly across his rain-soaked village. They stood silently by his side and after a few minutes Madron pulled his dripping furs tighter around his neck, sucked air across his teeth and cursed. "How many men did we lose to those turds?"

"About half."

"Then you will ride out this morning and seek your alliances."

Taraghlan smiled with relief. "Thank you. It is for the survival of our people."

"I know," he snapped impatiently. "Go straight to the Corieltauvi tribe."

Caderyn stepped uneasily in front of his chief. "They may need a trade, but we have nothing to give them of big value."

Madron looked sadly towards the great hall. "We do. Algar, their chief, has a young son about three summers. I have a new-born daughter." He paused to let the significance permeate.

"T-that is too big a trade surely?" stammered Caderyn.

Madron's eyes narrowed and, ignoring Caderyn, he turned to face Taraghlan. "His name is Taranis. You will promise Catherine to him. If Algar accepts then I want the boy brought here when he is ten summers old. He will be trained to fight and he will be schooled in how to be a good husband to my daughter. Tell Algar they will be married when Catherine is thirteen summers; not before. Tell him she is the greatest gift I can offer."

Taraghlan knew better than to argue. "I'll need a dozen men to ride with me. Caderyn will stay behind to keep the village safe."

Madron nodded. "Don't come back until the alliance is agreed."

oOo

Antoinette Deselle flopped back onto her seat, tears in her eyes. "I, I don't know what to say, mon cher enfant." She reached for a tissue. "I think you should be sectioned under the Mental Health Act." She dabbed at her eyes. "But I believe you. What you have told me is so fantastical, it *has* to be true; at least I want it to be."

"I promise you it is all true. I've seen things that no one else in living history has experienced."

"And what about the language they speak?"

"I would say it is Old Brittonic."

"And you understand it?"

"That's another fantastic thing about all this. I can understand them perfectly; I know it's essentially a foreign dialect, but it's like they're almost speaking modern English."

Antoinette held up her hand. "And you say you tried, but failed to intervene?"

"Yes."

"There is a reason for that. The slightest change you make to the past will alter the future completely. Maybe not for you, but let's assume you had managed to prevent the raid on the village. The timelines, the family trees, of all those people who survived because of your intervention, would be altered.

"If you had stopped the attack, what would have happened to their descendants; to the ones who currently exist because the attack actually *did* go ahead? Would they have just simply disappeared to be replaced by new bloodlines?

Charley looked forlornly at the floor. "The butterfly effect."

"Exactement. You can never, never intervene. Do you understand?"

Charley tilted her head to one side. "I can never intervene? That sounds like you are giving me an instruction for the future?"

Antoinette Deselle smiled and handed her the artefact bag. "It is too dangerous for you to keep using the brooch in your trench. You could have drowned in the mud on your first trip."

Charley took the bag and laughed. "That's a bit of an exaggeration, Professor."

"I'm serious. We need to see if you can go back from the safety of my tent."

Charley smiled with gratitude. "I can't tell you what it means to know that you believe me."

"I do believe you Mon Cher, but we need to make these time-jumps in a more controlled environment. I have no interest in your connection with Catherine or her troubles. I'm only interested in historical data so there is one condition to my allowing you to return again."

"Anything."

"You are to record everything you can. I want to know historical data. If you come back from a trip with nothing to offer, then that will be the end of it."

"I wonder if a modern day video camera would work?"

Antoinette smiled. "I doubt it. I'll keep the brooch in the high-risk artefact safe. If you feel up to it, we can try again tonight."

CHAPTER 18 - 443AD
Iúil (July)

Madron smiled at his daughter and stroked her dark hair. "You have grown so fast. Did I ever tell you how fair your hair was when you were born?"

"Yes, many times."

"And you look so much like your mother."

"You have told me that many times, too." She giggled and took his hand.

Madron gave a squeeze. "And now you have reached twelve summers. You are nearly a woman. Soon the child you are will be no more."

Catherine looked petulantly at the floor. "And do I still have to marry Taranis next year?"

Madron laughed. "Yes. It is arranged. Why, do you not like him?"

Catherine scowled. "He is a pig."

Madron's eyes twinkled. "Did he beat you at sword play again?"

"Yes he did. Father he is older, bigger and stronger than I. His sword arm is well muscled but you won't let me train for real. How can I ever beat him."

"You cannot. Nor do I want you to."

"You want me to learn my mother's skills instead."

"Her healing skills, yes I do. There will be no more sword play"

"I can be a good with a sword too, Father." She thought for a second. "No I can be *great* with a sword and still learn the old ways. I can still be a priestess."

Madron hushed his daughter and looked tentatively at the door.

81

"You must not mention being a priestess. Timancius would not allow it and I don't trust him. His magic is dark."

Catherine straightened her long grey cotton dress. "His magic is not magic at all, father. I know this."

"I wonder sometimes. I do not like him and I do not trust him, but he is our priest and as such commands your respect.

Catherine gazed up at her father's dark eyes. "I will never respect him."

Madron looked at her, concern etched across his weathered face. "We have talked about him many times, Catherine; I have told you what he intended when you were born and I believe you are still in danger."

Catherine nodded. "I know this, but our paths seldom cross outside my studies."

Madron shook his head sadly. "That will not last. He has seen you grow, he sees your mother in you and that disturbs him. He knows you want to be like her and that *really* frightens him. I fear that the next year will be very dangerous for you."

Catherine tilted her head, "Why?"

"Because he only has until your wedding to Taranis, to harm you."

She frowned. "I don't understand."

Madron blushed slightly. "Because you will no longer be intact after you and Taranis are joined together. Timancius can only appease his gods if you are intact."

Catherine pulled away from her father. "Then *please* let me learn how to fight."

Madron laughed, "You will not need to wield a sword to defeat Timancius. Not for as long as your mother is with you." He smiled and reached for her hand again. "Despite his hatred for you, your education is his responsibility. He will never teach you enough to become the Avertci priestess, but his teachings about herbs and plants will be important; just as they are for all the girls in the village. He will teach you how to use them to cure ills. If you have truly inherited your mother's abilities, his teachings will be a good foundation for you to build upon."

Catherine stared at the floor again and wondered if she should tell him that Timancius had never allowed her to attend his teachings on herbs and healing. Everything she knew had been self-taught. She hated him with every fibre of her being and she knew her magic was more powerful than his, but she was not ready to show him… not yet. The time was not right and she would have to rely on her mother's guidance to tell her when it was.

Movement at the doorway stopped her thoughts and a young man entered the hut. He was 14 years old, about 5'7" with a mass of dark floppy hair. Although quite slim, he displayed a finely honed young body with some good muscle definition in his strong arms; evidence of his constant training. His greatest wish was to be allowed into battle against the Picts. He was trying to grow a beard, but it just refused to show. He unbuckled a sword and propped it just inside the doorway, smoothed his dark brown tunic and bowed slightly.

"Lord."

Madron smiled. "Ahh, Taranis. We were just talking about you." Catherine dug him hard in the side but Madron ignored it. "Have you come to challenge my daughter to another fight?"

The boy grinned at Catherine. "No Lord. She is too slow for me. It is too easy to beat her."

Catherine pulled herself away from Madron's grasp and stomped to the door. "I *shall* beat you Taranis. I swear."

Taranis and Madron laughed loudly as she flounced out of the hut. Madron beckoned the boy to join him and poured him a cup of ale. "Tell me why you are here."

"I have a message for you, from Taraghlan. He is asking you to meet him in the hall; there is a challenge amongst the men that he can beat you in sword play."

Madron's eyes widened. "He has *never* beaten me in a fight."

"Lord, he is claiming that he lets you win, because you are the chief."

Madron downed his ale and reached for his sword and shield.

"He lets me win?" he roared. "Then the little turd will be meeting his gods." He winked at Taranis and strode from the hut.

oOo

Antoinette Deselle handed Charley the brooch. "Lie back. I'll be here all the time."

The last of the daylight had been squeezed out of the sky and now, as darkness took over, the camp was quiet. Most of the team had gone to bed, exhausted after another long, hot day in their trenches. Charley had fully uncovered the bones that she believed were Catherine's, but she struggled emotionally with their removal and storage. It felt disrespectful to disturb them and she wished she hadn't found them. It also felt very personal, as if part of *her* life were being mistreated.

Greg Collier had been particularly annoying. He hadn't been rude or unpleasant, but he just kept getting in the way. He had been paying far too much attention to her section of the dig and he kept bombarding her with questions about every aspect.

Eventually Charley had to tell him to go away. "I can't concentrate, Greg. You're really beginning to piss me off."

"As you wish," he muttered and begrudgingly sloped off.

It had been quite a successful few days for all concerned. A new trench had been opened-up on the landward side of the old river bed and it had given up evidence of a potential burial site. Certainly two graves had been found along with a selection of 'grave goods:' weapons, coins, jewellery and decayed fragments that may have been wooden bowls that would have contained food at the time of the burials. More importantly, the finds were confirmed as being Saxon.

Antoinette sat back in her chair. "Remember, I want details; clothing, language, how they lived, everything."

Charley nodded and slipped the brooch over her neck. She lay back and was immediately hit by the first jolt. She yelped and grasped Antoinette's hand. "The second one is usually worse." It hit her as the words left her mouth and she didn't even have time to scream before she lost consciousness.

Antoinette looked at her in shock. It had happened so fast. She quickly felt for a pulse. It was there and extremely rapid. "I hope I've done the right thing," she said quietly.

"How so?" asked a voice from the doorway.

"Sainte merde," swore Antoinette as she jerked around to see Richard. "What the hell are you doing? You don't just wander into my tent."

Richard stood in the doorway, the tent flap held back in his left hand and a bottle of wine in his right. "I'm so sorry. I just wanted to give you this." He held out a bottle of supermarket red wine. "It *is* French."

Antoinette eyes him suspiciously. "Why are you giving me wine?"

"For not telling you what Charley was up to."

Her eyes narrowed. "You know about this?"

"Yes. I know everything."

"You know about the brooch too?"

Richard nodded and suddenly noticed that Charley was out cold on Antoinette's bed. "Is she OK?" He took a step into the tent but then stopped abruptly and looked accusingly at Antoinette. "Is she using the brooch now?"

Antoinette nodded. "She is."

Richard handed her the bottle and moved to Charley's side. "Surely there's a risk?"

Antoinette placed the bottle on the floor and ran her fingers through her grey hair to untangle some wayward locks. "I do not see it as a risk, well not a big one. She is merely asleep and dreaming."

"She can interact with the environment. Did she tell you that?"

"Yes, but…"

"If she can do that, then to all intents and purposes she's not dreaming, she's really there."

Antoinette looked down sadly at Charley's unconscious form. "Then let us hope she comes through this visit unscathed."

Richard frowned. "Did she tell you that we're only friends?"

The question took Antoinette by surprise. "Er, yes, but why is that relevant?"

"Because I wanted more and I'm used to getting my own way."

"So you're not happy about the situation?"

"No I'm not, but as her friend, I'm telling you to make sure she survives this."

Antoinette glared. "You do not speak to me like that. You are the school's caretaker; you are not part of this dig."

Richard pulled back the tent flap and disappeared into the cold night air and Antoinette turned back to Charley and shivered. For the first time, real doubt coursed through her and she prayed she had done the right thing by letting her return.

CHAPTER 19
Iúil (July) 443AD

The summer sun was beating down on the village. After a long, wet winter and spring, the villagers despaired of ever feeling warm again. Early crops had been washed away and now the ground was bone dry and crops were failing through *lack* of water.

Timancius had recklessly promised rain before the next full moon, but had no idea how to make it happen.

A young boy had entered his hut with some news. Timancius listened. He could not believe what he was hearing. "How badly injured is he?" he demanded.

"It is bad I think. He was in a contest with Taraghlan and he tripped and fell on his own sword."

Timancius clasped his bony hands together in delight and dismissed the youth. This was wonderful news. For twelve years he had patiently waited to get rid of Catherine, but while Madron lived, the opportunity was unlikely to present itself. He also knew that if he waited until after the wedding ceremony, she would be unsuitable for sacrifice. Now however, he might have a real chance to dispatch Madron to his gods *and* rid himself of Ailla's accursed offspring.

oOo

Charley watched in horror as Taraghlan and his men hurriedly carried Madron to his hut and laid him on his cot. His tunic and furs were soaked in blood and she could see a ragged tear in his stomach.

"Leave me be!" he bellowed. "It is a scratch." He tried to climb out of his bed but Taraghlan held him down.

"It is *not* a scratch!" Taraghlan shouted back. "Lie still." He turned to one of his men. "Send for Timancius."

"No!" shouted a young voice and the man stopped mid-stride. "I will tend him; he's my father." Catherine pushed her way through the throng and ripped away the clothing around the wound and stuffed it into the slash. Madron cried out but Catherine hushed him. She might have been twelve, but was no longer a little girl. Her voice and actions were self-assured and mature. Hold this in place," she demanded of Taraghlan. "I will be back soon." With that, she ran out of the hut and Charley followed.

It was a heady mix of scents: Lavender, Yellow Rattle, Marigold were among the plants Catherine had gathered. She stood by the bank of the stream clutching the freshly-made posy in her young hands. The weather had turned on its axis signalling the end of the hot dry spell. A harsh Northerly wind had sent dark clouds scudding across the sky and as Catherine dropped her posy into the fast-running water, the first heavy and determined raindrops splashed onto her shoulders. She said a silent prayer to her favourite goddess, Brigit, who bestowed her with her healing powers and she then looked up sharply as a painful cry emanated from her father's hut.

Quickly, she gathered-up the fresh supplies and some Slippery Elm she had just foraged and swiftly splashed through the rain, back to the hut to make a poultice for Madron's wound.

It took a second or two for her eyes to adjust to the gloom. The villagers had left, to spare Madron's embarrassment, but Agnethena, her best friend and Brid, her aged nurse, were there, fussing around Madron's sturdy oak cot, whilst Taraghlan continued to try and stop Madron as he struggled to sit up.

Brid slapped his arm. "Enough!" chided the old lady. "You will surely split your wound wider if you do not keep still." But Madron would not keep still. As he tried again to sit up, Agnethena reached out to hold his shoulders.

"No!" he bellowed, "Let me be, aaaarrggh!" Pain shot through his stomach and he lashed out and struck Agnethena hard in the chest. She fell backwards with surprised cry and Catherine stepped quickly into her place.

"Father, look at me." she commanded, and grabbed his face tightly between her hands. "Look at me, father, LOOK at me." She held him firmly and forced his head round towards her. His angry, dark eyes met hers; bright sparkling blue and full of compassion and determination. As Catherine's held his gaze, her eyes suddenly flared an even brighter blue, so blue that they reflected back from deep within Madron's own eyes.

He tried to wrench his head away and break the eye contact, but it was too late and he fell back, unconscious.

Taraghlan stepped back, exhausted. "Thank you. I couldn't hold him any longer."

Brid smiled. "I tried to hold him too, but I just don't have the strength these days."

Catherine smiled. "There's many years of fight left in you yet Mamo."

The old woman smiled back. She loved the fact that Catherine referred to her as her grandmother. There were no blood ties, but having cared for the infant Catherine after her mother died and supporting and guiding her through her formative years, she felt part of the family.

"Here." Catherine beckoned to Agnethena and pointed to the basket of plants now strewn across the earthen floor. "Pound that and mix it with a little warm water to make a poultice."

oOo

Charley was fascinated by Catherine's self-assuredness. She was initially confused when she arrived in Madron's hut again, because she had expected to see a baby, not a confident young girl.

As the poultice worked its magic and Madron's pain began to subside, it was now more of a dull throb. "I will bind the wound when the poultice has done its work," said Catherine.

Madron laid his forearm across his eyes and sighed.

"Father?"

He removed his arm and smiled at his little girl. "Where do you

89

find your wisdom, daughter?"

She moved close to him and stroked his forehead, "You know where. She is with me, always."

A cold breeze riffled through the hut as Timancius swept through the heavy curtain and saw Brid and Agnethena busying about at the back of the hut. "You two, leave now!"

The women reluctantly hurried from the hut and Timancius then turned his attention to Madron "My Lord, I've only just heard; you are injured?"

Madron grimaced, "I was sliced by my own sword."

Timancius pushed Catherine aside, "No matter my lord I will administer to you immediately."

Madron put his hand up to silence the priest, "Unnecessary, Catherine has tended to me." He pulled away the clean strip of linen covering his wound. "The wound is good. I just need it closed."

Timancius glared at the little girl, "I have warned you not to meddle in such things. The gods will punish you."

Catherine glared back, "You refuse to teach me healing with the other girls, what do you expect me to do?"

Madron pulled himself into a sitting position, "You refuse to teach her?"

Timancius ignored the question. "The other children are not so free with the gods. They have respect for the powers I teach, whereas you do not."

"I have had to teach myself."

Timancius looked mortified. "You teach *yourself?* What demons possess you?"

"My mother guides me. Are you saying my mother is a demon?"

Madron grabbed Timancius's robe. "You refuse to teach her?" he repeated.

"As I said, she…"

"*She* is my daughter," he roared. "She is the future of our people. You do *not* deprive her of the skills she will need to administer to them."

Catherine touched her father's trembling hand, "I don't need Timancius. Tell him again, father, how is your wound?"

"It is good," Madron smiled at her.

"I did not learn this from Timancius."

The priest stepped closer to his chieftain, "My lord, I have brought you a remedy to hasten your recovery." He produced a small leather pouch and a cup from within his robes and handed them to Madron. "Let me close your wound and then you must drink this."

Charley watched in fascination from the other side of the hut as Timancius closed and bandaged Madron's wound. She could feel Catherine's powers as clearly as if they were her own. The sensation was incredible. At that moment, Catherine tilted her head, like an animal that had just detected a strange noise. She stared straight into the corner where Charley was standing and their eyes met. Charley instinctively recoiled into the shadows, but Catherine kept staring and then she smiled in Charley's general direction before turning her attention back to her father.

Charley swallowed hard at the realisation that Catherine knew she was there. It sent shivers down her spine. Whatever powers Catherine possessed, Charley knew they were a force for good. It was nature and the universe at its strongest and yet underneath, she sensed the overwhelming stench of treachery and evil. Charley just knew that it had to be emanating from Timancius.

Madron took the pouch from the priest. "What is it?"

"Just an infusion of simple herbs, it will restore you to full health before the night falls."

Madron poured the thick green liquid from the pouch into the cup and downed it in one swallow. "Father, no!" Catherine leapt up and tried to swipe the cup away, but it was too late. Madron suddenly gasped and grabbed his throat, "It burns."

Timancius stood aside with a thin, mean smile on his lips. "Don't fight it, my lord."

"What have you done to me?" Madron tried to heave his

91

massive frame from the cot, but fell back onto the furs that covered it. "I can't move." His breathing became laboured and raspy.

"Father!" screamed Catherine and she grabbed his head and pulled open his mouth, but before she could plunge her hand in to induce vomiting, she was grabbed by a pair of strong hands and pulled away from the cot.

Timancius pushed her to the door and into the grip of two of his junior priests. "Take her to the grove. It's time for her to meet her mother again."

oOo

Charley's hand flew to her mouth as she absorbed the enormity of what she had just witnessed. She felt strangely calm about Catherine's fate at Timancius's hand, because she knew she was destined to survive it, but it was Madron she was worried about.

She ran to the cot. Madron was barely breathing and there was slimy green foam on his lips. In desperation she tried to open his mouth, but her hands made no contact; they had no substance. It was like swiping her hand through a hologram.

"And yet I can move aside a curtain to enter a hut?" She looked on in despair and then made a decision. *"I can't help here. I need to find Catherine. I need to see what happens."* She turned quickly and ran from the hut.

oOo

"I've made a decision, Walter. I'm travelling down tomorrow. I should be on-site by eleven. Be there."

Smith blanched. "There's really no need, Rosemary. I have everything in hand."

"I want to see this monumental fuck-up for myself. Just make sure you're there." Walter's face reddened when he realised she had hung up on him. "Ignorant bitch,"

CHAPTER 20
Iúil (July) 443AD

Timancius threw Catherine onto the cold, stone table, "Hold her still," he snapped at one of the priests, who tentatively pressed down on the little girl's shoulders.

"My Lord, I'm not sure that…"

Timancius pulled a dagger from beneath his robe. "Hold her still or by the gods I'll cut you down where you stand."

The aide pressed down harder and Timancius stepped closer to Catherine's side. With the ground baked hard, the torrential rain began to flood the low-lying areas of the village and his feet squelched in the thick mud that now covered the floor of his makeshift temple. He looked into her eyes. They were the brightest blue he had ever seen and they seemed to flare even brighter as he looked down upon her. She might only be twelve, but Timancius knew that if he allowed her to live, she would be a stronger and more powerful priestess, than he had ever been as a priest.

"Timancius," her voice was quiet and knowing. He held her gaze, "Timancius you cannot kill me; my gods will not allow it and your gods will punish you for trying."

"What do you know of the gods, little girl? You are a stripling; you think they listen to you?"

Catherine smiled, "Then what are you frightened of? Why kill me?" Her eyes flared brighter still.

"Enough of this," Timancius snarled, "I should have killed you when you were first born. I told your father, but he wouldn't listen."

"And now?"

"And now, with our enemies so close, my gods must be

appeased or we'll be wiped-out."

Catherine frowned. "What enemies? The Picts?"

"Yes, the Picts. My scouts tell me they are returning to our region and means only one thing, battle, and people are going to die."

"And how will killing me help?"

Timancius scowled. "The gods have been displeased with me for twelve years for letting you live, but now I can make it right. Your powers are growing and I cannot allow that." He moved forward and held the dagger above Catherine's heart. "You can take comfort that you will be meeting your own gods very soon."

He held the dagger with both hands, raised it high above his head and then drove it downwards. As the blade plunged towards her heart Catherine reached up and touched his robe. An intense jolt shot through his body and down his arms, which were instantly paralysed. The knife stopped inches above Catherine's heart and no matter how hard he tried to press down, his arms wouldn't move.

"What is this sorcery?"

"I told you, Timancius," she smiled again, her finger still touching his robe, "you cannot kill me. Where are your gods, now?"

"No!" he shouted, "You *must* die."

There was a sudden blast of cold air and a large figure stumbled into the hut, "TIMANCIUS!"

The Priest snapped his head up and looked in fear at the huge form of Madron, standing in the doorway. "M-my Lord, how can this be? You are…."

"I am what, Timancius? Dead?"

"My Lord, I…"

"And what made you believe I was dead?" he held up his hand to stop the terrified priest from answering. "Brid made me vomit up your poison."

Timancius tried to straighten-up but to his horror, found he could not let go of the dagger. His feet started to slip in the mud and he struggled to maintain his balance. He shot a glance at Catherine, "Please, let me go."

Catherine smiled again, "As you wish, Timancius," and she moved her hand back to her side. The sudden release caused the priest to lose his balance. He fell and smashed his eye socket on the corner of the stone table. His scream was ear-piercing and he landed heavily in the mud where he rolled onto his back, crying and shrieking, blood spurting from the hole where his eye used to be.

Madron staggered to his daughter's side and was about to scoop her up, when she raised her hand to stop him. "What? What is wrong?" he asked.

Catherine smiled at her father and looked over the edge of the table at the writhing figure of the High Priest. "I say again, where are your gods now? I am not immortal and I will certainly die someday, but it will not be at your hand, Timancius. It will never be at your hand."

Three of Timancius's student priests ran to his side. They tried to haul the injured priest to his feet, but he was hysterical with pain and thrashing about in the mud.

Madron pushed them aside, grabbed Timancius by his cloak and pulled him to his feet. "Catherine, your choice."

Catherine smiled calmly. "If I had wanted him dead, Father I would have killed him myself."

Madron pulled the writhing man closer. "If I had my way, I'd gouge out your other eye before spilling your guts over the floor, you miserable turd. You can thank Catherine for your life." He pushed the terrified man to the door and threw him out into the cold rain.

"Be gone from my sight. I have a decision to make about you."

He turned back to his daughter, now standing and took her gently into his arms, "He shall not hurt you again."

Catherine smiled wisely, "He will try, but he will always fail."

Madron smiled back, "You have your mother's powers; I can

see it. I'm not sure what you did to him, but you can clearly protect yourself."

Catherine nodded, "The gods were with me today. I shall make an offering of thanks tonight." She squeezed him tighter still and then pulled away so that she could see him more clearly, "So *now* can I be a Priestess?"

CHAPTER 21
Iúil (July) 443AD

Charley had been physically sick when Timancius lost his eye. She stared at the green bile pooling on the muddy ground and wondered how it was that no one else could see it. It also seemed miraculous that no one had heard her retching; she knew from experience that she was the noisiest of her university pals when it came to being sick.

As Madron ejected Timancius from the makeshift temple, Catherine again looked directly at her and smiled. She muttered something that Charley couldn't hear and then then allowed her father to swallow her up in his bear-like arms.

"I need to do more research into the ancient Britonic languages." Charley thought. "I shouldn't be able to understand them, but I do...perfectly." She didn't question it too deeply. Nothing about these experiences was normal.

Charley waited for Madron and Catherine to leave the clearing and then followed them from a safe distance as they followed the track that led through the woods and back to the village.

Taraghlan ran from the gate as soon as Madron appeared and rushed to his side. "Lean on me Lord. We must get you back to your bed." He pushed his shoulder beneath Madron's arm and took his weight. Madron didn't argue and allowed his friend to steer him back to his hut.

Brid shuffled quickly through the gate and grabbed Catherine by her arms. "What happened? Are you hurt?"

Catherine hugged her. She was only an inch shorter than her former nurse. "I am well, Mamo."

"What did he want?"

97

"What he has always wanted since the day I was born." Brid's hand flew up to her mouth but Catherine smiled. "He now knows that was a mistake."

"He's dead?" Brid looked hopeful.

Catherine shook her head. "No, but he will always remember the day he tried to sacrifice me to his gods."

They walked on, arm in arm. "If you thought he was your enemy before this," Brid scolded, "then you have just made him your greatest enemy. He will not stop until you are gone. Why did you not kill him?"

"Would my mother?"

Brid didn't expect that question. "No. she would have shown the same mercy as you and let him live with a permanent reminder of what he had done." She smiled at her. "You really are your mother's daughter."

Charley suddenly felt weak and stumbled. She fell against the palisade and watched Catherine and Brid disappear through the gate and into the settlement. There was a tightness in her chest and her vision started to blur. "It's taking me back. Bloody hell, why can't it just let me stay a little longer." The thoughts had only just flitted through her brain when she blacked out and fell to the ground.

oOo

"I owe you an apology." Richard was back in Antoinette's tent. "I was very rude to you."

"No, it's fine. You are worried about her. I understand that."

Charley gave a moan and Antoinette quickly placed her hand on her forehead. "She's cold. Pull the blanket over her."

Richard suddenly stopped as he pulled the blanket up from the bottom of the bed. "Look at her jeans; they're covered in wet mud. It wasn't there a few seconds ago."

Antoinette rubbed the goose bumps that had just surfaced on her arms. "We are meddling in things we don't understand."

Charley moaned again and slowly opened her eyes.

"How are you, Mon Cher Enfant?"

Charley looked about the tent, clearly confused about her surroundings but then her eyes settled on Richard. "Hello you."

Richard smiled "Hello to you too. Are you OK?"

"I think so." She looked up at Antoinette. "How long was I out?"

Antoinette looked at her watch. "About an hour. What happened to you, you're covered in mud."

Charley managed a weak smile. "Again? Seems to be becoming a habit. Can I have some water please?"

She propped herself up on one elbow and drank gratefully from the bottle Antoinette passed her, then slumped onto the bed again. "I saw Timancius try to assassinate Madron, and then he tried to kill Catherine. She's twelve now. The brooch has missed out eleven whole years."

"Maybe it only lets you see what it wants you to see."

Richard snorted mockingly. "Oh come on, it's an inanimate object. It doesn't have a brain, it can't think for itself."

"And it shouldn't be able to transport someone back over a thousand years either," snapped Antoinette, "but it does."

Charley carefully sat up; she still felt a bit woozy. "She's right, Richard. It's obviously got powers of some sort, but it's beyond our science."

He shrugged and sat down on the edge of the bed. "It's a conundrum for sure."

"I would suggest, Mon Cher that nothing of any note happened to Catherine when she was growing up. This was probably the first major event to occur. I suspect when you return next time, her life will have moved on to the next big event."

Charley raised her eyebrows. "I hadn't considered that; like a potted history of her life?"

Antoinette beamed. "Exactement. So what else happened?"

"She's betrothed to a lad called Taranis. He's from another tribe. Part of a deal to support each other I think."

"Blimey!" Richard's mouth gaped. "Twelve's a bit young to go getting engaged."

Charley smiled. "She'll be married to him when she reaches thirteen."

Richard's mouth gaped even more. "Seriously? That's just not right."

Antoinette shook her head. "Many girls were married sooner, if their periods started earlier, but thirteen was considered the optimum age. I can see you need schooling in the ways of the ancient tribes." She grabbed a notebook and pencil from her table. "Tell me all about the people. What they were wearing, hair styles, tools, accommodations. I need to know how accurate our understanding is."

Charley tapped Richard on the knee. "This will *really* bore you. Fancy making me a cuppa?"

oOo

Timancius had not been seen for nearly a month. He had become a recluse, or so everyone was saying. Madron knew the truth however. He had decreed the priest should be banished from the tribe and the only reason it hadn't happened was because no one was brave enough to enter Timancius's dwelling uninvited. Everyone believed he had powers and everyone believed he was in close contact with the gods. To manhandle a priest was a very dangerous thing to do and would almost certainly bring down the wrath of the gods upon those who dared to defile him. And so, for Madron, it became a waiting game.

Catherine's revenge on Timancius's attempt to kill her was common knowledge and the entire village acknowledged that she possessed very potent and capable abilities. She knew that they were looking to her to match powers with Timancius when the time came to execute her father's decree. She also knew that her father would never allow it.

It was therefore a complete surprise when Timancius entered the great hall one evening. Madron's guards ran over to him.

"Let him be!" Madron shouted from the high table. He watched with hatred etched across his face as the priest approached.

Timancius stood before him, clutching a twisted staff of yew, his posture bent, so that he appeared to be at least five inches shorter than normal. His feet were bare and dirty, and his black robe was filthy and threadbare. It hung loosely on his scrawny frame. His one good eye was dark and sunken, and there was a ragged hole where his other eye used to be. The eye socket was healing over, but even so, the damage looked quite horrific.

"There is no need to restrain me my Lord, or to escort me from the village. I am leaving tonight." He looked along the high table. Taraghlan and Caderyn sat, one each side of the king and six of the village elders filled the rest of the table. Sitting to the king's right, at the far end of the table was Catherine. Timancius felt his heart quicken but he quickly looked away and met Madron's hate-filled gaze.

Madron pointed a half chewed sheep bone at him. "Do not stop until you are in the Southlands on the other side of the River Tem."

Timancius wrinkled his thin nose. "There is nothing there my Lord. I had planned to journey to Londinium."

Madron snorted. "Londinium? Even that turd-filled swamp is too good for you. No. You will go beyond the Tem and find yourself another tribe to conquer, but don't ever come back here."

Timancius pulled the cowl of his robe over his head and bowed. "As you wish."

He turned slightly to glare at Catherine and the sloped to the door. Under his breath he muttered a short plea to his gods. This last month of self-imposed confinement had not been wasted; he had spent the time plotting and planning. His sole aim in life now was to wipe out the Avertci and that damned whore, Catherine.

CHAPTER 22

"Good Morning Ms Forrester." Antoinette held out her hand to welcome the Director of the N.A.S. but the woman ignored her and swept past into the main marquee, hurriedly followed by the bloated form of Walter Smith.

Antoinette looked down at her empty outstretched hand and shook her head. "Elle a les manieres d'un cuchon," she muttered.

"So it seems," said someone at her side.

Antoinette jumped. "Sainte Mere, Greg you startled me. What did you say?"

"I was agreeing with you. She certainly does seem to have the manners of a pig. Who is she?"

Antoinette raised her brows in surprise. "You speak Francaise?" She hadn't expected anyone at the dig to have such a good knowledge of French.

Greg smiled. "Yeah. My mum was from Rouen."

"You and I must have a conversation one day. I miss speaking in my home language." She looked toward the tent and wrinkled her nose in distaste. "As to your question, that is Rosemary Forrester, from the N.A.S. I had thought that a formal greeting was appropriate but seeing that reaction from her, I think the gloves are off, no?"

"You know her?"

"Yes, very well. We have locked horns many times."

"What's she like?"

Antoinette wrinkled her nose again. "Hard-bitten, rude, ruthless. Think of an unpleasant adjective and it will fit her personality."

"Revengeful?"

Antoinette cocked her head to one side, a look of curiosity in her eyes. "Why do you ask that?"

"Oh I don't know. I've never met her; she just looks very mean-spirited."

"Oh she's that for sure. I hope you'll never be in a position to find out. Be warned, do not cross her, or you'll find out just how mean-spirited and revengeful she can be." She took a step to the doorway. "I'd better go in. Come along if you want."

Greg looked through the entrance. "No Charley?"

"She'll be along presently. And Greg…"

"Yes?"

"Don't get any ideas."

He laughed. "You don't need to worry on that score, Charley can't stand me."

Antoinette smiled. "Probably just as well. I think you would probably be trouble for her."

Greg feigned hurt and followed her into the marquee where they found Forrester examining the artefacts found so far.

"Is this all?" she demanded.

With a clear look of dislike on her face, Antoinette paused to look Forrester up and down. "Still wearing Primark business suits I see, Rosemary?"

Greg smiled. It looked as if the gloves were well and truly off.

oOo

"How long do you have left on site?" Forrester demanded and took a tentative sip of tea from a plastic mug. "God this is swill." She pushed the mug across the table.

Smith was seated opposite Forrester and Antoinette was to her left. Greg pulled up a chair and positioned himself at the end of the table, so he could see both 'Combatants.'

Antoinette shuffled some papers. "Well I'm sorry that the tea is not to your taste, Rosemary, but the red wine doesn't come out until the end of the day."

Forrester ignored the barb and repeated her question.

Antoinette pushed the papers to one side and checked wall chart that had lain beneath them. "Until August 31st. The school reopens on September 5th and we must have the site back to its pre-dig condition before then. I guess in practical terms we'll have to finish around the twenty-fifth."

Walter Smith took a large slurp of his tea and banged the mug down onto the table which caused the tea to slop over the brim. He tutted and unsuccessfully tried to wipe it away with his fingers. Antoinette sighed and tossed him a small packet of tissues. "Thank you Ms Deselle. Tell me, where is that awful protégé of yours?" He kept eye-contact with Antoinette as he wiped up the spilt tea.

"If you mean me, Mr Smith, I'm right behind you." Charley slapped him on the shoulder causing him to slop his tea again. "And don't be so rude, a girl could be offended." She took the chair next to him and sat back with undisguised delight at having caught him out. Smith cursed under his breath and wiped up the fresh tea spill.

Antoinette glared at him and he had the good grace to look away. "Rosemary, this is Charley Chandler-Price. I know you've not met before, but I'm sure you've heard about her."

Charley's and Forrester's eyes met and both women gasped. Forrester scrambled from her chair and took several paces back. What little colour she'd had in her face drained away and she drew her thin lips back into a virtual snarl. "You!"

In contrast, Charley was rooted to her chair. Shock and awe flooded her body and all her senses were screaming at her to run, but she couldn't move. Somehow, she knew this repulsive woman. She had been in her presence before and it leached malevolence.

Greg hurried to Forrester's side to steady her; fearful that she would fall over, but Forrester pushed him away. Antoinette too, went to her aid. "Rosemary, whatever's wrong?"

Forrester broke eye-contact with Charley and staggered towards the exit. "I – I'm sorry. I don't know what came over me. I have to go."

"But Rosemary you should take a moment to recover." Antoinette tried to guide her back to her chair but she pulled away.

"I need to go. Walter?"

"Can't I finish my tea first?"

"Now, Walter, you fucking moron." Smith took a final quick slurp of his tea and followed her into the morning sunshine.

Antoinette stared after her. "What the hell was that about?" She looked at Charley who was still sitting motionless, staring into the distance. "Charley?"

Greg took his seat again and touched Charley's arm. "What's up?" he asked gently.

Charley looked over at Antoinette and tears filled her eyes. "I need to be on my own." Her voice was shaky and she was on the verge of letting out a big sob.

"Charley?"

"I have to go." She pushed her chair back and ran from the marquee.

"What's up with those two?" asked Greg. "It's like they both saw the same freaking ghost."

Antoinette cleared-up her papers and pinned the wallchart back on the notice board. She was thinking…hard. Something had passed between those two women, but what the hell it was, she couldn't imagine.

oOo

Charley rushed into her space in the dorm tent, flung herself onto her bed and let the tears flow. What had just happened? Who was that evil woman? "I know she's Rosemary Forester," she chided herself, "but who is she, really?"

There was no explanation in her mind for what she had felt when she saw Forrester. She had never met her before; she had never seen a picture or had any sort of contact with her, and yet she felt…angry. Why would that be? And where did that woman's malevolence come from?

Antoinette tentatively poked her head around Charley's curtain. "Charley? Are you ok?"

Charley sat up and wiped her eyes with the heel of her hand. "Yes…no…I think so."

"Do you want to explain what that was all about?"

105

"I wish I knew."

Her mentor entered the bed space and plonked herself on the end of Charley's bed. "I think we have known each other long enough now for you to call me, Annie, Don't you?"

Charley managed a weak smile. "Thank you... Annie." She drew up her legs and sat cross-legged, facing Antoinette. "It was so strange. I felt as if I'd known her all my life, and hated her all my life. How can that be?"

"Did you see Rosemary's reaction when she saw you?"

"Not really. I was enveloped in some sort of cloying sense of evil."

"Her reaction was far more dramatic that yours."

"I was aware that she'd stood up."

Antoinette laughed. "Stood up? Mon Dieu, she fell out of her chair. I've never seen her so rattled."

"Rattled?"

"Charley, she was terrified - terrified of *you*. She couldn't wait to leave. She even left her handbag behind."

"I don't understand any of this," Charley wailed. "What's going on?

Antoinette reached out and stroked her cheek. "I will call her in an hour or two and let her know I have her bag. Perhaps I can find out more."

"I hope so, Annie, because this is freaking me out."

oOo

It wasn't until Rosemary Forrester's car joined the M25 that she became aware of her surroundings. She had been so shocked and so deep in thought, that the journey up to that point had been a blur.

The moment she had set eyes on Charley, Forrester knew her. She knew her well and it had scared the shit out of her. All she wanted to do was get away before Charley recognised her. She mentally slapped herself. "Stupid woman, that's utter nonsense. We had never met before. How could she recognise me? What would it matter if she did?"

And yet, underneath that initial terror, Forrester also knew that she hated Charley with every fibre of her body. It still made no sense; despite how she felt, the unassailable truth was that they had never met before and yet Forrester felt such hatred and a burning desire for revenge; but revenge for what?"

To top it all, she was no closer to finding out about the brooch that Charley had supposedly unearthed and without that, she had little hope of closing down the dig before... before what? Again she had no idea.

"Pull into the first service area you come to," she ordered her driver. He just nodded in reply. He knew from bitter experience not to vocalise any responses unless this odious woman asked him a direct question.

She searched around the back seat for her handbag. "Oh shit fuck. Roger, is my bag in the front with you?"

"No ma'am."

"Oh fuck it! Pass me your mobile; I have to make an urgent call."

oOo

Walter Smith clambered out of his car. The last thing he'd anticipated was a return to the dig. He just wanted to return to London and skive-off to his apartment for the rest of the day. He made straight for the main marquee and found Antoinette studying the latest geophysical results.

"Walter? What brings you back?"

"Rosemary forgot her bag. Apparently I'm now her errand boy."

Antoinette chuckled. "You've never been anything else in her eyes. It's on that table over there." She pointed to the beige handbag but Walter made no move to get it.

Antoinette raised her eyebrows. "Something up?"

Smith sidled closer and lowered his voice. "What happened back there? I've never seen that bitch behave like that."

Antoinette shrugged. "I have no idea. And frankly, now that she's out of my hair for the time being, I really do not care."

CHAPTER 23 – 444AD
Bealtaine (May)

Taranis swung his sword at Catherine's head. "Die, you sorceress."

Catherine ducked beneath the blade and hit his ribs so hard her wooden sword snapped in two.

"Arrgh, that hurt."

Catherine giggled. "It was meant to."

Taranis took the broken sword from her. "I think that's enough for now. If your father discovers I am teaching you how to use a sword properly, he will rip out my intestines."

"I will make a new sword when he's not around. Thank you Taranis."

She started to walk away but Taranis caught her arm. "Don't go." He swept his arm around the clearing. "This is a magical place."

Catherine looked about. Of all the clearings in her woods, this was her favourite. The landscape sloped sharply to this small level, grassy area. A rocky outcrop provided a majestic backdrop and where the grassy area fell away, was a small ravine that dropped about fifteen feet to a wide fast–running stream. Tall, magnificent trees around the edge of the clearing provided welcome shade from the hot sun and everywhere there was lush vegetation clinging to the rock faces.

She wrapped her arms around him. "It is. I'm glad you think so too."

Taranis kissed her lightly on the lips. "We should be married by now. You're thirteen and my father grows impatient

Catherine pulled away and danced lightly to the edge of the small ravine. The joy in her face was replaced by sadness as she stood looking at the high rock face on the opposite side.

"I'm not ready."

Taranis swept his dark brown hair from his eyes. "Will you ever be ready?"

She sat on the grass and half turned to look at him. "I don't know. I feel that my destiny lies elsewhere, not just as a wife and mother."

Taranis shook his head and let out a derisory snort. "You are a chief's daughter; you will never *just* be a wife and mother. You have status; that's why the marriage was agreed. That's why my father wants the deal to be sealed."

Catherine looked up sharply. "Is that how you see it; a deal that must be sealed; an opportunity to achieve status?"

Taranis glared down at her. "I have status. I am a chief's son."

"You haven't answered my question."

His eyes softened and he squatted down next to her. "I wasn't happy about the arrangement, you know that. I didn't want a silly little girl for a bride, but this past year..." he paused, wondering how to phrase what he wanted to say, "I've grown to really like you. You are far advanced beyond your summers and you possess logic and powers that frighten me a little. I'm not sure I can speak of love, but I enjoy your company, I miss you when you're not around and I think about you lot. Arrangement or not, I'm glad we have been matched."

Catherine smiled. "I think our fathers need to speak; they need a pact that will hold fast even if we do not wed."

Taranis's posture slumped. "That saddens me."

"What? That I talk about us not being wed?"

"Yes. I want to marry you. I want to lie with you..."

Catherine put a finger to his lips. "I am sorry Taranis, I might seem older than my years but when it comes to marriage or allowing you to bed me, I am not ready; I feel too young and until my mother says the time is right, I shall lie with no man."

A dark scowl crossed his face. "Your mother is dead. She cannot tell you anything." He jumped to his feet. "We *will* be married and you *will* lie with me."

Catherine stood up also and Taranis expected her to round on him and unleash her famous temper but instead, she looked at him with compassion. "So is this the true Taranis? You want to control me? You know that will never happen; and this sudden desire to lie with me? You say you enjoy my company and then you speak like all the other boys in the village."

Taranis turned on his heels and marched across the clearing to the path that meandered home. "Make your new sword and we'll meet here again in two days."

"We need to talk," Catherine called after him as he strode off.

"Talk to your mother!" he shouted back.

oOo

Richard smiled at Charley's recumbent form as he entered her bed space and sat wearily in the camping chair next to the bed.

She opened her eyes and smiled. "Hi. What time is it?"

"About midnight."

She sat up in horror. "Midnight? Christ, I've been asleep for hours" She twisted round to reach for her watch on the side table and checked the time for herself. "Aww shit." She flopped back on her pillows with a forearm across her eyes.

"How are you feeling now?"

"You heard about my 'episode'"

"Antoinette told me. What the hell happened?"

Charley pulled herself up and let Richard plump the pillows for her so that she could sit up and lean against them. "I honestly don't know. I just saw that Forrester woman and…" She paused and stared at her blanket. "I guess I just froze. I had such a profound feeling of hatred for her."

"And this was the first time you'd ever met her?" Charley nodded and Richard frowned. "This is all getting too weird. The sooner the dig finishes and you're out of here the better."

Charley managed a smile. "Are you trying to get rid of me?"

110

He grimaced. "Maybe."

"Go and get some rest, Richard. You look knackered."

"I will, if you don't mind." He heaved himself to his feet. "I'll see you in the morning."

He had just let himself in to his house when his mobile phone vibrated. He recognised the number. "Hello? It's a bit late for a phone call isn't it?"

Walter Smith was in no mood for small talk. "The dig ends on the 31st but they intend to pack up on the 25th. You don't have long. Ms Forrester wants them off-site within three days."

Richard blanched. "That's far too soon. I'm not sure I could even do it by the 25th let alone in three days."

"You're being well paid and the first instalment is already in your bank account. Make it happen or we'll blow your personal life and your job to kingdom come."

"Now wait a minute…" shouted Richard, but the line was already dead.

CHAPTER 24
Deireadh Fómhair (October) 444AD

Taraghlan cocked his head on one side. Something had caught his attention, but he didn't know what. Whenever something happened that he couldn't explain, he always had just one thought, Timancius. He was convinced the disgraced priest would return for vengeance and it worried him.

The hairs on his neck bristled and goose bumps appeared on his arms. "Hey, you!" he yelled at the guard patrolling the rampart on top of the gate, "Anything to report?" The guard shook his head and Taraghlan shivered and pulled his cloak around him; it was time to speak to Catherine.

He found her in Madron's hut, fashioning a wooden sword from a branch of Elm. "Catherine?"

She looked up and smiled. "I felt it too."

Taraghlan's shock was quickly replaced by wonder "What did you feel?"

"I told you, I felt the same as you."

"Fear, foreboding, something unknowable?"

Catherine smiled again. Well, perhaps not exactly the same as you then. I felt no fear. But foreboding?" She stopped whittling and thought about it for a moment. "Yes, foreboding, but it's not unknowable."

"Timancius?"

She giggled, "You place too much importance on that man. No, not Timancius."

"Then what, who?"

"An army. A large army. Maybe three days away."

"I need to ready my men."

Taraghlan made for the door but Catherine raised her hand. "There is no need. It's a royal army. There will be no war."

"Vortigern?" Taraghlan whispered the word and Catherine nodded.

"The King of the Britons is coming here?"

She nodded again.

"But this sense of foreboding…"

"He brings news; news that means trouble for everyone in Britain."

Taraghlan wiped his sweaty face with the edge of his cloak. "What news?"

Catherine went back to her whittling with a mischievous grin on her face. "How could I possibly know that?"

Taraghlan was suddenly galvanised into action. "I must find your father and tell him." He headed to the door again but as he drew back the heavy fur, he looked at her once more. "Vortigern? You are sure?"

"Three days," she said as she whittled and smiled.

oOo

Charley stared at the brooch and shook her head. "I don't think I can, Annie. Meeting that Forrester woman has really rattled me and I'm convinced it's something to do with the past."

Antoinette took her hand and gave it a gentle squeeze. "Forrester can't hurt you in the past, no one can. You have an opportunity like no other, to make discoveries about that period of history."

Charley suddenly felt very angry. "You were against this at the start and now you seem to be unconcerned about my safety, just so long as I bring back research material for you. We have no idea what can or cannot happen to me in the past."

At first Antoinette looked shocked by Charley's outburst but quickly realised that she spoke true. She had got carried away by the thought of so much first-hand knowledge at Charley's fingertips. "I'm sorry, Mon Cher. You are right. I apologise."

Charley smiled. "From what little I've seen, Catherine has trials to face that I can't imagine. If she can show strength, then so can I. I'm not going to let that bitch Forrester stand in my way."

A flicker of concern passed across Antoinette's face. "Stand in your way? Of what? You're not planning to intervene are you?"

"I can't, not yet."

"Not yet? Non, non, you mustn't intervene...Ever. Observe only Charley, promise me."

"I can't promise anything, Annie." Tears glistened in Charley's eyes. "I am so drawn to Catherine's story and I know she dies. Maybe I can help her."

"No!" Antoinette sounded almost panicky. "You must not. Everybody dies at some point, Mon Cher, whether by accident, design, illness or old age, everybody dies and you must not influence the past."

"But..."

"But nothing; think about it, what if, through your actions, Catherine is saved, and defeats the Saxon hordes, then our whole history, architecture and development would change. Think about the millions of people descended from Saxon and Anglo Saxon stock. What would happen to them, to their pasts, to their lineage? What if saving Catherine triggers the equivalent of a time-slip genocide."

"I- I hadn't thought of it like that."

"Go back by all means, observe and report, but do *not* intervene. Do you understand?"

Charley pouted. "Yes."

"I'm serious, Charley. If you give me any cause to doubt you, I will secure the brooch away from your grasp."

Charley looked crestfallen. "I understand, Annie, I really do, but it's going to be so hard to just watch."

"Then you must not go back," said Antoinette determinedly, "and that's an end to it."

"Annie, I must."

Antoinette snatched the brooch away. "This goes into the artefacts safe."

"Annie, no!" Charley could feel bile rising in her throat. Never seeing Catherine again was unthinkable and as Antoinette left the tent, Charley grabbed her waste bin and threw-up in it.

oOo

Richard Armitage was feeling down. He didn't like the fact he had so readily agreed to sabotage this dig, but Smith was right; Casinos like The Piccadilly are unscrupulous and it wouldn't be long before the "Heavies" were knocking on his door.

He had been losing steadily on his last three visits but was convinced that a big win was close. The night that Walter Smith had spotted him, Richard had drawn the last of his savings from his bank. Normally he'd play Blackjack because there was at least a modicum of skill involved, but for some reason on that fateful night, despite knowing it relied completely on chance, he opted to play the roulette wheel instead.

He had lost all his money within an hour - £3000. It was then that a supervisor approached him and led him to an office.

"I've been authorised to offer you a loan at a very competitive rate."

Richard looked suspiciously at the man. "Firstly, who are you? Secondly, why? And thirdly, I can't afford a loan"

The supervisor sat at his desk and pulled some spectacles from his pocket which he began to clean with his pristine white handkerchief. He smiled benignly. "My name is Andrew Thomas and I am the Senior Floor Supervisor. I answer directly to the M.D.

"As for why, well you are a good customer. You've been coming here for some months and you either win or lose small amounts or break even, but you've really been hammered this week. We like to look after our regulars."

Richard shrugged. "Well, like I say, I can't afford a loan."

The supervisor smiled again. No regular repayments are necessary; when you win big, you can pay it back."

Richard rolled his eyes. "When I win big? Well that will be some time never."

"What I mean is, when you win any amount above the total

115

repayable. To be honest, the best way is to repay, is to hand back half of your winnings each time you visit. You'll pay it off in no time."

Even as he signed his name on the agreement, he knew he was making a big mistake. Even more so when he was handed five thousand pounds in cash. "Why don't you just credit my account?"

The supervisor shook his head. "Because we're not authorised or regulated to give loans. We can't have a paper trail."

And so it was that Richard, with five grand in his pockets, returned to the tables and lost the lot!

Dejected and despondent he headed for the exit only to be stopped by Thomas. "Well that was very stupid. You now have no means to keep on gambling. We had anticipated you would ration your spending across several visits."

"I'll get some more, don't you worry."

"Oh but we do worry, Mr Armitage, which is why you now have four weeks to pay it back."

Richard was incredulous. "What the hell do you mean? You said I could pay it back when I win."

"Win using what? You're broke."

"If I'm broke, how do you expect me to pay back five thousand pounds?"

"Seven thousand Mr Armitage" Thomas smiled meanly.

"Seven? I only borrowed five."

"It's called interest, Mr Armitage. Four weeks please. Don't make me call on you to collect." Thomas patted him on the shoulder and walked away.

Yes Smith was right in everything he said. He was desperate for the money.

oOo

Richard put a comforting arm around Charley's shoulder. "Cinders *shall* go to the ball."

Charley wiped her eyes and stared at the floor. "What do you mean?"

"She's put the brooch in the safe?"

"Yes."

"Then I'll get it back for you."

"Don't be stupid, Richard. How could you possibly do that?"

"Oh ye of little faith. Leave it to me." He rose to leave but Charley grasped his hand."

"What are you going to do? Don't put your job at risk for me."

Richard smiled. "It's a crap job anyway."

Charley couldn't see how he could possibly get the brooch, but then the faintest smile touched her lips. "It's a very sweet thought though," she said to herself as she watched him leave.

Richard stepped into bright early morning sunshine, a plan formulating in his mind. If he could get Charley to go back, perhaps he could take the brooch from her while she slept; perhaps she might not be able to return. He saw the headline in his mind, *"Promising archaeologist falls into a coma."* It might be enough to end the dig there and then. Once it had been abandoned he could visit her in hospital and put it around her neck again and bring her back. It was a risk for sure, because no one knew the science behind it, and although he felt embittered by her rejection he still hoped she would survive. His immediate problem however, was how to retrieve the damned brooch.

He entered the main marquee and found Greg Collier just closing the safe. "Morning."

Collier looked up and nodded. "Can I help you?" He didn't particularly like the handsome caretaker, especially as he obviously had designs on Charley. He had to admit to a few pangs of jealously.

"Just looking for Ms Deselle."

"Gone into town; back in about an hour."

Richard thanked him and left, but he didn't go far. He moved quickly to the end of the marquee and peered through an eyelet in the wall. He watched as Greg slipped the safe's key into the breast pocket of his shirt and then busied himself with a small cardboard box of rubble.

This would have to be a waiting game…

Two hours later, Collier pulled off his shirt and swore under his breath. The marquee was getting unbearably hot. He wasn't particularly tanned, but his finely honed, muscular torso brought forth a wolf whistle from Kim Chambers, a student volunteer as she entered the big tent with a mature student, Shelly Price.

Greg chuckled. "That's sexual harassment young lady."

As they sat at one of the artefact-laden tables, Kim flicked her dark hair behind her ears and pulled on a hair band to keep it there. "So, sue me. You old men love it."

Greg feigned hurt. "Old? Thank you very much."

Kim giggled. "You're at least as old as my dad."

"So how old are you?"

"Seventeen."

"Oh god, now I *do* feel old."

Shelly laughed a deep throaty laugh. "Don't worry Kim; I'll keep you safe."

"You will?"

"Hell yes. I want him for myself." She winked at Greg who openly blushed. At nearly fifty, Shelly was the oldest student at the dig. Divorced, with two grown-up sons, she had thrown herself into archaeology with gusto. Everyone had taken an instant liking to this blonde, vivacious woman.

Charley appeared at the door. "Greg, have you seen Richard?"

He shook his head. "Briefly, a couple of hours ago. He was looking for the boss."

Charley tutted. "Fancy some lunch? It's being served up."

"Sure, why not."

Shelly dropped a fragment of pottery back into its cardboard box and scraped back her chair. "Hang on you two, I'm coming too."

Richard watched as Charley, Greg and Shelly strolled across to the mess tent. "He's not put on his shirt." He sprinted into the marquee. Greg's shirt was on a table at the far end. He ran over, grabbed it and searched for the top pocket. He gave it a shake and the key fell into his hand.

"What are you doing? That's Greg's shirt."

Richard's heart jolted in surprise and he spun around to see Kim at her table.

"Er, I know. He sent me over to get it. It's the key to the safe. He didn't want it left where someone might find it."

Kim wrinkled her nose. "He sent *you*? I know he's a lazy git, but why did he send *you*?"

Richard knew the ice he was skating on was getting thinner and thinner. "Oh for heaven's sake, here," he threw the key across the tent. "*You* take it to him if you're that concerned."

Kim shook her head and carried on working. "God, you men are all like petulant kids."

Richard ignored the barb and retrieved the key. This was bad news. That girl knew he had taken the key from Collier's shirt, and whilst she was in the marquee, he couldn't access the safe. "I need to get rid of her."

He walked to the door. "Hear that?"

"What?"

"What's your name?"

"Kim."

"I thought so. Someone's calling you. I think it's Ms Deselle."

"Oh shit. I wonder what I've done wrong. Thanks." She hastened to the door and disappeared into the bright sunshine.

Richard ran to the safe and hurriedly opened it. The brooch was there. He grabbed it and stuffed it in his pocket.

He'd only just locked it when Collier strode into the marquee. "What do you think you're doing?"

Richard stepped away from the safe. His legs felt like jelly and he doubted he could run, even if he'd wanted to. He had to think on his feet, and fast. "I found it on the floor as I was tidying up."

"Bollocks you did."

"No, truly. I recognised it as the safe key and was just trying it in the lock to confirm. You shouldn't leave it lying around where anyone could get it."

Collier grabbed the key from him. "What are you doing tidying up in here? This marquee is nothing to do with you."

"Force of habit I guess. I only came back looking for Charlie again. I'm sorry ok?"

Greg grabbed his shirt front. "Or are you supplementing your salary with a little thievery?"

Banking on Collier being unaware that the brooch had been placed in the safe, Richard continued to brazen it out. "Check the safe then. Nothing's missing. I've not taken anything."

"I don't believe you." He tightened his grip on Richard's shirt.

Richard tried to walk away but as Greg pushed him hard against a support pole, his military training and instinct for survival kicked-in and he responded with a roundhouse punch to the back of Greg's head.

Greg, however, hurled him across the tent a nano-second before the punch made contact, and Richard crashed over a table and landed by the entrance, just as Charley walked in.

"Greg! What the hell?" She dropped to Richard's side, a livid bruise and swelling already visible under his left eye. "Richard, what's going on? Are you ok?"

She helped him sit up. "I'm fine." He scowled at Collier. "That big arse just attacked me."

Collier stepped forwards. "He threw the first punch. This was self-defence. More importantly, he's been in the safe."

"What? Don't be ridiculous." She looked hard at Richard. "You idiot," she whispered.

"That's not true," he said loudly, "I was clearing up found the key on the floor. I tried it in the lock to confirm it was the safe key, that's all. I was going to bring it over to you."

Collier took another pace but Charley held up her hand. "Back off Greg. Where's the key now?"

Richard pointed at Collier. "He's got it."

"Greg, you'll be thrown off the dig for this."

"Oh c'mon Charley, he's lying his arse off. He had no reason to test the key. He should have just returned it."

"I thought I was doing the right thing."

"Bollocks. You saw an opportunity to make some cash and you took it."

"That's enough!" shouted Charley and her eyes flared in anger. "You shouldn't have left the key around, this isn't Richard's fault; it's yours and your flying fists. Come on sweetheart." She helped Richard to his feet and to the door. "You'll pay for this, Greg; I swear to God."

Richard cast a glance back at Collier and gave him a sly wink. It had turned out well after all.

CHAPTER 25

"I'm so sorry." Charley dabbed a small cut under Richard's eye with some damp cotton wool. You got hit for trying to help me."

"Yeah well, it was worth it." He adjusted his position in the armchair and pulled the brooch from his pocket.

Charley's eyes widened in disbelief. "Oh my god, you got it!"

"Greg caught me just as I was about to put the key back in his pocket. If he hadn't come in no one would've been any the wiser."

"Oh Richard, this is all my fault, I'm so sorry." She stood up. "I must go."

"Why?"

"I've got to sort things with Greg before he reports you to Antoinette. I don't want you to lose your job over this."

"You're not going to tell him the truth, surely?"

"Do I have a choice?"

Richard felt a slight panic welling up inside. If she told Collier the truth, then she'd have to give back the brooch and that would mean an end to his plan to trap her in the past. He'd wrestled with his conscious over the plan, and although he liked her, his feelings of rejection were growing fast and at times the hostility he felt inside was almost too much to bear. Once the deed was done he was sure he'd feel better. He just had to convince her to take another trip. "If you confess to Collier, he'll tell Antoinette and you'll never get the chance to go back. Think about it. This could be your life's work; don't throw it away. If they report me for assault, I'll take my chances. Honestly."

She smiled sweetly. "You'd do that for me?"

Richard feigned embarrassment. "I'd do *anything* for you."

She kissed him lightly on the cheek. "Then you can watch over me when I use the brooch to go back again... tonight."

oOo

Greg Collier sat in the mess tent picking at a rather wilted chicken salad. He had missed lunch, thanks to Richard and although he thought he was hungry, the altercation had chased away his appetite. What was Armitage doing with the key? The artefacts in the safe weren't valuable per se; you couldn't really sell them. Their value lay in the story they could reveal. They were items that were in very good condition and would be of enormous interest to the profession. Perhaps he thought it contained money?

Antoinette entered and plonked herself wearily on the chair opposite him. "Is there much left for lunch?"

Greg stretched out his legs and arched his back, trying to stretch-out the tiredness and stress he was feeling. As he relaxed back onto the chair he decided to tell Antoinette about his run-in with the school's caretaker.

"Ms Deselle, I have something to tell you and I don't think you'll be very pleased."

Antoinette looked over the top of a pair of half-moon spectacles and sighed. "What now?"

oOo

"Greg this is terrible." Antoinette couldn't quite believe what she'd just heard. As far as she knew, Richard was sound. Charley liked him and Antoinette knew her protégé's intuition was usually pretty much spot-on.

"The point is, Ms Deselle, that there's nothing in the safe of any intrinsic value. I just can't work out what he might have been after."

Antoinette's eyes widened. "Mon Dieu, I know exactly. Why did I not think of it sooner? I locked the brooch in the safe and forbade Charley to use it. I suspect Richard was trying to retrieve it for her. Do you know if it's still there?"

"I checked the safe after the incident. There was no brooch there."

"Oh Greg, she's planning to go back."

123

Greg glared at her. "This is the second time I've heard reference to Charley 'going back.' Back where? What does it mean and what's the brooch got to do with it?"

Antoinette scraped her chair backwards. "Too many questions, Greg and I do not have time to answer them yet. Come with me, quickly."

oOo

Antoinette burst into charley's bed space. "Mon Dieu, she is not here." She ran to the doorway.

"Antoinette, stop please, just for a second."

She stopped and turned back to face Greg. "I don't have time for questions; I told you."

"One question, please, just one."

"OK, go on…"

"Is she in danger?

"Yes possibly. Every time she goes back, she comes back weaker. I'm afraid she'll take one trip too many and it'll kill her. I'm also really worried she'll do something stupid and change the course of history."

Greg shook his head, trying to clear his thoughts. "Please Antoinette. What's all this talk of trips and going back?"

"No time to explain, Greg. Later, I promise. Now, where can she be?"

"Richard's house." He nodded in the general direction. "She'll be at Richard's house. Let's go."

oOo

"Are you ready?"

"Let me get comfy." Charley lay back on Richard's bed. "Ok, I think I'm ready now. Pass me the brooch."

Richard watched with morbid pleasure as the time-slip jolt knocked Charley unconscious. She jerked upwards like someone being defibrillated and then fell back on the bed her eyes closed and her breathing ragged. He found it quite puzzling that his feelings for her could have been turned around so fast by her only wanting to be friends and, of course, the promise of money. He

124

hauled her up and pulled the brooch and chain from her neck.

"Charley!?" A voice from downstairs.

Richard's heart thumped hard in his chest. "What's Deselle doing in my house?"

"Charley where are you?" A man's voice that time.

"That bastard Collier." Richard had no time to hide the brooch so he simply pushed it into Charley's hands and leapt away from the bed.

There were thumps on the stairs and more shouts before the bedroom door was flung open and Greg burst in quickly followed by Antoinette.

Greg flew across the room and pushed Richard away. "What have you done to her?"

"Nothing. Nothing, I swear. I tried to stop her."

Greg pushed him hard against the wall and grabbed him by the throat. "Fucking liar. You stole the brooch so she could do this."

Antoinette grabbed the brooch from Charley's hands. "What is this doing here? Why is it not around her neck?"

"Time to play the victim," Richard thought. "I - can't - breath," he croaked.

Greg relaxed his grip slightly. "Answer her question."

"I don't know how she uses it. She was just holding it. That's all I can tell you." Antoinette shook her head. "That makes no sense. It's always been around her neck. And where's the chain?"

Richard darted a look at the brooch. The chain was missing.

Antoinette started hunting frantically around the bed and bedding. "We must get the brooch around her neck, quickly."

"What happens if we don't?" asked Greg, still holding Richard by the throat.

"That's the problem, I don't know, but it's always been around her neck when she's gone back."

Greg pressed Richard harder against the wall. "Stay there and don't move. I haven't finished with you yet." He released his grip and moved to join Antoinette in the search, but stopped almost immediately. "Ms Deselle. I've found it."

Antoinette looked up and saw that Greg was pointing at Richard and there, caught on his belt buckle, was the chain.

Greg snatched it away. "You and I are going to have a little talk." He tossed the chain to Antoinette who hurriedly threaded it through the brooch.

Richard's resolve not to retaliate evaporated. "The time for talking is long past," he snarled and shoved Greg backwards. Greg lost his balance and fell to the floor, his head narrowly missed Richard's iron bedframe. Before he could get up, Richard pounced on him and delivered blow after blow to his head and face. Greg could hear Antoinette screaming but it seemed distant and unreal. The next thing he knew was being showered in glass and Richard's full bodyweight slumped across his chest. He rolled out from underneath and groggily tried to stand. He got as far as his knees before he had to sit back down on the floor.

Antoinette threw down the remains of the vase and stepped quickly to Greg's side. "Take it easy. If you can stand I'll help you over to that chair." She helped him to clamber unsteadily to his feet and wedged her shoulder into his armpit. "Here, sit. Mon Dieu you are a mess."

He dabbed at his bloody nose with a handkerchief and looked at the glass debris on the floor. "Did you just clump him with a vase?"

"I did. Look, he's coming round."

Richard had rolled over and was heaving himself into a sitting position. "What happened?" He touched the top of his head and splinters of glass fell onto his lap.

"You attacked me," said Greg angrily.

Richard glanced at him and gave the merest hint of a smirk when he saw Greg's puffy eyes and swollen cheek. "I guess I did a good job then."

Greg wanted to retaliate but felt too spaced-out to stand again. "Forget what you did to *me* for a moment, what were you doing to Charley. Something's not right; there's something else going on. If you were trying to hurt her…" He let the sentence hang.

Richard feigned indignation. "Hurt her? I love her you moron; I'd never do anything to hurt her."

Antoinette looked down at Charley, tears welling up in her tired eyes. "Why did you remove the brooch, Richard?"

"I – I didn't."

"You did. There's no other explanation. I hope you've not harmed her."

CHAPTER 26
Deireadh Fómhair (October) 444AD

Charley awoke in the lee of a byre, just in time to see a large man ride into the Avertci village at the head of a great column of mounted soldiers and walking servants. Ten wagons brought up the rear of his procession, all laden with produce including grain, fabrics and wines, all taken as taxes from the tribes along the way.

Similar in stature and appearance to Madron, the man was probably half a head shorter and his face slightly thinner. Behind his bushy beard, his expression was set and determined. His long greying hair fell around his shoulders and merged into the pale fur collar of his mantle – a richly dyed cloak of russet red, fastened at the neck with a golden brooch. Beneath the mantle he wore a stiff leather jerkin studded with small iron rivets and on his head was a highly polished conical helmet. From his hip was slung a fine sword, engraved with images of wild birds. His status was obvious and Charley scanned her memory to catch her mental notes about the period and realised with amazement, who this man was: Vortigern, King of the Britons!

She had studied this particular figure from history. Many Britons considered themselves to be of noble birth and jumped at the opportunity to promote themselves once the Romans had left Britain. Many of those Britons sought favour with the Romans before their withdrawal and Charley believed Vortigern might have been one of them. For a start, it was rumoured he had the patronage of the Emperor Magnus Maximus, who died in 388AD. Vortigern's marriage to the Emperor's daughter, Sevira, would appear to corroborate that and may have been instrumental in Vortigern taking overall control of Britain for himself.

Although Christianity was spreading through the lands, Vortigern still followed the teachings of Pelagius, a Briton who held that it was humans, not gods, who held the key to eternal salvation. Charley thought he may have been more worried about the rise of the Roman Catholic Church; he probably feared if the faith solidified, they would seek greater ties with Rome and that might bring the Romans back to his shores, and what would happen to his status then?

Charley searched the crowd of villagers gathered along the route to the great hall, but could not see Catherine or Madron anywhere. The column stopped but Vortigern and the two riders who flanked him continued to ride forward until they reached the Great Hall.

Charley's heart lurched as she saw Madron and Taraghlan appear on the hall's large veranda. A second or two later, Catherine stepped onto the veranda and Charley breathed a sigh of relief. She still appeared to be about twelve or thirteen years old, so maybe not too much time had passed since her last visit. All three moved forward to greet their important guest. Vortigern and the other two men climbed the stairs and Charley watched as Madron greeted his king.

"I need to get closer," she thought and stepped out from under the thatch of the cow shed. She walked purposefully through the throng of villagers and up the steps until she was actually standing next to Catherine. It was an action that took great courage and faith in her belief that no one could see her.

Catherine however, looked at right her and a faint smile touched her lips. Charley gasped. "She knows I'm here."

"These are my sons, Vortimir and Catigern." Vortigern swept his arm past the other two men who nodded at Madron. "My younger sons Pascent and Vortiger are back there." He waved dismissively in the direction of his procession.

Catherine strained to seek out Vortiger, who was about her age, perhaps a year or two older, but not much. She spotted him at the head of the colonnade and nudged her father. " Could
Vortiger join us? It would be good to have company my own age."

129

The King overheard and roared with laughter. "Catigern, go fetch your brothers."

Madron smiled. "Why don't we get some food and drink, and you can tell me what brings you to my village, my Lord, apart from robbing what little we have left for your taxes."

Vortigern slapped him on the back and steered him into the hall. "That is a very good idea, my friend."

Vortiger and his brothers ascended the steps and followed their father and Vortimir into the hall.

Vortimir, Catigern and Pascent were escorted by Taraghlan, whilst Vortiger walked with Catherine, a big cheery and cheeky grin on his face. He leant over and whispered something to her and she giggled loudly and followed him into the hall.

Taranis, at the bottom of the steps with Brid and Elowyn, just stood and scowled; he would have to let that so-called prince know that Catherine was his and his alone.

Charley waited until the party had entered and then she too slipped through the doorway. It took a moment for her eyes to adjust to the gloom. The building was about sixty feet long and forty feet wide. The entrance was on its long side. In the centre was a large fire pit with logs of cedar that burned brightly; smoke from its heavily scented wood curled up to a traditional roof; not conical like the domestic huts. The floor was strewn with rushes and lavender, the scent of which competed intensely with the wood smoke.

Long tables were arranged around the sides, but only one was laid out for eating – The High Table which dominated the back wall. All the stools faced into the hall so the diners would sit with their backs to the wall, facing the big doors – protection against an attack from behind.

Fascinated, Charley watched as the King and Madron took their places, Madron allowed the king to take his large oak chair at the centre of the table and sat by his right hand. Catherine sat to the right of her father. Vortimir and Catigern sat to Vortigern's left and his two youngest sons sat next to Catherine. The village Ealdormen took their seats at each end of the table as Taraghlan directed other members of the party to their seats. He and Caderyn were the last to sit.

Vortigern looked along the table in both directions. "Madron, introduce me to those I should know."

Madron reached out to his right and put his arm across Catherine's shoulder. "This is my daughter, Catherine."

She smiled at him and Vortigern's eyes widened, "By the gods, you have a pretty one there, Madron." He faltered as she held his gaze. "Ailla would be very proud were she not with the gods now. She – she has something special about her."

Madron sighed, "This I know. It is hard work being father to a girl so confident in herself."

"When will she be married?"

Madron glanced at his daughter, "Soon enough… To Taranis, son of Algar…"

"Chief of the Corieltauvi," interrupted Vortigern. "And where is this, Taranis?"

Madron looked up at the throng of villagers that had entered the hall to watch the king eat his meal and spied Taranis skulking in the far corner. "Taranis!" he bellowed. Come here."

Taranis straightened his back and walked purposefully to the high table where he stopped in front of Catherine and bowed. Vortiger again whispered in her ear and again she giggled. Taranis felt himself reddening, hatred for the prince starting to build up, like bile trying to escape. The Prince must have said something belittling and Catherine had enjoyed the insult.

"Well, you are a lucky man, Taranis," laughed Vortigern. "Though if she has her mother's spirit I think you will not best her; it could be a lively union." He laughed again. "And who else have you here, Madron?"

Taranis melted back into the throng as Madron introduced the Elders and the rest of his household, finishing with his oldest confidant, Taraghlan.

Vertigern nodded with approval. "Ah, Taraghlan. I wish you

would come into my service. You would bring a great fighting spirit with you. I could make good use of someone like you."

Taraghlan smiled. "Thank you my Lord, but if I left the Avertci, Madron would gut me, and then all I could bring would be my entrails."

Vortigern roared with laughter and slugged down a horn of ale that gushed over the brim and soaked his great beard. "We will eat and then I must speak with you, Madron." He paused and looked around the hall with steel in his eyes. "Just you and Taraghlan."

Madron nodded. "As you wish."

oOo

Charley followed Madron, Vortigern and Taraghlan to Madron's hut. Vortigern had drunk too much ale and was verging on the aggressive, calling Taraghlan a maggot several times. The three men slumped onto fur covered seats and Vortigern called for more ale.

Madron frowned at the king. "My Lord, you have something important to say. Let us leave the ale until after. Why are you here?"

Vortigern frowned. "The Picts."

Madron rolled his eyes. "The Picts are a curse. They raided this village a few moons ago."

Vortigern's eyes flashed. "You drove them back?"

"We killed all of them."

Vortigern laughed loudly and slapped his leg. "That is *exactly* what I wanted to hear. I am riding north next week and you and your army will come with me."

Madron looked shocked and started to protest. "My Lord…"

"I am raising armies from all the tribes. I will slaughter the Picts and any that survive we will drive back to their high lands."

"My Lord, my army is largely untrained. They are not ready." He looked to Taraghlan for support.

"It is true, my Lord. We have been talking about how few men we have."

Vortigern stood up unsteadily, "Next week Madron, every fit

man will fight for me or yours will be the first head to leave its body. Now, where do I sleep?"

oOo

Charley was sitting on the floor just inside the hut and scribbling notes as she eavesdropped on the conversation. This was like living research. Talk about first-hand knowledge.

Catherine entered as Vortigern was being helped to Madron's own cot. As she pushed past the furs across the doorway, she stopped and looked down, directly at Charley and smiled at her again. Charley nearly fainted with shock. There could be no doubt, surely, that Catherine had seen her.

Catherine walked over to her father who put a finger to his lips and pulled her away from the sleeping king. "Daughter," he said quietly, "the king wants us to send an army north to help him battle the Picts. What say you?"

"You want my counsel. Father?"

"I do."

A look of childish petulance crossed Catherine's face, reminding Charley that, despite her aura of maturity, knowledge and calm, the girl was indeed just a child. "So you acknowledge me as the tribe's Priestess?"

Madron glowered at her. "You are *not* the priestess. You will never be the priestess. You will be Chieftess of the Avertci one day. You cannot be both."

"Then I choose priestess," she hissed.

Madron grabbed Catherine by the arm and pulled her roughly from the hut into the chill outside, nearly stepping on Charley in the process.

Charley quickly followed and again, Catherine threw a glance in her direction. Madron swung his daughter round to face him. "Do not defy me on this," he bellowed.

Catherine didn't flinch. "It is my destiny. I can feel it in every breath I take. You can forbid me, father, but you cannot stop destiny, no more than you can stop the breeze with your hands."

Madron released his grip and his posture slumped. "If you

133

become priestess, you will die. Timancius will make sure of it."

"Timancius has no powers. He has no gods. I have both, plus my mother is with me too." She cast another look over at Charley.

"You are too young; only thirteen summers."

"When the tribe accepts me as priestess, I will be old enough, even if I am still young."

Madron sighed. "We will see. If the gods choose you, then I will be powerless to stop you."

Catherine smiled brightly. "Thank you father, and in answer to your question, send a token army to fight for the king, but do not send Taraghlan or Caderyn." She paused for a second and then added, "Taranis should go. He needs to fight and he is ready."

Madron nodded and trudged back to the great hall. "Good counsel daughter... as always."

Catherine returned to the hut and sat on the edge of her cot, ignoring the King's deep and thunderous snoring. She looked toward the door where Charley was standing. "I know you're there." Her voice was quiet, yet solid and determined.

Charley's hand flew up to her mouth and Catherine tilted her head to one side as if she were listening, "I can't see you, or hear you, except as a voice in my head, but I know you're there." Charley was rooted to the spot; she wanted to run away but this situation was as exciting as it was terrifying. Catherine gestured to a chair by the fire, "Sit," and then as an afterthought, added, "Please."

Charley felt compelled to comply and she tentatively crossed the hut and sat. "What do you want from me?" she whispered.

Catherine cocked her head to the other side, "I knew you'd come to me; I've felt you by my side so often."

"You have?" Charley was reassured by Catherine's calmness. She didn't seem angry at the intrusion, so Charley felt compelled to extend some sort of gesture of friendship. Without really knowing why, she stood up and crossed over to the Priestess, and placed her hand lightly on her shoulder.

The moment she touched her, Catherine drew a sharp intake of breath and her hand flew up to her shoulder. Charley snatched her hand away with a gasp of fright and then noticed that Catherine's eyes were flooded with tears.

"I know you're there," she repeated. "Thank you... mother."

CHAPTER 27
Deireadh Fómhair (October) 444AD

Charley staggered backwards, "Mother? Oh no, no, no. The poor girl thinks she's in contact with her dead mother. What have I done? This is so cruel." Charley quickly stepped in front of Catherine and hunkered down before her, "Catherine, I'm not your mother. My name is Charlotte. I'm *not* your mother. Do you understand me? Can you hear me? I'm *not* your mother."

Catherine simply smiled and rose to her feet causing Charley to topple backwards onto her haunches. Catherine walked to the doorway and just before she stepped outside, turned and beckoned, "Come."

She headed straight for Brid's hut; she needed the counsel of her old and dear friend, but wanted her mother present also. Charley followed her into the hut.

"Brid!" Catherine barked as soon as she was over the threshold, "I need you, quickly."

The old woman climbed out of her cot and scolded her future Priestess, "I'm not your nurse any more, Catherine. What's so urgent?"

Catherine sat in front of the fire and patted the seat next to her, "Sit here. I need your guidance." The old woman sat and Catherine suddenly choked back a sob.

"What's the matter? Why are you upset? This is not like you."

Catherine took her hand, "My mother is with me."

Brid chortled, "Your mother is *always* with you, silly girl."

Catherine bit back tears of frustration, "No, Brid, she is really here. I feel her presence and I hear her voice."

Charley clasped her hand to her forehead and turned a full circle, "No Catherine it's not your mum with you," Charley shouted, "It's *me.*"

Brid's eyes narrowed, "You *hear* her voice? Catherine this is very dark magic, the gods will not be pleased."

"In my head, Brid, not out loud, not in the air."

Brid looked relieved. "That is good. These are just dreams, Catherine."

"No, they are not. She touched my shoulder, I felt her."

Charley looked at her hand, stunned. Had Catherine really felt her? What did that mean, that she was becoming a tangible presence and not just a ghost from the future?

Brid squeezed her hand. "How do you know it is your mother?"

"Who else could it be?" She scratched at her arm and Brid noticed.

"Does it bother you today?"

Catherine smiled, "Yes, it plagues me today; it itches so badly." She pulled up her sleeve to reveal a crescent of angry red eczema.

Charley's eyes widened and her hand flew to her left arm. She too had eczema there and it was itching like mad.

Brid smiled back. "Your mother suffered in the same way."

Catherine looked surprised, "Really? You never told me that before."

"It is the Priestess's Mark. Your mother's was behind her left ear, usually hidden under her hair."

"I did not know that. Mine itches when conflict is near."

Brid frowned. "And is conflict near?"

Catherine shook her head. "No, it also tells me when it's time to pray, but I cannot always tell the difference."

Brid patted her hand. "Then go and pray child and ask the gods if it really is your mother who speaks to you."

Catherine stood and kissed her old nurse on the forehead. "I will. Thank you Mamo."

Charley started to follow but the room started to spin. Before she could gather her thoughts, she had passed out.

oOo

Charley jolted awake, eyes wide and her breathing fast and ragged.

Greg fumbled for his phone. "I'm calling an ambulance."

Charley pulled herself up onto her elbows. "Annie, we're connected." Her voice was barely above a whisper.

Antoinette felt Charley's brow with the back of her hand. "Mon Dieu, she is so cold and clammy." Charley collapsed back onto her pillow, jerked violently and then lay still. "I think she's gone back again."

Greg stopped mid-dial. "What?"

"She's gone back."

"She could have something seriously wrong."

Antoinette shook her head. "No, look. She's totally calm again. Her breathing is steady." She grabbed for Charley's wrist and felt for her pulse. "Slow and steady too. She's fine."

"How can you say that? I'm still calling an ambulance."

"No, you can't do that. The paramedics will remove the brooch and then Charley could be trapped there. No, let's wait until she returns here again."

Greg turned back to Richard, now sitting moodily on a chair nearby. "If this is your doing…"

Richard stood up and walked to the door. "I keep telling you, I've done nothing." He headed downstairs where he poured himself a large whiskey and sat heavily at his kitchen table. He took a swig and felt it burn the back of his throat. He stared sullenly into the bottom of the glass. How could such a simple plan have gone so horribly wrong? Even if the French cow and that big fool couldn't prove anything, they would have him under close scrutiny from now on. The chances of trying again were slim.

But then his mood brightened. Something had happened to Charley; she'd been pulled back to the past by the brooch before she could properly regain consciousness. Maybe fate would step in and keep her there. Perhaps he could still claim the money. He allowed himself a sly smile and downed the rest of his whiskey.

138

Greg sat on the bed and also felt Charley's brow. "Enough playing around, Antoinette. It's time to level with me. What's going on? What's the deal with this brooch? You keep referring to her 'going back.' Back where? Come on, spill."

Antoinette pulled a hankie from her pocket and blew her nose. She dropped her hands to her lap and grasped the hankie tightly. "The brooch takes her back to Saxon times. She's been following the life…" she paused for a moment, "and death I suppose, of a tribal priestess called Catherine. The dagger that sparked off this whole wretched dig was used to kill her. Charley says it was Hengist himself who used it."

"The Saxon warlord?"

"Or Horsa. I forget." She looked up into Greg's disbelieving eyes. "The first time she went back, she was lying in the river mud face to face with the dying Catherine and the next time she witnessed her birth. Every time she's gone back she's witnessed some pivotal point in Catherine's life."

Greg shook his head. "Can you hear yourself? It's totally preposterous."

"I questioned it too, Greg, but when she came back from her first trip, she was covered in river mud and she had Catherine's blood on her face. She persuaded me to let her widen her trench to look for the remains of Catherine's body, and we found it."

"Premonitions, dreams, clairvoyance, I would accept all those, but time travel? Come on, it's ridiculous."

"So how do you explain the blood? It wasn't hers."

Greg tried to process Antoinette's story. Eventually he looked up forlornly. "Ok, so let's say I believe you, which I don't, what happens now? What if she gets hurt, or killed, back there. Would she also die here?"

Antoinette pull a face. "I hadn't thought of that. Time travel is impossible and yet it is happening."

Greg stroked Charley's face and then stood up determinedly. "It's time to speak to Armitage and find out exactly what he was up to."

CHAPTER 28
Mí na Nollag (December) 444AD

Madron beamed as he welcomed Algar and the elders of the Corieltauvi tribe into the Great Hall. The Corieltauvi occupied an area to the West of The Wash and to the distaste of neighbouring tribes, their capital bore the Romanised name of Ratae Corieltauvorum, known simply as Ratae. Centuries later it would be known as Leicester.

The two men were of similar size although Algar's beard was sparse and he wore his long fiery-red hair tied back.

"Good to see you again my friend," said Madron as they grasped each other's forearms.

"It makes a change for us to meet here." Algar's voice was deep and his breath stank of stale meat.

Madron showed his guests to the fur-covered seating arranged around the central fire. "Sit and I will get you ale." He signalled to Nessa who went in search of a large flagon of ale.

Algar unstrapped his sword and threw it to the ground by the nearest seat. "I want to see my son."

"Of course; I will send for him." Madron nodded at Mabyn and she scuttled away to find the boy. Madron took the biggest seat for himself and spread his arms wide. "You seem restless. Is there a problem, Algar?"

The big man leant forward, his left forearm resting on his knee. "Yes. Our alliance has been in place for many months now and the Picts have been constantly raiding our lands. Where is your army? Why have you not ventured north to help us?"

Madron looked puzzled. "Algar, King Vortigern was here three full moons ago and took what men I could spare. He was riding north to drive the Picts away. Did he not reach you?"

Algar shook his head. "He did not. I did not see him"

Madron frowned. "I heard that Vortigern had abandoned his plans and returned to Gwrtheyrnion but he could not have travelled very far north if he did not even reach you."

Algar roared, "I was told he had amassed a great army but that they did not find or kill a single Pict."

"Nor has he sent my men back to me."

"So still the Picts raid my lands!" He glared at Madron. "And still you do nothing to help."

"Algar, you know we have just a small army; about enough men to protect the village. This was explained to you. This was why I needed the alliance. You have many more men than I and we agreed that in return for allowing your son to marry my daughter, I could call upon *you* in times of need."

Nessa ventured tentatively to Algar's side carrying two pitchers of ale. He snatched one and pointed accusingly at Madron. "Then this alliance is very one-sided."

"My friend, you have sent no messengers asking for my help. If you ask, I will always send those men I can spare, but I fear they will be too few to make a difference."

Taranis and Catherine entered the hall. Catherine went to her father's side and Taranis walked over to Algar and stood before him, hands on his hips, chest puffed up and his features set and strong. "You wanted to see me?"

Algar slouched back into his seat and took a long swig of ale. He wiped his mouth with the back of his hand and then eyed his son up and down with barely concealed contempt. "I need you back at Ratae."

Madron raised an eyebrow. "Why?"

"Taranis is my son. He will do what I say and go where I tell him."

Madron's face hardened again. "Your son is bound to my daughter. He is in my service. She is now of age and once they are married and only then, if he chooses, he can return to Ratae."

"Then release him from the arrangement," Algar growled with venom dripping from each word.

Madron stood and led his daughter to Taranis's side. "Is that what you both want? To be released from the arrangement?"

The two youngsters looked at each other, studied each other's eyes and then they both smiled. "No," they said in unison.

Catherine took Taranis's hand. "Lord Algar, if at any time, married or not, Taranis chooses to return to Ratae, he will return alone; I will not go with him. My place is here." She glanced at her father who nodded his head in confirmation.

Algar's face tightened and his eyes narrowed. "Once you are married, girl, your place will be with your husband. You will do as he says and he *will* command that you return with him to Ratea."

Taranis shook his head. "Father I cannot make Catherine return with me. She is destined to be the Avertci's priestess and I will not stand in her way."

Madron wheeled around to face the boy. "Not this again!"

Taranis recoiled slightly. "My Lord I am only telling my father what Catherine has told me many times. I meant no disrespect."

Madron glared at his daughter. "Do not test me child. I have not agreed that you will be the priestess. You presume too much. It is a dangerous path for you to tread. If Timancius were to hear of it…"

"I have told you father, I can deal with Timancius. I have done it once as his blindness proves and I can do it again. If I am old enough to marry then I am old enough to take care of myself. You know my powers are strong."

Algar reached for his sword. "Enough! I have no interest in your child's future, other than as my son's wife. It appears that this so-called alliance can be broken as easily as it was made. You need me and my army, you have just said so. On the other hand, I do not need you; my people can survive without your warriors." He spat on the earthen floor, "If you can call them that."

Madron took an angry step towards Algar but stopped short when he felt Catherine's hand slide into his and squeeze.

"This alliance is ended. You can keep your daughter and I can claim back my son," Algar growled,

"Why?" Catherine said gently. Algar took a sharp intake of breath. There was something about her voice that, with that one simple word, had instantly deflated his anger. He looked at her, bewildered and she moved to stand before him. "Why do you want him back? You clearly hate him; it is written on your face."

Algar appeared flustered. "He is my son. His place is with me. He must be trained to lead."

"Trained to lead? Why now?" A sudden look of understanding crossed Catherine's face. "You don't hate *him,* you hate yourself." She met his gaze and searched his eyes. "You hate what is happening to *you.*" She studied him for a few seconds more and her blue eyes narrowed. "Ah, I see it now; you are dying and you need Taranis prepared as your successor."

Taranis stepped forward. "What is this?"

Algar roared with disapproval. "What godless magic is this? Hold your tongue, girl. I am *not* dying."

Madron stepped forward. "Show me."

"Show you what?"

"Algar, there is fresh blood dripping from your fingers. Show me." Algar looked down at the blood that dripped from his left hand and his posture sagged. Madron's voice softened. "What happened?"

Algar slumped back onto his seat. "I took a blow from an axe some days ago. No one can stop the flow. I expect to be dead within the week."

Taranis knelt by his father. "Can I help?" Algar shook his head.

Madron looked crestfallen. "Catherine?"

She smiled and moved silently to Algar's side. "I can help you."

"You're just a girl. Go away."

"She's a girl with a priestess's powers, father," interrupted Taranis.

Catherine stood her ground. "I promise you, I can help."

Algar staggered back to his feet. "We are leaving. Taranis,

143

prepare for the journey, we leave before nightfall."

Taranis looked at Catherine. "I am sorry," he said bitterly, "but I should go with my father." Catherine nodded and stepped back.

Madron took Algar's arm. "Let Catherine tend to you."

Algar snatched it back. "This alliance is over." He walked stiffly to the doorway and signalled to Taranis to follow.

Catherine reached up and gave the boy a peck on the cheek. "I am sad to see you go, but I know that no harm will come to you and for that, I am happy."

Taranis smiled miserably. "I have learned not to argue about things you 'know.'"

Madron watched sadly as Algar and his party left the hall. "Stupid old fool." He looked unhappily at his daughter. "I'm sorry your betrothal has been broken."

Catherine smiled. "It hasn't and it won't be, unless I choose it so."

"Pray for him Catherine. He doesn't know it, but his life is in your hands."

Charley looked in wonder at Catherine. She was only thirteen but looked older, self-assured and regal. She will be a great priestess.

CHAPTER 29

Charley woke to find herself still in Richard's bedroom. She felt tired and discontent. The present day held no interest for her at that moment. The only place she wanted to be was by Catherine's side.

"Good. You are awake. We were both very worried about you." Antoinette passed Charley a tumbler of water.

"Both? Richard is here?"

"No," said Antoinette firmly. "Not Richard - Greg."

Charley wrinkled her nose in distaste, "That oaf? The only thing he worries about is where the nearest mirror is."

Antoinette steeled herself for the awkward conversation she was now going to have with her protégé. "Greg possibly saved your life."

Charley jerked her head back to meet Antoinette's gaze, her expression one of surprise and disbelief. "Saved me? Was I in danger? What happened?"

"You sent Richard to steal the brooch for you." Her voice had a hard edge. "And you used it to go back, against my explicit instructions."

Charley now averted her eyes; ashamed of her deceit. "Annie, I honestly didn't put him up to it. It was his idea. I tried to talk him out of it."

"Not hard enough!" Antoinette's temper was rising. "When he brought it to you, you could have simply brought it back to me, but no, you chose to use it. It might not have been your idea but you grasped the opportunity to go back without a second thought for the consequences and you might have died as a result."

Charley put the tumbler back on her bedside table. "What went

145

wrong? What happened?"

Antoinette's mouth tightened. "Richard happened."

"I don't understand."

"When we found you, Richard had removed the brooch from around your neck."

"Why would he do that?" Puzzlement flashed across Charley's face. "It would probably mean I couldn't return; we've talked at length about these trips and he knows that, I'm sure."

"Exactement."

"So why…?" Her voice tailed-off.

"We don't know why. He has not told us."

"And Greg?"

"Greg and Richard fought and I managed to get the brooch around your neck again, but Greg's pretty badly beaten."

"Is he ok?"

"I'm sure you'll see him soon enough; once he's cleaned himself up and perhaps had his nose reset."

"Oh my god. It was that bad?"

"It was. Then you returned for just a moment and then went back again. We didn't know why, or what was happening to you. What could we have done if Richard had been successful and got away with the brooch? We don't know how or if, we can bring you back. I can only assume if you get trapped back there, then your body here would remain in a coma until… well until…"

"Until I get the brooch back or someone turns off the life support," Charley whispered.

"Indeed." Antoinette patted her hand.

"Why would Richard do that to me? Do you think he meant to harm me…to…" She tailed-off.

"Kill you? I have no idea."

Charley's bewildered eyes filled with tears and Antoinette gripped her hand tightly.

"Stay focused because there's more. Here's the thing, as I just said, when you came round it was for only an instant and then you went back into the past again. That's never happened before. I can only assume there was some unfinished business and the brooch took you back again for some reason."

Charley shook her head. "I didn't return to the same moment. I think it was about three months later."

Antoinette looked relieved. "Well, at least you're safe. I am grateful for that." She stood up. "Give it to me please."

Charley looked shocked. "No, Annie, please."

"I'm not going to stop you going back, Mon Cher, but from now on it must be controlled and monitored." She held out her hand and raised a warning eyebrow. Charley complied. "Now, let's get you back to the dorm so you can get some proper rest. You look dreadful."

oOo

Forrester was reading Bede, a Benedictine Monk, born 672AD and a prolific writer of his time. His "Ecclesiastical History of the English People," a history of the Church of England, was completed about 731 AD and is widely considered to be his greatest work. But it was a lesser tome that Forrester had before her. She was reading Bede's history of King Vortigern. She knew that there was relevance there, she just didn't know what, or why.

When Smith had updated her about the Chandler-Price girl using the brooch to travel back in time, she thought it was totally preposterous,, but something had changed since she had met her and now she wasn't so sure.

Before that moment, all she wanted was for the dig to be shut down but now she knew any knowledge of the past, revealed by the dig, would harm her, although she had no idea how or why. For some unknown reason, she now had an intense hatred and malevolence for Charley. The dig was not as important as dealing with that bitch. Every sense she possessed was warning her that Charley should not have any contact with that brooch and should never be allowed to visit the past again. In Charley's hands the brooch would be a catalyst that would pose a real danger for her. The fear was extreme. She needed to formulate a plan, but her mind wouldn't focus on it.

She tried to solidify her thoughts. "Exactly what do I have to fear? How could she be a danger to me? That's ridiculous and yet..." She left the thought dangling in the air and then suddenly jolted upright. There is was... a solid thought, not a plan, but an outcome. Forrester had realised, with something akin to a mixture of guilt and pleasure, that she didn't just want Charley removed, or sacked or discredited...She wanted her dead!

oOo

Under orders from Forrester, Walter Smith phoned Armitage again. *"There's been a change of plan. You can forget about the brooch for now."*

Richard rolled his eyes. "Seriously? I retrieved it for Charley earlier and you wouldn't believe the trouble it's got me into."

"You moron, Forrester doesn't want her to have it now. Like I say, the plan has changed, although I don't think you'll have the stomach for it."

Richard's heart missed a beat. "Go on."

"Forrester wants her dead."

Richard snorted back a laugh. "You two have lost the plot. I'm not doing that."

"Then you won't get your money."

"Oh come on, you expect me to kill her? Don't be so ridiculous."

"Find a way; You're an ex-commando, it should be easy for you."

Richard felt sick. Yes he had killed enough enemy combatants during his military career, but Charley? His feelings towards her were certainly turning darker the more he sulked about her rejection of him, but did he really hate her enough to murder her?

But then he realised he could try again to take the brooch from her while she was in the past and let her fall into a coma, then wait until Smith had paid him before waking her up again. It would be a con but at least he wouldn't have to commit murder.

"I think I can help but I'm not going to kill her, that's for sure."

"I told you, Forrester wants her dead."

"And I'm telling you, I'm not a murderer; however, I can try again stop her getting back from a future jaunt, she'd be in a coma, maybe forever."

Smith smiled and nodded. *"That would probably suit Forrester's purpose but I need an assurance that's what would happen."*

"If I can take the brooch from her while she's asleep, I'm pretty sure that would trap her. We'd know by now if Collier hadn't stopped me."

"Ok. Give it a try."

"As long as you keep your promise to pay me; I really do need that money."

"Just do it," Smith shouted."

Richard hung up and wondered how he could make it happen. He doubted he'd be let anywhere near Charley now.

CHAPTER 30

A shadow crossed Charley's doorway and Greg entered the bed space. "Got room for a small one?"

Charley and Antoinette looked up and gasped. Both eyes were black and one was swollen shut; there was a livid bruise spreading across his left cheek and had a dressing across his nose.

"Bloody hell, Greg," whispered Charley. "Richard did that to you?"

"Caught me by surprise or he'd be in hospital by now. I must have been having an off-day."

Charley looked ashamed. "I'm so sorry. I understand I have to thank you for saving my life."

Greg smiled. "Yeah, I didn't want to, but Mademoiselle Deselle insisted."

The two women smiled and Charley reached out a hand. "Liar, but thank you anyway."

Greg gave her hand a squeeze then pulled up a chair. "So what's the goss?"

Charley lay back. The effort of bringing Antoinette up to date with her latest visits was exhausting her and she didn't want to go over it all again.

Antoinette carefully placed the brooch on the floor and tapped her notebook. "Before the brooch suddenly took you back again, you said something about a connection?"

"Oh my god, yes." Charley sat up again, excitement replacing her tiredness. "It was incredible. Catherine knew I was there." Antoinette raised an eyebrow but Charley grabbed her arm. "No really, it's true."

150

"How do you know?"

"She only bloody spoke to me."

Greg and Antoinette looked shocked. "Are you sure?" she asked.

"She said, 'I know you're there.' How much more sure could I be?'

"Is that all?" Greg smiled. "That not exactly proof."

"Oh come on. That's pretty conclusive I'd say."

Greg leant back and stretched out his legs. "So she can see you."

"No, she can't see me; she just senses my presence. But there's a problem, sort of. She thinks I'm her mother."

"How do you know?" Greg was still smiling and disbelieving.

"Because she called me her mother, that's how. She looked right into my eyes and said, 'I know you're there, mother.'"

Antoinette shook her head. "Oh Charley, that's not right. That's so unfair on her."

"Yes, I was quite upset by it at the time, but it isn't really unfair; it gave her comfort. And then something incredible happened. I squeezed her shoulder and she felt it."

Antoinette dropped her pencil. "Mon Dieu!"

"It was amazing…"

"No. Stop, stop, Charley. This could be very bad." Antoinette stood and paced around the small bed space, thinking out loud. "She could sense you…sense you enough to try and communicate… You touched her and she felt it? What does this mean?"

"It means…"

"Shhhh, be quiet; let me think." She paced some more and then suddenly sat down again. "How do you feel, I mean in yourself, health-wise?"

"Health-wise?"

"Yes, how do you feel now, compared to when you first went back?"

Charley looked puzzled. "I don't know what relevance…"

"Just fucking answer me, girl. How do you feel?"

Charley was shocked. She'd never heard her drop the 'F' bomb before. "I, er… I'm tired. Well, fatigued would be more accurate."

"Go on."

"The first time I went back was traumatic. I felt like I'd done three rounds with Mike Tyson, but subsequent visits haven't really affected me. I get tired but I recover quickly enough…"

"But?"

"But these last couple of trips have wiped me out. I just want to sleep. All I can think about is going back, but I'm so, so tired."

Antoinette leant back in her chair, apprehension written over her face. "I thought so. Charley I'm really not sure it's safe for you to go back anymore."

"Not again Annie. Make your mind up. One minute I'm allowed, then I'm not, then I am. What's going on?"

"I think you're losing your grip on reality."

Greg laughed. "Going insane you mean? Yeah I can quite see that."

Antoinette glared. "No not insane. I mean she's losing her grip on the here and now – on the present." She turned back to Charley. "It seems harder for you to return. You're exhausted when you do get back and you're now making physical and emotional contact with Catherine. It feels as if the past is absorbing you."

"This time travel lark is taking it out on me for sure."

Greg leant forward. "Well it's not time travel is it?"

Anger flashed across Charley's eyes. "Of course it is. What else could it be?"

"I don't know, but it's not time travel. Antoinette and I were discussing your trips and she called it time travel, but it really isn't. Your body stays here. It goes nowhere. If this was time travel your body would go too – you'd be a physical presence in the past. People would be able to see you, speak to you and interact with you, but they can't."

"Which means what exactly?" asked Antoinette.

"Which means Charley's body is not traveling through time."

Charley glowered, "That's just a theory."

"It's all just a theory you idiot!" Greg was frustrated. "Time travel isn't possible but if it were, it would have rules and you're breaking them."

"Rules? So what are these non-existent rules for something that's impossible?"

"Look, everyone knows that a single object can't exist in two places at the same time."

"Everyone knows?" Charley scoffed. "Until now, no one has proven time travel is possible, so how can anyone know what the rules are, you moron."

Greg grasped his neck in frustration. "OK, it's a widely-held belief. You said that on your first trip, you saw the brooch taken off the dead queen, right?"

"Yeah, so?"

"So you were wearing that same brooch. If you had really been there, if you had really time-travelled and dropped into that hut, something would have happened when those two brooches met-up."

"But…"

"But nothing happened because it wasn't there – It was here, in this time, hanging around your neck whilst you were asleep and dreaming."

Antoinette nodded. "That makes sense Charley. But it also means my fear about the past absorbing you, has some foundation. You are becoming a real entity in the Dark Ages. If you were to be absorbed completely, the brooch would also be real and tangible in the past. What might happen? Perhaps the two brooches meeting could set off some cataclysmic time and space event."

"I need to return Annie. Maybe I can help to save her life."

Antoinette rolled her eyes. "Not again, Charley. We've been over this."

"You want to change the course of history?" Greg looked alarmed.

"That wouldn't be so bad, would it?"

Greg's eyes widened. "Are you for real? The knock-on effect would be appalling."

Antoinette thumped the bed. "Charley, You mustn't do anything to change history."

Greg's bruised face was taut. "If she had lived longer, she might have had children," "And they in turn would have set up new lines of genealogy."

"That's a good thing, surely?"

"Yeah, there might be new generations for sure, but there would also be entire generations from other lines, that would never have existed had Catherine lived. What would happen to them?"

"They would be wiped-out I guess. Time travel genocide just like we discussed, Annie?" Charley's eyes filled with fresh tears.

"Greg speaks sense, Charley."

Charley slid down under the sheets. The eczema on her arm was itching like crazy. "I'm tired now. Please leave."

Alone again, it only took seconds for Charley to fall into a deep sleep. She was so tired.

CHAPTER 31 - 449AD
Márta (March)

"My Lady, there is someone here to see you."

Catherine had just finished applying a poultice to the leg of a villager who had been gored by a wild boar. "You should learn to keep away from the end that bites, Bryn."

"I will in future, My Lady."

As he hobbled to the door, Catherine turned to Taraghlan. "You look tired. Is my father too demanding of you?"

Taraghlan laughed and brushed his fingers through his now greying hair. "He always has been and always will be." Catherine beckoned him to sit and Taraghlan looked back at the door, an expression of uncertainty on his face. "But your visitor, My Lady?"

"He can wait."

"I am not sure he can, My Lady, it is…"

"He can wait," she interrupted. "You are my father's closest friend and my protector since I was a child. I need to be sure you are well."

"You have always been wise, even as a child, but now that you have reached eighteen summers, your strength and wisdom are unsurpassed. You are right. I do not feel well."

Catherine stepped over to his side and held her hands about four inches above his shoulders. Slowly she traversed her hands down his back and stopped at his kidneys. "There is little reason for me to be the Avertci's Priestess if I cannot sense my people's pain. Why did you not come to me?"

"I had much to do."

"You drink too much ale and not enough water. You must drink more water; at least two pitchers a day until I tell you to stop."

Taraghlan laughed. "And that is all I need to do?"

Catherine smiled." It is, for now. You can tell Vortiger he may come in now?"

Taraghlan laughed. "I should be used to you knowing everything by now."

The merest hint of a smile touched the corners of Catherine's mouth. "Not everything, Taraghlan, just the important things."

The fur across the door was swept aside and Vortiger, the King's youngest son strode through and bowed. "My Lady." He straightened up and inwardly gasped when he saw Catherine. It was no longer a child who stood before him but a tall, elegant and beautiful woman, whose long dark hair tumbled across her shoulders and almost reached her waist. She was dressed in a long white gown held by a belt of linen, interwoven with fine gold thread. She preferred plain clothes rather than the checks and squares favoured by most people of Celtic descent.

Catherine smiled broadly at Vortiger. No longer the gangly youth who had entertained her five years ago at her father's feast. Now he was tall and powerfully built. Unlike most men, his beard was not wild and woolly, but short and neatly trimmed as favoured by the Romans. He was wearing soldier's uniform, also fashioned in a similar style to those worn by the Romans but with an English long-bladed sword at his side. "Good to see you again my Prince."

Taraghlan headed for the door. "Thank you for your advice My Lady." Catherine nodded and threw him a surreptitious wink. He bowed briefly to Vortiger and left the hut with a grin on his face. Perhaps this amazing young woman had a match in mind.

Catherine refocussed her attention on Vortiger. "Please, sit." She directed Maybn to fetch some ale then and then sat opposite the handsome warrior.

Vortiger's eyes flashed appreciatively "You convinced your father to let you become the tribe's priestess then?"

"My poor father had no choice. The people demanded it, as did I."

"When did this happen?"

A flash of sadness crossed her face. "When I turned sixteen."

Vortiger accepted the ale from Maybn and took a small swig. "Why does that make you sad?"

"You know that my mother had been the tribe's priestess? I thought, for a brief moment, she had come back to me. I could feel her presence, I even felt her touch." Her hand involuntarily moved to her shoulder. "But then she left me again and I've not felt her since. It makes me sad." She shook away the memory and smiled again. "Tell me Vortiger, why have you come?"

"I have been sent by the king. I am to visit every tribe in Britain with some news. I have spoken to your father already, but I didn't want to leave without seeing you."

Catherine ignored the obvious invitation to ask why he wanted to see her in particular. "What news did you bring?"

"The Picts and the Scots are raiding into Ceint now and are also dropping down along the West coast to my father's lands. He has extended an invitation to an army of displaced Saxons to settle in Britain and help us drive the Picts back to north of the wall. They are a mix of Jutes, Angles and Frankish I think."

Catherine's bright blue eyes darkened and her face grew taut. "That was a very bad idea. It will not end well…for any of us."

Vortiger frowned. "Why do you say that? The Picts are fearless in battle and we need allies who are just as fierce. We need to meet might with might."

Catherine stood up. "Tell the king to withdraw his invitation." Her eyes flashed angrily.

Vortiger stood also. "I cannot; it is too late. The invitation was sent two moons ago and they have been arriving for some days now."

Catherine glared at Vortiger. "Then we will all pay the price for this foolishness. The gods will not forgive us for bringing those murderous warriors into our midst."

"You are wrong, my Lady. Father has given them the Isle of Inis Ruim and already they have driven the Picts away from there.

Once settled, father will bring them north."

"And then what? After the Picts have been sent home, do you believe that the Saxons will be happy to remain in Ceint? They will spread across our lands; they will force us to adopt their ways, their religions. Our tribes will disappear."

Vortiger's temper spiked. "We stood against the Romans and…"

"And we lost. Look at our past. The Romans changed everything."

"But we drove them away eventually."

"Is that what you learned from your schooling?" Catherine stepped close to him. "They left because they wanted to. They left because this was an outpost they no longer needed. Look at the scars they have left across our land – the ruins and that accursed religion of Christianity. Our gods are appeased for now, but if the Saxons attack us too, our gods will be like the Romans and they will leave us, like an outpost they no longer need."

Vortigern looked down into Catherine's eyes and suddenly, without warning, leaned in and kissed her hard on the lips. She gasped and drew back before delivering a stinging slap to his face. "Never do that again." Vortigern grabbed Catherine by the waist and pulled her into a tight embrace. "Do not!" she warned, but Vortiger ignored her command and kissed her again. And this time, she kissed him back.

oOo

Charley was again transfixed by the events unfolding before her. Catherine was now eighteen and was still unmarried which was unusual for girls of that time. According to her tribe's laws, she should have been betrothed at thirteen and married as soon as possible after. To be unbetrothed and unmarried at her age could have seen her condemned to a life of servitude, even if she was the Chief's daughter. Being the tribe's priestess obviously gave her protection.

She felt guilty that the brooch had chosen to leave out five years of Catherine's life and she felt sad that Catherine had missed her

158

presence. She frowned. Something about that last thought was off kilter. The brooch! The brooch didn't figure in this trip. Antoinette had taken it. She looked about the hut. Without the brooch, was she really here? There was only one way to find out. She picked up a sharp piece of flint and sliced a small cut on her forearm.

"Oh this is ridiculous," she said to herself. "Without the brooch it's impossible to return; I'm just dreaming." She reasoned that if this was merely sleep, then she could force herself to wake up... but she didn't want to.

Catherine removed Vortiger's hand from her breast. "No," she said firmly.

"No? I could just take you."

Catherine laughed. "You could, but only if I let you and only if you didn't object to my father gutting you like a fish."

Vortiger laughed too. "Oh yes, your father." He kissed her again. "I do not know what will happen with the Saxons but I promise you, unless you send me away, I will never leave your side."

She smiled at that. "You will, Vortiger; the gods have much in store for us and I know we will be wrenched apart, but until then..." She leant in and kissed him again, and this time allowed his hand to remain.

oOo

Catherine and Vortigern were sitting by the fire when Madron entered and stopped in surprise. "Vortiger? I thought you were leaving for the Trinovantes and Iceni."

Catherine rose and sidled up to her father. "It is late. I bade him stay until sunrise so that his horses may rest. His men will sleep in the byres with them. That is acceptable to you?"

Madron grunted and then turned to Vortiger. "I want to speak to my daughter."

Vortiger nodded and smiled, and Madron waited until he had left the hut before addressing Catherine. "I do not need your mother's powers to see that you have a desire for that boy."

Catherine blushed. "I did not know until tonight. It would be a

159

good match father. A good match for me and for you too; a prince married to your daughter?"

Madron laughed. "By the gods I feared you would never be interested in any man. He feels the same?"

"We have talked. He is a good man."

"He is still a boy. Has he even cut his teeth in battle?"

"He is kind, strong, determined and I believe he will be fearless in battle."

Madron shook his head sadly. "There is a difference between being fearless and being courageous. Fearlessness can get you killed too quickly. This might be a very short marriage."

"Father do not tease me. Do you agree to the match or not?"

"Of course I do but Vortiger must get the King's approval too, and there are two things I must do before I can announce your betrothal." He reached into a chest and pulled out a small roll of cloth. He held it by its loose end and let it unravel. A beautifully ornate dagger fell into his hand.

Catherine picked it up and gasped. "It is beautiful." She traced a finger around the intricate carving on the hilt and her eyes shone as she took in the beauty of the engravings on the blade.

"It was your mother's. She called it Fire-Sting and now it is yours. You may call it what you will."

Catherine's eyes filled with tears. "Fire-Sting is the perfect name for it, Father. Thank you." She flung her arms around his bearlike neck."

"And now there is one more thing to do before I can announce your betrothal."

Catherine cocked her head to one side, trying to read her father's mind, but it was closed to her. "What must you do?"

"Some call me King of the Avertci but to most I am a Chieftain. If you are to marry a prince, you must be a princess. I will therefore arrange for the village Ealdormen to proclaim me king." A pained look seeped into his dark eyes. "It means when I die, you will be the Avertci's queen."

I am not your wife, father, how can I be queen?

"Without a wife, the title goes to my surviving blood."

Catherine smiled. "A queen and a priestess? Timancius would be so proud."

oOo

"I can't wake her." Greg was shaking Charley's sleeping body but she refused to respond.

"Mon Dieu, Greg, look at her arm."

A livid red gash was gradually appearing on her left arm. As it materialised it started to bleed. "Throw me that towel, Greg." Antoinette dipped a corner of the towel in Charley's tumbler of water and then wiped away the blood. "Merde Sainte, she's gone back without the brooch."

"But that's not possible."

"It seems perhaps it is. Wherever she is, her arm has been cut and it is replicated here. Just like the mud and Catherine's blood on her face. I fear the past is not done with her yet."

There was a cough outside the bed space and Richard put his head through the doorway. He knew it was a risk. Greg might want payback, but Richard reckoned he would prefer to play the victim, not the aggressor. "I know I'm the last person you want to see, but I need to know how she is."

Greg leapt up and pushed Richard back through the curtain. "Feigning concern now?"

"I *am* concerned."

"She's travelled again and we think she's in danger; she's been hurt."

"I - I thought she didn't have the brooch anymore."

"She doesn't. We think she's managed to get back to the past without it. Whatever happened when you removed the brooch from her probably caused this to happen." He shoved him toward the exit. "You'd better sod off before I do something we'll both regret."

Richard raised his hand and stepped outside. "OK, OK. I can take a hint."

Greg glared after him. "It wasn't a hint!"

CHAPTER 32
Eanáir (January) 450AD

King Vortigern, dismounted and walked quickly to the great hall, leaving his army outside the settlement's gates. He was followed by Vortiger and Vortimir.

Madron, seated behind the high table, looked up in surprise. "I had no warning of your approach my Lord." He glared at Taraghlan and hurried to the king's side. Taraghlan in turn, hurried from the hall to interrogate the soldiers on watch.

"I need your counsel, Madron." He looked about the hall. "And the counsel of your priestess."

Madron chuckled. "I am sure my counsel will suffice."

Vortigern banged his fist on the table. "Fetch her!" He roughly pushed past Madron to warm himself before the fire that snapped and crackled in the Centre of the hall. "Vortiger has told me much about your daughter, Madron. He says she is a gifted priestess. He also tells me you have proclaimed yourself King, is that true?"

Madron smiled. "The Ealdormen have proclaimed me King, my Lord, but King of my tribe, nothing more. I think it may be a wise decision; I believe my daughter and Vortiger have thoughts of being betrothed."

Vortigern spun round to face his son. "Well?"

Vortiger blushed. "We have spoken about it Father. She is beautiful, intriguing and more than my equal. I would be happy to accept betrothal if it pleases her and of course, you."

Vortigern let out a short roar of laughter and slapped his son on the back. "A priestess in the family? Of course I agree."

Madron grinned. "Then let it be so."

Vortigern's smile however, vanished quickly and his features grew taut. "Enough of this talk of betrothals. I need to speak to her. She told my son I was ill-judged to bring the Saxons to Britain and I need to know why."

"You already know why, my Lord," said a gentle, yet firm voice from behind.

Vortigern wheeled round to see Catherine standing in a shaft of sunlight, a short grey jerkin tied around her and a long sword at her waist.

Vortigern's eyes widened in amazement, "You allow your daughter to carry a sword?"

"He does my Lord." Catherine answered for him. "And I am as good as any man."

Madron smiled. "She is, my Lord. None save Taraghlan has beaten her yet."

The king shook his head. "The gods will not approve."

"My gods approve, my Lord and they ensure my arm is swift and strong." She removed the sword and placed it on the table. "My Lord I fear that your position will be sorely challenged now those accursed Saxons are here." She saw Vortigern's eyes narrow. He would not want to hear what she had to say next. "I fear for you too, my Lord. Your time as King of Britain may be coming to an end."

Madron looked up sharply. "Hold your tongue girl…"

Vortigern raised his hand and stopped Madron mid-sentence. "This is why I am here. Madron. Go on, girl."

"The Saxons *will* move north but not to drive away the Picts. They will turn against you my Lord, to seize the lands for themselves."

Vortigern nodded sagely. "It has already started. This winter is hard. One of the hardest for a generation and they are foraging further afield. The Cantiaci have succumbed."

"Then you must fight them," said Madron flatly. "You cannot allow them to attack our tribes. Where is your army, Lord?"

"I am gathering my forces, but I do not want a battle yet. I still need Saxon help against the Picts. I will negotiate one more time before I resort to a fight."

Catherine picked up her sword again. "We are caught between the two; Saxons to the South and Picts to the North. We have no wish to appease the Picts, but perhaps, Lord King, you could share some winter stock from your kingdom with the Saxons? That would remove their need to attack the tribes."

Vortigern shook his head. "If we had sufficient for our own needs I would accept that as good counsel, but we don't. If I take from the tribes to give to the Saxons, there would be an uprising." He turned to Madron. "You know how it lies, Madron. Could you afford to give stock away?"

"I could not, my Lord. We can barely feed ourselves."

"Then the only answer is to fight them," Catherine suggested. "For they will strike further and further north, ripping the hearts out of all the farms and homesteads they find."

Madron agreed. "We have built up our army a little. If you need us to fight with you my Lord, we will."

oOo

Charley awoke with a start and immediately sat up. Antoinette and Greg were sitting in her cramped bed space comparing historical notes about Vortigern.

"Mon Cher," Antoinette smiled broadly. "I am so happy to see you back. How are you feeling?"

"Shocked and sad; I had a vivid dream." She wiped away a tear. "Dreams are not the same as being there in person." Greg and Antoinette exchanged glances that were not lost on Charley. "What?"

Greg looked pensive. "You *were* there, in person."

"No. Why do you say that? You know that's not possible without the brooch."

"Did you cut your arm in this…dream?"

"Yes. It was self-inflicted but…" Her voice tailed off.

"Look at your arm."

She glanced down at the small dressing and a look of fear

164

crossed her face. "Greg why am I bandaged, did the cut materialise here?"

Greg poured a glass of water and handed it to her. "Yes. You weren't dreaming Charley; you *were* back there."

"I realised I didn't have the brooch and cut myself with a piece of flint. I figured if I were dreaming, nothing would happen but..." she looked at her arm again. "That means I got there and back by myself. How was that possible?"

Antoinette patted her hand. "Things are at force here that we don't understand Mon Cher. Somehow you have made a connection to Catherine that is so strong that I fear you are losing any control you had. This could be very bad."

"Or very good." Greg grinned boyishly. "Think about it, free travel into the past whenever you want; this is a scientific marvel."

"Except I'm not actually time travelling though am I, as you so pedantically pointed out before."

"Maybe not, but you're doing something."

Antoinette rose and ushered Greg to the door. "That's enough for now, Greg." She looked back at her Protégé. "We'll leave you to rest. Try and get some sleep... proper sleep."

Charley bit her lip. "I'm too frightened to try."

Richard darted into the adjacent bed space as Antoinette and Greg exited the dormitory tent. His heart was racing as he processed what he'd overheard. "So that's confirmed then; she doesn't need the brooch to travel back." His plan to remove the brooch and trap Charley in the past would have to be rethought. Overt murder was not on his radar and would point straight to him; even if he made it look like an accident, it could still point to him. "I need to tell Smith about this new development and see what he suggests."

He peered into Charley's bed space; she was sleeping peacefully. His gaze fell upon her spare pillow, now lying on the floor, and his pulse quickened. Could he really do it? He tip-toed through the curtain and stood beside her, watching silently, her breathing slow and steady.

His thoughts were in turmoil. *"Leave now." "Do it." "Leave now." "Do it!"*

He bent to pick up the pillow and as he held it above Charley's face, she stirred and mumbled something incoherently. He stopped in his tracks and shook his head clear, tears in his eyes. No, overt murder was definitely *not* on the cards. It had never been on the cards. He turned quickly and left the tent. It was time to speak to Smith.

CHAPTER 33

Rosemary Forrester entered the artefacts tent and quickly scanned the tables. "No, it will be in the safe you stupid woman," she scolded herself, and that meant she would need the key. For once, Walter Smith had come to her with some useful information and now that she knew Charley could travel without the brooch, she wanted it for herself.

oOo

"Are you telling me Richard Armitage failed in his plan to trap her in the past?"

Smith swallowed. "Not exactly. He's had to abort that plan. There's more to it."

Forrester listened intently as Smith explained about Charley's new-found ability to go back without the brooch.

"What do you want him to do now?" A thin bead of sweat lay across Smith's brow.

"I still want her dead," she snarled.

"What can be so important that you're prepared to kill the girl. It makes no sense."

Forrester fixed him with an icy glare. "It makes no fucking sense to me either; I can't explain what's driving me, but it's got to be done."

Smith pulled himself as straight as he could and held her gaze. "Then find someone else and just be grateful I don't report you. I'm not going to prison for you, Rosemary and I doubt Armitage will help anymore."

"Rubbish. He needs the cash. You said he contacted you for advice, so give it to him. Tell him to kill the bitch!" No sooner had she finished the sentence than a new thought jumped into her mind. "No, wait... I'll do it."

"You'll tell Armitage?"

"No you moron, I'll *do* it."

"You?!" Smith was incredulous. "How on earth will you manage that?"

Forrester grinned, her mouth turning into a thin, mean smile. "I'm going to get the brooch, go back in time and kill her there."

Smith's mouth dropped open. "You're mad. How do you know you'll be able to travel back?"

Her smiled grew. "Oh I know, Walter. I don't know how I know, but I know."

oOo

Smith sat at his desk, deep in thought. This whole situation was totally crazy. Charley Chandler-Price was a know-it-all little madam, but how could Forrester's dislike have become so extreme? She was now talking of murder... and for what? The dig unearthed a Saxon dagger and that damned brooch, but nothing else of note. Smith chewed a hangnail and then reached for the phone. He'd made a decision.

An hour later, Smith was standing before Sir Roger Crane, head honcho of the NAS and Forrester's boss. Crane was staring at Smith in disbelief.

You expect me to believe that Rosemary wants to kill an archaeologist? Not just any archaeologist but one who is widely regarded as Antoinette Deselle's protégé?"

"Yes."

And for what motive, Mr. Smith? What motive could Rosemary possibly have?"

"As far as I can tell it's just jealousy. I can't think of anything other reason. She is like a woman possessed."

"And you expect me to believe that there is an artefact, a brooch that can transport people back to Saxon times?"

"I know it sounds fanciful, Sir Richard, but..."

"Are you on drugs?"

"No sir!" Smith was indignant.

"Are you an alcoholic or just simply insane?"

"Sir Roger, I really must object…"

Crane tugged at the cuffs of his shirt. "Very well. I will speak to her, though what the hell I'm supposed to say is beyond me."

oOo

"You fucking little piece of shit!" Rosemary Forrester slammed the door behind her as she stormed into Smith's office. "You total fucking piece of shit. You complained to Crane… about *me*?" Her voice rose to a painfully high shriek.

"Rosemary, please…"

She strode around Smith's desk and grabbed him by the lapels. "You told him I wanted that bitch dead and the stupid fucker believed you!"

"I didn't think he did!"

"He's warned me that if anything happens to her, he'll report me to the police."

Smith tried unsuccessfully to pry her strong, bony fingers from his jacket. He struggled to stand up but Forrester held him in his chair with ease. "You've lost the plot, woman, you're insane!"

Forrester reached across Smith's desk and grabbed a paperknife from a mesh pencil container and before Smith could even register what she was doing, she'd plunged it straight into his neck. "Cross me again and I'll kill you too."

She stepped away and looked in fascination as blood spurted across the office from his carotid artery.

Smith's hand flew up to his neck and tried to stem the flow of blood; his hand and sleeve instantly turned a bright crimson red. "What have you done?" He tried to stand but his legs buckled under him.

Forrester moved further away to avoid the blood that was spurting across the desk and pooling on the floor near her feet. "Oh dear, I hadn't planned for that," her words were dripping with sarcasm, "but never mind."

"God forgive you, you bitch, because I won't"

169

Forrester checked to make sure she had no blood on her clothes. "I don't need your god's forgiveness, Walter. I've got my own gods looking after me and they'll help me kill that bitch once and for all."

Walter slumped forward onto his blood-soaked desk. Everything was starting to feel peaceful. He was feeling detached from everything around him. He could just make out Forrester standing by his office door. "Why Charley?" His voice was weak and breathy.

Forrester laughed. "Charley? She's the least of my worries. I'm talking about Catherine. She's the one I'm going to kill!"

Smith's vision was fading. He was slipping into some sort of dream state. It was quite pleasant. He hated Forrester with a passion and as he died, he wondered if it was too late to choose a different career path.

Forrester left Smith's office and hurried out of the building. She had to get to the brooch. As she slid into the driver's seat of her BMW, a frightening array of thoughts flashed through her mind. She thought about the name of the person she felt driven to kill and muttered, "Who the fuck is Catherine?"

oOo

The banging on the front door was incessant. "Ok, ok, hang on," Richard walked reluctantly into the hall from his kitchen. It could only be Greg or Antoinette and he didn't relish speaking to either of them again...ever. He wrenched open the door and was almost battered out of the way by Forrester.

"Is the brooch in the safe?" she demanded, her nostrils flaring and her hawk-like eyes filled with hatred. She moved up close to him and stared straight into his eyes. "Well?"

Richard recoiled as the smell of her stale breath assailed his nostrils. "As far as I know."

"Who keeps the key?"

"Deselle has it."

"And where is she?"

Richard had had enough and pushed the vile woman back a step.

"Get away from me. Who are you?" As soon as the words left his lips, he realised. "You're Rosemary Forrester aren't you? Look, I don't know where she is and I don't care. If you want the brooch so badly, go find Antoinette and just order her to hand it over. It's nothing to do with me."

"That's a very good idea. Take me to her."

Richard shook his head. "I'm taking you nowhere; I told you, I don't know where she is, so piss-off out of my house."

Forrester pushed past him again and stormed out leaving the door wide open behind her.

Richard ran his fingers through his hair in frustration. Things were getting seriously out of hand.

CHAPTER 34

"I'm here for the brooch." Forrester stood in front of Antoinette, hands on hips and hatred in her eyes.

Antoinette looked up from behind her desk and sighed when she saw Forrester standing there. She pushed her work aside and glared at the hateful woman. She took in her grey two-piece suit with the jacket buttoned-up incorrectly. She noted too Forrester's white blouse, mid-brown tights and black flat shoes and decided she resembled a cross between Norman Wisdom and an evil Mary Poppins. An involuntary twitch of a smile escaped before she could stop it.

"What's so funny? Give me the brooch!"

There was something different about Forrester this time; she had always been rude and difficult, but this was something more, a touch of hysteria perhaps?

"It's locked in the safe."

"I guessed that. Go and get it."

Antoinette's hackles rose. "Why do you want it?"

"That's sod-all to do with you." She stepped menacingly towards the table.

"No way, Rosemary; it's probably the finest example of an ancient Celtic brooch ever found. It's staying put, where it's safe."

With a shriek of rage, Forrester literally flung herself across the table and crashed on top of Antoinette. Locked together by Forrester's bony arms, they crashed backwards and fell to the floor. The landing was hard and Antoinette's head hit the ground with a sickening crack. She was out cold, with a thin trickle of blood in her hair. Forrester rolled off and wasted no time in searching her for the safe key. She found it in the first pocket she checked and pulled herself painfully to her feet and smoothed her skirt. "Now where's that sodding safe?"

oOo

"I'm sorry Ms Deselle, the safe is open and the brooch has gone."

Antoinette was back at her desk in her makeshift office and holding a cold compress to the lump on the back of her head. "We need to call the police, Greg. This is a robbery, pure and simple." Her phone rang. "Oh Sante Merde. It is the big boss." She poked at the answer key. "Yes Sir Roger, how can I help you?"

"Hello Annie. There's little time for pleasantries so I must come straight to the point. I think Rosemary Forrester has gone insane. Walter Smith is dead and I think Rosemary may be responsible. Walter came to me today and told me she had made threats to kill Charlotte, and now he's dead."

"Whoa, just a moment, did you say she has *killed* Walter?"

"I think she stabbed him in the neck. Why would she do that Antoinette, why?"

"I really do not know. She used to abuse him all the time. He was a useless lump but he did not deserve to die; how awful."

"Listen, Annie, Forrester has obviously gone AWOL, not surprising under the circumstances, but in view of what she did to Walter and her threats to kill Charlotte, I think you should keep your protégé close to you. I've alerted the police here and they are going to liaise with the police in Kent."

"Thank you, Sir Roger, but I should tell you that Rosemary has been here already; she attacked me and has stolen a priceless artefact. I guess under the circumstances, I'm lucky to be alive."

"Attacked you?" The surprise in his voice was quickly replaced by anger. *"What the hell is going on with her, Annie? Is this to do with that so-called magical brooch?"*

"You know about that?"

"Walter told me."

"Wait, what? He knew about it?"

173

"Annie, what is going on? This brooch, is it for real?"

"It's complicated. I will explain everything the next time we meet. Is that OK?"

"I guess it will have to be. Have you checked on Charlotte recently?"

"Yes. She's fine. Sound asleep and yes, I did check she was breathing. Listen, Sir Roger, I've got a banging headache, thanks to Rosemary. May I call you later? We can discuss it more then."

He agreed and Antoinette wearily put her phone back on the table. "Let's go check on Charley again," she said to Greg.

oOo

Rosemary Forrester was in the Central hall of what appeared to be a semi-derelict Roman palace. It was around fifty paces long by thirty paces wide with painted walls and a solid mosaic floor. The tile roof was gone, replaced by thatch and the windows let in a fearful draught. She stood rooted to the spot, transfixed by what she saw. The hall was full of warriors, dressed in Saxon clothing, shouting and arguing. Suddenly swords clashed and more shouts rang-out as an argument between two warriors descended into violence.

"Enough!!"

The power behind that shout made Forrester jump and she suddenly became aware how vulnerable she was. They must be able to see her. Clutching the brooch tightly to her scrawny frame, she ran for cover behind a threadbare curtain that hung across a side door.

She peered out and could just make out the man who had shouted. He was standing on the top table his arms raised. Gradually the noise subsided and he looked at the sea of faces before him. He was powerfully built and wearing thick furs. His hair was light brown and hung below his shoulders.

"We have taken Cient for our own. Tomorrow we ride for the lands north of the Tem."

The crowd took up a chant of "Horsa, Horsa, Horsa," and continued until he raised his arms again. "Our new friend here assures us that victory is certain."

The hall erupted with more cheers and shouts as Horsa gestured to a man sitting at the end of the table. "Stand and be recognised."

Forrester recoiled for a split second as the man stood up. She knew him; somehow she knew him. As she took-in his wizened body, shaved head, thin mouth, hooked nose and his revoltingly empty eye socket, she began to feel an overwhelming sense of happiness. She was home at last.

Timancius nodded to the crowd, acknowledging their praise and adoration, and his one good eye settled on the very spot where Forrester was hiding.

CHAPTER 35 - 450AD
Sōlmōnath (February)

Catherine stopped abruptly and tilted her head to one side, listening. She suddenly staggered backwards and dropped her basket of freshly picked winter herbs. "NO!"

Maybn and Nessa ran towards her from the woods, both also clutching baskets of medicinal herbs and tree barks. "My Lady?" panted Maybn as she reached Catherine's side. "Are you unwell?"

Catherine steadied herself against the high wooden palisade that protected the village and calmed her breathing. She turned to her two faithful servants with a look of fear and uncertainty in her eyes. Nessa recoiled slightly. She had never seen those emotions in the Priestess and it unnerved her. Maybn touched Catherine's arm. "My Lady?"

Catherine stared southwards and put her hand to her chest to feel the comfort of her mother's brooch around her neck. "Timancius," she said, barely above a whisper.

Maybn and Nessa both took a step back. "What about him?" Maybn asked cautiously.

"He comes...and not alone."

The blood drained from Charley's face the moment Catherine had whispered Timancius's name. The possible return of the tribe's old priest worried her more than it should have. After all, Charley knew that Catherine died at Hengist's hand and not because of that awful, evil man, so why did his name trouble her so much?

She ran after the three women and followed them to the main hall where Madron was sitting, scowling at some coinage on the table before him.

"Roman shit!" he cursed and swept the money from the table. He looked up and glared at his daughter. "The King sent some coins to buy armour for the men, but no blacksmith will take that worthless shit. It is not even hack silver." The frown suddenly lifted, to be replaced by concern. "Step forward daughter; what is wrong with you? You look like a whipped dog."

Catherine swallowed. "Timancius is back."

Madron stood angrily and withdrew his sword. "Where? Where is that turd?"

"Not here, Father, not here…not yet."

Madron looked relieved and sheathed his heavy sword. "Then where?"

Catherine shook her head, as if trying to shake her thoughts free. "I don't know. Not far; maybe two or three day's ride."

"He is coming here?"

"I cannot be sure; my sight is clouded."

"Who is he with?"

Catherine thought hard. "Saxons. He has befriended the Saxons." She closed her eyes to concentrate. "They are riding north." She paused again and then her eyes widened. "Father, they are coming for us."

oOo

Vortigern, King of the Britons, looked forlornly across the icy lake, his youngest son by his side. "I have no idea how to deal with this situation." He sighed, his breath visible in the cold night air.

Vortiger glared. "A situation you created by not honouring your early promises to the Saxons."

Vortigern raised an eyebrow, "Careful…"

"I apologise, I meant no disrespect, but this uprising was unavoidable once you failed to keep them in food and clothing."

The old king knew there was some truth in that. "I thought the Isle of Inis Ruim would suit t their needs. I was wrong, but their treachery is nothing to do with broken promises; they turned on me long before their bellies complained through lack of food. This is the hardest winter for many years. Our animals are dying of cold, even in the byres; we can hardly feed and clothe ourselves, let alone those murderous warmongers." He looked up at the dancing lights in the sky and tried to change the subject. "I see that the Roman goddess, Aurora is busy tonight."

"The Goddess of the Dawn they called her. I have never seen her sky fires before."

Vortigern smiled wistfully. "I have seen them only once, when I was very young. The Picts in the North see them often. Maybe it is their gods speaking, not Aurora. Maybe they are warning us."

"The Romans believe she is just heralding a new day."

"Hmm."

Vortiger returned the subject to the Saxons. "I know we needed help against the Picts who have now reached the lands of the Iceni…"

"Which is far too close."

"Aye, father, but why reach out to Hengist and Horsa?"

"I had little choice!" Vortigern's temper was rising.

"But they had already been banished from their own lands. How could you possibly imagine that they would be compliant allies?"

"You say too much, boy."

"And you act too little." As the words left his mouth Vortiger knew he had gone too far.

With a bellow of rage Vortigern rounded on his son and with the speed and dexterity of a younger man, grabbed him by the throat and swept the boy's legs from under him.

Vortiger hit the ground heavily and Vortigern stepped astride him, drew his sword and pressed it hard onto his son's neck.

"Was that insolence born from contempt or was it simply youthful arrogance I wonder?"

Vortiger clutched the sword's blade. "If you think I have contempt for you then press down now, father; end it here. I'll even help you." He pulled down on the blade until it pierced his flesh.

"Enough, you maggot." Vortigern stepped back and sheathed his sword. "You are disrespectful, but you are resilient and determined." Vortigern turned away and gazed sadly over the lake. "It pains me to recognise there is truth in your words."

Vortiger looked up. "Really?" He hauled himself to his feet and declined the strip of cloth his father offered him; the wound was superficial.

The king shrugged and tucked it back in his belt. "It is true that Pictish raiding parties have been moving further and further southwards and I have been totally unable to repel them. My forces are too weak," he said flatly.

King of the Britons? He felt more like the king of nothing. The Iceni, normally a brave and competent tribe, had been demoralised following many years of resistance to Roman rule followed by the death of their queen, Boudicca, They no longer had the will to fight and they needed Vortigern's help against the Caledonian raiders.

The goddess's green dancing lights reflected in Vortigern's face. "I gave them Inis Ruim, but they have taken the whole of Cient for themselves. Now they are moving ever northwards, repelling the Picts as they go, but also taking villages and land for themselves. I cannot stop them, even though Madron and the Avertci had pledged to fight with us if we go to war. "

Vortiger leant forward – a gleam in his eye and his jaw set firm, "I can stop them."

"You?" The King burst out laughing. "And how will you do that?"

"We have an army in decline but we can raise an army from the tribes, if you command them to do so, and I will lead them."

Vortigern chuckled again and shook his head, "You have no battle experience. Hengist and Horsa have more of their kind arriving every day not just families, but warriors."

"We can raise an army that will vanquish them for all time."

Vortigern turned away from the frozen lake. A look of forlorn resignation had fallen across his face like a shadow. "An army of farmers and boys? It will take more than that. I admire your resourcefulness and optimism Vortiger, but you are naïve; it will not happen."

His son turned and walked away. "It will, father. It will if you command it so."

Vortigern stood alone on the lakeshore. Aurora's magic was waning and the sky was darkening. Low, heavy clouds were scudding from the East and as the first flakes of snow landed on his furs, the old king looked skywards. "It will be dawn in a couple of hours," he said aloud.

"Indeed it will," said a voice from the shadows.

"How long have you been there?"

"Long enough."

Vortigern turned and looked at his eldest son. "Long enough to hear your brother's suggestion?"

Vortimir walked across the shingle to his father's side. "Yes."

"Can it be done?"

"I will help to raise the army and we will fight, but we won't win."

"Then why bother?"

Vortimir drew his sword and plunged into the sand. "Because we are Britons. This is our land. If *we* fail perhaps other armies will rise one day and drive them from our shores. The Saxons will never rule here. The histories of our future generations are not about to be rewritten."

Vortigen smiled at his son. "A fine speech." He placed his arm around Vortimir's shoulders. "But I believe what Catherine of the Avertci told me; I fear the Saxons are here to stay."

oOo

The activity in the Avertci village was frantic as every man woman and child, busied themselves in preparation for the Saxon attack. Taraghlan was supervising repairs to the palisades whilst beyond the walls, Caderyn was overseeing the erection of sharpened tree trunks, all bedded into the ground at an angle of forty-five degrees and designed to prevent the mounted warriors getting close to the walls.

The blacksmith was busy making swords and new centre bosses

for the shields. Six of Taraghlan's men had been assigned to making new shields for the newly manufactured bosses. Used imaginatively, that round metal boss could crack skulls, dislocate jaws and fracture almost any limb. It was much more than a defence against arrows, swords and axes.

All the field animals were being moved to enclosures within the village and dry foodstuffs to a central storehouse, so they could be better protected, and Catherine had taken a group of fifteen girls into the woods to seek out plants for stemming blood and reducing pain. "We will need much," she told them, "and when you think you have enough, pick the same again."

A corner of the great hall was being prepared by Maybn and Nessa to treat the wounded and dying, of which there would be many. "What's up?" Maybn demanded, seeing a tear in Nessa's eye.

"Just thinking about Brid."

Maybn nodded. "She has been with the gods for weeks, yet Catherine hardly mentions her."

"She doesn't mention Elowyn either and she breast-fed her from the day her mother died."

"Maybe she has forgotten Elowyn?"

"No, Maybn, she knows every one of us and what we are thinking."

Maybn chuckled. "What we are thinking? Do not confuse her powers with magic. She is very wise and very clever, but she cannot read minds."

"She does, and you know it."

Taraghlan, Caderyn and Madron entered the hall and the two women scurried away to let the men talk.

"Is my army ready for battle?"

Taraghlan poured himself some ale and held the jug toward Madron. "Yes my Lord, just about."

Madron grabbed the pitcher roughly and poured out two more cups. "What does that mean, 'Just about?' " He downed his ale in one go and handed the other to Caderyn.

Taraghlan stared into his ale. "My Lord, most of the men are now armed with axes and swords. Most have helmets and shields but they are afraid. They only know of the Saxons from the stories told by travellers; how they cut their enemies in two, how they feast on hearts torn from the dead... and sometimes the living."

"Yes, yes, I've heard the stories too, but they are make-believe; made up stories left to fly on the wind and put fear in their enemies' hearts."

Caderyn put his cup of ale on the table. "*We* know that, my Lord. Your army knows it too, but the rest, the farmers and workers who make up the numbers, they are simple people."

"How many men do you have?"

Taraghlan shrugged. "Six hundred? We should outnumber them and we have the protection of the walls; it might be enough to win."

Suddenly a horn sounded from outside. Three times it sang it's mournful, tuneless note. "They are close," shouted Madron. "Mothers with children should go deep to the woods. Get men to the walls and defend our gates. Taraghlan, fetch Catherine."

CHAPTER 36
Sōlmōnath (February) 450AD

The army that stood before the gates of the village numbered around eight hundred men. About a quarter were mounted and were positioned to cover the flanks. Madron looked down on the horde from the palisade gate tower. He saw they all wore thick leather jerkins and heavy fur coats that offered protection against the cold, but which would hamper them in battle.

Two riders pulled ahead of the army and for the first time, Madron saw the formidable warlords, Hengist and Horsa. A third rider pulled forward and stopped next to the brothers, His one good eye scanned the top of the wall until he saw Madron. "I hear you are now a King. Well you should prepare to be dethroned."

Madron glared down at Timancius. "And you, turd of the gods, I heard you were happily spending your miserable life with other turds. You should feel most at home in Saxon shit."

Horsa said something to Timancius, who nodded. "My Lord Horsa and his brother speak little of our tongue, though I am teaching them, and they are learning quickly. For now, I will speak their words for them. My Lord Horsa wants you to know that no Briton's blood need be spilled today. Just open the gates and you will all be spared."

"As he spared the Cantiaci? They opened their gates and were struck down; put the sword and the axe. Many trampled underfoot as the horses rode over them. The women were raped and the children enslaved or killed. Is that your "Lord's" idea of being spared?"

Timancius translated Madron's words and listened intently to

Horsa's reply. "My Lord Horsa says that was merciful compared to the alternative. You have no choice. Open the gates now or you will all die." He cast his eye along the line of archers and swordsmen at the top of the wall. "*All* of you."

Madron turned to Taraghlan, "Ready the bowmen. Loose at my command. I want Timancius and those two Saxon turds to breathe their last with the first volley." Taraghlan hurried along the platform and briefed Ede, who was in charge of the archers.

Caderyn leaned in to talk quietly to Madron. "Something is not right, my Lord. Their army is well out of range of our bowmen, but the warlords are close. They are within range and they must know it. Why would they put themselves there?"

Madron's eyes narrowed, "I do not care. He pointed at Hengist, Horsa and Timancius, "So long as those three are killed."

"They must have another plan." Caderyn's chest tightened. "Something is not right."

oOo

Charley ran from the palisade to the great hall, to find Catherine. If Caderyn was right, something dreadful was about to happen. The moment Charley stumbled into the hall Catherine stopped what she was doing and stared straight at her. A broad, knowing smile spread across her face and she walked over to near where Charley was standing.

"I knew if ever the village needed your help, you would return, mother."

Charley almost stamped her feet in frustration. "No, you stupid woman; I'm not your mother, but you *have* to listen to me. Concentrate on me, hear my words, pick-up on my emotions or whatever it is that you do, but something is not right. I fear a trap of some sort."

Catherine frowned, "You are angry, mother, why are you angry?" She tilted her head. "You are angry with us? But why? We have done nothing wrong, we are simply preparing for battle." Catherine's mind was in turmoil. Her mother was trying to tell her something, maybe warn her about something.

184

"Come on, Catherine!" shouted Charley. "Work it out. It's a distraction. They are decoys, or... fuck I don't know, but something is wrong!"

Catherine's blue eyes flared. "It is a trap," she whispered. She ran to the back of the hall to where a small group of women were laying fresh straw on the floor and grabbed her sword. "Nessa, Maybn, take the other women and hide." Without waiting for an acknowledgement she ran from the hall with Charley in hot pursuit.

"Where are you going, girl? Madron was walking towards her. "The Saxons are at the gates *and* in range of our arrows."

"Do not fire upon them, father."

"I am about to give the command."

"Do not."

"Pah. It will be done." Madron spun on his heels and ran back to the gate tower. Taraghlan met him as he and Catherine clambered onto the wall.

"My Lord, Timancius has ridden to hide behind the army like the snake he is, but Hengist and Horsa have not moved."

"Then kill them!" roared Madron. "Ede, loose your arrows now."

"Father, no!" Catherine pleaded and grabbed his arm, but it was too late.

Thirty bowmen on top of the palisade released their arrows straight at Hengist and Horsa. The two Saxons and their horses didn't stand a chance. The men were catapulted backwards as their steeds fell screaming and thrashing in the mud.

Madron let out a bellow of a laugh and clapped Taraghlan on the back. "See? See how they are now leaderless. Now watch them crawl away."

Instead of crawling away as Madron hoped, the horde instead let out a thunderous cheer and started to strike their swords and axes on their shields.

"Why do they cheer?"

Catherine pointed to the horde and Madron saw two more riders moving through the ranks until they reached the front of the army, but out of range. They were joined once more by Timancius who raised a hand to silence the army.

"Madron, you godless cur, allow me to introduce you to my Lords Hengist and Horsa."

Taraghlan rolled his eyes. "Those men were decoys."

"I can see that, but why?" Madron growled.

Timancius continued, "My Lords had come in peace; they had no intention of invading your village. They just wanted to talk, but needed to know how you might react, and now they do."

Madron's temper was spiking. "Threatening to kill everyone is *not* coming in peace…"

Timancius grinned. "Actually, they didn't say that. That was my little embellishment. They do not know much of what I said. I told you, their grasp on our language is yet slight."

"Then bring them in. Just them," Madron was almost purple with rage.

"It is too late for talking; you have just slaughtered two of his men in cold blood and that is an act of war for which you must pay."

"You turd! You have tricked me into starting a battle that could have been avoided?"

Timanicous shook his head. "All I tricked you into doing was to show that you wanted my Lords dead - and you took the first opportunity do it. They will not forgive you for that, so prepare to die."

His one eye suddenly caught sight of Catherine and his face grew taut and his mouth curled into a thin, mean snarl. "And you, bitch of a whore mother, you will die last and at my hand."

Catherine just smiled and turned away.

Charley was scanning the horde from the top of the palisade. She had never seen such a sight before and it was both spectacular and terrifying. Suddenly her heart skipped a beat. There was a face in the crowd, a female face in that sea of men, that was strangely familiar. She rubbed her eyes and looked again but now could not see her; the woman had vanished.

Timancius spoke quietly to the two brothers and then rode back through the ranks out of harm's way.

Hengist held his arm raised for a few seconds and when he brought it down again, eight hundred Saxon warriors charged.

The noise of the Saxon onslaught was thunderous. Charley ran to one of the corner towers where she felt slightly safer but Catherine and Madron hurried down the ladders to be with their army on the ground. Taraghlan had now placed a hundred archers on the platforms that ran along the top of the wall. Sentries were posted to the rear of the village and would raise the alarm if the Saxons attempted to breach the palisades there.

Catherine, surrounded by several hundred Avertci men, hitched up her long robe and tied it tightly in place. Caderyn thrust a round shield in her hand and she stood, hair flying in the wind, sword drawn and for all the world, looked like a warrior queen.

The Saxons raised their shields to fend off a relentless onslaught of arrows. On the flanks, the mounted warriors had abandoned their horses in the face of the deadly spiked defences, and were running back to join the main attack.

Taraghlan ordered his men into straight ranks facing the gates. This was the Roman way. His father Tarag had often told him tales of the formidable, solid ranks of centurions, generally unbeaten in battle due to the formations they employed. He ordered the first two ranks to close-up and form a solid shield wall. Then he called out to Madron and Catherine. "My Lord, my Lady, please seek the safety of one of the towers. If you are killed here today, then all will be lost."

Madron nodded. "Daughter, you will do so."

"And you will stay here? No! If you stay then so do I."

"If I am killed, you need to lead our people after this is over. If we are both sent to the gods, there will be no one. Now go!"

She was about to argue again when Caderyn grabbed her. "Listen to him. Come with me."

She allowed herself to be led away from the immediate danger, up the ladders and into the tower where Charley was sitting with her hands over her ears. She tried to see the future; she tried so hard to see the outcome but no visions came. She was alone; the gods had abandoned her and without them she felt powerless.

The heavy oak beam across the back of the gates began to splinter under the weight of the Saxons. "Let them come to us," shouted Taraghlan. "Hold your lines." Around him the stench of sweat hung heavy in the air, quickly combined with reek of faeces and urine as those who were new to battle and barely trained, shat and pissed themselves. A young lad, no more than sixteen was standing next to Taraghlan. His knuckles were white on the hilt of his sword and his teeth were chattering.

"Courage boy. What is your name?"

"Inir." The boy's hair was worn short and his green eyes looked out from beneath a muddy fringe. "Am I going to die?"

Taraghlan smiled. "Your name means 'honour.' Did you know that?"

"Yes."

"Then I expect you to live up to your name boy. Understand?"

Inir cast his eyes to the ground. "Yes, I understand."

Taraghlan looked up at the splintering gates. "Then fight hard and whether you live or die do it with honour and the gods will reward you, in this life or the next."

At that moment the gates succumbed and hundreds of Saxons charged through, swords, axes and shields held high and with such a thunderous vocal roar, that it sounded as if hell itself had opened its own gates that day.

CHAPTER 37
Sōlmōnath (February) 450AD

The front two ranks succumbed to the onslaught almost immediately. With little experience of battle, they didn't have the skills to hold back the horde. They knew, roughly how to create a shield wall but knew nothing of its mechanics; of how to interlock their shields, of how to create gaps to allow the enemy to be quickly impaled. They also didn't know that long swords are of little use in a shield wall, where they become unwieldy and a hindrance. A long sword, thrust into an enemy's stomach would be lost; gripped by the stomach's muscles, it would be impossible to retrieve. The Romans knew that, which is why they used short stubby swords. Pierce by four inches, twist and disembowel in one swift movement. It was a skill that most Brittonic armies had not acquired.

Taraghlan joined the front of the shield wall as the first wave hit and quickly thrust the sharpened metal boss of his shield into the face of a snarling Saxon, splitting the man's face in two. As he fell, his place was taken by another who thrust his short sword at Taraghlan's eyes. Taraghlan ducked out of the way and thrust his sword up between the Saxon's legs and he too fell screaming into the mud.

"Forward! Move forward!" Taraghlan shouted but already the middle of the line had collapsed and the Saxons were setting upon the second rank like ravenous wolves.

Caderyn and Madron ran from the gate tower and began to hack at the Saxons as they pushed through the gate. The archers turned their attention to the Saxons in the village, rather than those still

189

outside and arrows rained down, indiscriminately killing Avertci and Saxon.

"Caderyn, get back on the wall and stop those bowmen."

Rank after rank of Avertci fell in the wake of the attack and the mud turned red with the blood of the dead, dying and injured. Saxon axes cleaved men in two, severed limbs from their torsos and separated heads from their bodies.

Taraghlan found himself being set upon by three Saxon warriors. He used his shield to parry an axe blow that threatened to crush his skull. The force of the strike badly jarred his arm, which immediately went numb. He had intended to ram the shield into the Saxon's face, but instead his arm, carried by the weight of the shield, dropped uselessly to his side. The Saxon seized his chance to finish him off and swung his axe again but Taraghlan thrust his sword into the Saxon's exposed armpit and drove it up through his neck and into his throat. He quickly pulled out the sword and the warrior fell, wide-eyed and gurgling as the second Saxon aimed his sword at Taraghlan's legs.

With his left arm still unusable, Taraghlan quickly whirled his body anti-clockwise, causing his shield arm to fly upwards. The shield connected with the Saxon's chest, propelling him backwards where he suddenly stopped in mid-flight. He looked down, puzzled and saw a blade sticking out of his chest. "Die you Maggot!" shouted Madron as he pulled his sword clear and kicked the Saxon to the ground.

Taraghlan only managed the briefest of smiles before the third Saxon launched himself at him, yellow teeth snarling and his eyes wide with the joy of battle. His sword sliced through Taraghlan's left bicep and with a yell of agony Taraghlan dropped his shield. The Saxon swung again, this time scything his sword in a wide arc, intending to sever Taraghlan's head. He never completed the swing because Madron barged him to the ground and then with two hands, plunged his own sword through the Saxon's throat.

Madron stretched out his hand to Taraghlan. "Get up you maggot, this is no time to…" His sentence was cut short as a Saxon attacked him from his left flank and buried his axe in the middle of his back. Madron turned upon his assailant with a roar of pain and anger and drove his sword through the man's stomach. He sawed the blade upwards and the Saxon's guts spilled into the mud.

Madron dropped his sword, his spine severed and his legs numb, and he fell to his knees. His vision became blurred and the noise of the fighting was fading. The main battle had moved ever forward and was now half-way across the village.

Taraghlan yelled to Catherine who was still on the high wall. She was ferocious in her sword fighting as Saxon after Saxon climbed over the palisade to be met with a swift death by the keenness of her blade. Her face, hair and robes were covered in the blood of the dead and dying as she screamed her defiance in their faces.

When she heard her name called she looked down to see Taraghlan cradling her father's body. With a cry of anguish she scrambled down the ladder and ran to her father's aid. She slid down in the mud beside him and pulled his face round to hers. "Father, no!" Her eyes flared the brightest blue.

"It is too late for that, daughter," he whispered. "I am going to the gods."

Her tears fell on him, creating clean rivulets through the grime and blood that caked his face. "Not yet, you cannot leave me yet."

Madron smiled. "Your mother would be very proud of you." He reached for his sword. "This is now yours, daughter."

She took it from his hands and laid it beside her. Madron's sword was made of fine steel and he had always kept it razor sharp. He had named it, "Blood-Taker." She cast a glance over at Hengist and Horsa. "I promise you that I will avenge you and take much Saxon blood with this sword. I promise."

Madron's breathing faltered and his body juddered, and as he let out one last long sigh, his head dropped back and he lay in Taraghlan's arms, his eyes slightly open, but seeing nothing.

Catherine looked up at the dark rain-filled clouds that rolled across the sky and let out a long, heartfelt and agonised scream.

191

It took the Saxons barely twenty minutes to finish what they had come to do. Around a hundred Avertci were dead and another three hundred lay wounded or dying in the mud. Saxon warriors stabbed and hacked at the dying and picked over the bodies of the dead, looking for trinkets and weapons. Acrid smoke from torched dwellings hung in the air as the first drops of rain fell from the leaden sky.

Hengist saw one of his men on the steps of a demolished house, trying to rape one of the village's women. He rode over and from his saddle, kicked him in the back. "Leave her alone. The women and children must not be harmed!" he shouted. "Spread the word."

The warrior cursed and spat at the warlord. "I found her, she is mine"

Hengist drew his sword and the warrior shoved the half-naked woman onto the ground and stepped away from her. Hengist leaned over and snarled, "Spread the word; no harm must come to the women and children. Round up any you find and hold them in there." He pointed to the great hall.

Horsa rode up alongside. "You cannot deny the men their spoils of war, brother."

"Have you not heard the stories?"

"About their priestess? Of course but Timanicous is determined that she must die."

"If the stories are true, then she is powerful, much more so than that crook-nosed little bastard. Until we have her measure, we must be satisfied with the victory. The spoils can come later." He kicked his horse and started to walk it deeper into the village. "Come, let us see if we can find her."

Horsa laughed. "She is probably in the woods gathering posies."

oOo

Charley had thrown-up several times during the battle. This was not like Braveheart or Game of Thrones; this was real violence, real bloody carnage and very real death. When she heard Catherine's cry and saw her run to her father, she felt indescribable loss. It stabbed her in the heart and tied up her stomach in a tight

192

knot and she too let out a wail of despair. She scrambled down the ladder and ran to Catherine's side. She looked down at Madron's lifeless body and at Catherine, now cradling his head in her arms, tears flowing fast and freely.

Caderyn slid down beside Taraghlan. "You are wounded?"

"I am." He raised his arm to show a bloody gash through the fabric of his tunic.

"We need to go."

"Go?"

"We must get Catherine away. She is Queen now and those Saxons will want her head too." Caderyn hauled Taraghlan to his feet. "Taraghlan, we must take Catherine, now!"

Catherine looked up, her eyes angry and vengeful through the tears. "I am not leaving my people to the mercy of these dogs." She turned at the sound of approaching horses and saw Hengist and Horsa riding towards her.

Charley involuntarily moved behind Catherine for protection, forgetting for a moment that no one could see her.

Hengist gasped as Catherine stood and faced them defiantly. Filthy and bloodied, her clothing torn, one breast almost exposed and her long dark hair flying in the wind that drove the rain harder and harder, Hengist marvelled at her beauty.

The brothers reigned-in their horses but they did not dismount. Horsa grinned down at the small group gathered around Madron's body. "You must be the priestess." His accent was thick and he chose his words carefully. He was thick-set and muscular with long dark hair and a long moustache, set with beads that drooped past his mouth. His white tunic was covered by a coat of thick animal pelts and he wore a conical helmet adorned with the black wings of a raven.

Hengist was of similar build with strong features behind a full dark beard, flecked with grey as was his flowing dark hair. He too wore thick furs and a conical helmet, only his had ram's horns mounted upon it.

Catherine stood firm and strong, her long sword clutched in both hands and raised above her left shoulder. "I am Catherine, *Queen* of the Avertci."

"Queen?" Horsa looked puzzled for a second and then noticed the dead body of Madron. "Ahh, he was your king?"

"He was my *father*."

Taraghlan and Caderyn moved to her side. "She is also our priestess," said Caderyn. "She is more powerful than you can know and you can be sure she will take her revenge against you for killing her people."

The brothers whispered to each other, trying to understand what had just been said and then Horsa looked past Catherine and beckoned to someone. "Timancius, here."

A cold chill enveloped her and she turned to see her old adversary riding slowly towards her, his lips curled in a hateful sneer. He rode past her and stopped next to Horsa. "Why have you not killed her?" he demanded in their Germanic tongue.

"I would, but my brother says her death is not our purpose... yet."

Timancius leant round in his saddle, "Hengist, I promised to help you on the understanding that you would kill this godless whore." He wheeled his horse around to face Catherine's group.

Hengist smiled. "And maybe we will, but for now, we need to talk with her and you will speak our words to her and hers to us." Horsa grabbed the mane of Timancius's horse. "And be sure to speak true or you will be the first to die. We know what you did out there."

Timancius tried to look puzzled, as if he didn't know what Horsa meant.

"You started this battle, Timancius," said Hengist. "You did not speak our true words."

He pointed at the great hall. " Tell her we will speak in there."

Timancius sulkily complied and conveyed Hengist's words to Catherine and she stepped towards the disgraced priest, sword still held high. "Have you forgotten your manners, Timancius? You have not acknowledged me, except to bark an order at me. I am queen *and* priestess of the Avertci and as such you *will* show me respect."

Taraghlan stepped to her side and gently pressed her sword down. "You will refer to our queen as 'My Lady,' or you will die, right here, right now."

Horsa leant over towards the priest. "I understand these words, I think, and you *will* do as they say."

Timancius was horror-struck. "I will not! I would rather die than show her respect." He pointed at his empty eye socket. "She did this to me, do not forget. She gets no respect."

Hengist laughed, "Then priest, you die here. Is that not what that man said?" He beckoned to Taraghlan. "Finish him," he said in English.

"Taraghlan took a pace forward and Horsa gave Timancius a hard shove that unsaddled him. The priest tumbled from his horse and into the slippery bloody mud where he scrabbled and scrambled to his feet. "No!" he cried. He looked pleadingly at Horsa. "You must stop him."

Taraghlan raised his sword above his head and took another pace. "No, please, My *Lady...* " This time he begged to Catherine. "Order him to spare me, please."

Taraghlan had just steeled himself to deliver the fatal blow when Hengist pulled his horse into the space between him and Timancius. "Not today," he said in English. "Him we need."

Taraghlan smiled. He had already guessed this was a bluff to quieten Timancius and get his compliance. He pushed his way around Hengist's horse and found Timancius kneeling and trembling in the mud. "Tell your Saxon friends that we will meet in the Great Hall, once we have taken care of our king."

Timancius nodded and Catherine turned back to her father. At the sight of his bloodied, battered and bruised body, she let out a huge juddering sob and once more, fell to her knees by his side.

CHAPTER 38
Sōlmōnath (February) 450AD

Charley followed Catherine, Taraghlan, Caderyn and another dozen villagers as they carried Madron's body to his dwelling. Once inside he was laid on his cot and Maybn, Nessa and Agnethena stripped and washed him.

Catherine sat alone by the fire and stared into its flames. "Thank you for coming back." She looked at Charley.

"Can you see me now?"

"I can sense you still, as before. I sense your presence and I sense your words and emotions but..." She paused and twisted around to look at her father before turning back to the fire. "But you are not my mother."

"I know." Charley protested. "I tried to tell you."

The yellow and amber flames danced and flickered in Catherine's eyes. "I thought you were, but you are not. You are someone else, someone close to me; someone I should know." She clenched her fists and thumped her knees. "Aargh, it is closed to me. I know not who you are, but I will."

"How do you do it?" Charley asked. "You stood there, fighting for your life and your village. You severed limbs, you killed - and I hid. I knew I could not be harmed, but I still hid away."

Catherine cocked an ear. "I sense you are troubled but I cannot help you." She rose wearily and went to help Maybn, Nessa and Agnethena instead.

Maybn let her tears flow. "The Saxons have captured all the women and children from the woods and have left them to tend to their dead menfolk." She spat on the ground. "And Timancius lives on."

"I do not understand," ventured Nessa. "Every place they conquer they rape the women and kill the children, but not here. Why?"

Agnethena nodded at Catherine. "Because of our priestess; they are frightened of you, My Lady."

Catherine shook her head. "They are wary of me, that is all. They will have heard stories. I must command, I must be fierce or they *will* kill us all."

oOo

Hengist and Horsa had installed themselves at Madron's top table, along with their generals and of course, Timancius. Catherine and her entourage entered the Great Hall and she bade all but Taraghlan and Caderyn to sit on a vacant table just inside the entrance. Then the three of them walked purposefully to the top table.

"You are in my seat," she stared straight a Hengist, sitting in Madron's high-backed oak chair. Her tone was imperious and her bearing regal.

Timancious translated and the hall erupted with Saxon laughter and jeers, but Hengist held up his hand to silence them. "This chair?" he asked with a mocking smile. He said something to Timancius who again translated. "My Lord Hengist says it is a very beautiful chair, but as your father no longer needs it, he is minded to keep it for himself."

Catherine smiled back. "Please tell your lord Hengist, that if he does not give that seat back to me, I will remove him from it."

Timancius relayed her message and again the hall erupted with laughter. Hengist beckoned to Catherine to step closer. "Why so important?" he asked.

"Because it was my father's seat for many years and now that he has been killed it passes to me, so get your stinking fat arse *off my chair!*"

Again there was laughter as Hengist contemplated his answer.

"You may have this chair." He winked at his brother, "You may have it when you are my wife."

The hall was filled with laughter again and someone called-out, "Bed her now." The cat-call caught on and very quickly the hall was ringing to the shouts of "Bed her now, bed her now," as the Saxons banged their fists on the tables.

Hengist raised his hand for silence. "Enough." The hall fell silent. "What say you, *Queen* of the Avertci?"

oOo

The August sun was relentless as it beat down on the dig site. The dormitory tent was uncomfortably hot. "She's asleep," said Greg with relief.

Antoinette looked pensive. "I think not. Look at her breathing. It is uneven. I think she might have gone back again."

"Perhaps she's just dreaming?" Greg ventured.

"We need to open the sides of the marquee and get some air in here. Greg can you manage that whilst I get some water to sponge her down?"

A flash of concern crossed his face. "Not too cold and just wipe her face. She could go into shock if you chill her down too quickly."

Antoinette looked at Charley with sadness. "Wherever she is, I hope she is safe."

oOo

"Well, 'Queen,' what is your answer?" Horsa asked in his native tongue. "Will you wed and bed my brother?" He roared with laughter which again set the hall alive with jeers and catcalls. Catherine looked to Timancius for a translation, but he just smirked. It was not too hard to guess the gist of what the Saxon said. She walked up to the table and held Hengist's gaze as she addressed Timancius. "Tell this man that if he can best me in swordplay, I will wed him."

Charley's hand shot to her mouth. "No!" she gasped. "What are you doing Catherine?"

Timancius grinned broadly as he relayed the message and Hengist's eyes nearly popped out of his head. "She must have terms? Ask her what her terms are." He wanted to look away but somehow could not bring himself to break the gaze.

"My Lord Hengist asks…"

"He wants to know my terms for the contest." Catherine interrupted and her eyes flared. "Tell him if he can disarm me by the time you," she pointed at Timancius, "have run around this hall three times, I will wed him."

Timancius looked horror-struck. "I will tell him no such thing."

Horsa leant over to the priest. "What does she say?"

"Nothing My lord, she is just jesting. Might I suggest your brother just finishes her off here and now? There is no need to prolong the inevitable?"

Horsa grabbed Timancius by the back of his neck and smashed his head down onto the table. "*What does she say!?*"

Timancius screamed in pain as his hooked nose hit the table and bled. Horsa released him and Timancius quickly pulled a strip of linen from a pocket in his robe and held it to his nose to stem the flow. He passed her message to Hengist who managed to break his uncomfortable gaze with Catherine and stand up. He drew his sword. "Then start running Priest."

"My Lord Hengist," Timancius protested, "I am injured."

"You could try running without any legs, Priest," he snarled as he walked around to the front of the table where he stopped and stared in wonderment. This beautiful woman was as good as his.

Taraghlan ran forward with Blood-Taker. "You do not have to do this, My Lady."

Catherine took the sword and smiled. "Yes, Taraghlan, I do."

Horsa pulled Timancius to his feet and shoved him away. "Run or die."

Timancius looked over at Catherine with pure hatred in his eyes. She would pay for this ultimate humiliation and pay with her life. He started to lope along the back wall.

Hengist slowly approached Catherine, constantly turning his sword through three-sixty degrees. Catherine stood defiantly with her sword raised over her left shoulder with both hands on the hilt, mirroring the pose she had struck when Hengist first met her.

He began to circle around her and Catherine turned on the spot, matching his speed and keeping her body towards him. Suddenly he swung, targeting below the pommel of her sword, aiming for her wrists. Catherine twisted her blade down and the two swords sang as they clashed.

Timancius was half way round the hall as Hengist swung again, this time aiming for her sword's cross guard. If he could make contact hard enough it should deaden her arms and cause her to drop the sword. Catherine side-stepped the blow and again met his blade with hers.

As Hengist raised his sword again, Catherine suddenly lunged and drove the point of her blade through his trousers and nicked his flesh, close to his groin. He looked down in surprise. "What you do?" he demanded.

As a breathless Timancius loped past, she grabbed him. "Tell him he owes me a debt. I could have ruined his wedding night." Timancius spat on the ground and carried on loping around the hall. "Oh well," she said with a wry smile, "I think I had better finish this."

She swung at Hengist's head but he parried the blow and countered with a lunge to her heart. She jumped back. It appeared that this was now a fight to the death.

Hengist swung high and Catherine ducked beneath his sword and brought hers up diagonally. This time when the swords rang out, her blade caught the tip of his cross guard. Quickly twisting her hands her sword plucked Hengist's straight out of his hand. It flew across the hall and skittered to a stop by the top table.

Catherine quickly followed through by pressing the point of her sword into Hengist's tunic, above his heart. "Timancius, you can stop now," and the priest stumbled up to her, panting hard.

She smiled at Hengist, lowered her sword and walked around the table to her father's chair. She was about to sit when Horsa leant back in his own chair and put his feet on Madron's chair.

"Let her have it," Hengist called out. "She won it."

200

Reluctantly Horsa withdrew his feet and Catherine took her place at the table. She beckoned to Hengist to take the chair next to her and then turned to the dishevelled and sweaty priest. "Timancius, Tell these two men that we can talk as equals or they can surrender to me. The choice is theirs."

Timancius shook his head despairingly but agreed. He waited until Hengist was safely seated and unable to reach him, before he offered his translation. Any sort of alliance or peace between the Saxons and the Avertci did not suit his plans at all. He needed conflict if Catherine were to be slain. He contemplated lying but knew his own death would be swift were he to be discovered so, reluctantly, he translated word for word.

To his surprise, neither Hengist nor Horsa laughed or sneered, nor did they seem to take offence. Instead Hengist sat back with a fresh cup of ale and regarded Catherine with a look of new-found respect. "You are beautiful," he said in English, "and you are a true priestess and queen."

Catherine nodded imperiously and Horsa leant forward. "And that is why you must die."

CHAPTER 39
Sōlmōnath (February) 450AD

Charley was standing behind Horsa and heard every word and although shocked, she comforted herself with the knowledge that Catherine was not destined to die just yet. She still marvelled at how she could understand all the dialects she was hearing.

A movement from the far side of the hall, near the doors, spiked in her peripheral vision. She looked up and froze. There, creeping cautiously along the far wall was Rosemary Forrester.

"How is that possible?" Her mind was in chaos. Was there some kind of time portal involved? Had someone actually invented a time machine? Then she noticed something bright hanging around Forrester's scraggy neck. "The brooch, she's got my brooch!"

Forrester was looking furtively about the hall; clearly out of her depth and unsure of her own safety. Charley decided to confront her and hurried across the hall in her direction.

Forrester spotted her and shock resonated through her body. She turned back towards the door and fled into the night. Charley crashed through the doors, just seconds behind her, but she was nowhere to be seen.

oOo

Charley juddered awake and started coughing. Antoinette quickly helped her into a semi-sitting position and gave her a tumbler of water to sip. "What happened? Are you ok?"

Charley drank and then swung her legs out of bed to sit on the edge of her mattress.

"Someone else was there with me."

"Rosemary Forrester?"

Charley's eyes widened. "H-how did you know?"

"She's taken the brooch."

"I saw it around her neck. How is it possible? Does this mean anyone who wears it can be transported back?"

Antoinette shrugged. "I do not know Mon Cher." She pulled a protein bar from her pocket. "Here, eat. You need food. We will go to the mess tent in a moment and I will prepare you egg and chips, yes?" Charley nodded and unwrapped the bar. Antoinette waited for her to finish the first mouthful and then asked, "What did you see?"

Charley's expression softened. "Oh Annie, she's eighteen now and so beautiful and strong and…" Just then the memories of the bloodletting and horrors she had seen suddenly engulfed her and she started to shake.

"Whatever is wrong?"

"I was in a battle."

"In a battle?" Alarm spread across Antoinette's face. "You were *in* a battle?"

"I hid. Hengist and Horsa attacked the village. Oh Annie, it was utterly horrendous. The violence, the relish when they eviscerated and decapitated each other was just appalling. I've never seen anything like it."

Antoinette put her hand to her mouth. "Oh my god; I can't imagine the horror of that? You will need some counselling I think."

"What scared me the most was the realisation that maybe I could have been killed? I know they can't see me, but I felt so vulnerable. Can you imagine if I had been hacked to death? It would have been replicated here. How could you have explained that away?"

"You are talking yourself out of another trip, Mon Cher."

"I have to go back at some point."

So the Avertci have been conquered?"

Charley shook her head. "Not exactly. Madron had been elevated to the position of King by the tribal elders, so with his death, Catherine is now their priestess *and* their queen. You should have seen the way she stood up to them. She was ultra-self-assured. So much so, that Hengist and Horsa seem quite overwhelmed by her. They still say they're going to kill her of course, but at least they are all talking to each other at the moment."

Antoinette laughed, "You seem to have had quite a time of it, but no more travelling until you are fed and rested. You will need your strength and your wits if you go back, particularly if Rosemary Forrester is there too."

Charley smiled. "OK, let's get something hot inside me. Where's Greg?"

"Charley!"

"I meant to talk to. Good grief Annie, get your mind out of the gutter. Anyway, he's not my type."

oOo

Antoinette had business to attend to so Charley sought out Shelly for company. Just as she mopped up the last of her egg yolk with a large chunk of bread, Greg entered the mess tent. "Thank god you're ok," he said as he plonked himself down beside her.

"I don't remember inviting you to sit," she replied, without looking up.

"Having saved your life I didn't think I'd need an invitation."

Shelly looked quizzical. "You saved her life? How?"

Greg ignored the question. "Seriously, are you ok?"

"I'm fine thank you." This time she looked directly at him. His bruising was even more livid. "Does it hurt?"

"A little."

Shelly touched him on the shoulder. "I heard you fell into a trench."

Greg winked at Charley. "Yeah that's right."

"So how did you save Charley's life?

Greg had to think on his feet. "I didn't, not literally. I just lent her some money."

Shelly frowned and Charley quickly intercepted the

conversation. "For some ladies essentials, if you get my drift?"

Satisfied, Shelly picked up her plate. "Well I'll leave you two lovebirds to your billing and cooing."

Both Charley and Greg protested at Shelly's interpretation of their relationship, but she just laughed and walked to the kitchen area.

As soon as Shelly was out of earshot, Greg looked at Charley, concern etched across his face . "Tell me what happened on your last trip back."

"You really want to know?"

"Hell yeah. This is great stuff, but I'm also worried about you."

Charley smiled. "Forrester is there too. She has the brooch."

"Where? Back in the past?"

The look of surprise on Greg's bruised face made Charley snigger. "I tried to catch her but she vanished."

"Seriously, Forrester was there? You could see her?"

"Yes, and then she disappeared. She probably woke up."

Greg looked about the empty marquee. "No Antoinette?"

Charley shook her head. "She's on the phone to Sir Whatsisface."

Greg pulled Charley round to face him. "Hey!" she complained, but Greg just looked earnestly into her eyes.

"I was really worried about you. Promise me you're alright."

Charley tilted her head back and looked down her nose, as if trying to get him in focus. "Are you trying to get in my knickers?"

Greg sat forward. "I'm *trying* to have a serious conversation with you."

"Ah, well that's where you're going wrong. You wouldn't know how to have a serious conversation." She stood up to carry her plates to the washing up station but before she could pick them up Greg grabbed her. "Oi, you big lump, let me g…"

Greg pulled her close and kissed her full on the lips.

Charley pulled away and aimed a hefty slap at his face but Greg caught her wrist before she made contact. "I've been hit enough for one day, thank you."

"Then you shouldn't sexually harass people." Charley tried to pull away again. "Let me go you great oaf!"

Greg released her hand and she glared at him for a second and then leapt into his arms. Their lips locked in a deep and passionate kiss, her hands roving over his back and tugging at his shirt. He grabbed her backside with both hands and lifted her up so she could wrap her legs around his waist. She was as light as a feather to him and, continuing their kiss, he carried her out of the marquee, into the warm evening air and headed for the dormitory tent next door.

oOo

Richard slammed down his phone on the kitchen worktop. Why wasn't Smith answering? He paced the room. Smith was supposed to call back and tell him what to do but he'd heard nothing. This ridiculous business had to stop. How could he have become embroiled in this hare-brained plot to commit murder? The things being demanded of him were extreme and although he might be in debt, he'd rather stay that way than kill anyone.

He sat and wrapped his arms tightly around his stomach. He felt utterly miserable. He'd burned his boats where Charley was concerned, which upset him more deeply that he imagined it would. There was no way she would forgive him and Greg certainly wouldn't. What a mess. Somehow, Richard decided he would have to make amends.

oOo

Forrester awoke with a start. Her pulse was racing and her breathing was erratic. She forced herself to calm down by taking long, slow, deep breaths. Eventually she sat up and looked about her room. It was pretty much the same as every budget hotel; simply furnished with a hard bed. This was not Forrester's usual choice; she preferred to spend lavish amounts of NAS money on four star hotels, but this time, she had just wanted to try on the brooch as soon as possible, so any old dump would do.

As she recovered, she realised that she was actually feeling exhilarated. The enormity of what happened was not lost on her.

She had travelled back in time and seen Hengist and Horsa. And then there was that other man. What was his name? Tim something? Not that it mattered too much. All she knew was that she had to seek him out; there was a strong bond between them and Forrester believed it was the key to killing Catherine.

She halted her thoughts to question the direction in which she was being drawn. Why did she want Catherine dead? She had absolutely no idea, other than it was some sort of primeval instinct. She shook her head clear. No one can see me. No one knows I'm there, so how can I influence what happens?

Then there was that Chandler-Price bitch who *had* seen her there. Could she influence what happens? Forrester realised she had a lot more thinking to do.

oOo

Charley, gleaming with the sweat of their lovemaking was straddling Greg's hips and pulling gently at the hairs on his muscular chest. She gazed down at him. "I would never have imagined this happening...ever." She slid off and lay next to him.

Greg half turned towards her and kissed her on the nose. "Nor me. You and Armitage were an item only a few days ago."

She glared at him. "We were *not* an item. I'm not easy if that's what you're thinking; I'm not the type to sleep around, but Richard..." She paused to gather her thoughts. "Well let's just say in my view, betrayal of trust is the biggest sin in a friendship."

I wasn't suggesting you're easy, but this, whatever 'this' is, has moved very quickly."

"So what now? You know I still hate you."

"Yeah you made that pretty clear when you were ripping my clothes off."

"Me? I think it was you who was sexually assaulting me. I should report you."

"Yeah," he agreed, "maybe you should; after all you've done it before." He pulled her close and they melted into another kiss.

oOo

Rosemary Forrester found herself following Timancius along a

207

path outside the village. It meandered into the woods and eventually came to a clearing where a derelict building stood. She watched as Timancius walked around the outside, running his hand along the wattle and daub walls.

"I did not think I would see you again little temple." He looked in Forrester's direction. "This is where she took my eye." Forrester recoiled and quickly stumbled behind a tree. Timancius pulled a decayed scrap of cloth from the doorway. "I do not know who you are, but I feel you to be no threat. Come, come and see where I fell."

Forrester tentatively approached Timancius's old makeshift temple and stopped at the door.

"Come in," he cooed and Forrester stepped past him into the gloom. As she passed, Timancius tilted his head back, closed his eyes and inhaled deeply. "Ahh, yes, I will soon know who you are."

Forrester gasped. "You will?"

Timancius pointed to a corner of the stone table in the centre of the hut. "That was where she took my eye, right there." He picked up a piece of rock from the floor and smashed it down on the corner, which broke away and fell into the mud. "There was mud on the ground, that day too. I fell and even though I was in agony, clutching at the jelly that used to be my eye, blood pouring from the socket, that bitch and her father did nothing to help me." He looked in Forrester's direction again. "Madron is dead but you, whoever you are, whichever god you serve, you will help me to rid the world of Catherine."

oOo

"I'm going back."

Greg hunkered down beside her in the trench. "When?"

"As soon as I can."

"I'll be with you."

Charley smiled. "I'm glad."

At that moment, Antoinette and Shelly Price ambled up. "Hello again, lovebirds," laughed Shelly.

Antoinette raised an eyebrow and Charley stood up and stretched. "It's all your fault, Shelly. I was quite happy being single again until you put that ridiculous idea in his head."

Antoinette rolled her eyes and walked away. "Mon Dieu, I can't keep up with you, Charley."

CHAPTER 40
Aibreán (April) 450AD

Hengist grabbed his horse's mane and heaved himself onto its back. It whinnied in protest and tried to shy away, but Hengist patted its neck and pulled it round to face Catherine.

Flanked by Taraghlan, Caderyn and a small group of villagers, she stood by the open gates, waiting for the Saxon warlords to depart.

"Vortigern is of no concern to you now." Hengist said in English. "*We* now rule here," he waved his arm to indicate the lands to the East and south, "And we rule the Avertci. You are no longer a queen."

"My people disagree," she said defiantly. "And I will still be here, long after you have left Britain."

Timancius accompanied by Horsa, rode up to the gate. "I want to kill you now but Hengist disagrees. He says you should still be priestess to your people."

Catherine looked at Horsa and her eyes flared blue. "And what do you say?"

"I say that if you resist our rule, you *will* die." Confidence restored, he kicked his horse and cantered through the gates to join his army.

Hengist smiled. "You truly are a great priestess, but my brother is correct. Resist and you will die… by *my* sword." He nodded at Timancius and together they too cantered through the gates.

"Close them." Taraghlan barked at his guards. My Queen, we must talk."

"Indeed we must. Summon the village elders and your

commanders to the Great Hall." She turned and walked back to her dwelling where she found Maybn, Nessa and Agnethena preparing her supply of medicines. "Please leave. I need time alone."

Maybn and Nessa headed for the door, but Agnethena stopped next to Catherine. "You look troubled."

"It is nothing."

Agnethena shook her head. "We have been friends since we were very young. I know you better than anyone. What is happening to you?"

Catherine smiled sadly. "I have been troubled these past few moons, since the arrival of the Saxons and the slaughter of our men."

"That is understandable." Agnethena gave a crooked smile. "Hengist was true to his word though; no one was harmed after the battle, no woman was raped, no child killed. For that we must be thankful."

Catherine looked at her friend sharply. "I am thankful for nothing! They attacked us and they killed many good men, and now they want to rule our lands?" Her eyes flared blue and Agnethena flinched. "While I live, and for as long as I have the gods on my side, I will resist them, I will fight them and I will destroy them."

Agnethena touched Catherine's arm. "And I will be by your side. Teach me how to fight as you do."

Catherine smiled. "I will not. You have a husband who survived the battle, and a child. I will not put you in harm's way. Go now; the others are waiting for you." She nodded to the door where Maybn and Nessa were still standing. Agnethena squeezed Catherine's arm again and joined the other two women.

Catherine sat on her cot and looked about the hut. Nothing about it had changed since Madron's death except it was now devoid of his clothes and possessions, all gone to the funeral pyre. These past two months had been the hardest of her life. With Hengist and Horsa's larger-than-life presence in the village, she had been unable to properly grieve for her father. She had watched as

February had given way to March - Seen the muddy morass across the village dried by the gales that followed, into a deeply rutted and uneven terrain. She had seen the warm sun of April harden the ground so that planting crops became a real challenge for the remnants of her farming community, so brutally decimated by the battle.

She looked miserably at the corner of the room. "What do I do?" she asked. "What can I do for my people now?"

Charley stepped out of the shadows and knelt before her. "I don't know. Why ask me?"

"Because you are not of this world; you possess wisdom and knowledge beyond mine."

Charley fell back onto her haunches in shock. "You can hear me?"

"Yes but I still cannot see you." Catherine reached out hoping to touch Charley, but found nothing but thin air. "You visit me at times of need; I always know when you are here and each time, our connection is stronger. Maybe one day I will be able to see you."

Charley burst into tears. This was too much to take-in. She felt such deep loyalty and love for this amazing woman that for her to suddenly acknowledge her presence as something tangible *and* communicate with her, was overwhelming. She reached behind to steady herself and something jabbed her palm. She flinched and checked her hand. There was a sliver of flint glinting through the skin. Through her tears she picked at it with her nails and managed to pull it clear. She shifted her position and sat cross-legged before Catherine and let out a juddering sob.

"Why do you weep?"

"Because I am so invested in you and your story."

Catherine frowned. "I do not understand the words you say. You speak my language but...but it is different. Which lands are you from?"

Charley wiped her eyes on her sleeve. "I am from Britain, but not of your time. I come from a time ahead, but I cannot control when I come into your life; it is up to fate I think."

Catherine shook her head sadly. "It is up to the gods. I do not understand, nor do I want to. You use powerful magic. I must be content that you are with me." She stood up and adjusted her robes. "Now I must go to the Great Hall. You will come too."

It was an order, not a request so Charley walked with her to the meeting with the elders.

oOo

"Vortigern cannot help us!" shouted Cedryc, one of the six village Elders, a scrawny soul who was partially blind. He and Taraghlan had been arguing for several minutes when Catherine arrived.

The Ealdormen and assembled villagers stood when she entered. "Sit, all of you." She looked earnestly at the Ealdormen, all at the top table. "It is I who should stand for you. All my young life I have held you with high respect and being queen does not change that. You will never stand for me again." She looked severely at Taraghlan. "What were you arguing about?"

Taraghlan waited for Catherine to sit at the table. "I was saying that we should send a messenger to Vortigern. He needs to know what has happened here."

"And I say again, Vortigern - cannot – help - us." Cedryc banged his staff on the floor to emphasise each word.

"But he *does* need to know," said Catherine decisively. "Caderyn, you will take ten men and ride to Vortigern. Tell him of the Saxon's treachery and of my father's death. Also tell Vortiger that, if it pleases him, I wish to see him. Tell him I wish to arrange our marriage. Ask him to ride back with you."

Caderyn smiled. "Now that you are Queen, should you not seek a king for a husband?"

Catherine laughed. "Now that I am a queen I can marry any one I choose and I choose Vortiger." She beckoned Taraghlan to her side. "We should also tell the Catuvellauni and Algar of the Corieltauvi, if he is still alive."

"And if he is not?"

"Then tell Taranis. He will have taken his father's place as

213

chieftain. Then ride east and warn the Iceni and Trinovantes."

"My Lady, Hengist said he had conquered the East. A trader told me the land of the Trinovantes is now known as East Seaxe, the Land of the East Saxons."

"That saddens me. Both of you ride out tomorrow. Do what you can." She looked about the hall. "Where are your commanders?"

"I set them to supervising the repairs to our defences, my Lady. I thought it a better use of their time."

Catherine nodded and turned to the elders, all seated to her left. "What counsel will you give me?"

Arne, a small man who always wore an expression of anxiety, looked dolefully at his queen. "Will the Saxons return? Will they take our food and livestock? After that winter we have little to feed ourselves."

Catherine looked worried. "I am certain they will return but not until there are crops in the fields again."

The old men looked at each other, bemused until Aurl, a bald man with a face flushed from too much ale, tottered to his feet. "My Lady, we should kill them all."

"Oh, you mean as we did last time?" jeered another man. Within seconds all six Elders were arguing between themselves. None of them noticed Catherine leave the Great Hall with her two protectors.

oOo

Charley was so used to her timeslips that she could now decide for herself when to return to the present day. She knew that given the opportunity, she would probably stay in the past forever, so strong was the connection she felt, but she knew that she had to share her findings with Antoinette. The brooch had always taken her back to pivotal moments in Catherine's life and judging by her recent solo timeslips, she could do that for herself.

She suspected there was going to be a lull in Catherine's adventures for the time being, so this was probably a good time to return to the present. Besides, it would be quite nice to see that big oaf, Greg once more.

214

CHAPTER 41

The next morning at the dig was sunny and agreeably warm; a pleasant change from the thirty degree heat of the past couple of days. Activity was now centred on filling-in those trenches that had failed to yield any artefacts. No one on site knew of Charley's adventures and her recent absences had been explained away as a severe urinary infection. However, the arrival of two police cars and a CID officer was the cause of much gossip and speculation.

"Detective Constable Hallam." The young man offered his hand and Antoinette shook it. "Are you Ms Deselle?"

Antoinette regarded his boyish looks. He was wearing a blue and red checked shirt with short sleeves that revealed two full sleeves of tattoos on his arms. "I am. Shouldn't you be in school?"

DC Hallam's cheeks flushed, "I know I look young for my age, but I'm actually thirty two and I've been a detective for eight years. I can always get a CID officer who is nearing retirement if you'd prefer." He dropped his notebook, pen and car keys on the table. "May I sit?" he asked testily.

"Of course."

"Thank you. Perhaps you'd care to tell me what's going on?"

Antoinette sat too. "I'm sorry I was rude to you. Things here are rather…" She paused trying to think of the English word she needed, but gave up and resorted to her native language. "Rather bouleversante."

Hallam smiled. "Overwhelming? Yes from the initial report, it sounds like it."

Antoinette beamed. "Overwhelming yes. Tu parle français?"

"Oui. Je suis un francophile passionné."

C'est bon." Antoinette sat back in her chair. "So, what do you

215

want to know?"

"I understand the Forrester woman made threats against a worker here? Charlotte Chandler-Price?"

"Charley, yes. She is an exceptional archaeologist and is under my tutelage."

"And why does Forrester want to harm her?"

"None of us knows. She met Charley for the first time recently and just ran out of the door in a panic. She came back yesterday."

"So I've been told. She didn't make any attempt to harm Ms Chandler-Price while she was here?"

"No, but she bashed me about quite well." Antoinette pointed to the bruising on her face.

"So I see. And she stole something?"

"Yes, a valuable artefact; a brooch."

"How much is it worth?"

"I would suggest it is pretty much priceless."

"Would you know where she is now?"

Antoinette smirked a little. "No, I don't know exactly, but there's a good chance she is well out of your reach."

"Meaning what?"

"Meaning you wouldn't believe me if I told you." Antoinette smiled again. "The best I can do is call you if she shows up again, but I doubt she will." She rose and pulled a box file from a nearby shelf.

Charley popped her head around the door. "What's going on? Is this about Rosemary?"

Antoinette grinned. "You're back. You'll have to fill me in once the police have left."

Hallam stood and extended his hand. "Are you Ms Chandler-Price?"

Charley entered and shook the detective's hand. "I am. Has she been caught?"

Hallam shook his head. "Not yet, but her description has been circulated."

"That'll make interesting reading; sharp-nosed, pinch-faced, scrawny fucking bitch. Is that about it?" Charley laughed.

Hallam smiled too. "Not far off I imagine. Some officers will take statements from you shortly. I'd better get back to the nick."

"What about Richard?" asked Charley.

The detective stopped and turned back. "Who's Richard?"

"The caretaker here." Antoinette explained. "We think he tried to kill Charley too."

Hallam was taken aback. "I wasn't told about this. What did he do?"

The two women looked at each other, suddenly both aware that the truth would be hard to believe; that Richard had tried to steal the artefact from Charley and trap her in the past.

"He tried to strangle me," Charley suddenly blurted out, desperate for something to say.

"What?" Antoinette's reaction popped out before she could stop it, causing Hallam to throw her a quizzical look. Antoinette quickly regained her composure. "Well you see, Charley was asleep in Richard's bedroom and Greg and I entered to find him bending over her. We thought he was trying to hurt her and a big fight broke out. He battered Greg. He needs to be arrested for assault at least."

"You were in his bed? Are you in a relationship with this, Richard?"

"Not any more. He's changed. He's definitely got it in for me."

"Why?"

"To be frank, I don't really know. We were getting along fine then he suddenly became moody and aggressive. The next thing I know he's attacked Greg."

"So did he try to strangle you or not?"

"I thought he did, but it's all so hazy, I'm sorry."

Hallam shook his head. "I'll get the statements sorted. I think I'm going to regret this case. Nice to meet you both…I think."

Charley watched him leave. "Nice arse there Annie."

Antoinette tutted. "You need to control yourself young lady." She took her seat again and removed an old exercise book from the box file. "OK, so now tell me what happened on your latest timeslip."

Charley's face positively glowed. "She not only knows I'm there... she can actually *hear* me. We've been talking!"

Antoinette dropped her pencil. "Oh mon bon dieu! Surely this was just a dream. Without the brooch you must be dreaming surely."

Charley held up her hand. There was a small gash and traces of blood on her palm. "I did this in Catherine's hut when she told me she could hear me. This is as real as all the other times."

Antoinette sat back with a look of wonder on her face. "If this is true, then there must be other powers at work. Powers we do not understand. Charley we... you...must be very careful from now on. Once again, I'm not sure if we should continue. The dig has more or less been a failure and we are now running out of time. Next week we shall be packing up." She had expected Charley to protest but instead she just gave a little wry smile. Antoinette cocked her head. "What? What are you not telling me?"

"Annie, I don't think it matters that the dig is ending. I don't think the location is relevant; Rosemary Forrester went back and she was probably in London when she used the brooch, and..."

"And if you don't need the brooch, I can't stop you from returning to the past." She shook her head sadly. "If the past can physically hurt you like this..." she took Charley's hand and turned the palm upwards, "then your physical self and maybe your very life, is in great danger."

"Yes Annie, I'm sure you're right, but..."

"Let me finish, Mon Cher, I understand how you are now obsessed with Catherine and her story, but you know how it ends..."

"But it doesn't have to..."

"It does, you know it does. We've had this conversation so often. You must not change the course of history; the ramifications would be catastrophic."

"You don't know that, Annie." She snatched her hand back.

218

"I do. Common sense knows it...*You* know it."

In the awkward silence that followed, both contemplated what the other had said. Eventually Charley spoke. "Would it really matter if I died in the past? My body would still be here, in the present. My family would still have a body to bury and grieve over."

Antoinette climbed unsteadily from her chair. "How can you be so callous? Your parents would be devastated, as would I. Charley, consider this: You were injured, albeit a small injury, yes?"

"Yes."

And whenever you get injured in the past, the injuries manifest on your body in the present, yes?"

"Again, yes. What's your point Annie?"

She sighed and slumped back into her chair. "For heaven's sake, you said it yourself; you were scared by the realisation you could have been killed in that battle. You even acknowledged that your injuries would be replicated here. What was it you said happened to people back there, eviscerated, decapitated? What do you imagine the police would make of that?"

Charley snorted derisively, "We've already discussed that but Hengist can't see me. No one can see me, let alone interact with me or decapitate me."

"Yet! You said yourself your connection to Catherine is getting stronger. How much longer before she can see you, and how much longer after that before she can touch you?"

"I don't know!" Charley's temper was beginning to spike.

Antoinette stood up again. "Well think about it. Your stubbornness will get you killed."

Charley didn't watch her mentor leave the tent; she was in too much of a funk to care, but something Annie had said, stuck in her mind; that her parents would be devastated if she died. She hadn't thought about them in a very long time, except for the occasional 'Thank you for my allowance' text. Her father disapproved of her career. Not due to the nature of the job, but because at twenty eight, she was still a student. It was very unsatisfactory and meant that he had to keep sending her money.

Her mother Gwendoline, was the snob of the family. She had insisted in keeping her maiden name when she married and also that it should come first. He didn't argue. It was pointless and he knew it. Charley decided that on one hand, her parents would probably be upset by her death, but on the other, her father would be grateful he wouldn't have to keep sending an allowance each month, and her mother would just find the whole thing an irritation that would get in the way of her next bridge tournament. In truth, Charley thought that Annie would probably be the only person who would truly mourn her passing and of course there was now Greg to consider too, but was that fledgling relationship likely to go anywhere? The thought of Greg sent a tingle through her. This time last week she could never have imagined being attracted to him, let alone involved. She decided to go and find him. She could do with the distraction.

oOo

Charley rolled off Greg and pulled sweaty strands of hair from her face. "Phew, that was…"

"Amazing? Great? Sublime?" Greg ventured.

"I was going to say, adequate." She giggled and turned onto her left side to face him. She nestled into his armpit and began to tease his chest hair. "Considering I hate you, who'd have ever thought we'd end up sleeping together?"

"Yeah, twice. One kiss followed by a bunk-up and the next thing you know we're an item."

Charley frowned and tilted her head up to look at his face. "Is that what we are… an item?"

He stroked her hair. "I know it's probably too quick for you, but I'd like to think so."

She snuggled down again. "I thought you were the biggest oaf in the world; totally self-centred, chauvinistic, cruel and a general all-round bastard."

"Gee, don't hold back there." Greg feigned hurt and clutched at his heart.

"But you know what? These past couple of days you've shown more concern and compassion to me than any man has...ever. And the way you stood up to Richard? Well that was a complete surprise. I think that's when you won me over, so yes, I'm happy to be an item with you."

Greg kissed the top of her head. "I think we need a shower, don't you?"

Charley grinned. "Do you think Richard will let us use his?"

"What do you fucking think?" said a voice from the doorway. Greg and Charley scrabbled at the sheets to cover themselves as Richard stepped into the bed space. "That didn't take you long did it? You go bed-hopping like this often, you fucking bitch?"

Greg climbed, naked, out of the bed. "Ok that's enough."

Richard turned back to the doorway. "And to think I came over to apologise and put things right; well you can both go get fucked."

"Too late," shouted Charley as Richard stormed out, "we already have!"

oOo

"Don't worry Annie, I am quite rested."

"And I'll be by her side the whole time, I promise," added Greg.

"Ok, ok, you win, just stop badgering me." Antoinette raised her hands in surrender. "The police have just taken Richard away for questioning so I guess with Greg here, it should be safe for you to go back again, but Charley, please remember what I said about your safety. Please take care."

Charley gave her mentor a hug. "I will, Annie, I swear."

CHAPTER 42 - 451AD
Meitheamh (June)

Vortigern ruled Britain from Theocsbury on the confluence of the Rivers Avon and Severn. It was a very defendable location; protected to the East, South and West by the two rivers as they curved around the settlement.

Vortigern smiled across the Great Hall of his castle and caught Catherine's eye. She returned his smile and moved through the throng to sit by him.

"I am told that Hengist and Horsa are moving west towards us."

Catherine gazed out at the mass of people who had come to see Vortiger's bride of three months. They had married at the Avertci village but at the end of the celebrations, Vortiger had returned to Theocsbury on the welsh borders, to help train the army needed to rout the Saxons from Britain. Twelve weeks later Catherine followed, accompanied by Taraghlan, so that the tribes of the West could meet her.

"Do you know how many men the Saxons command?" she asked the king.

Vortigern shrugged. "I do not know for certain, but I am told he has about three thousand on the road."

"And we have how many?

"Perhaps two, if I can raise the farmers."

"Then we need surprise on our side."

Vortigern was about to laugh but he saw the earnestness in Catherine's eyes and refrained. She might be a woman, but her counsel was always faultless. "What do you suggest?

"Let them come. Amass your armies, lend me your eldest son, Vortimir, and five hundred men."

"And your husband of course."

Catherine laughed. "Of course, My Lord."

Vortigern stroked his fat beard. "And what will you do with my five hundred men?"

"We will ride south to Venta Belgarum."

Vortigern snorted, "That stinking hole? Why there?"

"Because it was one of the Romans' largest towns. It is still a strategic site."

"But the buildings are falling down, the Roman sewers have collapsed and most of the people have moved to higher ground."

"That is so my Lord, but it still has good walls and many Saxons have settled there. Hengist has placed a small number of warriors in the town to oversee rebuilding."

"And you know this how?"

"I sent a rider to find out."

"When?"

"Many days ago."

"You have been planning this all along?"

Catherine shook her head and smiled. "*Preparing* for it, My Lord. We will attack, kill them and then ride east to the coast below Ceint. We will attack all the Saxon settlements we find along the way."

"You intend to attack the Saxons by stealth?"

"We will nibble away at them piece by piece. We will snap at their heels like rabid dogs and we will dig away the foundations of their power."

"And undermine their ability to rule."

"When we reach Ceint we will attack their stronghold at Cant-wara byrg and finish the small force he will have left behind."

Vortigern shook his head. "When Hengist and Horsa have finished with us here, they will return to the island of Inis Ruim, probably before you get there."

"I believe that word of our attack on Venta Belgarum will reach them and they will ride to their aid, not to Inis Ruim. My Lord, it can be done if we leave tomorrow, while Hengist and Horsa are still days away." Her eyes flared blue and Vortigern sat back in his chair.

"You trouble me girl, but I trust you. I will speak to Vortimir and Vortiger."

Inis Ruim was the name by which Thanet was known and Charley congratulated herself on her ability to remember such trivia.

oOo

Charley bit her lip. If Catherine was going to ride out, how could she follow? She wondered if she could avoid the journey by returning to the present and then time-slipping back again, but would she come back to the right time? What if she missed out a great chunk of Catherine's life? A sudden idea flashed into her mind; she knew she could interact with inanimate objects, could she do so with animals? She ran from the hall, out of the keep and hurried to the inner bailey. There she found several horses grazing on the sparse grass.

She cast her eyes over them and then approached a large grey stallion. It whinnied and shied away. "It knows I'm here," she thought. Its wild eyes were staring straight at her and she suddenly felt very uncertain about her intentions. "I've never liked horses much."

As she slowly advanced, the big animal seemed to settle a little, although it was still pawing at the ground. She stretched out a hand to stroke its nose and it grunted at her and jerked his head away. "Steady boy," she said quietly. "I'm not going to harm you."

She tried again and this time the horse allowed her to make contact with his muzzle. She could feel the bristly hairs around its mouth and its warm damp breath on the back of her hand. "Fucking hell," she said aloud. "I just don't get it." It still didn't really solve her problem; she still had to find a way to ride with Catherine's small army and at the moment, she was all out of ideas.

oOo

Richard Armitage stepped out of the police station, into the cold

224

evening air and shivered. When he'd been arrested he was wearing just jeans and a T-shirt and it hadn't occurred to him to grab a pullover or jacket before he was hauled off to the waiting police car.

He eyes were dark and resentful; his temper was simmering and heading ever upwards to boiling point. The bastards hadn't even offered him a lift home. Richard thought the officer who interviewed him looked about fifteen.

"You're sure you don't want a solicitor present?" Hallam had asked after the pre- interview formalities had been completed and the tape machine was running.

"I've done nothing wrong. Why would I want a solicitor?"

"Assaulting Greg Collier?"

"He attacked me first. He grabbed me by the throat. I was only defending myself."

"Why did he grab you by the throat?"

"I don't know. The man's a fucking maniac."

"He grabbed you by the throat for no reason?" He produced three photos of Greg's injuries. "A tad extreme wouldn't you say?"

"I was in fear for my life. I thought he was going to strangle me."

"With Ms. Deselle in the room?"

"They're in it together?"

"In what?"

Richard was about to respond but realised he couldn't tell the truth. That was probably the quickest way to the Funny Farm. No one would believe him if he started spouting stuff about time travel.

Hallam waved some statements at him. "According to Ms Deselle and Mr Collier, you were trying to steal a brooch from Miss Chandler-Price while she slept."

"That's a lie!"

"Why was she in your bed?"

"Why do you think? We were screwing. She was always coming round."

Hallam pushed the papers away. "It's all academic anyway. You've admitted assault."

"I've admitted self-defence."

"*And* I've got statements from the victim and witness *and* I've got photos that show the force you used was excessive."

Richard's lip curled. "So fucking what?"

Hallam smiled. "So I'm going to take you back to Custody, hopefully for charging... that's what."

Richard looked up at a dark, foreboding sky. It was going to rain and he was facing a long walk home. Those bastards at the dig were going to pay for this. If they thought he was a problem before, they hadn't seen anything yet!

CHAPTER 43
Meitheamh (June) 451AD

It had been a bumpy and uncomfortable ride in the back of the supply cart. Charley had settled herself on some sacks of flour and grain, but even so, she was being bounced around and bruised. She looked ahead and could see the gates of a city, originally the stronghold of the local Belgae tribe until the Roman occupation. It was the Romans who changed its name to Venta Belgarum and under their supervision a substantial city arose. Following their departure however, Venta fell into a serious decline and over the years many of the buildings collapsed or were destroyed. It was the arrival of the Saxons that saved the city and, renamed Wintanceastre, it would become their centre of government and the court of their kings. In years to come it would be known as Winchester.

It was indeed in a sorry state and the only people on the streets seemed to be beggars, the sick and the lame. Dirty, dressed in rags and infested with lice, most watched the newcomers with suspicion; some ventured forth, holding out their hands for coins. One of Vortiger's mounted warriors kicked out at a young woman who approached his horse, a child at her flat breast. She cursed as she stumbled back.

Catherine saw. "You!" she shouted at him angrily, "Do that again and I will tear your eyes out!"

Taraghlan smiled. "I almost believe you would."

A faint smile touched Catherine's lips. "Ask Timancius if you disbelieve me."

Vortiger twisted in his saddle. "Where is everyone?"

"I told you; most people have moved out of the city to higher ground. They feel safer there."

Taraghlan gazed up at the walls. No sentries were posted. "I sent Adwurl to see if any soldiers remained on guard in the city and he said he was able to ride in without challenge."

Catherine wheeled her horse around and rode to the back of the supply cart, behind which trudged five hundred weary foot soldiers. "Well done," she shouted to them. "We have arrived at our first city. We shall rest tonight and tomorrow, we kill Saxons!"

Her words were met with a feeble cheer. "They are tired," said Charley.

Catherine snapped round to look at the cart. "You are here?" She was slightly taken aback. "I did not know. I did not sense you."

"You were too busy."

Catherine's face broke into a smile. "With you here, I know all is well." And with that, she kicked her horse to the front of the column again.

"You look happy," observed Vortiger.

"I am. Where do you think the Saxon army will be skulking?"

Vortimir rode in between Catherine and his brother. "I sent scouts ahead, posing as passing travellers. They say that the army is up in the hills with the townsfolk, building a small settlement. They say the Saxons there are lazy and do not believe Britons would have the wit to attack, not with the might of the Saxon army on the move to the North. The local population is mainly Saxon so the army is unconcerned and is sitting on their arses with their backs to the enemy."

Catherine smiled. "And for that they will die. How many?"

Vortimir smiled too. "About seventy."

Catherine sat back in her saddle. "Praise the gods."

The narrow street opened into a huge square with a broken fountain at its centre. Catherine looked sadly at the decay around them. "The Romans knew how to build. We are still living in houses made of mud."

"We should attack now, under cover of darkness," said Vortiger.

Vortimir looked as his brother in surprise. "I have taught you about warfare, or were you not listening? The men are too tired to fight now, but in the morning, before sunrise, when they are rested and the Saxons are still sleeping, *that* is when we will attack."

Catherine glanced around the square. "There is enough room for us to camp here."

Vortimir agreed. "But no fires. Bellies must be filled with bread and cheese tonight."

Vortiger turned his horse, "I'll post sentries and stand guard with them." He saw Catherine's quizzical look. "I am too excited to sleep."

She smiled. "You need to be calm, not excited."

Vortiger winked and rode back to the column.

oOo

Charley looked up at the dark sky. To the East it was just starting to lighten. It must be around five o'clock, she thought.

Catherine was sitting next to her. "I need to know. Are you a gift from the gods? I need to know your purpose." They were sitting on the remains of a garden wall. Once about six feet tall, it had been raided for building materials and was now just a knee-high crumbling ruin of loose bricks and heavy stones.

Charley shrugged. "Do you still hear me in your head, or am I real to you?"

Catherine smiled. "You are real to me, in my head or no. Tell me why you are here."

Charley felt her eyes stinging. "I-I don't know. I first came here by accident the day..." She stopped abruptly. How could she tell this amazing woman that she witnessed her death? "The day you were born."

Catherine's eyes opened wide. "You saw my mother?"

"Not before she died, no." Charley paused and then smiled. "You once thought *I* was your mother, remember?"

Catherine looked sad. "I do not know who you are and that troubles me. My magic does not work on you. I cannot read your

229

mind nor know how you look, nor know why you are here. All I know is that I get such a feeling of peace when you are with me."

"I wish I knew why I was here." She thought about the brooch. Should she tell Catherine that the brooch clasped tightly to her garments was the very one that brought her into Catherine's life."

"You like it?"

Catherine's question bit suddenly into Charley's thoughts and she jumped. "Do I like what?"

"The brooch." She fingered the precious ornament.

"I thought you said you couldn't read my mind."

Catherine raised her eyebrows. "Hmm, perhaps I can." She looked in Charley's direction, unsure of exactly where this strange, ghostly presence was actually sitting. "You have something to tell me? Something about..." the subject was tantalisingly close but she just couldn't quite grasp it. "Ahh, I do not know." She stretched out a hand into thin air as if reaching for her. "Tell me. Tell me what it is and tell me now."

Charley gulped. Antoinette had cautioned her against interfering because of the ramifications it could have on countless future generations, but the more she thought about it, the more Charley realised she had to say something to Catherine about the manner of her death. "I do. I have something very important to tell you. I was here when you..."

"Catherine." Vortiger's arrival cut across Charley's words and she shrunk back into the shadows. Vortiger knelt before his wife and took her hands in his. "My princess, my love, I need to tell you something."

Catherine smiled at her husband. "That you will protect me in the battle to come, that you will die for me, that you love me beyond life itself?"

Vortiger sat back on his haunches and laughed. "I need not tell you then. You know it all."

Catherine stroked his cheek. "And I love you beyond life itself too. And I will protect you in battle also."

"I'm sure you will try." He laughed again.

"My Lady." A harsh whisper from Vortimir stopped their playful conversation. The King's eldest son, accompanied by Taraghlan, bowed to his Sister-in-Law. "There is movement in the Saxon's camp on the hill. We need to awaken the men and hide them within the ruins. We might still have surprise on our side if the enemy is venturing into the city."

"If? Are your scouts not watching them?"

Taraghlan answered. "My Lady, the news came from Adwurl. I sent him and Aedluf back to watch them. He tells me two soldiers are preparing their horses and the rest of their camp is being roused. I suspect the riders are scouts. I will know more when Aedluf returns."

As the words left his lips, Aedluf cantered his horse into the square. "Two scouts are on their way. The rest of the army have just started a slow march down towards the South gate."

Catherine frowned. "Get the men into the buildings."

Taraghlan shook his head. "That would be a mistake; men cannot fight in confined spaces." He called to Vortimir, "Take a hundred men through the south gate and hide in the woods beyond."

"And what will you do?"

"Vortiger and I will take another hundred along the road to the gate but stop about two hundred paces before it."

Catherine looked back at the ruined buildings behind them. "I shall take the rest of the men and conceal them behind those houses."

Taraghlan smiled. "You read my mind, Lady. If any escape our trap you must stop them. I do not want them to escape the city and report our true numbers." He turned back to Vortimir. "You should see two scouts attempt to ride into the city…"

"And ride out again when they see their way blocked? Do you wish for us to kill them?"

Taraghlan shook his head. "No, I do not know how far behind them the other Saxons might be. Stay hidden. When the army is through the gate, move closer, *quietly,* and wait. The Saxons might turn and run when they see they are outnumbered but I doubt it. They love a good fight, but if they do run, that is when you kill them."

"And if they do not run?"

"They will have decided to fight us. I will blow my horn and that is when you can rush them from behind."

Vortiger smiled at his wife. "I am pleased you are staying with the rest of our warriors. I do not want you to fight." Catherine opened her mouth to object but Vortiger leaned across and planted a kiss firmly on her lips. "I love you and I do not want to lose you so early in our marriage. You will *not* fight today."

For a split second he thought she was going to argue but instead she kissed him back and then followed the men into their hiding places within the ruins.

Taraghlan looked anxiously in the direction of the gate. "Now go Vortimir, quickly."

And so it was that the fight Catherine had hoped to take to the Saxons, came to her instead.

CHAPTER 44
Meitheamh (June) 451AD

The two scouts did indeed turn and gallop out of the city as soon as they saw the Britons blocking the road. They fled back to the main body of soldiers as the ragged formation marched down the hill. It took the Saxons half an hour to reach the gates, by which time their senses were more alert and their appetite for blood and killing whetted. They were led by Beorhtric, an experienced warrior, who was weary of the quiet life that had been forced upon him and who, like the others, relished the idea of gutting some Brittonic tribesmen.

They entered through the gate and rounded a slight bend in the road where they encountered Vortiger's army of around a hundred men. The Britons blocked the road with their numbers, but Beorhtric knew from their lack of a disciplined formation that his seventy men had the upper hand. Saxons might not have the orderly marching skills of the Romans, but in battle, they were disciplined and deadly.

"Shield wall!" he shouted.

Vortiger looked puzzled by the activity ahead. "What are they doing?" he asked Taraghlan.

"Forming a shield wall; two rows of shield bearers with short swords, spear throwers in the rear ranks."

"I have never seen that before."

Taraghlan glowered at him. "That's because you've never fought before. We tried to use a shield wall when Hengist and Horsa attacked us."

"And we know how that ended," grumbled Vortiger bitterly.

233

"we had never tired it before; we never had need of it, but done properly, like that," he nodded at Beorhtric's wall, "it is how Romans and Saxons fight... and it's how we die."

Vortiger kicked his horse forward a few paces. "We outnumber them, shield wall or no." He pulled his long sword from its scabbard. "Look at their swords; no more than big daggers. We must attack."

"Do that and we *will* die, Vortiger. We would lose half our men trying to break through that wall, and then other half will be outnumbered and die too."

"But..."

"You are a wetling, Vortiger and you would rush us into death. Those swords are short for good reason; a short sword can spill your entrails."

"So what do we do?"

Taraghlan reached for a horn. "We spring our trap."

Beorhtric took a position in the front and centre of the shield wall, his round metal-rimmed ash shield clasped tightly in his left hand and his short sword in his right. "Look at them. See how frightened they are? You can feel their fear from here."

A long mournful note from a horn echoed along the street and Beorhtric heard a great roar from behind as another hundred Brittonic warriors charged through the South gate and rushed the unprotected rear of the shield wall.

"Shields to the rear!" he shouted, but it was too late, Vortimir and his men crashed into the Saxons, their long swords now a distinct advantage. With the wall in disarray, Taraghlan also charged. Caught between two hundred men, the Saxons didn't stand a chance.

Nevertheless they were ferocious warriors and they fought with a level of violence and blood lust that King Vortigern's armies had never experienced. Taraghlan, galloping towards the Saxons, was met by a spear that embedded itself in his stallion's throat. The animal screamed in shock and pain and collapsed onto the road, blood pouring from its wound. Taraghlan threw himself off before the horse hit the ground and was immediately trampled on by his own men who were also rushing the broken shield wall.

All he could see was a clamour of feet and legs. If he didn't get up now, he would be crushed to death. A hand came from nowhere and he found himself being hauled to his feet.

It was Vortiger. "No time to rest, Taraghlan," he winked, and charged on. The shield wall was broken and in confusion, but it was still a formidable obstacle. Vortiger found a huge Saxon towering over him, his clothes torn and his face and arms covered in blood and about to bring an axe down on his head. Taraghlan barged Vortiger out of the way and plunged his sword into the man's belly. He ripped it upwards and it cut through his ribs. As the big man fell, a spear was hefted from further back and Taraghlan raised his shield just in time to fend it off.

As Vortiger reached the confusion of the shield wall, someone thrust a short sword at his face. The Saxon on the other end looked so young, maybe fifteen. Vortiger disarmed the boy with the superior strength of his long sword. But then when it came to finishing him off, he hesitated for a second. The lad looked terrified.

Before Vortiger could react, a sword was thrust into the boy's heart and he fell, gurgling onto the blood-soaked road, a dagger revealed in his left hand. Taraghlan pulled his sword back. "Hesitate like that again, boy and you will be dead."

"I –I am sorry. I.." Vortiger ran out of words to say. He was witnessing the reality of battle for the first time and his initial joy at fighting had been suddenly tempered by the sordid truth, that battle was anything but joyous.

Charley ran forward to watch the fighting. She thought she might now be immune to the shock and horror of combat, but quickly realised it was probably something to which she would never become desensitised. She was used to the sanitised, drone-led warfare that was now prevalent across the globe, but what she was seeing here was close-quarter violence – vicious and inhumane - hacking, stabbing and slicing - spilled intestines and bodily fluids - the intense metallic smell of blood and the stench of shit and piss.

She lasted only a couple of minutes before she fled back to the market place and sought comfort next to Catherine.

It was all over in fifteen minutes. Those defeated Saxons not already dead, were put to the sword, except for Beorhtric. Taraghlan had identified him as the commander by the way he berated his men as they fought. "Keep him alive," he ordered. "I will speak with him later." He walked over to Vortimir. "How many men did we lose?"

"Twenty, but many are wounded."

Taraghlan looked sadly at the warriors, bloodied, shocked and weary. For many this was also their first time in a battle, although Taraghlan knew it had been little more than a skirmish.

Unless put out of their misery, those men who couldn't travel would die slow, agonising deaths, or perhaps live long enough to be tortured for information by Hengist and Horsa. He nodded to Vortimir. "You know what to do."

Catherine was shocked. "I can help them."

Taraghlan shook his head. "They cannot be saved. Even though your powers are strong, they need treatment you have no time to give. We have only days to do what must be done and they must be with their gods."

Charley was still standing next to Catherine. "What about the others?"

"Those who can walk will walk," said Catherine sadly. "We have horses for the few who cannot. Some will ride in the supply carts, but many might not make the journey. I will treat as many as I can as we travel."

Charley felt sick and Catherine sensed her fear. "You are troubled?"

"Until the battle where your father was killed, I had never seen such brutality."

Catherine gazed in the direction she thought Charley might be. "Nor I."

Charley let out a huge juddering sob. "I had never even seen a killing before."

Catherine looked puzzled. "How can you not?" A sudden realisation hit her. "I do not know your name. How are you known?"

Charley calmed her breathing and answered softly, "I am called Charlotte but I am known as Charley."

Catherine sniggered. "That is a funny name. I was told by my father I bear the name of a woman who lived and died across the seas, tortured and killed by a Roman Emperor many, many years before the gods brought me into the world and took my mother. He learned the story from the tales of a Roman musician who would sing and dance across the tribal lands. He was witless but my father enjoyed his stories." She was silent for a moment but then added, "I wish I could see you."

Charley suddenly felt faint again, but this time she knew it was not the effects of the battle. She was being taken away; taken back to the present. "Catherine, I have to go, but I will be back again, I promise…"

Catherine reached out, but as usual she grasped thin air. "No…come back."

oOo

Rosemary Forrester moved through the huge newly built Saxon village at Sturigao which would become the Saxon capital of Ceint. She was totally absorbed in the Saxon lifestyle and language. As a historian, she already knew that Sturigao roughly translated as 'Region of the Stour,' which was the river that ran near the present-day primary school. A frisson of excitement riffled through her as she realised each step she took was set in history.

She was shadowing Timancius, who had justified his fear of battle by claiming he was remaining behind to build a temple to the Saxon gods.

The village was quiet. Four hundred warriors were billeted there and three hundred of them had gone with Hengist and Horsa, leaving the rest to protect the village, their families and a population over a thousand people.

Timancius sat on a bench by the village's great hall. "Why do you haunt me?"

"Have the Saxons have settled all over Kent?"

"Get out of my head." Timancius pounded his temples.

"Cant-wara byrg, Raven Geat, Reculbium and Sondwic have all fallen to them and been renamed, but still the Saxons do not outnumber the local tribes."

"Leave!"

"But no one will fight them, not even the Cantiaci." Forrester knew that the ruling tribe, the Cantiaci could drive out the Saxons if they had a mind to. "Cowards," she thought. "The people of Kent have been subdued with very little blood spilled and you helped. You are no Briton, Timancius."

The accusation stung and Timancius wheeled round to face her. "You have no mind as to what I am."

Forrester grinned slyly. "You're like me Timancius; an opportunist. You care only for yourself, as I care only for me. I think we will make a good team."

Timancius glared. "You speak strangely and I do not understand. Leave me alone!"

Forrester's grin only faded once Timancius had oozed out of sight. She recognised him as an odious creep, but nevertheless had decided she had found in him, a kindred spirit.

CHAPTER 45

Charley woke to find herself curled-up in Greg's arms. He was stroking her hair and humming to himself. "Jeez, stop that caterwauling will you? What time is it?"

Greg leant down and kissed her on the forehead. "I dunno, about 7am? Welcome back. Are you ok? What happened?"

Charley stretched and heaved herself from the bed. "I'm fine." She pulled on a robe, switched on the kettle by her bed and plonked herself back down on the hard mattress.

Greg noticed her eyes were glistening and within a second a heavy tear tipped over and trickled down her left cheek. "Hey," he said, his voice full of concern, but as he shuffled across the bed to her, she raised a hand to stop him.

"No, Greg. I don't need comforting. I just need some time to process what I've just seen." She stood up and began to pace around her bed space, muttering. Greg detected that her musings were becoming jerky and breathless, her words becoming almost frantic. Enough was enough. He rose and grabbed her arm. "Steady, you look like you're working yourself into some sort of panic attack."

Charley rounded on him, her eyes angry, her face upset and her fists clenched. "For the second time I've just witnessed the brutality of combat. Severed limbs, decapitations, gut spilling into the dirt, horses speared and screaming, the stench of blood and actual shit. I've heard the screams of men and boys, and I'll ever forget any of that as long as I live." Greg tried to put his arms around her, but she pulled away "I told you, I don't need comfort, I just want to be alone so I can sort my head."

"But…"

"Piss off and leave me alone!" The moment the words left her lips and she saw the hurt on Greg's face, she knew she'd gone too far. He hadn't deserved that. "Greg, I…"

"Fine, I get it. You want to be alone. Shame you didn't just tell me that from the get-go."

He pulled back the curtain to leave.

"Greg…"

"See you later." He didn't look back.

Charley looked at the empty doorway and slumped back onto the bed. She closed her eyes and brought the images of what she'd seen, into sharp focus. She didn't want to put them out of her mind, she wanted to see them again, to put them into perspective, to desensitise them. She fully intended to go back and she knew that there would be more battles to see. She had to toughen-up. Her legs felt weak and her heart was pounding. Was toughening-up even an option?

oOo

Richard Armitage was now in a blind jealous rage. He had just wrenched open a kitchen drawer so violently, it had flown off its runners and crashed to the floor. Knives, peelers, measuring cups and mixing spoons spilled across the quarry tiles. Quickly he hunkered down and rummaged through the debris of utensils until his hand closed around the blade of a large carving knife. As he pulled it free, the blade stung his palm as it sliced a nasty gash across it. "Shit!" He grabbed a dirty tea towel and wrapped it around his hand but quickly discarded it when he realised he couldn't hold the knife properly.

His heart was racing, his temples were pounding and his vision was distorted by tears. First on the list was Greg Collier, then Charley. How could she have driven him to this? He had never wanted to hurt her. He tried to convince himself that he could never have killed her for the money he'd been offered, but now the bitch had humiliated him once too often and he was now planning the ultimate revenge.

240

oOo

"Charley, Mon Cher, how are you feeling?"

Charley crossed the marquee to the artefacts tables where Antoinette was packing up some pottery pieces. "Getting them ready for transport to the university?"

Antoinette drew the sealer across the box and cut the tape. "There are a few more to do. You haven't answered my question."

A couple of student volunteers walked past and one clapped Charley on the shoulder. "Hey Charley, welcome back. Are you over your trauma?"

A look of shock came over Charley's face. *They know?* "My what?"

Antoinette quickly cut into the conversation. "He means your medical condition."

"Oh, yes, thank you Tim," she replied, relieved that she had misunderstood what he meant. "A lot better."

My Nan had one of those urinary things and it sent her nuts. They do that apparently."

"I'm not sure Charley would like to be put into the same category as your nan," laughed Antoinette.

Charley waited until the students were out of earshot and then reached out to her mentor. "Can I have a hug please?" The moment Antoinette's arms encircled her, Charley burst into tears and sobbed, and sobbed.

"Hey, is it all getting too much for you?"

Charley didn't answer. She couldn't. There was no way she could have fitted any words between the sobs, even if she had wanted to, so Antoinette just let her cry it out.

It took two or three minutes for her emotions to settle down and gradually she began to catch her breath again. After what felt like an eternity to Antoinette, Charley pulled herself away and sat on a chair by the artefacts table. Antoinette pulled up a second chair and sat next to her.

Charley accepted the tissue that Antoinette offered and dabbed her eyes and blew her nose. "I'm shell-shocked by what I saw,

241

Annie, and then, about an hour ago I was horrible to Greg when he was just being concerned and lovely."

"You do realise these events you're witnessing could trigger some sort of PTSD? They might have already. No one these days should see violence on that level."

"But it still happens, Annie."

"Pah! Where? No that sort of bloodletting has been consigned to history."

Charley shook her head. "Rwanda, Darfur, Taliban torture in Afghanistan? It still goes on Annie; I just can't get my head around why people actually seem to enjoy it."

Antoinette nodded. "There is a phenomenon called 'Battle Joy.' It's that moment in battle when all your primeval instincts take over – when you are beating the opposition and realise you have a chance of survival. It's what gets you through the violence, desensitises you to the carnage *you* are creating. As a bystander, you will never know that feeling, so all you are left with are the sights, sounds and smells that your brain has to process and make sense of and Charley, it probably won't' be able to. I'm really worried for your sanity."

"You do know I'm still going to go back don't you?"

Antoinette looked crestfallen. "I know you will but I still prayed you would not."

"I promise I'll do my best to stay away from danger."

Antoinette nodded and patted her hand. "You had better find Greg. Make your peace with him before your next timeslip."

"I will. In fact I'll go and find him now. Thank you, Annie."

Antoinette watched her go and dabbed away a tear. "I don't think you should be thanking me for anything, you silly girl," she whispered to herself. "If I was any kind of friend I would have put a stop to this a long time ago."

oOo

Richard strode across the dig site to the trench-works that the digger had started to fill. A small group of volunteers were watching from the side-lines and several others were folding muddy tarpaulins. "Any one seen Collier?" he shouted.

"Gone to the bog I think," someone shouted back.

Armitage turned on his heels and strode purposefully back towards the school, where the toilets were open for the site's workers. He crashed through the double swing doors into the boys' toilets, but they were empty. "Shit!" He pushed through the doors again and into the corridor. "Collier?" There was no reply.

He almost ran to the mess tent. "Where's Collier?" he demanded of a young girl who was cleaning down the cooking area.

She shrugged. "Not here. Everyone should be out working now."

He glanced around the empty marquee. Two lads were cataloguing the last of the artefacts for transit, before they were packed-up. "You two, have you seen Collier?"

"Not recently."

Richard stormed out and hurried to the dormitory tent. "Collier?" He swept aside the curtains at each bed space but they were all empty. "Shit, where is he? Where are Charley and Deselle for that matter?" He checked that the carving knife was still hidden in his waistband and then hurried out of the tent again.

oOo

"Thanks for the lift, Greg."

"I don't get why you want to visit the library. What's wrong with the Internet?"

Charley opened the campervan door and swung her legs out. "It's local history I'm after and there's a local historian based here at Ramsgate. Any chance you can pick me up again in an hour?"

"Sure. I'll go get a coffee."

Charley leant back and kissed him on the cheek, then trotted into the ornate brick building. A few minutes later she was being introduced to historian Marjorie Turner; mid-fifties, dark brown hair with silver roots highlighting her centre parting. Charley had expected her to have a sallow complexion, as if she were confined to dusty vaults all day, but the woman before her was tanned with lively green eyes and an obvious enthusiasm for her chosen career.

243

"How can I help?"

"My name is Charlotte Chandler-Price and I'm an archaeologist. I'm looking for some information about the Saxons in Kent and the Isle of Thanet in particular."

"Ahh yes, the Anglo-Saxons. My favourite period of British history."

Charley shook her head. "Well, no, not the Anglo Saxons. I meant the original Saxons who invaded in the 5th Century."

Marjorie laughed. It was a throaty laugh, full of character and amusement. "You'll be lucky. They weren't called the Dark Ages for nothing."

Charley smiled back. "No, obviously I'm aware of that but there are references in some works. Have you heard of the Avertci tribe?"

"Britons you mean? Vaguely, not from round here I think."

"You're right, they were from north of the Thames. What do you know of them?"

Marjorie shrugged. "Nothing really. Come on; let's grab a coffee in the staff room."

Charley followed her through to a kitchen where a jug of fresh-brewed coffee sat on its hotplate. "Help yourself."

Charley poured herself a mug and ignored the sugar and milk. "I'm particularly keen to learn if there are any references to the Avertci's queen or priestess from around that time. She was known as Catherine."

Marjorie took a sip of her strong, over-sweet coffee and frowned. "Why ask me? Surely you should be making your enquiries in the Home Counties from where the Avertci hailed?"

"I have evidence to suggest Catherine came to Kent to do battle with the Saxons; Hengist and Horsa to be precise."

Marjorie looked slightly disbelieving. "Hengist and Horsa?"

"They attacked her village and killed her father who was the tribal king. She then became queen and soon married Vortiger, youngest son of King Vortigern. She led his army down to the south coast and into Kent to try and rout the Saxons from the

244

land."

"Another Boudicca, a warrior Queen in the making eh? How do you know all this? I've never heard that story before. What's your evidence?"

Charley chose to sidestep the question. "We found her body at a dig here. The thing is I was hoping there might be something somewhere that recounts any of the battles."

Marjorie grimaced. "Well... Vortigern is certainly quite well documented. Bede, for example, documents his disastrous pact with the Saxons. His marriages are recorded and details of his sons, Vortimir, Catigern and Pascent, but I've not heard of Vortiger. I would have thought that Catherine's marriage into that family would have been documented but I've never heard of her either. What do you want to know? It seems you probably know more than I do."

"I was hoping there might be a note of her death; a date perhaps, just a year would be useful."

"Carbon dating would tell you that pretty accurately wouldn't it?"

Charley looked crestfallen. "Well I had hoped for some background too. And carbon dating takes time. We leave the dig soon."

Marjorie stood and guided Charley toward the door. "I'll see what I can find out. I know where your dig is and I've got your number if there's anything to tell you."

Charley thanked the amiable historian and wandered through the main hall to the reference section. "Well, why not, now I'm here," she thought and quickened her pace.

Twenty minutes later she gave up. Not one reference to the Avertci anywhere and certainly no mention of Catherine.

"Any luck?" Greg asked as she climbed back into the campervan.

"No. Let's go."

He selected a gear and squeezed her thigh before he drove away. Charley looked at him, crossly. "Not now Greg."

"Not now what?"

"I've got too much on my mind to get fruity with you."

Greg was genuinely perplexed. "Who said anything about getting fruity? I'm driving."

"You squeezed my leg; I'm sorry, I thought were making a pass."

Greg laughed. "Oh get over yourself woman. You're not even my type."

Charley laughed at that and settled back in her seat to plan her next timeslip.

CHAPTER 46

The rest of the day was uneventful. Charley felt compelled to make up for her absences on the dig by throwing herself into the clean-up operation, barrowing earth from the plywood sheets protecting the grass, into the smaller trenches, whilst the digger tackled the larger ones.

The mood on site was cheerful and slightly boisterous as the younger student volunteers became a little demob-happy, realising their life under canvas was coming to an end.

Charley returned to her quarters at 5pm to grab her toiletries for a well-earned shower, but as she drew back her bed space curtain, someone spoke.

"Hello Bitch."

Standing in the corner was a thin, pinch-faced woman, wearing a long coarsely woven dress. Saxon? She stepped into the muted light that spilled in from the doorway.

"Forrester!" Charley gasped and turned to run, but Forrester leapt forwards, grabbed her hair and pulled her back into the bed space. Charley screamed as a handful of her long dark hair was pulled out by the roots and she toppled across her bed. Forrester was on her in a flash, hands forming claws and trying to rake her sharp nails across Charley's face.

Charley grabbed the demonic woman's wrists and tried to push the talons away from her eyes, but Forrester was surprisingly strong. "Help! Somebody help me!" She pushed upwards with all her strength and then twisted her body sideways so that Forrester's hands were no longer over her face and then rolled as hard as she could to topple Forrester off the bed.

Too late Forrester realised what was happening and with a
tortured scream fell onto the floor. Charley leapt from the bed and
ran for the doorway but Forrester grabbed her ankle and clung on.
Charley tried to kick backwards with her free leg but completely
misjudged and overbalanced. As she crashed to the floor Forrester
was on her again, this time with her gnarly hands around Charley's
throat.

"Get off me," Charley gurgled, quickly realising that they were
probably the last words she would be able to utter.

Forrester squeezed tighter and tighter as Charley thumped at her
arms and thrust her hips, trying to dislodge the mad woman, but
every time she thrust her hips upwards, it caused Forrester to fall
forward more, increasing the pressure on Charley's windpipe.

A kaleidoscope of colours was bursting behind Charley's
eyelids as she fought to stay conscious; she could feel herself
becoming weaker and weaker. It was like tumbling down a dark
tunnel. She considered time-jumping but quickly realised if she
died in this plane, she would probably die in the past too.
Somehow she had to stay awake, but she knew unless there was a
miracle, she was going to die at any second.

Suddenly there was a sickening crunch and Forrester emitted a
strange whimper before she fell heavily across Charley's body.

Through her bloodshot and tear-filled eyes, Charley could just
make out the distorted shape of someone standing in the doorway
holding a shovel, raised above their shoulder, like a baseball bat.
Then she passed out. The miracle, it seemed, had happened.

oOo

"Wakey, wakey sweetheart."

Charley opened her eyes to find Greg sitting beside her on the
bed and stroking her forehead. She tried to speak but her throat
burned like hell."

"Don't say anything; it'll take a day or two for your windpipe to
recover."

Charley gestured, trying to ask what had happened and Greg
understood. "Forrester attacked you and before you ask, we've got

248

her; she's tied up next door and isn't going anywhere."

Charley pointed at Greg and signed, "Thank you." at which point he laughed.

"Don't thank me. I didn't do anything." Charley mimed swinging a club and Greg laughed again. "It wasn't me."

"Then who?" she mouthed.

"That would have been me, Mon Cher," smiled Antoinette from the doorway. "That bitch was straddled across you, trying to choke the life out of you."

"Police and a paramedic are on their way," said Greg, "So you just rest. Here, take a sip of water."

Charley sipped and then whispered, "Did she come here just to kill me?"

"What else?" Greg stood so that Antoinette could take his place.

"Maybe she thinks that killing you will somehow interfere with Catherine's plan to attack Saxon settlements along the South coast. What's her final target, assuming that Hengist and Horsa don't return early?"

"Cant-wara byrg." Charley's voice was barely audible.

"Where?"

Annie smiled up at him. "Canterbury. They hope to lie in wait and finish them off."

oOo

Sitting on the floor next door and separated from Charley's bed space by a simple screen, Forrester's eyes widened as she overheard Charley discussing Catherine's plans. She now had a mission far more important that killing that bitch, but first she needed the brooch. She wrestled with her bonds until they were just slack enough for her to access the left-hand pocket of her robe. Gingerly, she withdrew the brooch and grasped in in her hands. Immediately she felt the time-jolt and fell on her side, unconscious.

oOo

"You had a lucky escape I reckon," said the Paramedic, packing-up his equipment and stowing it in two huge holdalls.

"I'm not going to hospital," Charley rasped.

249

"I don't think there's any need at the present time. Your windpipe is bruised…"

"Not crushed?" interrupted Greg."

"No. She'd be on oxygen and on her way to hospital if it had been. You need to rest though Miss." He looked sharply at Greg. "Can you make sure she does?"

Greg winked at her. "I can try."

A movement at the door made them all look round. A young, worried looking policeman was standing there. He gestured to the Paramedic. "Er, I think you'd better come and look at the prisoner; she's unconscious and I can't rouse her."

As the ambulance man hurried to the bed space next door, the policemen looked accusingly at Charley. "What did you do to her?"

She opened her mouth to protest but Greg jumped into the conversation to save her using her voice. "She did naff all. Have you forgotten already that Forrester attacked *her* and nearly killed her?"

The policeman glared back at Greg. "Well someone did something 'cos she's got a sodding great lump on the back of her head and blood all down her neck."

"That would have been me, Officer." Antoinette stepped forward. "As I've already explained to your colleague, I hit her with this shovel to stop her strangling Charley." She held out the shovel. "You want to arrest me now, or are you content to treat me as a witness?"

A steady blush crept up the young officer's neck and spread across his cheeks. "Either way, you will have to be interviewed down at the station."

Greg was livid. "Seriously? This whole thing was self-defence. We're the victims here."

The officer was unmoved. "Tell that to the injured woman's family if she dies."

"Dies?" Antoinette looked shocked.

"Better to deal with this now while the events are still fresh in your mind. Same for you Miss." He nodded at Charley.

"If you haven't noticed, she can't talk! She…was…strangled!" Greg sarcastically separated the last three words to emphasise them.

The officer turned on his heels and went to join Forrester and the Paramedic. Greg followed and watched as she was administered oxygen.

"She appears to be in a coma. I need to get her to hospital straight away."

"She's gone back," whispered a voice in Greg's ear.

"What?"

Charley clung to his sleeve and pointed to the brooch in Forrester's hands, "She's gone back."

"Oh shit!" Greg looked back at Charley, "How do we explain this away?"

CHAPTER 47
Meitheamh (June) 451AD

Forrester found Timancius in his temple. He wheeled round and glared in her direction. "By the gods will you not leave me alone?"

She hurried to his side. "Can you see me yet?"

"No. Nor do I wish to. Which god sent you? Why do you torment me?"

"No god sent me, you old fool; I sent myself. Listen to me. I have news about Catherine."

Timancius froze. "What news?"

"Catherine has an army and they are attacking settlements along the south coast. They are heading for Canterbury to ambush Hengist and Horsa when they pass through on their return."

Timancius screwed up his sharp nose. "Where? You speak in riddles."

"I meant Cant-wara byrg." She reached out and shook Timancius by the arm. "You must send a messenger to warn Hengist and Horsa."

Timancius screamed and lurched away from her. "Argh you...you touched me." He glared in her direction but then his eyes widened. "I...I can see you."

oOo

"Annie, did you warn the Paramedic not to separate Forrester from the brooch?"

Antoinette drew the tape sealing gun across the box in front of her, "I tried but I couldn't think of a legitimate reason for not taking it away. All her personal effects will be by her hospital bed for sure, but unless that brooch is touching her skin, I don't see her

252

ever waking up."

Greg winked. "I don't see that as a problem. She should go straight to Hell."

"Stop it, Greg," Antoinette scolded, "You will go to Hell yourself for remarks like that." She carried the box to a pile of similar cartons and placed it on top. "How is Charley? Resting I hope."

"She wants to go back."

"With Rosemary there too? That could be suicide. You must stop her."

"Not so easy, Annie; now she can time jump whenever she wants."

"And we won't know she's gone until it's too late."

"Precisely. I just wanted to thank you for saving her."

Antoinette smiled. "You really do like her, don't you?"

Greg looked embarrassed. "Yes I do and I need to get back to her. See you later."

He left the marquee and headed to the dormitory tent, but when he drew back the curtain to Charley's bed space, the covers were on the floor and the bed was empty. "Charley?!"

oOo

"Rosemary Forrester?" Charley whispered hoarsely at the nurse.

"Still being assessed I think. Are you a relative?"

"She has none. I'm the closest thing she has."

"Let me check for you."

It was a typical triage area; maybe thirty beds, all screened-off into cubicles and all occupied. Many of the cubicles had curtains drawn and there was a general murmur of conversation in the air, punctuated by the occasional yelp or scream of pain.

"Cubicle sixteen," said the nurse. "She was brought in unconscious and she hasn't come round yet, but you're welcome to sit with her for a while."

Charley drew back the curtain and gazed down at Forrester. For a heartbeat, she felt total fear, but it was quickly replaced by something else... a strange sense of compassion. As much as she had good reason to hate her, she didn't want this vile woman to be trapped in the past *and* in her comatose body.

She noticed a sealed polythene bag on a chair by the bed. It contained Forrester's personal effects and Charley could see the brooch within. Quickly, she opened the bag and grabbed the brooch. Forrester was lying on her back covered by a blanket but with her arms outside. An oxygen sensor was attached to one of her fingers and electrodes were fixed to her chest were monitoring her heart and other functions.

Charley slid the brooch under Forrester's free hand. "You really are bitch, Timancius."

The realisation of what she'd just called Forrester hit her like a sledgehammer. "Oh jeezuz. Timancius? You're *him?*"

Charley felt panic rising inside. "I have to get out of here." She ran from the unit, back to the car park and back to the safety of Greg's campervan. She jumped in and started the engine. She had to get to the school and explain to Greg what she'd just done.

oOo

"But she'd tried to kill you!" Greg was incredulous.

"I know, but to sentence her to life in a coma would have been inhumane, especially as I had the key to her survival." Charley lay on her bed. "I know why she hates me."

Greg's demeanour softened and he sat on the nearby chair. "Go on."

Charley could still only manage a hoarse whisper. "I've seen Timancius, you remember that, yes?"

Greg nodded.

"Who am I describing: Pinch-faced, hooked nose, skinny as a rake with bony limbs?"

"You've just described Forrester, so what?"

Charley laughed. "I was actually describing Timancius."

Greg's eyes widened. "Really? You think they're ancestrally related?"

Charley shook her head. "That's too vague to have generated that much hatred in her, and don't forget I reacted to her too. It

254

really shook me up when we first met. No, I think Forrester *is* Timancius."

She waited for Greg to laugh at her, but instead he stared at his feet and wrung his hands. "And now Timancius past and Timancius present are both in the past. Both hate your guts and both would see you dead in a heartbeat."

"Except, we don't know if Timancius hates me. Forrester yes, but Timancius has never met me. It makes no sense…"

"And you're obviously planning to go back."

Charley nodded. "I am. I have to, Catherine needs me."

Greg's face flushed. "No she doesn't. She's a warrior, you're not. There's nothing you can do to help her and her destiny is already written."

"And maybe so is mine." Charley tried to raise her voice but it hurt too much. "I'm not going to abandon her on the eve of victory."

"For heaven's sake Charley, what happens from now on is academic. Whatever she does, she's still going to end up in the Stour with her throat cut."

His words cut her deeply. "Leave me alone, Greg."

"What?"

"If you can't or won't support me then I need you to leave."

"Not if you're planning to time-jump."

"Just go!" she screamed. The effort ripped through her vocal chords and burned her throat. "Just get the hell out," she whispered and tears of pain and unhappiness trickled down her cheeks.

Without another word Greg shrugged and left the bed space. Charley lay back with her forearm across her eyes. She had a thumping headache.

oOo

Charley stared in wonder at the city before her. Canterbury under the Romans had been a thriving metropolis dominated by an enormous circular theatre, around which had sprawled palatial villas, baths, the homes of the rich and the slums of the poor.

All that remained now was the theatre and the roofless ruins of

255

the city. Amongst those ruins a new city was slowly evolving. Utilising materials from the Roman buildings, new thatched houses were being built.

"Cant-wara-byrg must have been quite something in its heyday," said Charley.

Catherine smiled. "I still find your language strange, but I believe I understand what you mean."

Taraghlan appeared through the trees. "We do not need to go into the city, My Lady. The road into the city follows the bottom of this hill and we have the advantage of height"

Catherine smiled, "Very well. Post guards on the road and send scouts west." She waited until he was out of earshot before speaking again. "You came back, as you promised."

"I did. Has your campaign been successful?"

"It has. I am told Hengist is rushing his army back to do battle with us at Sturigao."

"But you will attack them here instead?"

Catherine smiled and patted her horse's neck. Suddenly her smile widened even more. "I can see you." Although her pulse was racing and her breathing had quickened, her voice was calm and steady. "My gods are with me. I can see you."

Charley gasped. "You can see me?" Her voice was strong and normal.

oOo

"You are not solid like me," said Catherine. "I can see right through you. You are like a whisper on the wind. Surely you come from the gods." Catherine knelt down before her and held up her hands. Clutched in her fingers was a posy of Forget-me-nots. "It's my offering to you."

Charley squirmed with embarrassment. That this amazing and powerful young woman should be on her knees before her was too incongruous for words.

"Get up, please. I am no gift from the gods but I have come to help you." Her eczema was flaring-up through the stress of the past few days and Catherine noticed her rubbing her arm.

"Show me."

Charley pulled up her sleeve to reveal the crescent of irritation and Catherine's eyes widened with surprise. She pulled up her own sleeve to reveal an identical crescent.

Charley felt an icy chill run down her spine. "What does this mean?"

"That we are bound. I do not know how, but we are bound."

oOo

As the sun rose the next morning a scout returned. "The Saxon army is coming."

"Many?" Taraghlan started to kick earth over his fire.

"Less than expected; perhaps two thousand?"

Vortimir smiled broadly. "They have only sent a small force; they do not anticipate much opposition from us. How far away?"

"About seven leagues."

Vortimir glared. "Roman leagues? You answer with Roman leagues?"

The scout dismounted and faced his prince. "I meant er, about ten miles, my Lord."

Vortimir pointed to the rest of his army, camped throughout the wooded hillside. "Spread the word; Douse the fires, clear the camp and prepare for battle."

Charley watched in fascination as Catherine gave her sword and dagger one last clean. "They are beautiful."

"Yes. They are very special to me." She held out the sword. "It is called, 'Blood-Taker.' It belonged to my father. And this…" she produced her beautifully ornate dagger from within her shirt, "is called 'Fire-Sting.' It was my mother's."

"Blood and Fire. I wish I could hold them," marvelled Charley. She wanted to trace the intricate engravings along the length of sword's blade and hold the golden hilt that was wrapped with gold cord. "They are beautiful. The Danes believe they must die with their swords in their hands or they will not enter Valhalla."

"Who are the Danes?"

"They come from lands to the North, across the sea. They too

257

will come to Briton, not for many years."

"And where is Valhalla?"

"It's their afterlife."

A horn sounded and people started scurrying about the camp with urgency. "Are they here?" asked Charley, a shard of fear gripping her chest.

"No, but they are near. I must go."

Catherine left a bewildered Charley standing in the clearing, and sought out Vortiger who was sharpening his sword. "Husband, they are coming."

He rose and pulled his wife close. "We have not been alone for so long."

She kissed him full on the lips. "And this is not the time."

Vortiger looked Catherine up and down and frowned. "You are dressed as a man."

"My gown hampers me in battle. It would also mark me as Queen of the Avertci. If I am to kill Saxons, I must look no different to our warriors."

She had ripped her gown in half at the waist and wore the top half as a shirt. The bottom half she had fashioned into leggings which were held in place with strips of cloth torn from the hem. Over her shirt she wore a leather jerkin, reinforced around the chest. Around her waist hung Blood-Taker and she intended to use it to kill as many Saxons as possible.

Vortiger saw the determination in his wife's eyes. "Then be sure to tie your hair up too."

Taraghlan and Vortimir had ridden to the top of the hill and were surveying the battleground below. The hill faced due north and was relatively steep. A wide road traversed along the bottom of the valley, following the line of the hill. On the other side of the road was a narrow meadow beyond which the River Stour ambled unconcerned, on its way to the sea. At the top of the hill, green meadows carpeted with white clover and yellow dandelions, rolled southwards. The deep wood, that concealed the Britons, covered the lower reaches.

"It is a good place for an ambush Taraghlan."

"It is, Vortimir. When we charge from the trees, the Saxons will have nowhere to go but into the river."

"Which is too deep at this time," smiled Vortimir. "We could win this. Come, let us re-join the men and ready ourselves."

As they rode back down the hill to the tree line, two new riders appeared across the distant meadow behind them, cantering towards the top of the hill.

CHAPTER 48
Meitheamh (June) 451AD

Horsa and Timancius abandoned their horses in some heavy undergrowth to one side of the meadow and quietly and carefully made their way to the brow of the hill.

"Your information was good, Timancius. See them skulking in the woods, waiting to ambush us?"

"And no guards protecting the rear. How will you attack?"

"Hengist, with his half of the army, should arrive soon. I will bring my half here and we will wait to hear the Briton's battle cheer. As they run down the hill to meet Hengist, we will run down behind them and help them to meet their gods." He stifled a laugh. "Come. We must return to my men."

oOo

"Excuse me?"

Antoinette looked up from her table to see a pleasant-looking woman standing at the entrance to the marquee.

The woman stepped forward and offered her hand. "I'm Marjory Turner from Ramsgate library. I'm looking for Charlotte Chandler-Price?"

Antoinette accepted the handshake. "I'm afraid Charley is indisposed. I'm leading this dig, Can I help?"

"Mademoiselle Deselle? I am so pleased to meet you. I've followed the accounts of your digs for many years. Miss Chandler-Price came to visit me today and I have some information for her…I think."

"Go on."

"She was enquiring about the Avertci tribe and their queen in

260

particular. I knew of no tomes that might have mentioned them, but then I fell upon a work by an Anglo-Saxon historian, Eadmund. He doesn't mention the Queen Catherine or the Avertci, but he does make reference to a battle between the invading Saxons and the Britons."

"Where was it, this battle?"

"It's not clear, but the consensus of those more knowledgeable than I, is that it was near Canterbury."

Antoinette sat forward. "And does Eadmund provide an outcome?"

Marjory looked sad. "Yes, he does. Apparently the Britons had set an ambush, but the Saxons split their forces. When the Britons attacked one half, the rest of the Saxons attacked from the rear. They were wiped-out.

"They must have been warned." Antoinette's only thought was how to let Charley know the Briton's plan had been compromised, but she knew that unless Charley woke up in time, there was nothing she could do.

oOo

"Don't forget," Taraghlan whispered, "that the horsemen go first, then the rest of you follow down to the road. Don't give them a chance to set up a shield wall and make as much noise as you can. Pass it on. Vortiger…"

"Yes Taraghlan?"

"Can I suggest you position yourself to receive the last message? Make sure it is the same as the first."

Vortiger laughed and began to spread the new instructions around the camp. Catherine rode up alongside her friend. "Taraghlan, is everyone ready?"

"Yes my Queen."

Catherine blushed at that. "You honour me, Taraghlan. I am the same little girl you have always known."

He smiled wistfully. "I pledged to your father I would protect you until death, and I will." He reached for her hand. "It is your destiny to lead your people to better times and mine to help you. I love you as my own, Catherine and always will."

There was a sudden whinny from the road and Taraghlan held up his hand. The Saxon army could be seen almost sauntering along the road below. The entire Brittonic army held its breath, waiting for his arm to drop.

"Fight true and strong my Lady… and *live!*" He dropped his arm and a mighty roar issued forth as the Britons charged down through the trees to the horde below.

oOo

Antoinette looked anxiously at Greg. "That must have been the battle Charley was talking about. Is this when Catherine dies?"

"I don't know, Annie, but more importantly, what if Charley gets killed?"

Antoinette stroked Charley's forehead. "Oh Mon Cher, what have you done?"

"What have *we* done?" Greg corrected her. "We should never have allowed her to return after her last trip."

"Or the one before?" Antoinette suggested. "I wish I knew what was happening."

oOo

Hengist hadn't warned his men that an ambush was expected. He wanted their surprise to be genuine lest their preparedness tipped off the Britons that their plan had been undermined. So the sudden roar and appearance of two thousand screaming warriors caught them completely off-guard. As planned, the Britons were amongst them before a shield wall could be established and along with several hundred riders, Catherine, Taraghlan, Vortimir and Vortiger, were among the first to crash into their ranks.

Catherine took first blood, slicing Blood-Taker through the first helmeted head she encountered. Within seconds she was surrounded by baying Saxons. Her horse screamed as they hacked at it. Catherine sprang onto its back and, standing on the saddle, launched herself through the air just before the poor creature fell to the ground. She landed on top of two Saxons and drove her sword through one and then sliced through the hamstring of the second.

262

Taraghlan rammed his shield down on the head of a Saxon warrior who was just about to spear Vortimir, who in turn hurled his axe past Taraghlan's horse at a warrior about to slash its throat. They barely had time to acknowledge each other when the second wave of Britons, those without horses, waded into the fray.

Another horn sounded and Vortiger looked back up the hill; no second horn blast had been planned and to his horror saw hundreds more Saxons running through the woods towards them. So great was the noise of battle, there was nothing he could do to warn the other Britons. He searched desperately for Catherine, but her disguise was too good. A yell in his right ear startled him and he found a young Saxon charging at him. He rammed the boss of his shield into the Saxon's face and then plunged his sword through the lad's neck.

The Britons suddenly became aware of the Saxons' ambush and many tried to retreat but were quickly cut down.

Vortimir still mounted, found Taraghlan on the ground, driving his sword into a Saxon's stomach. "How did they know?"

Taraghlan pulled his sword free. "There must be a traitor close to us."

"We must retreat or die," Vortimir shouted.

"We chose this spot too well," Taraghlan shouted back and wiped his bloodied face with his sleeve. "There is nowhere to run. The river is too deep and the hill is cut off."

"Then every man must save himself." Vortimir blew one long note on his horn and then turned back to Taraghlan. "Come, get up behind me."

Taraghlan shook his head. "First, I must find Catherine. I vowed to keep her safe."

"Look back, Taraghlan; you think you can keep her safe now? She is gone."

"You go, Vortimir. I must find her and Vortiger too."

Vortimir nodded. "If you make it, we'll meet back at the Avertci village; it is closer than father's castle."

Taraghlan raised his sword in salute as Vortimir kicked his

horse and galloped from the scene. With one last look down the road, Taraghlan dived back into the melee, hacking, slicing and stabbing as he searched for the young couple.

He saw Hengist and Horsa sitting proudly on their horses just below the tree line, savouring the annihilation of King Vortigern's army. He squinted at the horseman next to them and bile rose in his throat as he realised it was Timancius. Was he the connection? Was there someone in the Avertci tribe who still kept contact with him?

A large Saxon barged Taraghlan to the ground and plunged his spear at his throat, but Taraghlan rolled into his legs and plunged his dagger into his knee, behind the kneecap. The Saxon screamed and fell next to him and Taraghlan drove the dagger through the warrior's eye and into his brain.

"Taraghlan!" It was Vortiger. "Taraghlan I cannot find Catherine anywhere." He grasped Taraghlan's hand and pulled him to his feet. "What do we do? If we stay any longer we will die here." There was panic in his face and tears in his eyes. "Where is my Catherine?"

"Vortiger, you must go. Your father needs his heirs alive. Go and I'll stay and look for her. I am on my oath to protect her."

"Then as her husband I release you from that oath. If she is alive you and I will be of no use to her if we are both killed here."

The road and the meadow were littered with the dead and dying, most of whom where Britons. There were dozens rider-less horses cantering in all directions through the battleground, ears back, nostrils flaring and whinnying in panic.

The fighting was waning quickly and Taraghlan knew Vortiger was right, no matter how much he felt it was a betrayal of Catherine and Madron. They had to escape now or be captured and put to the sword.

"Vortiger, look to the meadow; those horses look calm enough." They tumbled off the road into the meadow and ran for the horses.

oOo

Charley had watched the whole battle from the safety of the

woods, close to the tree line. Her heart raced with joy as the Britons plunged deep into the Saxon army, taking many lives in the process. But then a twig snapped from behind and made her spin around to look up the hill. To her horror, there were hundreds more Saxons walking down through the woods. Suddenly a horn sounded and they charged. They raced down the hill and as they reached Charley and the tree line they started to roar and shout. She clung to a sturdy elm tree as the horde thundered past her. The ground shook as the warriors charged past, oblivious to her presence. She tried to shout a warning. Maybe Catherine would hear, but her voice was feeble compared to the terrifying noise of the Saxons.

As the last of the warriors exited the woods and charged down onto the road, she heard a whinny and turned back to see two riders approaching. Horsa and Timancius. She quickly flattened herself against the tree. "What if Forrester is here too?" She scanned the ground above but it was quickly apparent they were alone.

An intense feeling of hatred boiled-up inside her as she watched Timancius pass within feet. Instinctively she reached for a large stone. Her fingers closed around it. It felt solid. She lifted it, took aim and hurled it with all her might at the odious priest.

It fell short but struck his steed on the rump which caused it to rear. Timancius was thrown backwards and fell heavily to the ground. Horsa roared with laughter as Timancius lay on the hard earth.

"I am hurt!" Timancius whined angrily and showed Horsa his bloodied fingers. "My head."

Charley grabbed another stone and rushed the priest, intending to pound it onto his head and finish him off, but her foot caught on a root and which sent her sprawling across the ground. The stone flew from her hand and whistled past the priest.

As Charley slithered to a stop right next to him, Timancius suddenly jerked his head round in her direction and glared right at her. She froze in terror; surely he could see her.

The anger in his face was replaced by concern and then

something akin to fear and he reached out towards Charley. "You are there, I know it, you accursed sorceress."

Timancious's hand was millimetres from her face when he closed his fingers as if trying to grasp her. "You will die here today, Catherine and cowering in the wood like the coward you are, will not save you."

Horsa pulled his horse around to Timancius. "What are you doing? Get back here."

Timancius glared at Charley once more and clambered to his feet. "Just make sure Catherine does not survive."

Horsa gave Timancius a look of barely disguised contempt. "She is our greatest prize." His horse snorted and pawed the ground. "Here comes Hengist. This is a great day for us."

Charley scrambled to her feet and ran into the clearing below the tree line. The battle was in full swing. The screams of men and horses filled the air, but she ignored them. She was frantically searching the battle for Catherine, but she knew it was a lost cause. To spot one person in a field of thousands would be impossible.

She was exhausted and knew she should return to the present, but it was becoming harder. It took more effort each time. It was if the past didn't want to let her go. Besides, she needed to stay a while longer; she needed to be sure Catherine had survived.

She watched as the battle peaked and waned. She stayed until it finally ceased. Saxons were clambering over the dead and dying, putting to the sword any Britons they found alive. Other warriors were rounding up all the horses that were alive and uninjured. It had been a good day.

She had no idea how many Britons had escaped, but judging by the corpses being piled-up in the meadow, it couldn't have been many. Suddenly she was overcome with grief and she slid to her knees and let out an anguished cry of despair. Catherine was almost certainly dead. Charley knew that somehow she must have changed the course of history after all.

Then a thought struck her: whenever she travelled to the past, she always returned to where Catherine was. Maybe she could wake herself up, then come straight back again; if Catherine was alive, surely she would find her again.

"I have to get back to the present.... now."

CHAPTER 49

"It was terrible." Charley cupped the mug of tea in both hands.

"It was a trap, yes?" asked Antoinette gently.

"Yes, how did you know?" Her throat was painful and her voice raspy again.

"Marjory from the library came by. She'd found an account of the battle. It's on your chair. Apparently the Saxons found out about Catherine's ambush."

Charley looked perplexed. "But how?"

Greg sat next to her on the bed. "Forrester would be my guess."

Antoinette rolled her eyes. "Forrester? Really?"

"She was next door after we captured her. She must have overheard Charley telling us the plans and she skipped-off back in time to warn them."

"That can't be true, surely?" Charley croaked as she blinked back tears. "That would make all that carnage my fault."

Antoinette banged her fist on the back of the chair. "And that, you stupid girl, is why you don't time travel and don't mess with the past. Who knows what damage has been done - what changes to history have been caused by your careless talk and Forrester's shenanigans." She swept back the curtain at the doorway and stepped through. "You don't go back again. I forbid it."

"Oh don't start that again, Annie. Reflecting on it, I don't think I changed anything. You just told me that Marjorie has a record of the battle, so it's already written into history...our history. Nothing has changed here has it?"

"That may be true, but as you said, all that carnage is your fault." Antoinette stormed off leaving Charley again overcome with grief.

"What have I done, Greg? All those bodies in the field, all those dead animals? Catherine is probably dead, Taraghlan and Vortiger too."

Greg squeezed her hand. "Well at least you're speaking to me again."

Charley looked puzzled for a second but then remembered. "Oh. I was a complete bitch to you wasn't I? If you want nothing more to do with me I'd understand. I keep pushing you away. I'm so sorry."

Greg smiled. "I'm getting used to it, although I don't see why I should have to."

"That horrible person is not me Greg; please believe me. Maybe Annie is right and I'm suffering from some sort of PTSD." She lay back in his arms and let out a huge wracking sob.

oOo

Richard Armitage turned the knife around in his hand. His chest felt tight and he was struggling to breath. He was wrestling with some very mixed emotions. He hated Charley but also missed her, big-time. He had decided that she was a manipulative cow and all he wanted to do was hurt her, but when he was offered good money to kill her, he realised he couldn't do it; he still had feelings for her.

Perversely, the more he hated her, the more he yearned for the friendship they'd had only a few short weeks ago. Now she was screwing around with that Greg Collier tosser and that upset him more than anything. The feeling of rejection was intense.

Then there were his debts. Smith had already paid half of the seven grand into his bank account, but it wouldn't enough to appease the casino. In a couple of weeks he would be facing a beating or broken kneecaps or worse. It didn't bear thinking about.

He had no family to speak of, a crappy job and a whole load of shit in his life that he really didn't need.

He thought about his feelings for Charley once more. It was now clear that this feeling of hatred was far stronger that any feelings of love. He still wanted to hurt her and now, with nothing left to live for, he had just executed his final revenge – the one last trick up his sleeve - one that would hopefully send her over the edge.

He lay back against the wall in the warmth of the shower spray and watched in fascination as light swirls of red spilled across the tray and spiralled down the drain. Before long the swirls had combined and the colour of the water was deep crimson and uniform.

His wrists stung, but he hardly noticed. He closed his eyes and tried not to dwell on his shortness of breath. It would be over soon and he could relax for good, and Charley would hopefully suffer from guilt for the rest of her miserable life.

oOo

"Feeling better?" Greg kissed Charley on the cheek.

"Yes. I can see things more clearly now. I can't blame myself for what happened. If that battle was recounted in an ancient text, then it had already happened. It is consigned to history."

"It must have been hard to witness, nonetheless."

"It was. It was a massacre. The Saxons charged down the hill behind Catherine's troops and just destroyed them." She paused in thought for a moment. "Catherine had the most amazing sword and dagger. Blood and Fire she called them. They were so ornate and beautiful."

"Tell me about Catherine and Vortiger? You have no idea what happened to them?"

"None."

"You're going back of course."

"Yes, of course. If Catherine is still alive then I should be somewhere near her when I arrive back." She pondered for a moment. "Of course if she's dead, maybe I won't be able to return. I am certain that my time-slips are connected to her and her alone."

"I don't see how she could be dead. You witnessed her death. I doubt this battle changed that. Come on, let's get you fed and watered, then we'll hunt out Annie and you can try to make peace with her before you go back."

"She won't be happy, Greg; she's forbidden me to go back again."

"As she has many times before, but she knows she can't stop you."

"No but she could throw me off the dig, maybe end her mentorship or throw me out of Uni?"

Greg helped her up. "I don't think she'd do that. She's too invested in you to end your friendship."

Charley wrapped her arms around him and leant on his shoulder. "I'm not so sure."

oOo

The Marquee was buzzing with activity as the whole dig team collected their meals and joked and jostled each other around the tables. Greg and Charley took their trays of shepherd's pie and peas back to the table they had commandeered.

Antoinette and Shelly joined them.

"I'm sorry for my outburst earlier, Mon Cher," she said to Charley.

Shelly looked up, surprised. "You ranted at Charley? My god, don't tell me the Golden Girl is falling from grace."

Charley smiled. "It's a long way to fall, Shell, when you're as special as I am." She stopped with a forkful of mince halfway to her mouth. "You know, Annie, I think we could bring Shelly into our circle of trust. We could do with an extra member on the team."

Shelly stopped eating too. "What's this?"

Antoinette looked horrified. "No Charley!" She looked at Shelly. "Forget what she just said."

"Oh come on, you can't exclude me now"

"Think about it, Annie," said Charley with undisguised enthusiasm, "You can't keep your eyes on me all by yourself, not with the clear-up to supervise, and Greg can't do it all either. We need someone else, someone we can trust and I think Shelly could be the one."

Shelly's eyes nearly popped. "Trust with what?"

271

Antoinette glared. "I might have overreacted before, but my stance hasn't changed, Charley. You're not to go back."

"Go back where?" Shelly pleaded.

Greg raised a calming hand. "We are so close to finding out what happens to Catherine and the Avertci. We can't give up yet."

Shelly glanced from Greg to Antoinette. "Who's Catherine? Give up what?"

Antoinette shook her head. "It's just too dangerous. For all we know her actions have already changed the present, let alone the past?"

Charley banged the table. "My actions? If anyone changed anything it was Forrester and *her* actions, not mine."

"Are you talking about Forrester from the NAS? Oh come on guys, what's going on?" Shelly grabbed Charley's hand. "You've got to tell me now."

"Yes I will."

Antoinette threw her fork onto her plate of unfinished shepherd's pie and pushed it away. "I give up. This is a big mistake Charley. If this gets out, we are all in big trouble."

Charley grinned. "Or we are all heroes who have revealed unknown truths about the Dark Ages."

"If anyone believes us," she countered.

"Us? Does that mean you're still on board?

It was useless to try and fight against this particular current; it was too powerful. "Ok, ok."

The look on Shelly's face was pure frustration. "Unknown truths? Jumps? For heaven's sake what is going on?"

"Finish your meal Shell and we'll tell you everything," laughed Charley.

oOo

All the colour had drained from Shelly's face. "You're all mad."

Charley laughed. "I'm not surprised you feel that way. It's a lot to take in."

"And Forrester is supposedly time-jumping too?"

Greg frowned. "Forrester is a big risk to Charley in my

272

opinion."

"Let's say I believe you all, what happens now? What do you want me to do?"

"Someone has to be with me when I jump back in time. They need to keep me safe from..." she paused as she thought about Richard, "er, outside interference, oh and health issues."

"Such as?"

"Well, as I explained, if I get hurt in the past, it manifests here in the present too. So if a sodding great gash appears in my stomach and my intestines fall out, you'll have to dial 999." Charley laughed again.

"Don't joke like that," scolded Antoinette.

"That could happen?" Concern was etched on Shelly's face.

"It could," confirmed Greg.

"Will you help us? Please say yes," pleaded Charley.

"Of course I will. But why do you need to go back again?"

I witnessed the Britons being ambushed and slaughtered. They were wiped out but I have to know that Catherine is still alive."

"But she must be; you witnessed her death and that happened here in Thanet, not at Canterbury."

"It's not as simple as that now, Shelly. Forrester might have changed history by warning the Saxons. Perhaps her treachery caused Catherine to die prematurely."

"If that's so," said Shelly, her brown eyes fizzing with excitement, "then her skeleton will have disappeared from the artefacts collection." She laughed at their puzzled looks. "If her place of death has now changed from here to Canterbury, then you couldn't have found her bones. They will never have existed here, so they should have disappeared."

Greg leapt up. "Shelly I could kiss you."

Charley glared. "Don't you frigging dare. You're mine now." Charley's throat was still bruised and her voice sound like a growl.

"I'm going to check," he said and left the dormitory tent.

Charley stood too. "I should go and find Richard. I think we need to clear the air."

Antoinette shook her head, "Not without me. It's not safe for you to go anywhere near him on your own."

Shelly looked up at the two women. "What shall I do?"

"Anything you like," replied Antoinette, "So long as you keep your mouth shut."

Shelly grinned broadly. "You have my word."

oOo

"The back door is open, Annie."

Antoinette moved Charley out of the way and stepped into Richard's kitchen. She called out. There was no reply. They walked into the hall and Antoinette placed a hand on the bannister and looked up at the landing. "Richard, are you home? It's Mademoiselle Deselle and Charley. Hello?"

Charley put her hand on Antoinette's shoulder. "Annie I have a bad feeling about this."

They tentatively climbed the staircase with Antoinette calling out for Richard every few steps. Once on the landing, they peered into his bedroom. It was dark; the curtains were still drawn, but there was enough daylight leaking past them to see the bed was unmade and unoccupied.

"I'll check the bathroom," said Charley. She pushed open the door and gasped.

"What is it?" Antoinette pushed past her and stared into the room. "It's empty. He's not in here either."

At that moment a terrified scream echoed across the site. Antoinette froze. "What the hell has happened now?"

The two women rushed out of the caretaker's house and sprinted across to the marquee and tents, where a crowd was gathering. "What's going on?" Antoinette demanded as they ran to the front of the throng.

"In there," pointed a young teenage student, her face as white as the T-shirt she was wearing. Charley and Antoinette entered the steamed-up shower tent and pulled open the curtain of the nearest cubicle.

"Oh my god, Richard." Charley dropped to the floor and

274

checked for a pulse in his neck as Antoinette turned off the flow of water.

"Someone call an ambulance!" shouted Antoinette.

"Don't bother," said Charley, her chin quivering and her tears mixing with the shower spray that had soaked her. "He's dead."

CHAPTER 50

DC Hallam looked exasperated. "I don't know what's going on at this dig of yours, but it's all becoming too much like Midsomer Murders. How can you have so many serious incidents in one place over such a short space of time?" He looked across the field to the car park. "My guvnor is on his way; Christ knows what I'm going to tell him."

"That Armitage committed suicide I imagine," retorted Greg.

"With the history you lot have got with him? I doubt this will be treated as a simple suicide."

Greg burst out laughing. "You muppet, you think one of us killed him? Now who's channelling Midsomer Murders?"

"What about Rosemary Forrester, is she still unconscious?" asked Antoinette.

Hallam shrugged his shoulders. "As far as I know; and that's something else I think you lot know more about that you're admitting."

A tall, sharply-dressed man strode across the field towards them. In his wake was a rather dishevelled detective sergeant.

Hallam leaned in to whisper. "That's Detective Chief Inspector Burton and Sergeant Taylor."

Charley stifled a laugh. "Burton and Taylor? Are you kidding me?"

Hallam grinned. "Shh. It's a running gag at the nick and the boss is getting pretty fed up with it. Someone left a photo of Anthony and Cleopatra on his desk the other week and he's pretty-much conducting a witch-hunt to find out who did it."

DCI Burton was in his late forties. He wore a sharply-trimmed moustache that was slightly more ginger than the salt and pepper sported by his hair. His suit was tailor-made, his shirt was from Harrods and his tie was pure silk. It was evident that his image meant more to him than anything.

DS Taylor on the other hand obviously cared nothing for image. Although his slacks were smart and his sport jacket fitted his frame, he still managed to project an air of slovenliness. His curly grey hair was overly long and one curly strand kept blowing over his left eye, so he was constantly swatting it away.

"Why have you called me to a suicide, Hallam?" Burton demanded.

"The deceased is Richard Armitage. He was arrested the other day for assaults on Miss Chandler-Price and Mr Gregory Collier."." He pointed at Charley and nodded towards Greg.

"And now he's dead, eh?" Burton opened the flap to the ablutions tent and peered in. "Have Forensics finished in there?"

Hallam nodded.

"And the body's gone to the morgue?"

"Just before you got here, Sir."

"So why is this a CID matter?"

"Just a gut feeling, Sir. These people here all seemed to have an axe to grind where Armitage was concerned."

"Now hang on a minute." Greg stepped forward. "That maniac could have killed Charley. We're angry, but not stupid."

Hallam ignored him. "Plus there is the matter of Rosemary Forrester. She is some big shot at the National Archaeology Society and she also attacked Miss Chandler-Price."

Burton's eyebrows shot up in surprise. "It sounds like you've been busy upsetting people, young lady."

"Not my fault," she croaked.

"What's up with your voice?"

Antoinette put her arm around Charley. "Forrester tried to strangle her."

DS Taylor spoke up for the first time. "And where is this Forrester woman now?"

277

"In hospital, in a coma," Hallam interjected.

"And how did that happen?"

Hallam looked at the group for an answer.

"We don't know," said Antoinette. "We found her like it."

Burton shook his head "This is ridiculous. Well, if forensics cast any doubt on this being a suicide, you'll all be coming in for questioning. Hallam, be sure to update me when you get the autopsy results, and keep me posted about the Forrester woman; I want to speak with her when she wakes up." He signalled to the detective sergeant, "Come on Taylor; I haven't got all day."

Charley tugged at Greg's sleeve. "Can we go now?" she whispered. "I really want to get back to find Catherine."

Greg shot a glance at Hallam who was now talking to a couple of uniformed officers. "Let me check with Dick Tracy over there." He sauntered over. "DC Hallam, Can we go? Miss Chandler-Price is supposed to be taking it easy."

He nodded. "Don't leave town, as they say in the movies. I might need to speak to you again."

Greg flushed a little as his temper spiked. "That's going to be hard as we're vacating the site tomorrow."

"Shit. Ok, I'll get those two officers to collect the contact details of everyone on the site."

Greg returned and took Charley by the arm. "The police have finished searching through the school house. I suggest we convene in Armitage's bedroom for your next time-jump."

Shelly rubbed the goose bumps that had suddenly surfaced on her arms. "Ooh I'm not sure I like that idea. Not in *his* room."

"Greg's right," Charley agreed. The guys and gals are going to be packing and stripping down a lot of the dorm ready for packing-up tomorrow. There's less chance of being disturbed at Richard's house."

Shelly shivered. "Well if his sodding ghost shows up, I'm outta there."

CHAPTER 51
Márta (March) - 452 AD

Sturigao lies at the old Roman junction of the road from Canterbury to Thanet and Reculver, at the point where the Romans built a fort to protect the crossing of the river. Hengist and Horsa had rebuilt and refortified the old garrison and were using it as their base, in preference to the more substantial coastal fort at Reculver.

Hengist looked into the cell constructed for their guest. "Your husband has just led another assault." He laughed. "That is three times he has tried, yet he knows not if you are here or alive."

Catherine rolled over on the stinking straw that covered the hard mud floor and blinked at the light that spilled through the doorway behind him. She stared at Hengist for a moment and then rolled back again.

"We tried to kill him. His father needs to lose at least one son." He laughed and then cocked his head and studied Catherine's recumbent form. "I thought a powerful priestess such as you would have flown away like a bird, but still you lie there. Maybe your gods have no patience with failure."

She pulled up the filthy length of hessian she used as a blanket and curled into a foetal position. After nine months as the Saxons' captive, she had no doubt that her gods had deserted her.

The only thing she remembered about her capture was lunging at a huge Saxon warrior who grabbed her sword by the blade and head-butted her. After that, she knew nothing until she woke up, tied to a post in the middle of the Sturigao Fort.

She had been stripped of her leather jerkin and makeshift

leggings and wore only the shirt that she'd fashioned from her dress. It was just long enough to cover her modesty and, although still dazed, she was satisfied she had not be defiled by her captors.

The fort was stone-built with high walls, surrounded by deep ditches. Within the walls were some stone-built buildings, some whole, others in various states or ruin and collapse.

Men were working within one of the more complete buildings and Catherine would find out soon enough that they were preparing a cell for her. They were building a partition wall so that the building would consist of two rooms instead of just one large space. One room would be for her guards and the other would be her prison.

She remained tied to the post, standing, for three days, with no food, but regular sips of water brought by guards, who without exception, took the opportunity to let their hands wander. Catherine was too weak to use her magic.

Once the cell was finished, she was manhandled across the grounds and thrown into her new accommodation. It was Horsa's idea to feed her just every few days. He was worried that she would use her magic if she regained her strength. Over the next few weeks, Hengist regularly visited her to ensure she was not getting any stronger.

She didn't speak to him, except for the first time he visited. "What do you want with me?"

He laughed. "I am keeping you as a symbol of our power and strength; as a warning to your tribes that they must submit or die, just as your army died."

"To do that you must tell all the tribes that I am alive and your prisoner. I feel you have not."

"That is true. I will, when the time is right. Your little prince is convinced that we have you. He had a messenger come with a demand that we release you."

"What did you do?"

He laughed again. "I sent him back with his head in one saddlebag and his heart in the other."

As soon as Hengist left, Catherine prayed to her gods. She prayed for forgiveness and she prayed for Vortiger and her friends, and she prayed that Charley had not deserted her.

A few days later, a dark shadow fell across Catherine's recumbent form. She knew who it was without looking. "What do you want of me, Timancius?"

"I have brought someone to meet you. Can you see her?"

Catherine sat up and saw a shimmering form, almost solid but not quite. It reminded her of the first time she saw Charley. "Who is this?"

Timancius smiled a thin black-toothed grin. "She is a gift from my gods. She does not have a name.

Forrester stepped closer. "So, this is the bitch that Chandler-Price was talking about."

Catherine gasped; the likeness between the apparition and Timancius was uncanny.

"Who is Chandler-Price?"

"You know her as Charlotte or Charley," Forrester sneered.

"You know my Charlotte?"

Forrester smiled meanly. "I do and soon I hope to kill her." With that she just melted into the background and Timancius turned to leave.

"Wait! Timancius!" she begged, but they were gone.

oOo

The following six months were boring and uneventful. She was allowed no exercise outside and had to content herself with pacing her cell. She had mused that they could have allowed her unescorted exercise because she had little enough strength and certainly not enough to consider escaping.

The heat of the summer gave way to the cool of autumn, followed by the chill of winter. The biting December air froze everything it touched; frost clung to the ground most days and freezing air tumbled into Catherine's cell from her small window.

It was around the middle of that month that an elderly Saxon man entered the outer room and peered into Catherine's chamber.

"So you are the Queen of the Avertci."

He was dressed in a brown linen shirt and breeches. His long, straggly grey hair hung over his shoulders, his blue eyes peeked through the strands that almost covered his face. He wore a long grey beard that was braided and inset with colourful beads. Catherine thought he looked wise and kindly and she smiled for the first time in weeks. "Who are you?"

"I am Wælheard. I teach the children but I am now to be one of your guards. Apparently you are no threat to an old man like me."

"You speak my language well."

I am a scholar. I studied Roman history and their language and have learned many languages, including yours.

Catherine rose from the floor and walked shakily to the stout, barred door. "Why are *you* guarding me? There is a reason. What is it?"

A rueful smile touched Waelheard's mouth and eyes. "I am to befriend you, to find out about your powers. I am old and they believe you will trust me." He delved into a sack and produced some bread and dried meat. "Here, this is for you."

She eyed the food suspiciously. "Your time would be better spent teaching; you will learn nothing from me."

The old man smiled again. "I will not do as they ask; I am here because I want to be."

Catherine decided it was safe to take the food, but she knew it would come at a price. She looked into his rheumy eyes. "Then what *do* you want?"

Waelheard faltered. He wanted to consider his response so he could frame his answer honestly, but for a moment the words of this foreign language had escaped him. "I will try to explain, but forgive me if I speak your tongue badly. I have heard many things about you; how you read minds, turn people to stone, boil them alive with just a stare. I want to know what is true and what is just idle talk and untruths. Is it true you took the eye of that false priest?"

Catherine hesitated. "Why do you say he is a false priest?"

He spat on the floor. "Timancius cares only about himself. He will not aid the sick or counsel those in need. He schemes with Hengist and Horsa and they give him gold for his advice. Did you take his eye?"

"I did."

"Is it true you turned him to stone first?"

Catherine smiled. "If I had turned him to stone, I would have left him as a statue."

Waelheard laughed at that. "I believe you. Tell me about your gods."

"I will, but first I need clothing and warmth. I need a fire. And you must tell me about your gods too."

Waelheard removed the bar from the door and pushed it open. "I have a brazier here, come, sit with me so we can talk."

Over the following months, Catherine and Waelheard spent many hours talking about their respective gods, about medicine, about philosophy and many other topics of mutual interest. They formed a bond of trust and Waelheard enjoyed his time spent with this entrancing woman. He ensured she had extra food, smuggling fruit and roasted meat into her cell daily so she could rebuild her strength.

Catherine's friendship with the old man was in stark contrast to her night-time guards. They were coarse and rude, constantly making lurid remarks about her. Even with her strength restored and her powers reignited, there were times when she was genuinely afraid for her safety. She dared not use her skills to protect herself in case it alerted Hengist and Horsa to her recovery. She had felt deserted by her gods for so long, she couldn't be sure that her powers would be strong enough to overcome any forceful attempts to subdue her.

Neither Hengist nor Horsa made any attempt to visit her during those months. They were away much of the time, taking control of the Southlands and welcoming the hundreds of Jutes, Angles and many Germanic tribes who arrived daily to settle-in under their rule.

Catherine began to rely on Waelheard's visits to keep her sane and despite enjoying his company there was one thing that troubled her: the lack of contact from Charley.

During one of their conversations Waelheard noticed a look of pain in her face. "What ails you?"

Catherine had never told anyone about Charley, so why she chose to confide in the old Saxon was a mystery to her, but confide in him she did. She told him about every visit and every conversation she had had with Charley and when she had finished, he gazed at her with watery eyes.

"And you do not believe she is one of your goddesses?"

"She tells me she is not. She says she is from my future. She knows about things that have not yet happened."

"Yes, so you told me. Who do you think she is? You thought she was your mother?"

"Not anymore," she said sadly. "I wish she were. I never knew my mother, but I miss her all the same."

The old man nodded sagely. "I can understand that." He stared at the floor, temporarily lost in thought.

Catherine touched his arm. "What is it? You too have something on your mind?""

"I do." He looked tentatively towards the outside door to ensure no one was within earshot. "In a few moons I will bring you clothes, shoes, a hair comb and other things you will need to disguise yourself when you escape from here."

Fear crossed Catherine's face. "Escape? What do you mean? I can't escape." Her time in captivity had badly damaged her confidence.

Waelheard leant forward earnestly. "You can, you will, you must. Your strength is improving and I'm sure your powers are too. By Marta you must be ready."

"But how am I to leave here?"

"The clothes will be Saxon. Look from your window and see how the women fashion their hair; you must learn to copy it. In Márta when the winds blow and the flowers appear, that will be the time. Every day women leave the fort for many reasons. Some work in the fields, some wash clothing at the river and in Márta many are hunting for plants for dying linen. I will bring you a basket and you will just walk out of the fort. Where you go after that is no concern of mine."

Catherine's eyes filled with tears. "Why?"

"Because I am your friend; because it is wrong to keep a butterfly in chains."

"But how will you explain my escape?"

"I am an old man. I shall just tell them I fell asleep."

"But they will kill you."

"They might, and if they do, at my great age, I will welcome the journey to my gods."

oOo

Just as Waelheard predicted, when the March winds began to blow, groups of women would leave the fort at dawn every day, to collect plants for medicines and for dying fabric. This, he had decided, was the right time for Catherine to escape. He pulled a bag from underneath his chair. "Here, hide this."

Catherine looked puzzled. "What is it?"

"The clothing I promised you. "Tomorrow when the women leave, you must go too. I will send the night guards away early and let you out." He then held out a large package bound in linen.

"What is this?"

Waelheard just smiled and watched as she unwrapped the bundle. Within the folds were a finely-crafted sword and a beautifully ornate dagger. "Blood and Fire," she breathed softly as she saw them. "I never thought I would see them again."

"Wear them under your gown."

Catherine looked at the old man with gratitude. "Where did you get them?"

"Do not ask. They belong with you." The old man embraced her and then stepped away and locked the cell door. "The night guards will be here soon. Hide everything I have given you."

Catherine turned back into her cell and hid everything under the grimy straw-filled mattress that Waelheard had provided. As she lay down, something stirred in the darkest corner of the chamber.

oOo

The surroundings took Charley by surprise. She was in a dank, smelly room where a small solitary window cast a muted ray of daylight onto a straw-covered floor. In one wall was a stout door which consisted of a thick oak frame and iron bars. On the other side of the door an old man appeared to be dozing in a chair.

A movement near the centre of the cell caught her eye and she inwardly gasped as she realised there was a woman lying there. The woman stirred and propped herself up on her elbows - Catherine!

"Oh my god, Catherine. What's happened?"

Catherine let out a shriek which roused Waelheard. He came to the door. "Are you alright?"

"I am, thank you Waelheard, it was just a rat. It surprised me."

With a grunt, Waelheard returned to his chair.

"Charlotte?" Catherine whispered.

"It is. What's happened to you?"

"Where have you been?" Tears stung Catherine's eyes. "I thought you had left me for good."

"Catherine how long has it been since you saw me last?"

"Nine moons I think."

Charley looked shocked. "Nine months? Catherine for me it has been only one or two days. I cannot control when in your life I appear to you. I'm so sorry it has been so long." She crawled over sat on the ground next to Catherine and reached out to her.

Catherine reached out too and when their hands touched, a bright blue aura flared around their fingers. Charley pulled her hand back in fright but Catherine didn't move save for a smile and a look of utter peace that spread across her face.

Tentatively, Charley reached out again and this time, when their fingers touched and the aura flared, she allowed Catherine to interlock fingers with her. Within a nano-second, Charley knew everything that had happened to Catherine in the intervening months. It wasn't like mind reading or thought-transference; it was as if Charley had lived through all of Catherine's experiences too. She just *knew* what had happened.

The aura faded leaving the two women sitting with their fingers still interlocked. "I can feel you," said Charley. "Can you feel me?"

Catherine nodded. "Finally you are real." A look of concern suddenly flashed across her face. "If I can see you as a real person maybe other people can. You could be in great danger." She pointed to the corner where Charley had appeared. "Hide there." She waited until Charley was enveloped in shadow again and then went to the door. "Waelheard."

The old man rose to his feet and shuffled to the door. "The night guards will be here soon, what do you want?"

Catherine lowered her voice to a whisper. "Remember I told you about my friend Charlotte?" Waelheard nodded. "If I told you she had come back and was in my cell, would you believe me?"

He peered through the bars and studied the cell. "It is empty. There is no one there."

"No one can see her but me but I think perhaps if you look hard enough, you *will* see her. Look into that far corner."

Waelheard squinted and shook his head. "Nothing but straw; you were dreaming." He turned back to his chair and settled down. "Get some sleep."

Catherine returned to Charley. "He cannot see you. Tomorrow you walk out with me."

oOo

Antoinette looked down at Charley's sleeping form. "Tomorrow we leave the site. What if she has not woken by then? We can't move her."

Greg looked around Richard's bedroom. "We'll be ok here for a couple of days."

"And then what?"

Shelly clicked her fingers. "Charley's flat." She beamed at the others. "Charley has an apartment in Greenwich, near the indoor

287

market."

"We can't move her," repeated Antoinette.

"I'm not suggesting we do; we'll have to stay here until she finishes this time jump and then she can take us to her flat so we can continue there." She looked at Antoinette's doubtful expression. "Annie, we need a plan…and this is a plan."

Greg concurred. "It's a good plan; better for Charley to be on familiar turf and it'll be safer too should Forrester come looking for her. She won't know about the flat."

Antoinette looked down at Charley again. "J'espère que Dieu la ramènera en sécurité" She saw Shelly's quizzical look. "I said I hoped God will bring her back safely"

Shelly smiled. "Amen to that, Annie."

oOo

"I am ready." Catherine adjusted Blood-Taker under her thick woven clothing so it didn't show.

Charley smiled. She had studied Saxon clothing fragments from other digs and what she was seeing here did not align with what she thought she knew.

The age of a woman would dictate her everyday clothing, usually a long dress, over which, if she was of child-bearing age, would be worn a Peplos; a long garment held together by a brooch at each shoulder. The dress under the Peplos would be tied with a strip of cloth, from which would hang the woman's tools of her trade, but Catherine's attire did not match this. Instead of a long over-head dress and a Peplos, she wore a long front-fastening garment over which was a Frankish-inspired front fastening jacket, secured by four brooches

Catherine noticed Charley's perplexed expression. "What ails you?"

"Your Saxon clothing is not as I believed it would be."

Catherine nodded. "I said to Waelheard that this is not clothing I have seen worn by the women, but he has told me it is favoured by the Saxon women in Ceint. Most of them are Frankish and this is how they dress."

This was history coming alive for Charley, which is exactly what she wanted to happen. "What now, Catherine?"

"Waelheard has resumed guarding me, so we wait for him to let us out and then…"

There was a scrape of metal as the door was unlocked; it silenced the women and they watched as Waelheard heaved open the heavy door. Wordlessly, he beckoned to Catherine and she slipped past him and into the courtyard of the fort. He didn't follow; he was supposed to be guarding her.

The courtyard was alive with activity as forty or more women gathered up their baskets and headed for the main gate. These were not menial women or slaves. These were wives and businesswomen who were collecting for their own trading benefits, or simply because they were enjoying the freedom given to Saxon women.

Catherine, with Charley in tow, joined them and pressed her way into the middle of the throng. As they reached the gates, a Saxon guard spotted her. "Hey you!" he shouted and took a pace forward. Catherine froze. She hadn't even made it through the gate before being recaptured, although her thoughts were with Waelheard who would be severely punished, if not killed, for allowing her to escape.

The guard pushed his way through the crowd and grabbed Catherine by the arm. "I do not know you. I know most of the women here."

Catherine batted her eyelids, "Only most? Well the gods must be smiling upon you now."

The guard leered. "Come find me when you return."

"I will," she replied and smiled at him coyly as she moved on with the rest of the crowd. They passed through the gates and hurried along the road that would take them north. "We are free Charlotte and now I have a very long journey home.

oOo

Waelheard stepped into the pale sunlight and shuffled over to Hengist who was standing in the lee of Timancius's chapel.

289

Hengist smiled at the old man. "It is done?"

"It is."

"And she suspected nothing?"

"Nothing my Lord."

"And is she going to find her husband?"

"Just as you said she would."

"That is good. We cannot get near King Vortigern, nor his other sons, but Vortiger is still searching for his wife and that makes him vulnerable. She is being followed so I am hopeful she will lead us right to him."

The old man scratched his head. "My Lord, I advised her to take her time and to be alert for spies. She may not be back with him for several moons."

"I am using my very best trackers. You have done well, Waelheard."

A look of regret crossed Waelheard's face. "I enjoyed her company; I will miss her."

CHAPTER 52
Márta (March) 452AD

Catherine darted up a side street away from the women who were headed for the woods to the West of the town.

"Where are we going?" asked Charley, breathless with the excitement of the adventure and the fact that Catherine could see her, hear her and touch her. She could not have been more real to the Priestess and yet be so invisible to everyone else.

"Waelheard cautioned me about returning directly. He said there may be spies about so I should take my time. Maybe find work in the fields."

Charley looked shocked. "But it's only about a hundred miles from here to Luton."

"Where?"

"Oh, I'm sorry. In the future, the location of the Avertci village will be called Gaddesden, after the River Gade that flows past it. There will be a big city nearby called Luton."

"A hundred miles will take four or five days to walk, but I must make that walk last at least until Meitheamh."

Charley searched her memory. Meitheamh was June, three months away. "Oh Catherine, I don't think I can stay with you for that long."

Catherine smiled. "I know but I have much to do on my way."

"Such as?"

"I must visit all the tribal villages on my way, to get support for King Vortigern."

Charley's face tightened. "You must be very careful; the Saxons control Kent and all the tribes this side of the Thames. Waelheard

291

could be right; there may be many spies or even common workers who would sell you back for a handful of coins."

"You speak true but I have no choice. The Saxons are spreading like a pox and I must stop them."

Charley nodded. "Many tribes will now be loyal to the Saxons, just so they can stay safe."

Catherine agreed. "There are only two tribes in Ceint; the Cantiaci, who I fear may be loyal, and the Atrebates, who have ties with the Catuvellauni north of the Tem. I must speak with them both."

Charley smiled. "Then we should not waste any more time."

oOo

Forrester rounded on Timancius. "I want to know exactly where Catherine goes."

The priest was weary of this apparition; no longer afraid of it, just tired to the bones of constantly being harangued and nagged. Forrester's image was now clear to him and it disturbed him how physically alike they were, as if they could be related.

She had taken to wearing Saxon styled clothing in the present, so that she appeared correctly dressed in the past. She felt at home in the period, as if she were in her comfort zone and although she gave Timancius a hard time and was still consumed with hate for Catherine and Charley, she actually felt less angry and more at peace.

"If we were married I would divorce you," he sneered. "I am going to visit Hengist and Horsa; do not follow me."

Forrester cackled. "As a good wife I must follow you...everywhere."

oOo

"Catherine, we are being followed." Charley jerked her head backwards. "Don't look back yet or they will know we've seen them."

They had just entered a small market square where a Christian church lay in smouldering ruins; the charred body of a priest was tied to a pillar outside. Charley pinched her nose and Catherine smiled. "The smell of burnt flesh is hard upon you?" Charley gagged in reply, which brought another smile from the priestess. "You have much to learn."

Despite the gruesome sight, the square was reasonably busy, with three or four stalls selling a limited range of goods and there were some townsfolk milling around. Most were dressed in Saxon garb, but there were many who were obviously Cantiaci tribes-people. Charley knew that this Kentish tribe, known as Kentings to many people, were good, solid fighters but sadly most had knuckled-under and submitted to Saxon rule. In fact she knew the Saxons would rule Kent for another three hundred years until the Danes arrived and took Thanet for themselves.

They stopped by a stall where a heavily pregnant woman was trying to sell some mouldy fruit. Catherine glanced back. "Where are these men you speak of?"

Charley turned to look. "I – I don't see them anymore."

"Perhaps you were mistaken."

"I wasn't," she replied more coldly than she intended.

Catherine flashed a look of anger at her and was about to say something about respect, but changed her mind; Now was not the time; she knew she was lucky to have such a woman as Charley by her side. "Come, we must hurry. I want to reach Faeferham before nightfall."

"Faversham," Charley mused and they strode towards the other side of the square. "In my time that town yielded the largest recorded find of Saxon glassware."

Catherine glanced back at her. "I still do not understand so much of what you say. You speak so..." She stopped mid-sentence, looking past Charley towards the stall they had just left. "The men you saw. How many?"

"Two." She looked back too. "That's them, Catherine. Should we run?"

Catherine pushed her out of her way and turned fully to face the two men. "I do not run. If they are only following us, they will stay where they are until we move on."

293

"And if they mean us harm?"

"They will answer my challenge." She reached into the folds of her clothing, pulled Blood-Taker free and began to walk slowly across the square.

At the sight of the determined priestess, sword drawn, jaw set firm and her eyes staring right into their souls, one of the men ran away. The other after his initial shock, grinned broadly and stepped away from the stall.

"Jeezus , it's like the gunfight at the OK Corral," Charley muttered as she moved cautiously off the square and into the lee of a nearby tannery. The stench of the urine used in the tannery process assaulted her senses and for the second time she gagged. "Remind me again why I love this period of history," she said to herself.

Charley watched as Catherine and the Saxon soldier circled each other in the middle of the square. He was a large man with long, light brown greasy hair. His face was badly scarred from too many battles, as were his bare arms. When he smiled he exposed a surprisingly intact set of clean, white-ish teeth.

"I recognise you," he snarled. "You were a prisoner at the fort."

The second man returned, shorter than his friend by a head and a half and sporting more fat than muscle. "She's a priestess, Goda, be careful. They say she has powerful gods."

Goda glanced at Leofa. "I know the stories, but if they were true, she would not have been Hengist's prisoner for so long."

"She's free now."

Goda grinned at Catherine. "No, Leofa you are wrong… she is *dead* now." He charged at her and swung his sword diagonally downwards to cleave Catherine's head from ear to chin, but Blood-Taker parried the strike with ease and sang out as it clashed with the Saxon's blade.

Catherine spun around on the spot, allowing Blood-Taker to scythe horizontally through the air. She was aiming to cut through the Saxon's leather jerkin and inflict a deep life-changing gash through his belly and into his kidneys. Goda read the move

294

perfectly and brought his own sword down hard to deflect Blood-taker. He used so much force that the sword was wrenched from Catherine's hand and skittered away across the ground.

He leapt forward, grabbed Catherine's hair and pulled her in close, his sword at her throat. "Hengist will pay me well for taking you back. Or I could just kill you here. No one would care." He looked about at the now deserted market place, but he had no doubt that there were many pairs of curious eyes watching the events unfold. "Maybe I should have some fun with you first, oh great priestess; what would you say to that, eh?"

He reached down below Catherine's waist and delved into her clothes and Catherine immediately plunged her hand down there too. Goda grinned again. "You can't stop me now." Unexpectedly, his fingers closed around something cold and sharp; a look of confusion spread across his face.

"You asked me what I'd say?" Catherine thrust her face up into Goda's. "I'd say goodbye." And she drove Fire-Sting into his stomach.

Goda's eyes opened wide in surprise as he tried to understand what had just happened, but his thoughts failed to solidify before he fell onto the hard earth. Leofa simply turned tail and ran.

Catherine watched Goda rolling around on the ground, clutching at his clothing. She watched as he bled-out, turning the hard earth into a dark crimson pool of mud. Slowly the villagers began to emerge from their hiding places and she heard someone say, "Be kind, finish him."

She looked up at the crowd that was gathering and nodded. She knelt and put a hand over his heart. Her eyes flared bright blue and Goda drew his last breath.

oOo

"You realise that Leofa will raise the alarm," panted Charley as she tried to keep up.

"He will not." Catherine was confident. They were heading towards the ruins of Canterbury with the intention of travelling the now famous Roman road, Watling Street, all the way to

Faversham. It was a journey that would take around five hours. The road they were on was moderately busy, mainly with wagons and carts and Catherine was considering hitching a ride to shorten their journey.

"I need a pee, Catherine."

The priestess looked puzzled so Charley crossed her legs and gave an exaggerated expression of pain. Catherine laughed and pointed to the tree line. "If you need to piss I will wait here for you." She moved to the side of the road where a large tree trunk lay. She sat down and said, "You can show yourself Leofa."

The Saxon emerged from the undergrowth. He was nervous; his face covered with sweat. "How did you know I was following you?"

Catherine didn't look at him. "You are not very good at hiding. Tell me, why do you follow me?"

Leofa stepped in front of her. "I wish to sit."

Catherine nodded to the tree trunk. "Then sit with me."

"You will not kill me?"

"Should I? Do I have reason to kill you?"

"No, but..." He paused, searching for the right words. "You killed Goda with just a look. I don't want you to look at me that way."

Catherine laughed. "Then do not give me cause. My dagger killed Goda. I simply helped him to meet his gods without pain." She studied the tubby the little man. He was obviously Saxon; his attire consisted of the usual coarse linen trousers, cotton shirt and fur tunic, but his hair had a Romanesque cut which jarred with the rest of his appearance. His small but alert eyes were deep set and overshadowed, literally, by big bushy eyebrows. His nose was large and pockmarked and his mouth was full and round. His facial features just did not match his Saxon origins.

"You are not a Saxon and I do not think you have ever been in a battle. You have no scars; your hands are not hardened. Who are you?"

Leofa stared at his feet. "I was captured by the Saxons when they first come to these shores. Until then I was known as Egnatius Drusus."

Catherine's eyes narrowed. "Roman?"

"My family was killed by a Saxon raiding party and I was taken as a slave but then they discovered I am educated. I can read, write and speak many languages, so they changed my name to Leofa and set me to teaching."

"I ask you again, why were you following me?"

"Goda recognised you. He said there would be a reward for returning you to the fort. That's all I know."

"He was correct. I am Catherine, Queen and Priestess of the Avertci."

"That much I know. Where are you going?"

Catherine reached out for Leofa's face. "Look at me." He obeyed with trepidation. Her eyes flared and he recoiled. "That is good Leofa. You are telling me the truth. I do not believe you will betray me."

At that moment Charley returned and stopped in amazement when she saw who was sitting on the tree trunk with Catherine. "Leofa? What the hell?"

Catherine raised a hand. "It is good, Charlotte. He will not harm or betray us."

The look on Leofa's face changed from puzzlement to fear. "Who are you talking to? There is no one there. Is it one of your gods."

A sly thought crossed her mind. "Yes, Leofa, it is one of my gods and she will be watching you."

Leofa cast his eyes to the ground. "I understand."

Charley sniggered. "So I am a god now? You praise me too much, my queen."

Catherine smiled broadly, enjoying the joke and then addressed Leofa. "We are going past Cant-wara-byrg and then to Faeferham."

"No, you cannot go near Cant-wara-byrg. There is a large army there helping to rebuild parts of the city. If Hengist and Horsa are looking for you, those men will have been told."

"Then how should we travel?"

Charley searched her memory. She had spent several childhood holidays at Whitstable and if they could get there, the A299 would take them straight to Faversham. She inwardly laughed at herself for referencing a modern major trunk road, but there was an excellent possibility that there would be another Roman road there or a cart track at least. "We go north," she said. "We can go to the sea and then to Faeferham."

Catherine looked doubtful. "It will add much time to the journey."

Leofa frowned. "What will?"

"Yes, but we can't continue along this road. North is our only option, *and* you're not in a hurry are you; you want to take your time, right?" said Charley.

"Yes you are right."

"I am? About what?" asked Leofa.

"Not you, Leofa. I was speaking to my God, Charlotte." She looked north. "We must go towards the sea and find another route to Faeferham."

"Then let me come with you." There was urgency in Leofa's eyes. "I cannot return to Sturigao. I need to be free. I can guide you on your journey."

Catherine stood up, "Very well, come with us Leofa and consider yourself a free man."

CHAPTER 53

Annie woke from her doze in the chair next to the bed to find Charley sitting up. "Oh my God, you're back. Are you ok?"

"I can't stay, I have to get back but I need something." Charley clambered from the bed. Richard had an OS map of Kent in the kitchen. I need it."

"I'll fetch it for you," said Annie and she hurried from the room.

Greg stretched and roused himself from a kitchen chair he'd taken to the bedroom. He looked doubtful. "You can't take it back with you. If you lost it…"

"If anyone found it, it would mean nothing. They would throw it away again."

"Why do you need it anyway?"

Catherine and I are travelling on foot to Faversham, but we need a circuitous route to avoid Canterbury. The Saxons are looking for her since her escape."

"Escape?"

"She's been a prisoner of the Saxons for months. I'm sorry but I must get back. Oh, and she can not only see me fully, but we have touched – actually touched. It was amazing."

"How do you know you'll return to her at the same point in time?"

"I don't, not for certain, but I seem to be taken to times when I'm needed and I'm definitely needed now."

Annie returned with a newish map and Charley grabbed it. "Thanks Annie." She spread it out on the floor and traced her finger across it until she found Sturry and Canterbury. "We need to take that road to Tylers Hill."

She traced from Tylers Hill north until the road bisected the A299. "How will I know which road to take to Faversham?"

"Look for the road that's been travelled the most, said Greg. "All east/west routes to a large town will be heavily used." He pointed eastwards to Reculver. "There's a coastal fort there founded by the Romans. There will be a connecting road for sure.

Charley climbed back into the bed and lay down, hugging the map to her chest. "How the hell I'm supposed to sleep now is beyond me." She looked up at Greg. "I love you big man. See you soon."

Greg leant down and kissed her lightly on the lips, but she had already gone.

oOo

"No, no, no, where is it?"

Catherine looked up. "You are back."

Charley looked around and was relieved to see they were still by the fallen tree. "How long was I gone?"

"Not long. You said you had to go back. I was sorely feared that I would not see you again."

Leofa looked quizzically at Catherine. "Your god?"

She nodded. "Charlotte, what have you lost?"

"I went back for a map. I wanted to see the best route. We need to turn right and then turn left and go to Tyler's Hill, though what it is called in this time, I don't know. Leofa, do you know a place called Tyler's Hill?" He shook his head and Catherine stood up.

"We must turn right and then go towards the sea."

"There is such a road about a mile ahead." He heaved himself to his feet. "This way."

What is now Tylers Hill was then just a collection of farmsteads and homesteads spread across the surrounding countryside. There was a small inn and several cottages, made from a mix of stone and straw. There appeared to be no one about as the three travellers passed through.

Leofa was now used to Catherine's apparent one-sided conversations with Charley; he paid no heed to anything she said

300

unless she addressed him directly.

"The sun is high. How long will this journey take?" asked Catherine.

Instinctively Charley looked at her wrist but her watch was not there. She'd left it behind realising that it was far too risky to bring such an object from the future into the past. "Maybe another four or five hours?"

Catherine seemed satisfied by that. "Leofa, when we get there I will seek out the chieftain."

"He is Faefer." Leofa replied.

"Of course," said Charley excitedly. "In my time we thought that this town's name was derived from the Latin, 'Faber' which means metal. Faversham was well known for its metal working."

"And now?"

"Many towns were named after their chieftain, in this case Faefer. Ham means home or village. Faeferham. Wow it all makes sense now."

oOo

Faeferham was a large town, much larger than Catherine's Avertci village. It too was encompassed by a high wooden palisade but here, the gate towers and sentry towers were made of stone and brick. The road was busy with traders and their carts and wagons and the town's gates were open. As they passed through, Catherine was immediately aware how many of the buildings had stone foundations or stone walls and she wondered if the Avertci had been too hasty to decry everything that the Romans had brought to Britain. Utilising stone would give her village much more resilience against attack and keep the interiors much dryer and warmer.

She approached a group of men standing outside a blacksmith's forge. "Where is Faefer?"

The men turned and looked appreciatively at her; despite the ravages of her captivity she was still a beautiful woman. "Who wants to know?" asked one.

"I am Catherine, queen and high priestess of the Avertci, north

301

of the Tem."

He looked her up and down and shook his head. "Queen? A queen without a horse or an army is not a queen."

Someone else shouted, "A queen dressed as a Saxon? Be gone, woman."

The men laughed and a particularly large man stepped forward to shove her in the chest. At the last second he spotted Fire-Sting in her left hand. "Ha! The lady has a dagger."

"Best you take if from her then, Broga," said one of the other men.

"Shall I take your pretty dagger, my queen?"

"You can try," said Catherine as she raised Fire-Sting towards him.

He roared with laughter, "Maybe I should just stick you with my own dagger." He thrust his hips forward and grabbed his crotch, looking to the other men for approval. Broga's laughter however was brought to an abrupt halt by an uncomfortable sensation in his groin. The other men stopped too when they saw shock and uncertainty on Broga's face. He looked at Catherine who flicked her eyes down and up again. He followed down where her gaze had been and saw Fire-Sting sticking into his trousers at crotch level.

Catherine applied a little pressure so that Fire-Sting's point pierced the fabric and nicked his flesh. "I will ask you one more time and if you fail to answer, I promise you will sire no more children. I expect your poor wife would be grateful for that. Where is Faefer?"

Broga moved backwards out of stabbing range and grabbed an iron rod from a rack by the forge. "Oh you want to play with Broga, yes? Well come on, let us play together." With a yell of rage he swung the rod at Catherine's head. In what seemed like a split second, Blood-Taker appeared in her other hand and she met the iron bar full-on. With a quick twist of the blade and a flick of her wrist, the iron bar was wrenched from Broga's hand and landed at Leofa's feet, He quickly kicked it out of Broga's reach..

Catherine held the point of Blood Taker's blade to Broga's throat. "Do not make me ask you a third time. Where is Faefer?"

"I am here. Who are you?" The voice, deep and resonant, came from behind her.

She lowered the sword and stepped away from Broga. She turned to see who claimed to be the Chieftain of Faeferham.

She gasped. Faefer reminded her so much of her father, Madron. He must have been similar in age and had the same large build, long hair and bushy beard. He was roughly the same height and he had the same granite eyes.

"I am Catherine, Queen of the Avertci."

Faefer looked at her in astonishment and then beamed from ear to ear. "Indeed you are. And you look even more like your mother than the last time I saw you."

"You know me?"

"I do. I was sorry to hear that your father has gone to the gods. Killed by Saxons?"

"Hengist and Horsa's army," she replied bitterly. "They attacked our village."

Faefer nodded sadly. "I heard. They attacked here too a long time ago. Come, we shall go to the Great Hall; we have much to talk about and there is someone I want you to meet."

He beckoned to Broga. "You insulted and attacked my guest, a guest who is also a queen." He drew his sword. "On your knees you turd." Faefer grabbed Broga by the neck and forced him to the ground. "Catherine, take his head if it pleases you."

Catherine stepped in front of the frightened man and looked over to Charley. "Well Charlotte, shall I take his head?"

Faefer and the other men looked about, confused. Leofa pointed in Charley's general direction. "She is talking to her goddess, Charlotte."

Charley looked horrified. "No, Catherine. Please don't."

Catherine smiled down at Broga. "Today will not be your last. My goddess Charlotte has decreed I should forgive you." She winked at Charley and tucked Blood Taker and Fire-Sting back into the folds of her clothing. "Get up and be gone."

For a moment it looked like Broga, beaten and embarrassed, was going to leave, but as he took a pace away, he suddenly drew his own sword and with a scream of rage, swung it at Catherine's neck.

She had no time to retrieve Blood Taker or avoid the blade that was scything through the air towards her; the blade that in a Nano second was going to end her life and send her to join her father and mother, Ailla.

Everything seemed to slow to a snail's pace. She saw Broga's face contorting with rage, his eyes narrowing, his nostrils flaring, his lips drawing tightly across his teeth, his mouth distorting into a fearsome snarl. She saw the blade slicing a wide arc through the air towards her. She saw the sunlight glinting on its polished surface; saw his fingers grasping the hilt so tightly his knuckles had turned white.

Then there was another movement; a second blade, this one wielded by Faefer, also slicing an arc through the air, but this one was not aimed at her. Just before Broga's blade reached Catherine's throat, Faefer's blade reached the back of Broga's neck. It sliced through flesh, sinew and vertebrae before Broga could even register what was happening. His head, cleanly separated from his body, spun into the air and landed at Catherine's feet.

But for Catherine it was too late. There was no way she could avoid Broga's sword, which had reached her throat. His headless body, propelled by momentum, would have completed what he had started, but for a third blade that suddenly appeared and clashed against Broga's. Both steel blades sang loudly as Broga's sword was deflected downwards. The sword and his body fell to ground.

Catherine staggered backwards, blood trickling from her neck and two strong arms grabbed and steadied her. "Still as headstrong as ever, my queen?"

She turned and gasped. "Taraghlan? By the gods, is it really you?"

"It is my lady," he laughed as she flung herself into his arms and hugged him tightly.

"I never thought to see you again." She kissed him full on the lips. "You are my saviour, Taraghlan, just as you were my father's." She pulled away and looked around excitedly. "Where is Vortiger? Is he here as well?"

"No my Lady. I have not seen him for several moons."

Faefer stepped between them. "This is who I wanted you to meet. Come. It is time to talk."

oOo

"So Vortiger knows I am alive?"

"He does, my lady. He never believed you were dead, although there were many who claimed you were. He sent spies into Cant-wara-byrg and Sturigao many times. He knows you were captive at Sturigao and I have heard he has tried at least twice to rescue you, but was beaten back before getting close to the town."

"But you have not been with him?"

"I had the Avertci to protect. We have formed an alliance with the Catuvellauni but with more Saxon and Jutes arriving each day, they are reluctant to fight them; as the Saxon numbers grow, opposition fades away."

Faefer nodded in agreement. "I lost many good men when they attacked here but they spared us. They want to rule and they want King Vortigern's head."

Catherine's cheeks flushed. "They shall not have it. I am making my way home, but I intend to gather a loyal army on the way."

Taraghlan took a swig of ale. "My lady, you cannot win."

"I can try."

The great hall was large, but compared to the warm outside temperature, it felt quite chilly inside. They were seated on wooden benches pulled closely to a roaring fire.

Something behind Catherine suddenly caught Taraghlan's eye and he squinted past her. "Who is that?"

Catherine turned and realised with shock that he was talking about Charley. "You can see her?"

"Of course I can see her. Who is she? Why is she dressed so?"

Faefer saw her too and rose from his bench. "Who are you? Come forward."

Charley looked down at her jeans and T-shirt and felt the world closing in on her. What should she do? She couldn't run or hide and she didn't want to return to her present yet. "Catherine, help me?"

Catherine stood and walked calmly to Charley's side where she placed an arm around her waist. Facing the two men she smiled benignly. "This is the earthly form of my goddess, Charlotte."

Shock and awe registered on Taraghlan's face and he dropped to his knees, but Faefer glared angrily. "A goddess? What magic is this?"

Taraghlan tugged at Faefer's sleeve. "Catherine is a powerful priestess, my lord; more powerful than you can imagine. If the gods come to *her,* then her magic is beyond anything we have ever seen. You should kneel."

Catherine beckoned to Taraghlan to stand. "This is the first time Charlotte has been seen by anyone but me. She has great wisdom and knowledge of the future. Be respectful and she will not harm you." Catherine threw a secretive wink at Charley who, emboldened by Catherine's confidence, took a step forward. She pointed at Faefer and at the floor. Faefer hesitated for a moment and then, with uncertainty leaking from every pore, slowly got down onto his knees.

"You may stand," said Charley, her voice surprisingly strong considering that her tummy was doing backflips.

Catherine guided Charley to the benches and they all sat again. Are the Cantiaci tribes loyal to Hengist and Horsa, or just obedient through fear?"

"You would do well to seek out the Atrebates tribes," Faefer replied, unable to take his eyes off Charley, who seemed to have a slight shimmering aura around her. "Most of the Cantiaci tribes will not help you."

Taraghlan agreed. "The Atrebates, to the West, are already

rebelling against the Saxons, but they are in disarray; they need a leader to guide them."

Catherine nodded. "When the Romans left, the Atrebates began to take back control of the land as far as Durocornovium."

"Close to King Vortigern," added Taraghlan.

"They are loyal to Vortigern," confirmed Faefer, "but he has already drawn most of his army from them. They have no more to give. That is why they are in disarray."

Charley coughed quietly and Catherine nodded at her to speak. "You should use a small army, maybe only a couple of hundred men. Send them out to bite the Saxons' heels. They can be defeated through stealth."

"We tried that!" snapped Taraghlan bitterly. "That's how Catherine was captured."

"I mean that you should send them out in small groups, maybe four or five men to each group. Send them into the heart of the Saxon strongholds, Cant-wara-byrg, Sturigao, Reculver, to the east and others to the West. Let them infiltrate, get to know people, ask the right questions. Maybe we can find out their weaknesses."

"Spies?" Faefer did not look impressed. "Spies get caught and tortured. The Saxons would learn of our plans very quickly."

Charley agreed. "But you also use them to dismantle their power bases."

Catherine, Taraghlan and Faefer looked blank. "What does she say?" Faefer asked Catherine.

Charley rephrased. "You use them to attack the Saxon strongholds. They can set fires, they can disrupt supplies, destroy winter crop stores. It is as I said... they should bite at Saxon heels."

Although Charley spoke with earnestness and enthusiasm, she knew that the course of history was not about to be changed. The Jutes were settling across the south, the Angles were taking over much of the East, and more were coming every day; not with spears and swords, but with wives, children and chattels. It was, for the most part, an economic invasion, an inveigler's invasion, a bloodless invasion.

As she brought these facts into sharp focus, she felt a stab of pain cut through her heart. For the first time, she accepted that she couldn't and shouldn't do anything to prevent Catherine's death at Hengist's hands. Antoinette was right; any change, no matter how small, would have devastating consequences for current and future generations.

Taraghlan thought about Charley's plan and then broke into a smile. "My Lady I think your goddess is right. We could learn much and maybe destroy their morale if nothing else. If you agree, I will leave for King Vortigern's castle tonight and start arrangements."

"Do you know where I can find Vortiger?"

Taraghlan shook his head. "Not really. The last I heard he was hiding in an old stone cottage in woodland south of Saedingburga"

"Sittingbourne," thought Charley, although woodland was pretty sparse there in the twenty-first Century.

"Then I must go to him."

"It will take you about three hours if we walk," volunteered Charley, "or less than two if we ride."

Catherine shook her head. "You are not coming with me."

"But..." Charley was horrified.

"I command you to go with Taraghlan or go back to your own time. You may choose, but come with me, you will not."

"Why, Catherine?"

"My time with Vortiger will be private and you can serve me better by staying with Taraghlan and advising him. If you cannot do that, then go home."

Faefer looked shocked. "She commands a goddess?" he whispered.

Taraghlan looked afraid too. "I fear she does, Faefer. Her magic is beyond anything you know. I have learned not to challenge her, beyond giving wise council."

Charley's eyes narrowed. For the first time she felt hostility towards Catherine. She didn't appreciate being side-lined, especially after everything she had done for her. She did not want to return to her own time, but at that moment, she felt petulant enough to just sod-off and leave her to fend for herself.

Catherine lowered her voice. "Or, you can find that other woman from your time."

Charley's mouth gaped. "You mean Forrester?"

"She visited me when I was Hengist's prisoner. She is evil and is under Timancius's power."

Charley snorted. "More like he's under her control."

"She is a threat to me. She will get me killed. If you really want to serve me, then find her, in this time or yours... and kill her!

CHAPTER 54
Márta (March) 452AD

Rosemary Forrester awoke with a start and a sharp intake of breath. For a moment she couldn't remember where she was, but as she looked around her room in the stone-built house she had adopted for her own, she was reassured that she was still in Sturigao. She shivered; something had woken her. A dark feeling of foreboding began to envelope her, like the thundery clouds outside that were spreading their malevolent shadows across the dawn landscape.

She rose from her bed, slipped her gown over her head to cover her scrawny body and stepped outside, into what promised to be a stormy day ahead. No one but Timancius could see her, but the townsfolk could feel her presence. No one would go near the house she had chosen to live in; it was possessed by evil spirits they said. That amused Forrester; she liked the idea that people perceived her as evil.

As the first determined raindrops fell, she padded barefoot across the street to Timancius's temple. Before long there would be a deluge that would turn the streets to thick, cloying mud.

"Someone wants me dead," she said as she strode into Timancius's room at the back of the temple.

The priest sat up in his cot and rubbed his eyes. "That would be me, you old crow. It is still dark. What do you want?" He relit a reed torch from the embers of his fire.

"It's daytime," she snapped and pulled the wooden shutter from the window. "Someone wants to kill me. I dreamt it and it woke me."

Timancius groaned. "Why tell me this? Why should I care?"

"Because I believe it is Catherine who wants me dead and if I let her find me you could be rid of her once and for all."

Timancius smiled. "Use you as bait and set a trap?"

"She won't come back to Sturigao, but what if we travelled north of the Thames? She will be making her way back to her beloved Avertci. We could find a town, lay a trap and let it be known I am there."

Timancius shook his head. "A long time could pass before she learns you are there. I do not have time for that."

"Then I will find her instead."

"And do what? Her magic is powerful."

A slow smile spread across her gaunt face. "I could kill Chandler-Price instead. That would attack Catherine's heart - maybe weaken her."

"You told me you tried and failed to kill her before."

"Not this time. This time I *will* kill her."

There was movement at the door and Hengist strode in. He faltered at the sight of the woman standing next to Timancius's cot. "Who is this?"

Timancius was shocked. "You can see her?"

"Of course I can see her. A lot more bony than your usual women... and a lot older too." He stepped forward for a better look. "A *lot* older." Forrester stepped forward to protest but Hengist waved her away. "Leave us."

Timancius saw the anger in her eyes and raised a hand to stop her from saying anything. "Do as my lord Hengist says or it will be bad for both of us."

Forrester glared at the two men and swept from the room with her pinched nose held haughtily high.

Hengist shook his head in disbelief. "By the gods, you can do better than that sour-faced vulture."

"She plagues me, day and night."

Hengist drew his sword. "I can deal with that for you."

Timancius laughed. "My Lord, I promise you would fail. She has some magic about her."

311

Hengist's eyes narrowed. "Should I be concerned?"

Timancius shook his head. "No my Lord, she will not harm any of us. She has her sights set elsewhere."

Hengist shrugged and sheathed his sword. "Horsa is riding west with a small army. We have had word that Catherine is at Faeferham."

Timancius clapped his hands together. "That is good news indeed my lord. Maybe now she will die."

Hengist looked puzzled for a moment and then he remembered that Timancius had not been party to Catherine's escape plan. "Ahh, Of course, I did not tell you, but I do not want her dead… not yet."

"My Lord?"

"Catherine did not escape; I let her go. I need Vortiger dead and have wasted too much time looking for him. He no longer comes to us, so I need her to lead us to him."

Timancius was shocked and angry that the Saxon brothers had excluded him from their scheme. He thought he had their trust, but it seemed that trust was only apparent when they wanted something from him. "Then why is Horsa riding out to capture her?"

"He is not. We just need her to think we are still searching for her. I do not want her to settle in Faeferham for too long. I want her flushed out and on the road again."

"And you have spies?"

"She is being followed, yes. You will ride with Horsa. It will look more convincing if her greatest opponent is looking for her too."

Timancius inwardly shuddered; he hated horses. "When do we leave?"

Hengist chortled. "Now."

oOo

"Catherine, if I kill Forrester it will change nothing. You are not destined to die by her hand…" Charley faltered and cursed herself for giving too much away. She was sitting at Catherine's feet in the chamber that Faefer had made available for them.

"But she can change the future by her actions, is that not right?"

"Yes, but..."

"Then you must stop her. You tell me her body is still in the future, as is yours?"

"Yes. It's hard to explain but..."

"Will dying in the past, kill her earthly body in the future?"

"Yes I believe so. I have had many injuries here that were still present when I woke up in the future."

"Woke up? So your earthly body is asleep?"

"Yes."

"And vulnerable. She could find and kill you in your future, while you sleep."

"I have people protecting me."

"Does she also have people protecting her while she sleeps?"

Charley had to think about that. Forrester was still in hospital in a 'coma,' but would she be under police guard? "I can't be sure, but probably, yes."

Catherine bit her lip. "Then you must do it here, in my time."

Charley could feel her eyes tearing-up. "Catherine, I'm no warrior. I've never ever killed anyone. I don't know how to use a sword..."

"But only you and I can see her so I cannot send Taraghlan; it has to be you."

Catherine suddenly stood and walked to her window, her head cocked to one side. After a moment she turned back into the room and her eyes flared blue. "Saxons are coming. They know I am here."

Charley leapt to her feet. "Then you must leave; take Taraghlan and go now - *please.*"

Catherine just smiled. "You know how I am to die?"

Charley cursed herself again. "Yes."

"Is it here, today?"

"I don't know when exactly."

"At whose hand?"

313

Charley looked distraught. "Catherine if I tell you, then you might be able to avoid it. If you live after you are supposed to have died, it will change everything about the future."

"My death is written by the gods; it cannot be changed. It matters not if you tell me." Catherine took Charley's hand and stared into her face. For a split second her eyes flared an even brighter blue. "Ahh, I see it now. I will die at Hengist's hand." She turned away, deep in thought and Charley saw a look of pain appear on her face.

"I wish you hadn't done that, Catherine."

Catherine stared out of the window and blinked back her tears. "So I am to be defeated by the Saxons and killed by Hengist." She looked up at the stormy sky. "Then why am I doing all this? If I cannot free my people from the Saxons, what is the point of it all?"

Charley stood behind her, wrapped her arms around her waist and hugged her tightly. "The point is your people need hope, even when there is none. Every Briton needs hope. The Saxons have rampaged across the land burning towns and villages, raping young girls and killing whole families. They mean to beat you, and everyone else, into submission so they can take full control from Vortigern. They are invaders. They want to settle here and make this their home. They will breed and breed again, the Jutes, the Franks, the Angles; they will interbreed and they will breed with the Britons until they are merged and become known as the Anglo-Saxons. They will form the basis of British history, they will rule for hundreds of years, at least until the Danes invade and..." She stopped, suddenly acutely aware that her passion for history had taken over and that Catherine didn't want or need to hear about the future in such detail. "I-I'm sorry, Catherine, that must be hard to hear."

Catherine just stared up at the dark foreboding sky, still blinking back her tears, and said nothing.

"My Lady?" Taraghlan entered the room. "I've had a report that..."

"Yes, I know. The Saxons are coming," she said sadly and

pulled away from Charley's embrace.

Taraghlan smiled. "I should have known you would know before me." Catherine turned to face him and he saw a look of utter sadness on her face. Her normally bright eyes, were dull and dark. "My Lady?" He quickly crossed the room and reached out to offer some comfort, but she pushed his hand away.

"I am done," she said. "I have no strength or will to fight anymore." A shocked Taraghlan opened his mouth to say something but she raised her hand to stop him. "I will go home and send messengers out to find Vortiger. Maybe we can have a small future together before Hengist sends me to the gods."

"I don't understand, my Lady. What has happened?"

Charley turned away, tears streaming down her face. She felt destroyed. She had blurted out secrets that might not change the future, but had changed Catherine. She couldn't bear to see this strong beautiful and powerful woman so broken. She couldn't undo her mistake, but she could at least ensure she didn't make any more.

She slipped into a dark corner of the room and sat on the floor. "Time to wake-up," she whispered to herself. "And never come back."

oOo

"She's back!" Greg helped Charley to sit up as Antoinette and Shelly ran into the room.

"Oh thank God you're back." Antoinette started to pull the covers from the bed. "We can't stay here any longer. The site has been restored, everyone but us has left and the Chairman of the Governors is due here any moment to inspect the place."

"That's fine by me," said Charley despondently. "I'm not going back anyway." Greg and Antoinette both stared at her in amazement. Charley lay back again. "What? I *can* choose not to go back, you know."

Greg sat on the bed. "What's happened?"

"Nothing; let's just get out of here."

oOo

315

"You can drop me at the train station."

Greg threw the last of Charley's bags in the back of his Volkswagen campervan and opened the passenger door for her. "No chance. Get in."

"I'm serious, Greg." She clambered in. "I don't feel like company."

Greg climbed in to the driver's seat. "Well, you've got it and you're not getting out until you've told me what happened back there."

Charley stared down at her feet. "Nothing happened."

Greg depressed the accelerator and the aged beast struggled out of the school grounds and into the lane. "Don't lie to me. Something happened to make you fall out of love with time travel and I want to know what it was. We've all put ourselves out for you. We've got into all sorts of trouble because of you and people are dead…"

"Because of me?" Charley interrupted.

"I didn't say that."

"You were going to. Because I found the brooch, because I kept going back, Forrester got involved and Walter died. And because Richard fell in and out of love with me, he's dead too. All of it bound together by this bloody stupid time travel."

"Oh get over yourself. Forrester killed Smith, not you. She has free will, you didn't make her kill him, *she* chose to do that. The same with Armitage. Whatever went on with you two, he's the one who turned violent and he made his own choice to commit suicide. Again, you didn't make him."

"But…"

"But, nothing. I was going to say that we all put ourselves out for you, people have died in the process and now, suddenly, you don't want to know any more. It's not good enough; you owe us an explanation."

Charley continued to stare at her feet. She could feel her cheeks beginning to heat up and there were tears stinging her eyes. "I fucked-up," she said quietly.

Greg turned on to the local High Street and started to look for signage to the M2. "What did you do?"

"I inadvertently told Catherine that she dies at Hengist's hands."

Greg's eyebrows shot up and he stamped on the brakes. The driver of a thirty ton grain lorry behind them, blasted his air horns as he swerved and thundered past. Greg just stared at Charley in disbelief.

"Don't look at me like that; it wasn't intentional."

"Jeezus, Charley."

"I know, I know. Just drive, will you? We're getting funny looks."

As they set off again, Greg quickly glanced at her. "So what now? Have you been banished from the court of Queen Catherine?"

Charley glared at him. "You're making jokes? Really? If you must know, she took it with incredible stoicism. I told her she mustn't try to change what happens and she just said that if the gods had decided Hengist was to kill her, nothing she could do would change it."

"Something more than that happened, Charley; you wouldn't have come back just because you let the cat out of the bag."

Fresh tears trickled down her cheeks. "Something else did happen. My telling her has effectively destroyed her. She now knows she can't beat the Saxons, so she's just given up. She intends to return home and find Vortiger."

"Surely that's a good thing."

"That's not the point. It's what I've done to her I can't live with. The light has gone out of her eyes – literally – She seems to have lost her soul. I can't bear it." Charley let out a juddering sob, adjusted her seatbelt and curled up on the seat, her back towards Greg. For once the big man was lost for words.

"Oh and she wants me to kill Forrester."

oOo

The server returned to the table and held out the coffee pot. "Refill?"

Greg waved her away, but Charley held out her mug. "Thanks." She waited until the waitress had filled it and was out of earshot. "And that's about everything. What do I do? She expects me to kill her and I don't think she cares whether I do it here or back there."

Greg looked alarmed. "You're not considering it surely? Charley, you can't! We've just had a conversation about how Smith and Armitage's deaths weren't your fault, but now…?" He left the sentence hanging

"Of course I'm not. I'm a frigging archaeologist not a murderer."

Greg looked around the American styled roadside diner as he pondered on their next course of action. Greg had used this particular establishment many times on his travels and loved it. The service was quick, the coffee very tasty and food was delicious. Today however, he had no appetite and the coffee tasted insipid.

"Sweetheart, I really do think you need to go back." Charley was about to object but Greg put his finger to her lips. "Let me finish. Three things spring to mind. First, you can't leave it like this; you need closure or you'll rip yourself apart. You'll be wracked with guilt and you'll just keep going over it all until you implode."

Charley stared out of the window, her eyes were filling up again.

"Secondly, you owe it to Catherine. You entered her life uninvited and became part of her personal story. You can't just vanish and leave her to deal with the aftermath of the problems you might have caused by revealing secrets about her future." He placed his hand on hers.

She nodded and dropped her hand on top of his. "And thirdly?"

"And thirdly, I love you so much and I can't bear to see you so unhappy. You have an affinity with that era; it's almost as if that's where you belong, and you *need* to see how this all plays out. Remember your original reason for going back… to bring the past to life, to fill in some of the gaps in our knowledge about the Dark

318

Ages? You have unfinished business there."

"I'm scared." Charley's lip was quivering.

Greg reached up and rubbed away one of her tears with his thumb. "So am I."

She stared out of the window. "Where do you live? You've never told me."

"To be fair, you've never asked. I have a house in Essex, near Colchester. Why?"

"Can we go there? I don't want to go back to London at the moment."

Greg smiled. "Of course."

They began to gather up their things when Charley suddenly stopped and grabbed Greg's hand again. "Hang on. Did you just say you loved me?"

Greg just smiled and went to pay the bill.

CHAPTER 55
Márta (March) 452 AD

Faefer tapped lightly on the doorframe of Catherine's room. "I have some news." He entered with Taraghlan and waited for the sad and defeated Catherine to acknowledge their presence, but she just stared out of the window, so he continued. "My lady, my spies have news for you. The Saxons are close. If you leave now you will be safe, but delay and it will be too late."

"Let them come," she said quietly. "I will never be safe."

Faefer looked pleadingly at Taraghlan for help. "Say something, Taraghlan."

Taraghlan looked angrily at his queen. "What about Vortiger? I thought you were going to return to the village and wait for him."

Catherine turned back into the room. "My vision is clouded. I cannot tell if I will even live to see him again."

"You *will* die if you stay here. The gods did not plan for you to die here."

"You cannot know that."

"Then why did they tell you the Saxons are coming? They want you to live. It is not your time. My lady you must leave...Please!"

Faefer held out a small parchment scroll. "My Lady, my spies also had news about Prince Vortiger." He has moved further west and for the moment is living in woods by a small Roman village called Noviomagus. It is where the long Roman road crosses the River Cray."

Catherine rubbed her eyes with the heel of her hand and straightened her posture. "Faefer, thank you. That is good to know." The news about Vortiger seemed to have resonated. In her mind she was now formulating what to do next.

Taraghlan smiled. "You seem to have made a decision? The light is back in your eyes."

She returned his smile "Yes, you are right; the gods would not have warned me unless I was to live and find my husband." Catherine's familiar steely grit had resurfaced. "Faefer, how far is this place?" She began to push her few clothes into a bag and once again hid Blood-Taker and Fire-Sting beneath her gown.

"A day's ride to the West, close to the Tem," he replied.

"He must be intending to cross the Tem north of Darentford," offered Taraghlan.

"Get someone to fetch me a horse, Faefer." Catherine stepped up close. "Are you feeling unwell?"

He grimaced slightly. "To be true my Lady, I feel dead inside. I have no energy to fight anymore. Perhaps it is my age."

Catherine gave him a hug and her eyes flared blue. Faefer jumped away which made her laugh. "How do you feel now?"

He felt himself, like a man checking his clothes for loose change. "I feel strong. I feel powerful. Let the Saxons come. What did you do to me?""

"My gift to you, Faefer. Give good account of yourself and kill as many Saxons as you can.

He stepped back and bowed. Whatever magic this woman possessed, it was powerful.

"I'm coming with you, Catherine." Taraghlan was determined.

"You may, as far as the Roman road. But after that, I must go alone." Vortiger was so close, she could almost taste him. As she headed for the door, she stopped and stared into the darkest corner of the room. "You too, Charlotte; you will ride next to me. You give good counsel."

Charley's sad and dejected figure stepped from the shadows and stood before her queen, her eyes cast downwards with guilt and the weight of the world on her shoulders. She didn't know what to say. Was there anything she could say?

Catherine reached out and stroked her cheek. "I was too harsh with you. Forgive me?"

"Forgive you? It was I who crushed *your* spirit. It is I who needs forgiveness." She hesitated. "If it pleases you to do so."

Catherine smiled. "I forgive you. Will you come with me?"

Charley nodded. "I will come with you as far as Taraghlan is allowed, then you must be with Vortiger…alone."

"My Lady," said Taraghlan, "when we leave you, we will ride to the ford across the River Darent and will wait there for you and Vortiger. You may need my sword arm before you reach home."

Catherine smiled a bright, sunny smile. "No, Taraghlan. I want you to go straight home and tell the Elders and my people that I am alive and well. I will come to you there."

"You are happier now?"

"I am. The gods have decided my path, which now leads back to Vortiger and for the moment that is all I want. Soon I will be back with the Avertci and I shall live there as their queen until Hengist fulfils the Gods' wishes. Now come." She strode purposefully from the room and into the stormy weather.

oOo

"The Queen has left Faeferham my Lord." The scout dismounted and wrenched a horn of ale from a young warrior's hand. He chugged the contents and threw the horn back at the lad's feet.

Horsa smiled. "That is good. Follow her; take three more scouts with you."

The man sneered. "I do not need more men. They will delay me. I will go alone."

Horsa grabbed the scout and shoved him hard against a tree. "Argue with me and I will gut you like a pig." The man was about to struggle when he felt the sting of Horsa's dagger in his groin. Horsa leant in until he was nose to nose with his warrior. "If my blade slips, you will be cock-less, so say nothing to anger me." The man nodded and Horsa relaxed his grip. "You will be no match for Catherine if she uses magic. You *must* take three men with you… or you can argue and die. I can always find another scout to replace

322

you."

The man nodded again and Horsa released him. He walked away to jeers and catcalls from his fellow warriors and set about finding three more suitable scouts to ride with him.

Timancius scurried forward. "My Lord, I am told that the news of our arrival here has reached Faefer and that Catherine has gone."

Horsa glared at the priest with ill-disguised contempt. "I know that already. Tell me something useful, like, where they are going."

"I do not know, my Lord."

Horsa sucked air over his teeth and turned to his commander. "Now that I know she has gone, we shall continue to Faeferham and wait for news from the scouts."

His commander smiled. "Then we ride out to kill Vortiger?"

"Oh no," said Horsa with relish, "Then we return to Sturigao because the scouts will have already killed him."

oOo

An hour into their journey and the rain was lighter, although the wind was harsh and cold. It whipped the tops off the puddles that lay in the potholes and cart tracks and bent the branches of the trees that lined the roadside. The clouds were lightening and scudding more quickly across the grey sky.

Even though Catherine had lent Charley a thick woollen cloak, she was soaked to the skin. Her horse was a tired old dapple-grey mare that was grateful for the slow progress they were making. She was riding side-by-side with Catherine, whilst Taraghlan and Leofa, who had insisted on travelling with them, were riding ahead.

"So you are fond of your queen, Taraghlan?" he asked.

"I have known her since she was born. Her father was the King of the Avertci and my best friend. He was killed when Hengist and Horsa attacked the village."

Leofa rubbed his bushy eyebrows to dislodge the heavy raindrops that continually dropped onto his face. "I am sorry to hear that. How long to Noviomagus do you think?"

Taraghlan shrugged. "It will probably take a day in this rain. I am told you are Roman by birth, and educated too. Did you live in the Roman towns with their stone houses?"

"I did. How I long for that comfort again."

Taraghlan chuckled. "Not many left now. Most have been destroyed."

"The Saxons are rebuilding them. Look at **Durovernum Cantiacorum**, or Cant-wara byrg as you call it. You still live in homes made from straw and mud. I know which I prefer."

Charley laughed. "Listen to those two putting the world to rights."

Catherine shook her head. "You still use words I do not understand."

Charley agreed. "I know and I'm sorry. You speak a Gaelic dialect that no one would understand in my time and yet somehow I understand everything you say. I understand everything the Saxons say too. It's as if my brain has been wired with an in-built translator."

Catherine laughed. "Again, I understand many of your words, but not much of what you actually say."

The four continued on their journey north, heads down against the wind and all feeling chilled. Catherine's gods seemed to have their heads down too, otherwise she'd have known there were four more riders on that road, about half a mile behind them; riders who meant to kill her and Vortiger as soon as the opportunity presented itself.

oOo

Timancius paced angrily around the room he'd been given at Faeferham.

The arrival of the Saxon army had been greeted with little interest by the townsfolk; they knew they were now under Saxon rule and were compliant. Faefer had welcomed Horsa, his commanders and Timancius, and was showing them lavish hospitality; he was playing the long game; outwardly accommodating, whilst inwardly praying to his gods that Catherine would not give up her fight. The Britons needed a strong and charismatic leader and he knew she was it.

Timancius was not interested in Faefer's hospitality. When the army arrived in the town, Horsa had failed to introduce him or include him in any conversations with the Faefersham Ealdormen and he felt slighted, excluded and unvalued.

It was obvious that his usefulness as an advisor had come to an end. Admittedly he had been allowed to create his own temple in Sturigao but Hengist had recently made comments about dedicating it to his own gods. The brothers had even allowed building to start on a new Christian church in Canterbury after an appeal by some priests.

Timancius was plotting again and it felt good.

"You're a spineless turd, Timancius." Forrester stepped in front of him to stop his pacing. "I would never let Horsa disrespect me the way he disrespects you."

"And yet you stood there and did nothing…just like me, so be quiet woman."

Forrester stepped back and squinted at him. "You are planning something. What?"

Timancius sat himself on a cushioned bench by the empty fireplace. "Hengist and Horsa had no intention a capturing Catherine. They wanted to flush her out and have her run to her beloved Vortiger. I care nothing for him, but I want her dead…now."

"So what will you do?"

"What I do best; find some decent fighters, preach to them and put the fear of the gods into them. They will be too afraid not to do my bidding. They will be compelled to follow me."

"Follow *us,* where?"

"To find that Avertci bitch before she finds Vortiger."

Timancius's plan however, failed spectacularly. He found a small band of mercenaries at an ale house and attempted to bombard them with claims that he was the gods' priest on earth, and dark warnings about their fate should they disobey him.

Unfortunately for Timancius, the men were godless. They worshiped only the spoils they were paid for their services. Instead of fearfully complying with his orders to follow him away from the town, they laughed and jeered. Eventually one large warrior picked him up and threw him into the muddy street. Timancius had to skulk away with the sound of their cheers and Forrester's derision, ringing in his ears. He had no choice but to collect his pack, his sword and dagger, and ride out to find her on his own.

"Where do you think you're going?" Forrester screamed at him as he mounted his horse. "You're going nowhere without me."

In answer he kicked her hard in the chest and spurred his horse to the city gates. He was on his own now and he *would* find and kill Catherine.

CHAPTER 56
Aibreán (April) 452 AD

Charley looked up at the starlit sky and the new moon. "Another month begins," she said to herself. "What will happen I wonder?"

"I wonder that too," responded Catherine.

Charley winced. "Are none of my thoughts private anymore?"

Catherine laughed and stood up. "I will leave you to your thoughts," she said and wandered over to Taraghlan who was keeping watch at the edge of the forest clearing. "Is all in good order?"

He looked at her and smiled. "It would seem so." Are you going to tell me more about your 'Goddess' Charlotte?"

Catherine feigned hurt. You think there is more to know? Do you not believe what I have told you?"

Taraghlan laughed. "She has strange powers I am sure, but a goddess she is not. Who is she?"

Catherine cast a quick glance in Charley's direction. "I do not know. She came to me unasked. At first I could only feel her presence. Then I could hear her in my mind. Later I could see her and after that I could speak to her, and now all see her. Who else can she be but one of the gods?"

"Maybe I should ask her. She will answer to me." He placed his hand on the hilt of his sword but Catherine grabbed his wrist.

"No, Taraghlan. She is my friend. She is serving me in ways you could not understand. Leave her alone."

Taraghlan relaxed. "Very well. It is time you slept my lady. Tomorrow we complete our journey to Noviomagus and then you will be on your own."

327

Catherine nodded and padded back to where Charley was now lightly dozing. She settled onto the hard ground, close to the fire and closed her eyes.

About an hour later, she woke with a start. Something, or someone, was coming slowly through the woods. She looked about the camp; the fire had died down and was just a bed of glowing embers, Taraghlan and Charley were now asleep and Leofa, who was supposed to be on guard duty, appeared to be dozing too.

Slowly, she reached beneath her pack, pulled out Fire-Sting and peered into the woods. She gave a sharp intake of breath and her eyes flared blue. *Timancius.*

Carefully, she stood up and pulled a dark cloak about her, then slipped noiselessly into the cover of the trees. She could sense exactly the direction to take and she quietly followed a track further into the woods.

Suddenly he was there, right in front of her, His one good eye, narrowed and menacing, was staring straight at her. How had she not known?

With a croaky laugh he lunged at her with a sword. Catherine easily side-stepped the blade and sprung away out of its reach. He glanced down at Fire-Sting. "Is that all you have, that pathetic little dagger?"

Catherine began to circle the Priest. "It is all I need. Why are you here, Timancius? You are no fighter; you must know that you cannot match my skills and I sense you are alone, so why?"

In reply, Timancius lunged at her again. This time there was a tree in her way so she could not side-step the blade; instead, she had to jump backwards. Its point nicked some threads on her cloak, which she threw off; it was hampering her.

"You have wanted me dead from the day I was born, Timancius. Is that because I have real powers and you have none? Is it because you knew I would rise to be the priestess of the Avertci, the tribe you subjugated through fear? Or is it because you know my mother lives on in me and you are frightened of her? You know her powers are unstoppable."

Timancius snarled, exposing his yellow teeth. "I would have killed your mother too if you had not killed her first."

Catherine's grip tightened on Fire-Sting but she did not attempt to attack him. She knew he was goading her; trying to get her to make the next move so he could cut her down.

"Did you know that Madron was not her first?" he continued. "She slept with most of the men in the village. In fact I know that Madron was not even your true father."

"Enough, Timancius," Catherine's eyes flared and Timancius recoiled. "You are weak, Timancius; weak, cruel and ambitious, and that is a dangerous combination. Remember what happened the last time you threatened my life?" She pointed at his eye. "How does it feel to know a mere child did that to you?"

Timancius screamed like the tortured soul he was and lunged at Catherine one more time. This time she side-stepped the blade and crashed into him. As they fell to the ground, his sword skittered across the forest floor and they landed with Catherine on top. He screamed at her again and rolled her off. He was then on top of her in a flash with his hands around her throat, but as he attempted to throttle her, Catherine smiled and looked purposefully at his waist.

Timancius followed her gaze and saw Fire-Sting buried in his stomach. "NO! You bitch!" His sword was just within reach and he quickly grabbed it by the blade and held it across Catherine's neck. "You may have wounded me, but now, at last, you will die. I will send your head back to your beloved Vortiger, so he may weep over it."

He pressed down hard; the double-edged blade cut into his hands and his blood dripped onto Catherine's neck. In response, she pulled Fire-Sting from his stomach and plunged it into his neck. An arc of blood spurted from his severed artery and he looked at her in bewilderment. "What have you done?" He let go of the sword blade and reached up to his neck. His fingers found the dagger and traced the blade back to its hilt. "You have killed me?"

Catherine smiled again. "I have, Timancius. You may go and

join your gods…if you have any" She heaved his weight to one side and he tumbled onto the forest floor where he lay jerking and coughing. There was a look of sheer terror in his one good eye as his blood spurted and coloured the ground crimson. As the flow eased he fixed Catherine with one final malevolent stare. "Bitch," was the last word he ever said.

Charley, Leofa and Taraghlan ran into the clearing. Taraghlan dropped down by her side. "You are hurt?"

"No. It is not my blood. It is his." She gestured to the body beside her.

"Who is that?" He rolled the body over and gasped. "Timancius? You fought with him?"

Charley hunkered down too. "Why did you fight him? When you took his eye, you simply paralysed him."

Catherine reached out to Taraghlan who hauled her to her feet. "Tell me Charlotte, where would the fun be in that?"

oOo

"Her BP's dropped like a stone," shouted the senior ward nurse. "Crash trolley! *Now* please!" She rushed over to Forrester's comatose body and screamed. There was a deep puncture wound in her belly that was bleeding profusely and another in her neck from which blood was spurting, turning the bedding a sodden red and the floor crimson and slippery. How was this possible?

The crash team rushed in just as the monitor flat-lined. One of the nurses slipped and fell in the blood as others crowded around and attempted to stem the flow.

"It's too late," cried one. "She's lost so much blood she's almost dry."

Consultant, Alexander McGregor rushed into the mayhem. "Turn that damned machine off, I can't hear myself think!" He quickly surveyed the scene of carnage. "Step away from the bed. There's nothing we can do for her. Who is in charge here?"

The senior nurse stepped forward, shakily. "That was me."

"Was anyone else in here? Visitors, police, axe murderers?"

"No, no one. I-I was on my own."

330

McGregor looked at her over the top of his rimless spectacles. "Then would you care to explain to me how this patient has just been stabbed twice and bled to death?"

oOo

Taraghlan returned from a quick scouting mission. He had wanted to make sure that Timancius had been acting alone and didn't have Horsa's army in tow. "It is all clear, My Lady."

Catherine looked up at the lightening sky. The clouds had gone and it promised to be fair weather. She took that as a good omen. "Taraghlan, we should leave now. We can be at Noviomagus before the sun is high."

He nodded in agreement. "My Lady, does your goddess, Charlotte know how to fight?"

Catherine cast a glance over her shoulder to where Charley was dampening down the final embers of the fire. "I do not know. But should a goddess know how to fight?" She winked at him and went to gather up her things.

Just before noon they reached the village of Noviomagus. Being of Roman origin it was almost entirely stone-built. Some of the homes still sported tiled roofs, but many were now made of thatch. It was not a walled town, just a collection of dwellings clustered around the ford across the River Cray. A crudely drawn sign, depicting a leather drinking bottle, hung outside one of them.

"We can eat there," said Taraghlan and kicked his horse into a trot. "I am so hungry."

An hour later and they had eaten and drunk their fill, all except for Catherine. She had only eaten some bread and drunk a little water. "This is where I leave you," she said with a wistful smile. She looked at Leofa. "What will you do, Leofa?"

He scratched his belly and glanced out the window at the lush, fertile grasslands that benefitted from the enrichment provided by the meandering river. "I think I will stay here. See if I can find some land to farm."

Catherine nodded. "And you, Taraghlan, you and Charlotte will return to the Avertci and tell them I am alive and will be returning soon?"

"We will," he replied, "but I would be happier riding with you and keeping you safe."

Charley sniggered. "No offence Taraghlan but I honestly don't think she needs any help to stay safe. She totally blitzed Timancius."

Taraghlan looked at Catherine for help. "What did she say?"

Catherine laughed and shrugged. "I pray to the gods that by the time you get back to the Avertci, you will be clucking together like two old crones at the well."

Taraghlan rolled his eyes. "And I pray not."

oOo

"What can I do for you DC Hallam?" Greg put his phone on hands-free as he answered the door to Antoinette and Shelly.

"Rosemary Forrester is dead."

Greg nearly dropped the phone. "What? How?"

"I was hoping you would tell me."

Antoinette and Shelly stood, transfixed with their mouths open. Greg would have laughed had the situation not been so serious. "What are you suggesting, DC Hallam? I don't even know which hospital she's in, and neither does Ms Deselle."

"What about Miss Chandler-Price?"

"Impossible. She's been with me all day."

"Well, someone knows what happened."

"I can assure none of us do. What *did* happen anyway?"

"She was stabbed, twice, once in the stomach and once in the neck."

"And no one saw who did it?"

Hallam sighed. *"No. The nurse on duty claimed it just... happened. One minute she was fine, then next there was blood gushing everywhere."*

The colour drained from Antoinette's face. "Oh Mon dieu... Charley."

"Well I'm sorry DC Hallam I can't help you. But please, feel free to come and arrest me if you think I did it." Greg cut the call.

"What's up, Annie?"

"Forrester must have been injured in the past. This is definitive proof that anything that happens to them back then, replicates itself here. She must have been caught up in a battle or something."

Shelly's hand flew to her mouth. "And if it can happen to Forrester..."

"It could happen to Charley. "Greg finished her sentence for her."

"What could happen to me?" said Charley as she descended the stairs. Greg rushed over to her. "Are you ok?"

"Yes. I didn't intend to come back, but something made me. What's going on, why do you all look so shocked?"

Antoinette stepped forward. "Rosemary is dead."

Charley gulped. So is Timancius; Catherine killed him."

"How?" asked Greg.

"She stabbed him in the gut and in the throat. He was dead pretty quickly." Her three friends looked at each other in horror. "What's going on, what haven't you told me?"

"Let's go in the living room. At least we can sit in comfort," said Greg and he led the way. "Sit anywhere guys." He waited until Charley had plonked herself into his favourite armchair and then sat on the arm next to her. "The way you described Timancius's death...it's exactly how Forrester died. One minute she was asleep, gallivanting about in the past or whatever, and the next second her throat was slit and she bled to death."

Charley looked stunned. "I think Forrester was Timancious."

Antoinette looked doubtful. "As in reincarnation? Perhaps she was just so closely linked to Timancius that she died with him?"

Charley frowned. "They looked identical, Annie."

"I wonder what happened to Forrester in the past when Timancious died?" Greg asked.

Shelly raised her hand. "She probably just snapped back into her earthly body the second it happened."

Antoinette leant forward on the sofa. "The point, Mon Cher, is that however Timancius died is *exactly* how Forrester died. She was closely linked to him – just as you are linked to Catherine." She waited for her words to sink-in.

Charley's frown deepened. "So when Catherine dies in that river bed, if I am with her, I could die the same way?"

"Perhaps. Charley it is just too dangerous now."

Charley shook her head. "I disagree. I know how she dies and, more importantly, *where* she dies and she is nowhere near Inis Ruim. She is sending me back to the Avertci."

Antoinette thumped her knee in frustration. "So you think if you stay in the Avertci village you won't die when she does?"

"Maybe, but maybe there is also a way around this; a way to mitigate the risk to me."

Antoinette rolled her eyes. "How?"

"We know that Catherine dies after a single stab to the throat, right?"

"Yes," said Greg, "Just as Forrester did, kinda."

Forrester died because the nursing staff was not prepared for it. If they had been, they could easily have stemmed the flow and stitched her up."

The penny dropped for Greg and he stood up. "Oh no! no, no, no, Charley; you cannot be serious about this."

Shelly looked perplexed. "Serious about what?"

"Charley is proposing that we prepare for her to be stabbed when Catherine is stabbed and then we dive in like a clutch of Florence-fucking-Nightingales and save her life!"

"How about," Shelly ventured, "as soon as Charley recognises what's happening to Catherine, she returns?"

"No that doesn't work for me," argued Charley. "You know there's no way I'd leave Catherine at the very moment when she needs me the most."

Greg sat back down. "I was frightened you'd say that. Please don't go back, Charley. We can't protect you and we can't save you. Please don't."

Charley smiled, patted his hand and fell instantly asleep.

oOo

"This is where we part." Catherine turned her horse alongside Taraghlan. "Thank you sweet Taraghlan. You have been my protector for many years, but now that task must fall to my husband." She reached out and squeezed his hand. "If I need you before I return, I promise I will send for you." Taraghlan seemed appeased by that and squeezed her hand in return.

She waved to Leofa, "Good luck Leofa, I pray you find all you are looking for." He nodded and smiled, then turned his horse away and headed back towards the town.

Next she wheeled her horse around to face Charley. "You returned to your own time earlier. Why?"

Charley's brows rose. "You don't miss a trick do you, Catherine. Yes and I have news. Forrester is dead too."

Catherine smiled. "That is good to hear. You must ride with Taraghlan, unless you wish to return to your own time once more... and stay there?"

Charley shook her head. "I'm not ready to go back yet. I will stay and tease Taraghlan without mercy on the journey home."

Catherine reached out and took her hand. Her eyes flared blue and a surge, like electricity flashed up Charley's arm and into her chest. Her body jerked. "What the freak did you just do to me?" she yelped.

"If I call you, you will hear me. If I need you, you will know it. We are one together, Charlotte." With that Catherine kicked her horse and cantered off the road and into the dense forest that surrounded them.

Charley looked forlornly after her. "What will we do without her, Taraghlan?" she said sadly.

Taraghlan kicked his horse forward onto the road that would take them north to the River Tem. "We will wait for her and Vortiger at the village. Come on, this way."

Charley followed, her heart felt empty but her stomach was churning; something wasn't right.

CHAPTER 57
Aibreán (April) 452 AD

Catherine found Vortiger bathing in a shallow stream by an old, abandoned hut he had made his temporary home. She watched, hidden by the trees, as he splashed the cool water over his body. As he stood up to dress, her eyes roved over his naked body. She admired his well-defined muscles and strong torso. She didn't want him to get dressed.

A twig cracked under her feet and he spun around in shock at being caught off guard. When he saw it was Catherine, he fell to his knees, overcome with emotion. Through his tears he could see her walking slowly towards him. She dropped her cloak on the forest floor and then her gown. When she reached him she too was naked. She knelt down in front of him and encircled his neck with her arms and kissed him lightly on the lips.

"I thought you must be dead," he choked.

"Shh. I'm here now."

oOo

The hut was warm. Their lovemaking had lasted into the night and now they lay naked, facing each other before an open fíof peat and logs. His strong arms encircled her and for the first time in months she felt safe again; secure in his arms and protected by the man she loved so intensely.

She watched the amber reflection of the flames dancing across his face; his determined blue eyes now softly studying her earthy features. Catherine traced the curve of his mouth with her finger and caught a slight smile that twitched involuntarily. She smiled back and lifted her mouth to his and even though their lips barely touched, the pleasure she felt sent shivers to her core.

She trembled at the beauty of the kiss, for in truth she had begun to doubt she would see him again, and the fact that her gods had had been so benevolent, was not lost on her. She must make an offering as soon as the sun rose.

Eventually he spoke; his voice usually so strong and even, was now cracked and hesitant. "Where have you been all this time? Were you at Sturigao? I thought you were lost for forever."

"I think I nearly was," she replied. "So where were you?" This time there was an edge to his voice and she glanced up into his eyes again. They were no longer soft; the familiar steely determination was there once more. She loved his strength, but he had grown into a man who was not to be challenged, threatened or cornered.

"I do not understand what you mean. I was a captive at Sturigao. You *know* I was captive. I am told you tried to rescue me."

"News of your escape reached me in Márta It is now Aprilis."

Catherine pulled away from him, "You speak of Roman months? Have you abandoned our own gods? Does Aprilis replace Aibrean? After my escape I travelled as quickly as I could. It has not been that long. I had planned to take much, much longer, at least three moons."

Vortiger looked puzzled. "Why so long?"

"I planned to take my time, to mingle with other tribes, to work the fields to earn hospitality, to remain hidden as I made my way, because Hengist and Horsa would be looking for me."

"But you changed your mind?"

"I was lucky. I went to Faeferham where I was reunited with Taraghlan. All the time I was being harried by spies and chased by Horsa and his army. How can you doubt me? My one thought was to escape and find my way back to you!"

"Yes, you must have been well-guarded. Even with the help of our neighbouring tribes I was unable to get close. Every time we got near to Inis Ruim we were repulsed. Have you any idea how many good men were lost to the Gods trying?" His eyes were pained at the memory.

"How could I?" Catherine's eyes flashed angrily, "You speak as though it were my fault!" She turned her back and sat up. Resting her chin upon her knees she stared helplessly into the fire; tears stinging her eyes.

He reached up and touched her shoulder, "I could not get near you and yet you escaped. How?"

"I befriended one of the guards. He made my escape possible." She thought of gentle Waelheard and smiled.

"For what reward Catherine? What did he get for his help? It must have been something very precious - Precious enough for him to risk his life to help you."

Catherine could not believe what he was suggesting and she turned back sharply to face him, her eyes flashing angrily

"He was an old man. I gave him *nothing*. Even if he had been young and handsome, I had nothing to give! I could not give of myself, for I belong to you – Mind body and soul."

Vortiger looked away, deep in thought and Catherine punched him on the shoulder. "Is that what you think?" she spat, "that I hold my self so lowly that I would give myself to a guard, even one as old as time? Do you honestly believe he would have let me go if he thought I could be forced into satisfying his needs for some vague hope of freedom? My escape was his idea. He planned it for me."

Vortiger sat up, thinking hard. "No one would risk their life if there was no reward, no promises. Something is wrong."

In the distance a dog barked. It barked angrily - defensively,

Catherine's eyes widened. "Horses!" she cried. "Horses are coming, listen."

Vortiger sprang to his feet and hurriedly started to dress, "You didn't escape - They let you go!"

"That is not possible."

"It is. They need me dead. They failed each time I attacked them, but they need me dead as a message to my father."

"And I have led them to you."

"Grab your robes and head out into the woods. Stay there. Do not emerge until I come for you."

"I am *not* going to leave you!" she hissed as she dropped her robes over her head and tied them loosely around her waist. "Not again. I won't leave you." She strapped on Blood-Taker and tucked Fire-Sting into her belt.

Vortiger grabbed his sword and pushed Catherine through the door and into the night air. There was no mist and the clearing was bathed in cold moonlight.

He pushed her towards the woods. "Run," he commanded. "They are close now. By all the gods if you truly love me, run."

"I cannot - I will not. I have Blood-Taker, let me stay and fight beside you." She stood fast, her long dark hair blowing in the night breeze and her determined eyes again flashing angrily. He knew that it was useless to try and force her into hiding - Catherine was as stubborn as she was loyal, and she would rather die at his side than be separated again.

He knew she was a fearless warrior, she had proven that time and again, and at this moment, with the riders so close, he knew he had no choice but to put his love for her and his faith in her skills, to the test.

"Then pray that our gods love us Catherine, otherwise we shall both perish!" He raised his sword and ran to the centre of the clearing.

Four horses crashed through the trees, their riders wearing the unmistakable clothing of Hengist and Horsa's Saxon warriors. Two of the horses reared immediately and threw their riders heavily to the ground, startled by the sudden appearance of the sword-wielding couple in front of them.

The remaining two reigned-in their steeds. One leapt to the ground and drew his sword. Seeing Catherine defiantly facing him, her long hair flying at the will of the wind, and Blood-Taker in her hand, he screamed with rage and charged at her. The other Saxon unsheathed his axe and kicked his horse forward, preferring to keep the advantage of height and speed.

He rode toward Vortiger at full gallop, the axe held high above his head. He screamed wildly and swung the axe in a wide arc, intending to cleave him in two. As rider and horse reached Vortiger, he dropped to his knees and thrust his sword up through the Saxon's thigh and groin. The warrior's war cry was abruptly cut short and the axe fell from his hand. He tried to cling on to the mane but he toppled from his saddle as the horse careered into the woods beyond the clearing.

Catherine met her attacker with the full force of her well-developed sword arm. His war-like scream was also cut short as she severed his head with a single left-handed slice.

The two thrown riders were now on their feet and charging toward them, swords drawn. One stumbled and fell to the ground, but the other ran straight at Catherine. She neatly side-stepped him and brought her sword down across his back, slicing through his spine. His legs folded underneath him as the sword severed his spinal cord, and he tumbled across the clearing.

Vortiger leapt upon him and finished him with one clean stab to the heart; better that than a life of paralysis.

Catherine intercepted the remaining Saxon as he regained his footing and tried to run past her to reach Vortiger. She stepped straight into his path, plunged her sword into him and let it go. He stumbled on a few paces, before he fell to the ground.

Vortiger sheathed his sword and smiled. "By the Gods, you fight like a man."

Catherine smiled as she retrieved her sword from the fallen Saxon's body and wiped it on his fur vest. "I fight like a woman who knows how to fight!" she retorted and looked about the clearing. "We can't stay here now."

Vortiger agreed. "We should head north and west; try to find my father and raise an army to rid our lands of the Saxons once and for all."

Charley's history lesson flashed into Catherine's mind but now was not the time to explain to her husband that they would never beat them. "We should head back to the Avertci village first. Taraghlan and Charlotte will be waiting there."

"Charlotte?"

Catherine started to ready her horse. "It is a long story; one best saved for the journey."

CHAPTER 58
Bealtaine (May) 452

Taraghlan's wife, Germaine had died from a fever. The village elders wept, villagers wept and Charley wept, but Taraghlan did not weep.

"Do you know what the name Germaine means?" he asked Charley as the women of the village prepared her for burial.

"No. Something poetic I imagine, like 'Spirit of the Wind.'"

Taraghlan smiled. "It means, 'Woman with the loud voice.' The gods made sure she carried the name well." He left the hut and made his way to the Great Hall with Charley striding alongside.

"Was she a bit of a nag then Taraghlan?"

"I do not understand you, but if you ask if she shrieked and yelled when displeased then yes... And almost everything displeased her."

They entered the hall, which was bustling with traders. Taraghlan waved at Caderyn. "Where is this messenger from Vortigern?"

Caderyn pushed a tall thin man towards him. "This is Ansgar."

Ansgar stumbled but quickly regained his composure. He was well dressed but had severe Alopecia. He wore black his hair long, but it was missing in great clumps that revealed a red and blotchy scalp beneath. It was a source of great amusement to most who met him.

Taraghlan laughed and said to Charley, "Ansgar means 'Warrior.' Does he look like a warrior to you, Charlotte?"

Charley frowned. "Please don't tease him." Taraghlan looked at her for a second and grunted. She squeezed his arm. "Thank you."

342

"What have you to say, Ansgar?"

"The king has word from Prince Vortiger and the Lady Catherine."

Charley's heart missed a beat. "They are alive?"

Ansgar drew himself up to his full height. "Well they were not speaking through the gods," he replied haughtily.

Taraghlan grabbed him by his collar. "Show respect, maggot. This is the Goddess Charlotte in earthly form."

Charley nearly choked. She'd forgotten that Catherine had introduced her as such; everything just felt so normal. Everyone could see her and interact with her. She simply felt at home. In fact, she felt more at home here, than back in her own time.

Ansgar wriggled free and looked at Charley in disbelief. "I have never heard of a goddess called Charlotte. This is too much, Taraghlan. The gods will punish you for claiming she is a goddess."

"Our queen and priestess, Catherine says it is so - so it is so."

"And do not forget, Ansgar," added Caderyn, "that Catherine is now your princess."

Ansgar was turning redder with every second. "Do you want to hear King Vortigern's message or not?"

Taraghlan gave an exaggerated bow. "Please."

"King Vortigern wants you to know that Prince Vortiger and the Lady Catherine are now north of the Tem and should be with you soon."

Again Charley squeezed Taraghlan's arm. "That's great news."

He looked down at the excited girl and felt a frisson of something, he wasn't sure what, but with her mass of dark hair, pert figure and lovely features, he hoped that feeling would happen again. "It is great news, yes," he replied, as Charley locked eyes with him. He held her gaze for perhaps a moment too long and wondered if the gods would condemn him if he tried to involve himself with a goddess.

"Is there anything else?" asked Caderyn.

"Yes." Ansgar took it upon himself to sit on a nearby stool.

"King Vortigern is also coming to your village. He wishes to discuss the best way to negotiate peace with the Saxons."

Taraghlan's face flushed with anger and he kicked out at Ansgar's stool which sent him sprawling across the dirt floor. "Peace? You mean he wants to surrender!" he shouted.

Three of the village's Ealdormen hurried over. "Taraghlan! You forget your place, said one. "You command our queen's army and you protect us, but you should *not* be talking to King Vortigern's emissary."

"Did you hear what he said?" Taraghlan rounded on the Ealdormen. "The king wants to make peace." He looked at the three men and their unmoving expressions. "But you already know this."

"Of course we do. We have already talked about the king's wishes with Ansgar and we will pass them on to our queen when she arrives."

Taraghlan turned on his heels and strode out of the Great Hall. Charley hesitated for a second and then rushed outside to catch up with him.

He stormed into his hut, removed his sword and threw it across the floor. "Gods' teeth."

"May I come in?" she asked as she peered past the bearskin entrance.

"Yes. Come."

She stepped inside and looked about. Like most of the other huts, it was sparsely furnished; a large cot, some wooden boxes that he used as tables and stools, a fire burning in the centre, light blue smoke curling upwards. Taraghlan, fed up with constant mud, had raised the floor level with duckboards for when it rained – Something that Germaine had nagged him about for months.

Charley walked up to him. "Are you ok?"

He looked down at her and suddenly grabbed her around the waist and pulled her to him. Treating a goddess so, could bring the wrath of the other gods upon him so, if he was going to die at their hands, he might as well enjoy committing the sin.

Charley gasped. For an older man he was very well built, and ruggedly handsome. He kissed her quite ferociously but Charley pulled away. "Taraghlan, no."

"You want me as much as I want you," he panted and ripped at her gown.

Charley pushed him away and held the torn garment tightly to her body. "Taraghlan I am Catherine's friend and you are her protector." She thought of Greg. "I am also promised to another. You cannot bed me."

He took a pace towards her and she held up her hand. "Taraghlan, you cannot bed a goddess, not if you want to live."

His posture slumped and he sat heavily on the cot. "Forgive me."

"There is nothing to forgive, Taraghlan. Even though you claim you didn't love your wife, you *do* mourn her and people do strange things when they are in mourning. Let's say no more about this."

oOo

Catherine and Vortiger arrived at the Avertci village two days later to much horn blowing and cheers from the population. Taraghlan and Charley reached the gates just as they rode through and as soon as Catherine saw them, she reined-in her horse and slid from the saddle. She embraced Charley first and then Taraghlan. As soon as she touched him, pain flashed across her face. "Your wife is with the gods? I am sorry for you my friend. When did this happen?"

"Three days ago."

"I shall make sure she is honoured in this world. The gods will surely honour her in theirs." Catherine hugged Charley again and instantly pulled away. She glared at her and then at Taraghlan. "What have you done?"

Charley was shocked by the question. She knew instantly what Catherine meant. "We have done nothing, I promise." She looked at Taraghlan for support. "He moved close to his queen and spoke quietly. "Germaine hated me, my lady; she made my life a misery." He looked over at Charley. "Your goddess smiled upon me and I could not resist, nor did I want to, but she refused, my queen, I did not dishonour her or you."

"But you wanted to," Catherine snapped. "You dishonoured your wife, Taraghlan." She turned to her husband. "We should go and meet with the Ealdormen."

oOo

Charley and Taraghlan spent the evening in the Great Hall. It would have been unwise to spend any more time in his hut; Catherine would not have stood for it. They talked about everything but his attempt to bed her.

"I have something to tell you," she said quietly.

"What?"

"Catherine told you I was one of the gods; I'm not."

Taraghlan laughed lightly. "I think I already knew that, although I could not be certain."

Charley looked at him in surprise. "You did?"

"Yes. I have heard things you and Catherine have said. You come from our future? I do not understand it, but it is easier to think of you as one of the gods, for that way it all makes sense."

"The history of Britain is mapped out and one thing I know for certain is that you cannot win against the Saxons. No one can, not even Catherine, and I don't want you to die trying. Please."

"And you know this for certain?"

"Yes, I know this. The Saxons will settle here for good."

"He frowned. "Have you told Catherine?"

"I have. That's why she was so upset at Faeferham and why she and Vortiger have come back. Somehow they have to tell the king about our future and try to end the warring. She doesn't know he wants peace too."

Taraghlan grimaced. "I know now how the Saxons' minds work. They seek not peace, but domination and that will mean killing the King and all his sons."

"To break the will of the people?"

Taraghlan smiled ruefully. "The people have no will. Everything is decided by the gods. If the future is as you say, then it must have

346

been the gods' will."

Charley folded her hands on her lap. "Taraghlan," she said softly, "I know how Catherine dies."

His brows raised and his mouth dropped open. "Is that also in your history?"

She shook her head. "Very little is known about this time. No one made records; not many people could read or write. We called them the Dark Ages."

"Then how do you know?"

"I was with her." Tears tipped over the edge of her eyes and flowed freely down her cheeks. "The first time I came here, I found myself lying in the River Stour in Inis Ruim, face to face with her. She had been stabbed by Hengist."

Taraghlan stood up and glared at her. "If you speak true then she must never go to Inis Ruim again."

"Taraghlan you can't change history."

He stood angrily, grabbed his dagger from the barrel by the cot and pulled her to her feet also. "You were there yet you did not save her?" he snarled, tears now in his eyes too. "You did not save her." He grabbed her hair, tilted her head back and held his dagger to her throat.

Charley screamed out. She had never seen him so angry and she was terrified. "I couldn't save her. She couldn't see me, I couldn't touch her. I was like a ghost. Please Taraghlan, let me go. I would have saved her if I could."

"Liar. You just said history cannot be changed."

"TARAGHLAN!" shouted a voice from the doorway.

He looked up to see Catherine standing there. Her eyes flared blue and the muscles in both arms went into spasm. He yelled in pain, dropped the dagger. "She did not save you," he cried and dropped to his knees, his face contorted by rage and grief.

Catherine crouched next to him. "I know this, Taraghlan."

Charley looked down at Taraghlan, curled up in Catherine's arms like a distressed child being comforted by its mother. "I'm so sorry."

Catherine just nodded at the door, indicating that Charley should leave. She took one last look at the bereft Taraghlan and stepped into the chill night air.

oOo

Catherine found Charley sitting in front of the fire in the Great Hall. She looked up sadly at the Priestess. "How is he?"

Catherine sat next to her. "He is calm and remorseful. He is my greatest protector and with my father dead, he has taken that duty deep into his heart." Pain was etched in her face. "Why did you tell him?"

"He still wants to fight and I don't want him to die, so I told him what I knew about the future. I wanted to dissuade him from going into battle."

"Dissuade?" Catherine allowed a smile to touch the corners of her mouth. "I will never understand your words completely."

"Tonight he terrified me, Catherine. If you hadn't come in I'm sure he would have killed me. He was in such a rage."

"You called for me and I answered."

"I did?"

"Yes. You know we are connected. Taraghlan could not have hurt you. He was angry but I know he cares about you." A slight frisson of anger crossed her face. "Maybe more than he cared for his wife."

Charley bit her lip. "I thought about returning to my own time and never coming back. I don't want cause any more turmoil."

Catherine patted her knee. "I am pleased you stayed. Now, get some sleep, we are all meeting with King Vortigern tomorrow."

CHAPTER 59
Bealtaine (May) 452 AD

King Vortigern and his retinue arrived mid-morning and was now in the Great Hall. A large table had been placed in the centre, around which everyone involved in the talks were seated. Vortigern's Ealdormen sat at one end of the table and Catherine's at the other, She sat in the middle of one long side with Vortigern to her right and Charley to her left. Taraghlan sat on Vortiger's right, whilst King Vortigern and Vortimir sat opposite. Charley leant over to her. "What am I doing here? This is not my place."

"Your place is wherever I say it is; I need you here to advise me."

Charley had not had the opportunity to speak to Taraghlan and leant forward to attract his attention, but Taraghlan was engrossed in conversation with one of the elders and not looking in her direction.

Vortigern grunted with appreciation as servants brought wine and ale to the table. He took a large swig of ale and held up his mug for a refill. "We should begin." He looked directly at Catherine. "I do not have enough men to form an army big enough to crush the Saxons, not even with the men you can supply."

Catherine opened her mouth to respond but Vortigern cut across her. "The Trinovantes are too scared as they border Cient across the Tem. The Attrebates have joined with me in the past, but now refuse to lose any more men. The Belgae, Regni and Cantiaci are already under Saxon Rule, and the Corieltauvi and Catuvellauni have lost too many men to the Picts. And the Iceni are fighting their own battles with the Jutes and Angles landing on their coast every day."

Catherine again tried to speak and again Vortigern ignored her. "With no tribes willing or able to help, I just do not have an army big enough. I know this will displease you Catherine, but I feel our only option is to seek peace with the Saxons." He took another swig of ale.

Catherine sat back in her chair. "I agree."

Vortigern spluttered ale all over his beard. "You do? I thought you would want to fight to the end."

Catherine held the king's gaze. "This *is* the end, My Lord." She glanced over at her Ealdormen then back to the king. "I have already discussed this with the village elders and they agree with my views." There were nods and murmurs from the Ealdorman.

Vortimir looked over at Taraghlan. "You are in agreement also?"

Taraghlan stared moodily at the table top. "I am my queen's protector and commander of her armies. I do what I am told."

Next to him, Vortiger laughed. "You are much more than that. You advise her on all manner of things; you must have an opinion about making peace."

Taraghlan lifted his eyes and smiled a thin smile. "If my queen wants peace, I will help to protect that peace."

The king frowned. "Taraghlan, you are not speaking true, I feel it in my bones. Say what you want. This is the time to do so. Tomorrow it will be too late."

"Very well." Taraghlan pulled himself wearily to his feet. "The Saxons do not want peace. They want domination, and if they are to dominate us, they must kill you and all your family. And they must kill my queen, for unless she is dead, there will always be opposition to their rule. Surely my Lord you know this."

There were cheers of support from the Avertci Ealdormen and some jeers from Vortigern's elders. Vortigern also stood. "But we can talk. We can negotiate and get promises made." This time it was Catherine's Ealdormen who jeered.

"My Lord you are blind if you think that," shouted Taraghlan over the hubbub.

Catherine raised a hand and gradually the hall fell silent. "There is another way."

oOo

Vortigern looked horrified. "No. I forbid it."

Catherine smiled. "It is the only way."

Charley tugged at her sleeve. Catherine, you will be playing right into their hands. You cannot go alone."

"I am happy to offer my life in exchange for the lives of my new family." She swung her arm around slowly to indicate she was referring to her husband and his family.

King Vortigern thumped the table. "We will *all* go. We will take the biggest army we can muster and send messengers ahead to tell Hengist and Horsa that we are coming to negotiate peace."

Taraghlan smiled. "That is a good plan My Lord but a large army will suggest you have come to fight."

Vortigern laughed. "If they choose to fight instead of talk then we should be able to give good account of ourselves. And we will only die if the gods so decide."

Catherine slumped back in her chair. "I had hoped to spare the family," she whispered to Charley. "If I am to die at Hengist's hand then at least it would have been for a good reason."

"I don't want to think about that."

"Is it agreed?" Vortigern addressed all the Ealdormen. "We shall ride to Inis Ruim and try to negotiate peace."

Brod, one of Vortigern's Ealdormen stood. "My Lord, the Saxons will want much in return for peace. They may want all our fertile lands."

Taraghlan pushed away his mug of ale. "They will take whatever they want," he said, sourly. "They do not need to negotiate. They will take whatever lands they choose, they will rape our women and take them and our children as slaves, they will drive us out and populate our villages with their own kind. They are doing this in the East. The Icini have succumbed to vast numbers of Angles who arrive every day. It is now becoming known as the land of the East Angles. Where are the Icini? driven south, back towards the Roman town of Camulodunum. This will happen to us all."

Vortimir glared across the table at him. "And the alternative is what? If they will take everything from us anyway, then it is better to negotiate than do nothing."

The debate continued for another hour, before Vortigern enforced his decision to travel to Thanet. He announced he would travel back to Theocsbury the next day and return once he had raised as many men as he could.

That night, as Catherine and Vortiger lay together, they talked about Vortigern's plan. "You will go?" he asked, hoping her answer would be no, but knowing it would be yes.

"It is my destiny. Only the gods can stop me."

He rolled on top of her. "Then I will pray to the gods every day, they will." He kissed her on the lips but as he did, her eyes flared bright blue and she pushed him off and sat up.

"I know who Charlotte is."

Vortigern laughed. "Is that all? You have already told me who she is."

Catherine slid between Vortiger's thighs and bit him gently, her eyes still flaring blue. "No, husband, I know who she *really* is."

"Who?"

Catherine slowly wriggled up his body until her face was looking down on his. "That is only for me to know."

"Do you need to go to her?" he asked sadly.

"Oh no, right now Vortiger, I only want you."

CHAPTER 60
Meitheamh (June) 452 AD

Vortigern halted his army about half a mile from Durobrivae, which Charley knew was modern day Rochester. The town was located at the lowest point of the River Medway where the Romans had built a substantial bridge to carry their road across the river.

"We will camp here and wait for my messengers to return with the Saxon's response to my call for peace negotiations." He had only just heaved his heavy frame from his horse when a rider galloped into their midst. He leapt from his horse before it had stopped and ran over to the king. It was Cadric, one of the messengers and he was carrying a heavy sack.

"My Lord," he panted, "The Saxons have refused your request for talks."

Vortigern looked past Cadric for the second messenger. "Where is Briant?"

Cadric tossed the sack on the floor and a severed head rolled out. "There, my Lord."

A wave of shock ran through the onlookers and Vortigern grabbed Cadric by the collar of his jerkin. "What happened?"

"We announced who we were to the guards at Sturigao and they led us into the fort. Horsa came out to meet us. Briant gave him your message and he just laughed. He said they didn't need to negotiate peace; it would come as soon as you were dead and they ruled all of Britain. Then he stabbed Briant through the heart and cut off his head. He told me to bring it back to you with the message that would happen to every Briton who resisted their rule. He challenges you to battle at a place he calls Teneth. I'm sorry my

353

Lord I do not know where that is."

Charley knew. Teneth was the name the Saxons gave to Inis Ruim and Teneth was the name that slid to become Thanet.

She whispered what she knew, to Catherine who raised her arm. "My Lord, he means Inis Ruim."

Vortigern pushed Cadric away his fists clenched as tight as his jaw. "Taraghlan, spread the word, we leave at first light. If the Saxons want a fight, we will give them one."

"My Lord," Cadric called as Vortigern strode away. The king stopped. "Well?"

"I did not finish, my Lord; there is more to the Saxon's response." He approached Vortigern and whispered nervously, "Perhaps I should tell you this in private?"

"Tell me now!" Vortigern roared. "I am in no mood for delay. Tell me now."

Cadric gulped. "Hengist came into the courtyard and challenged Horsa's message. He said peace *was* possible but would not be given easily. He thanked you for the gift of Cient, but now they wanted you to gift them all the land south of the Tem. He also wants you to gift him the Land of the East Angles, as there are already many of his kind there. Then he laughed and said it mattered not if you refuse for they have already taken possession of many towns along the South coast. Everyone laughed at that, my Lord. But then he said..." Cadric paused, not certain how to tell his king the next part of the message. "...He said that to assure peace between you, he wants you to wed his daughter Rowena."

For a moment there was an earie silence as the shock of what had just been said permeated through those who were stood about. Then suddenly the camp erupted with jeers, catcalls and laughter.

Vortigern was unsure how to react at first but then he too burst into laughter. "Did you see her? Is she pretty or does she look like a cow's arse?"

"I did not see her, my Lord."

Vortigern waved his arms to quieten the laughter. "Was he serious or making fun of me?"

Cadric looked worried. "My Lord I think he was serious."

Vortigern's tent was now assembled and he beckoned to Catherine and her friends to follow him inside.

"Well, what do you all think?"

Charley gulped. From historical research she knew that Vortigern did indeed marry Hengist's daughter Rowena, much to Vortimir's disgust. Thereafter, Vortimir wanted nothing to do with his father. It was believed that Rowena poisoned Vortimir and his death caused Vortigern to fight back against the Saxons once more. At the battle of Episford, both Horsa and Vortimir's brother, Catigern were killed. Charley also knew that she could not tell them any of this.

Taraghlan slumped onto a large cushion on the floor. "You already know what I think, my Lord. They want our lands and they will take them with or without your cooperation."

Vortimir nodded in agreement. "They are ferocious warriors, father. They use tactics that are new to us."

"Like that shield wall," added Vortiger. "I've never seen anything so terrifying."

"Our army has about two thousand men," continued Vortimir, "a mix of battle-hardened warriors, mercenaries from Wales and inexperienced farmers and labourers."

Taraghlan raised his hand. "My Lord. Inis Ruim is a small island. Once we are there, the Saxons will close-off the causeway, leaving us trapped. There will be no escape/"

"Are you suggesting we cannot win?" Vortigern's anger spiked again.

Vortimir shook his head sadly. "I fear so, and if we *do* win, it will not have been easy; we will lose many good men. Maybe you *should* consider taking a wife?"

"The problem is," interjected Catherine, "two very different messages have come to us from Sturigao. Horsa wants us all dead, Hengist wants to talk. Who do we believe?"

"Maybe Hengist's offer of marriage is a trap; a way to get us within their walls?" suggested Taraghlan

Vortigern thought about that for a moment and then came to a decision. "We will take two bites from the same fruit," he said. "We will give Horsa what he wants and fight him. If we lose, then I will throw myself at Hengist's mercy and offer to wed his daughter in exchange for peace."

"And we still lose good men for no reason," grumbled Vortimir.

"Of course there is a reason," Vortigern shouted. "If we win, then that is an end to it."

Catherine move close to Charley. "How can I tell him we will never win?" she said quietly.

Charley kissed her lightly on the cheek, causing a crackle of electricity, and whispered, "You can't. All you can do is prepare for battle and pray to the gods that peace will follow."

"And this could be where I die."

"Don't!" Charley glared at her. "Don't even suggest that."

"Then battle it is," said Catherine loudly. "Tomorrow we leave for Inis Ruim, as King Vortigern has decreed. Now pray to the gods harder than you ever prayed before."

CHAPTER 61

Charley stirred and looked about. "Am I back?"

Greg was already by her side. "Hey, how are you?"

"Tired. Getting back was a real struggle. It was as if the past doesn't want to let me go. How long have I been out?"

Greg looked at his watch. "Only a couple of hours."

Charley swung her legs off the bed. "Really? I've been there for weeks."

"So what's happening back there?" He passed her a glass of water.

"So much has happened, but it's what's about to happen that has brought me back." She took a large sip from the glass.

"You've come back to be safe I hope."

Charley looked at him guiltily. "Not exactly."

"*Charley...*

"I know, I know, but things are coming to a head. Vortigern hopes to broker peace with the Saxons, but it looks as if we're going into battle first."

"We?"

"Greg, please understand; this maybe where the end comes for Catherine. I have to be there for her." She caught the distress that flashed across his face. "Don't worry, I'm not going to try and save her. I know that would be the wrong thing to do."

"Well at least they can't see you, so I suppose that will help to keep you safe..."

Her guilt returned and she couldn't hide it. "Actually they can see me; they all can. I can talk to them and interact with them. To all intents and purposes I am real to them now."

Greg looked desolate; this brave but stupid woman putting herself at risk. "How did that happen?"

"At first it was only Catherine and then… It's as if the past has accepted me."

Greg shook his head in despair. "Now you're visible, anyone could kill you…and even if they don't, remember what happened to Forrester when Timancius died; no one here could save her. If you're there when Catherine dies, you'll probably die from the same injuries."

"Greg, I'm going. If you're so concerned, then make arrangements to deal with whatever happens."

"Seriously? What do you expect me to do? Take you to hospital in advance and say, 'Can you please admit my sleeping girlfriend to ICU because she's time-travelled back into the past and is likely to bleed-out from a stab wound to the neck?' "

"Greg, this is why I've come back. I wanted to let you know what was happening and to tell you this might be the last time you see me."

"What?"

"I can't control what's going to happen, I'm also finding it harder and harder to return. I somehow feel that living in the fifth century is where I'm supposed to be."

Greg looked astonished. "You stupid selfish mare!"

"Greg!"

"Don't you realise that if you stay in the past, your body here will be basically in a coma. You'll be admitted to hospital and at some point your parents will have to make the decision to turn off any life support you might be on. If that happens you'll probably die back there too."

"But…"

"And what about your parents? What am I supposed to say to them? Think how they'd feel, losing their daughter to some improbable misguided adventure. For fuck's sake put other people first for once."

Tears coursed down Charley's cheeks. This was more than an

adventure; she felt it was her destiny but Greg's words had hit home. "I understand. Greg, I really do, but I can't abandon Catherine."

"You can't abandon your family either. You just have to decide which is more important. You can't make any difference to the past, it's already happened, but you *can* make a huge difference to the future, just by the things you do, the life you live and the love you share."

She knew deep in her heart that Greg was right, but travelling back in time had become such an important part of her life…no, it *was* her life. How could she give it up? She wondered if she could go back one last time to say goodbye to Catherine, but she knew that wouldn't work. Once back there she wouldn't want to return, she mightn't even be able to.

"Ok."

"Ok? Ok what?"

"I won't go back. I know you're right, but please, don't expect everything to go back to normal for me overnight. This is a very big deal for me and I know I'm going to have trouble processing it."

Greg pulled her to her feet and into a tight hug. "Thank you. I don't know what I'd do if I lost you." Charley's legs suddenly gave way. "Charley, are you ok? What's up?"

All the colour had drained from her face. "I don't know; I feel so weird." Her head lolled to one side and Greg hoisted her back into his arms. She managed to rouse herself a little. "Greg, I can't control it, I think I'm being taken back whether I want to go or not." Her voice was slurred and her eyes felt so heavy; she was on the verge of sleep.

"Charley no; don't you dare fall asleep." Greg kissed her on the lips. "Wake up, please wake up."

But it was too late. The past was not letting go.

CHAPTER 62
Meitheamh (June) 452 AD

Vortigern's army had traversed the narrow causeway across the Wantsum Channel onto Inis Ruim. They stopped and looked across at the Walland Marshes, flat, bleak and uninviting. When they crossed over the River Stour, Charley looked about to see if she recognised anything, but it was all so different to the modern day.

It was approaching mid-morning and the sky was a clear blue. The sun, with nowhere to hide, was beating down ferociously and the army, most of who were on foot, were feeling the effects of the heat.

Taraghlan rode up alongside Vortimir. "This is foolish. We've let the Saxons dictate the battleground; we are riding into a trap."

Vortimir nodded. "I agree." He peered across the countryside. "And yet, it is quite flat."

"Nor is there is any high ground for the Saxons to use," Taraghlan added, "Apart from way over there to the right."

Vortigern led his men to the edge of the marshes, where a tributary of the Stour meandered back to the estuary. "Vortiger, tell the commanders to rest the men, but keep them alert. Send out some scouts too."

As Vortiger rode away, Catherine pulled her horse alongside the king. "My Lord, my senses are on fire."

"Meaning?"

"Something is not right. Hengist and Horsa want us to fight them here, but look at the land. It is deeply rutted; there are streams and rivulets running every which way. There are hillocks and ditches. This is not a ground over which we can ride horses

360

and it is too uneven to fight upon on foot." She pointed back to the channel. "Escape from here is limited by the estuary and causeway. There is only one clear route which is to stay this side of the marshes and go to our right."

Vortigern looked to the right. "Between those two small hills?"

"Indeed my Lord; the only high ground for miles."

"And a perfect place for an ambush." He ran his fingers through his beard. "Taraghlan, Vortimir, come here."

Catherine explained again the cause of her unease and Taraghlan agreed with her. "That low ground is our only way and it is where they will be waiting for us."

Charley had been listening and rode clumsily over the uneven ground. "It is too obvious," she said.

Catherine looked at her with raised brows. "Explain please, Charlotte."

Surely any soldier worth his salt would recognise that as the perfect place for an ambush and avoid it."

Vortigern looked at his son with puzzlement. "Worth his salt? What does this woman say?" Vortimir laughed and shrugged his shoulders.

Charley tried again. "If you ride through there, where will all your attention be?"

"On the hillsides," replied the king.

"Yes, because you will be expecting an ambush there, but I think Hengist and Horsa have been cleverer than that."

Catherine threw her head back and laughed. "My wonderful Goddess Charlotte, you have seen the truth that I failed to see." She pulled her horse around so that she could address all three men together. "If we enter that small valley, the attack will not come from above; it will come from behind us and will be followed by more Saxons from the front, trapping us on that low lying land, where we will be slaughtered."

Vortigern stared at the hills. "Then we do not go that way. We will ride back across the river and wait for them to come to us."

"Or…" ventured Charley as she gingerly turned her horse to

face the two small hills, "we approach the one on the right, ignore the valley and we march up the hill. That will give us the high ground."

"Surely the Saxons will have thought of that?" Catherine squinted at the hills. "No, I think King Vortigern is right. We should ignore the obvious trap and go back."

"If they see us leaving they may try to stop us," said Vortimir.

"And that, at least, will reveal their positions," replied Catherine

Vortigern slapped his leg. "That is a good plan my Lady, a *kingly* plan. In fact *my* plan." He laughed and shouted to his men. "Back to the river! Back to the river and let them come to us!"

oOo

Charley surveyed the Estuary and the 2000 metre-wide Wantsum Channel that separated the Island from mainland Kent. In modern times, the Isle of Thanet was an island in name only as the channel had been silted-up by the 17th century. The scene before her was vastly different from the area where the school was located – the school that started this whole mad adventure.

The causeway was a narrow sandbank that allowed a muddy but passable crossing onto the island, and from which there suddenly came the whinny of a horse. There, making their way across and ready for battle, was at least half of Hengist and Horsa's army.

Vortigern turned to his sons in dismay. "They've cut off our escape. Get the archers to the front. Stop them reaching the island."

Catherine galloped over to him. "They have trapped us, look behind."

The remainder of the Saxon army was clambering out from the hillocks and ditches of the marshland where they had lain concealed, and were now spreading out on the dunes behind them.

"What do we do now, father?" Vortiger stared at the enormity of the Saxon army. "We are truly outnumbered."

"We fight them in halves," Vortigern directed. "Vortimir, take the archers and fifty warriors further along the dunes until you are opposite the causeway. Stop them getting onto the island."

Vortimir galloped over to the king's army, shouting orders as he went.

"Everyone else will fight the warriors behind us. We are now more evenly matched to kill them all!" He wheeled his horse around, drew his sword and charged through his men, screaming at the top of his lungs. It took a second for them to realise what was happening but then they too all charged.

Catherine leant from her horse towards Charley and grabbed her arm. "Do not follow me into battle. Stay here." She pulled a sword from a sheath on her saddle. "Take this."

"What the hell am I supposed to do with this?" she shouted, her eyes wide open with shock. "I don't know how to use a sword."

Catherine laughed. "You will find a way if you need to," and she galloped off to catch-up with Vortiger.

Charley looked at the razor-sharp blade in her hand and felt real fear. The two sides were now involved in a fight for their lives and the noise was deafening. Shields clashed together, swords rang out as blades met other blades, axes thudded through bones, muscles and skulls, daggers sliced and ripped at faces and stomachs. She wanted to drop her sword and run, but the fear had rooted her to the spot.

Catherine and Vortiger were fighting side-by-side at first but were quickly separated. She had both Blood and Fire drawn; Blood-Taker in her right hand and Fire-Sting in her left. A Saxon warrior leapt in front of her, his axe raised. He brought it down hard at her head, but she ducked under his arm and plunged Fire-Sting into his spine. As he fell, another took his place, swinging horizontally, determined to decapitate her. Catherine dodged his axe too. The warrior's, swing didn't stop until it met one of his own men and severed his head instead. Catherine stabbed him in the neck and ran on.

Vortiger stumbled against a Saxon who was repeatedly smashing his shield into the face of a fallen Briton. The Saxon turned with a roar and swung his bloodied shield at him, but Vortiger sliced through the man's legs with his sword and the Saxon fell screaming into a water-filled ditch.

Catherine found herself with space around her and took the moment to look quickly at the battleground. She could see three Saxons hacking at the already dead body of a young boy. Her eyes flared blue and the three men collapsed on the ground, clutching their throats. Immediately she felt nauseous and unsteady. She had misused her magic; her life had not been in danger, she had used it purely for revenge.

A fat burly Saxon slid down a hillock with both an axe and sword in his hands. He swung the axe and Catherine tried to dodge it, but was too unsteady. "This is it," she thought. The gods are about to punish me for using my magic."

Just before the axe reached her, she heard a woman scream and she was shoved hard from behind. As she fell to the ground, a sword was thrust past her shoulder and the blade pierced the Saxon's heart. He tumbled over, the sword still sticking out of his chest, and rolled into a ditch.

Catherine looked up to see Charley, her face splattered with blood and contorted into a manic snarl. Charley reached down and pulled Catherine to her feet.

"You saved my life, Charlotte."

"This is not your time to die," she panted.

Charley retrieved her sword just as another scream echoed out. She quickly parried a sword blow that was aimed at her face. She sliced downwards which ripped the sword from the warrior's hand, and then followed through with an upwards slice that cut up under his chin and severed his jawbone from the rest of his face.

Catherine looked at her in wonderment. "How did you learn to fight?"

Charley, now drenched in blood, stood firm. "I have never used a sword in my life but you said it yourself; we are connected."

The two women charged forward, slashing and hacking. Warrior after warrior fell in their wake. Vortigern's army was giving a good account of itself and the men were driving the Saxons back into the marshland.

An arrow thudded into the ground next to Charley. She turned and saw the rest of the Saxon army had breached the causeway and were running onto the battleground. The dunes by the causeway were strewn with the bodies of the Brittonic archers and soldiers. "Catherine, they're coming."

Catherine looked behind and scanned the dunes. "Where is Vortimir, I do not see him."

"He's not dead, Catherine. He lives long after this."

"Then so must we," Catherine shouted and turned back to face the oncoming horde, ready to take as many Saxons lives as she could.

The fighting began to peter-out as the Britons looked at the oncoming hordes and realised that they were now really outnumbered. Vortigern had been pulled from his horse early in the skirmish and had been fighting on foot with Taraghlan and a handful of warriors. He was an unmistakable target for the Saxons and had been in a constant fight for his life.

Now he too saw that the end was fast approaching and that surrender was the only option. The Britons stood facing the approaching army, swords pointing downwards. Dead, dying and heat exhausted men from both sides littered the marshes.

A horn was blown and Hengist and Horsa rode through the ranks of their army until they reached Vortigern.

"Now I will kill a king," snarled Horsa and started to dismount.

Hengist grabbed at him. "There is no honour in killing a king who has surrendered." He held Horsa's contemptuous gaze and then smiled. "Besides Horsa, I cannot allow you to kill my future son-in-law."

Vortigern stood his ground, his hands, face and beard drenched in Saxon blood and he spat on the ground. "I will not marry your daughter."

"There can only be peace between us if you do."

Catherine leaned in to Charley. "Vortiger; have you seen him?"

Charley looked about, a feeling of dread flooding through her. "No, not for a while."

Hengist swept his arm around. "Your men fought well, but

surrender without a peace pact is meaningless. Without a pact, there will be nothing to stop you rising against us in the future. He nodded to one of his commanders, and two warriors appeared, dragging a semi-conscious body between them. He had six arrows bedded deep into his legs and two in his back; blood still flowed steadily from the wounds.

Catherine's eyes widened, "Vortiger?!" She ran forward but Horsa quickly pulled his horse in front to block her way. She tried to duck under its flanks but three Saxons made a grab for her. She punched the nearest under the nose with the heel of her hand, the bone in his nose was driven straight into his brain. The next man, she stabbed in the eye with Fire-Sting but they were quickly replaced by other men who helped to wrestle her to the ground.

"Catherine, the warrior priestess," laughed Horsa. "Your husband was an annoyance whilst you were our guest – Like a little shit-covered fly, buzzing around a cow."

Catherine glared up at the warlord. "That would make you the cow's arse then."

Hengist laughed. "She has your measure, brother." He dismounted and picked up Fire-Sting. Vortiger was forced to his knees and he screamed out as the arrows in his legs scraped against bone. Hengist stepped behind him, pulled his head back and held Fire-Sting to his throat. "What is it to be, Vortigern? Peace and your son's life?"

Catherine looked pleadingly at Vortigern but he couldn't look at her. "I cannot marry your daughter," he said quietly, "But please, Lord Hengist, spare my son."

If you kill my husband," snarled Catherine, her features taut and her eyes flaring blue, "I will kill you too."

Hengist smiled again, his yellow teeth dull in the bright sunlight. "Last chance Vortigern."

Vortigern's shoulders slumped. All resolve had disappeared; his only thought now was to save his son. "Very well. I will marry your daughter, Rowena."

Hengist beamed. "See, my Lord King that was not hard to do,

but I can assure you that *this* is much harder."

Before anyone could process what was happening, Hengist pulled Fire-Sting across Vortiger's throat. A wide curved slit appeared, like a second mouth, and blood gushed from it and spilled onto the marshy ground.

Catherine and Charley screamed in unison as Vortiger fell face down into the blood-soaked mud. Both ran to him and Catherine slithered to the ground and pulled him over onto her lap where she cradled his head. He was gurgling and foaming at the mouth. Blood was also foaming around the slash in his throat.

His eyes were wide with terror and he grabbed at Catherine's shoulder with a bloody hand. He mouthed, "I'm sorry," as Charley plunged a large pad of material, torn from her gown, into the slit. It made no difference and he died in Catherine's arms, as the last of his blood soaked through her clothing.

Vortigern stood paralysed and numbed and looked from Hengist to Horsa, to his dead son and back again. "What have you done?" he croaked. "I had agreed to the truce."

Hengist walked over to the king and pushed Fire-Sting under his chin. "You needed to see that. You have to believe that this truce is a gift, one that can be taken away if I so choose. If you fail to keep your word, none of your sons will be safe."

He walked back to his horse to be met by the blood-soaked Catherine. "By all my gods, Hengist, you will die for what you have done here today." Her eyes flared.

"You will not use your magic on me." He growled and raised his hand to push her away but Charley stepped in front of her priestess. "Leave her be."

Before Hengist could react, Charley had seized Fire-sting from his other hand and passed it back to Catherine. "That dagger has been cursed by the blood of Vortiger. If it should ever draw your blood, Hengist, you will die, even from the smallest cut."

Hengist looked at Charley with a mocking smile but Catherine suddenly stepped up close to him and hissed, "She is a goddess in earthly form, you piece of horse shit. You should believe what she

367

says, because I vow to avenge my husband."

Hengist hesitated and then swung himself into his saddle. He looked down at Catherine and scoffed. "You think you can beat me with a cursed dagger and magic?"

Catherine glared at him with undisguised hatred. "You know I can."

"But can you beat me without using magic?"

"I promise you, Hengist, I will beat you without magic and without mercy." She spat on the ground.

"Then meet me here tomorrow morning as the sun rises and we shall see who is the better warrior." Another horn blew and Hengist and Horsa galloped away, followed by the remains of his army, as Catherine fell to her knees by the side of her dead husband, and wept.

CHAPTER 63
Meitheamh (June) 452 AD

In stark contrast to the day before, Vortigern's camp awoke to dull, overcast skies and a light drizzle. Catherine had hardly slept. She was grieving for her slaughtered husband and she knew that today was the day Charley had warned her about. Somehow, even if she was destined to die, she had to inflict a fatal wound on Hengist before she met her gods.

"Will you use magic?" Charley asked.

Catherine stared at her clothes, bloodstained from yesterday's battle and strewn across the floor of her tent. "I cannot."

"Even to protect your own life?"

"No. I would be using it for revenge. The gods would disapprove."

"I will go with you onto the island." Charley was not asking for permission. "Taraghlan too."

Catherine shook her head. "You will not. Hengist will meet me alone. If I take you and Taraghlan with me, it would be a sign of weakness."

"But I am destined to be by your side. That is how I first saw you. I *have* to be there."

Catherine thought for a second. "Very well, you and Taraghlan may escort me to the end of the causeway, but then you must back away and leave me to face my fate."

"And you will kill Hengist at the same time?"

Catherine smiled. "I know that you are forbidden from changing your past, but there is nothing to stop *me* from changing it, so yes, if I can kill him, I will."

Vortigern entered. "Daughter, I need to speak with you alone." He glared at Charley. "Be gone." Charley was startled by his directness but just bowed slightly and left the tent to go and find Taraghlan.

Vortigern sat on the edge of Catherine's cot. "Yesterday my son, your husband, was killed. I delayed, I held back and Hengist killed him. You are not just the Avertci's Priestess, you are mine too and I need to ask for your forgiveness, both as Priestess and daughter."

Catherine reached out and touched Vortigern's battle-scarred face. "I cannot."

Vortigern was dismayed. "Please, Catherine."

She smiled gently and stroked his beard. "My Lord, I cannot, because there is nothing to forgive. Hengist would have murdered Vortiger even if you had promised to marry Rowena when first asked."

"You cannot know that."

"I do. My husband's death was preordained, the gods had already decided." She lowered her hand onto her lap. "But as Priestess, I can take away the guilt you feel. The gods do not condemn you for being human."

Relief spread across Vortigern's face. "Thank you." He took her hand in his. "I wish you would not fight Hengist. I fear you cannot win and I will have lost two people I love."

"You are right, my Lord, I cannot win, but I hope, if I die, that all the tribes of the Southlands will remember me and maybe rise up against the them in the future."

"My army will come too."

"You must not cross to the island. This is now my fight and mine alone. You must not be near."

oOo

Charley found Taraghlan feeding his horse oats from a leather bucket. His strong features looked haggard and when he saw her approaching, his chin quivered.

"Oh Taraghlan." Charley ran forward and embraced him. He

370

buried his face in her neck and they wept together.

After a moment he pulled away and rubbed his fingers across his eyes. "She will die today."

"I know," said Charley, gently, "but she says we can ride with her onto the island, but then we have to leave her to her fate."

"I held her in my arms the day she was born. Madron was so proud of her. He loved Ailla so much. I thought he might blame Catherine for her death, but he didn't. He just loved her even more because she was his only connection to her mother."

"Do you think her death might spark an uprising?"

"If Vortigern marries Hengist's bitch of a daughter, then no."

A messenger rode into the camp, sent by Hengist. Taraghlan intercepted him and the man passed his simple message, "Please tell the Lady Catherine that my Lord Hengist is waiting on the island for her."

"This is it," said Charley, "The beginning of the end."

oOo

Although the morning was beginning to warm slightly, a thick mist hung determinedly to the shorelines on both sides of the small estuary. There was a vague hint of sunlight behind the clouds, but nothing strong enough to drive the fog away.

Vortigern and his army were gathered on the western shore, looking across at the island, where more than a thousand Saxons lined their side of the river. Rank after rank of archers faced the Britons, with orders to loose-off a devastating storm of arrows, should Vortigern attempt to cross the causeway.

The tide was out and, save for a wide channel of water that meandered past the island, the river was a sea of thick, cloying mud.

Taraghlan lifted his nose and sniffed. "I hate that stench of decaying seaweed and stinking river mud."

Catherine just smiled. She was wearing a light white gown under which she wore cotton leggings. The gown was gathered tightly at the waist by a thick leather belt. Over the top of the gown she wore sleeveless leather jerkin. Blood-Taker was in its scabbard

371

and Fire-Sting was tucked in her belt. She kicked her horse and started to cross the causeway with Charley and Taraghlan riding beside her.

Hengist appeared through the mist and dismounted at the river's edge. He dropped the reigns and stood watching Catherine's progress. When she was within hailing distance, he called out.

"Your escort must return. Only you should approach."

And your army?" Catherine shouted back, "They should leave also."

Hengist laughed. "This is *my* island, lady. You can turn away too if you wish."

The trio continued to approach and Hengist turned to his bowmen. "Ten of you, loose a warning shot."

The whistle of arrows through the air is unmistakable to those who have experienced battle. They are a deadly force that can strike down dozens of men in seconds. Taraghlan and Charley had no weapons and no shields. The arrows slapped into the mud around them and Taraghlan's horse reared in fright. He wrestled to keep control.

Catherine yelled across the remaining hundred feet or so. "They are unarmed. They are no threat."

Hengist raised his sword. "They must turn back or die."

Catherine turned to her friends. "Go back. There is nothing you can do for me." Taraghlan was about to protest but Catherine cut him short. "Please."

He cursed under his breath and then added, "I pray to the gods that they let you live this day."

A split second before he was able to turn his horse back to the western bank, came the whistle of a lone arrow. It flashed past Charley's face, its flight feathers leaving a livid red graze on her cheek and it thudded into Taraghlan's chest. The force of the blow sent him tumbling backwards from his saddle and onto the muddy causeway.

Catherine shrieked and leapt from her horse. "Taraghlan, Taraghlan." She snapped the arrow and ripped open his jerkin. The point was buried deep in his heart. "Taraghlan, look at me." She pulled his head round so she could look into his eyes. They were half closed and saw nothing.

Charley dropped down beside her. "Do something, Catherine, please."

Catherine closed his dead eyes and looked at Charley's distraught face. Her own features were taut and filled with hate for Hengist. "This must end now," she hissed. "This *will* end now." She drew Blood-Taker and stood up. "Hengist!" she screamed, "I am coming for you."

She sprinted across the final few yards of causeway and onto the beach. With sword raised she charged at him. He raised his sword too and met her blow with a solid deflection, the vibrations numbed Catherine's arm and she nearly dropped Blood-Taker. Hengist saw and instantly swung his sword backhanded at her neck. Catherine tossed her sword into her left hand and successfully deflected Hengist's sword strike. The blades sang-out as they clashed.

Catherine threw Blood-Taker back into her right hand and swept it in a wide arc to take out Hengist's legs but he leapt back and sliced at her right bicep. She parried the blow but not before the tip of his sword had nicked a deep gash in her flesh.

Hengist brought down his sword vertically, aiming at the top of Catherine's skull, but she stepped into the blow, right up to his chest so that his arm crashed onto her shoulder and his sword fell to the ground behind her. He pushed her away and then noticed Fire-Sting in her left hand. She smiled and nodded at his belly. Hengist looked down to see several of the metal scales that covered his jerkin had been cut loose and that blood was leaking through from a wound beneath.

He pushed her away and she lunged at him with Blood-Taker but he managed to meet her sword with his. They lunged, they sliced, they parried, neither gaining a solid advantage. Catherine ducked away from one blow but fell over a small hillock. Hengist was on her in a flash, his sword blade across her throat. "Time to die," Hengist growled as he pressed down.

Suddenly there was someone on his back, screaming in his ear, "Get off her, you fucking bastard!"

Catherine's eyes widened. "Charlotte!"

Hengist twisted and writhed but was unable to shake Charley off, so he clambered to his feet and reached over his shoulders with both hands. He grabbed a fistful of Charley's hair and heaved her over his head. She managed to land on her feet, but before she could orientate herself, Hengist punched her in the face and she tumbled into the river mud, where she lost consciousness.

Catherine clambered to her feet, Blood-Taker in one hand and Fire-Sting in the other. Hengist charged at her and their swords and daggers clashed repeatedly until Catherine lost her footing again. This time she fell off the dune and tumbled down into the river mud. Hengist leapt down beside her and struck her with his sword. The blade did not break flesh, but the blow significantly hurt.

She stumbled to her feet just in time to see the next blow coming. Hengist had produced an axe. It must have been tucked in at the back of his belt. She hadn't noticed it before. He swung the axe at her head, but missed as she slipped in the mud. The axe passed cleanly above her as she fell over again.

She sliced at Hengist's legs for a second time trying to sever his left hamstring. She cut a gash and he screamed in pain but refused to go down. Instead he came at her like a mill in the wind; arms flailing, sword in one hand, axe in the other. Catherine scrambled to her feet again and met his sword with such force that it was wrenched from his grasp. The axe missed her and momentum took it also from his hand.

Catherine tried to take advantage of the disarmed man and swung high and wide to decapitate him, but he stooped low, charged and body-checked her to the ground. The fall knocked all the air out of her lungs and as he fell on top of her, Hengist retrieved his dagger from his belt and held it to her throat. The point hovered a hair's breadth above the artery pulsing in her neck.

She pushed up with all her might against Hengist's hand as he

374

straddled her, but the blade didn't budge. "No, no, NO!" she spat through gritted teeth as she writhed and twisted to get away from the lethal shard of steel.

He leered down at her, exposing his broken yellow teeth. "You – are – going - to – die." he panted as he pressed down, determined to end her life.

"NO!" she spat again and her eyes flared the brightest blue.

The man quickly looked away. "No magic can save you now," he grunted as he leaned on the dagger as hard as he could. Her strength was ebbing fast. She saw visions of her mother, she saw her father too and her beloved Vortiger, and then, as the man fell upon her with all his weight as her strength finally gave out.

"Yessss," he hissed as he felt the blade pierce her skin.

She felt the sting of the cold steel as it sliced deeply into her neck, and as the blade sank through her flesh, it severed a thin leather cord around her throat and her silver Celtic knot fell into the river mud which swallowed it greedily. "Hengist... no..."

A wide arc of blood spurted from a severed artery and quickly pooled across the slimy brown mud that covered them both.

He leered again, his face now inches from hers; she could taste his fetid breath. "Yes Catherine," he snarled, "yes... at last."

Her vision began to fade and she could feel her life drifting away. She had to offer a prayer to her gods before it was too late. She had to ease her passage to the afterlife.

Hengist rolled off and pulled himself onto all fours. He was panting hard; it had been quite a battle. She was a fierce fighter and there had been times when he truly feared he wouldn't survive this final encounter.

A nervous whinny came from the riverbank. Until now his horse had been standing dolefully grazing on sparse clumps of samphire. Now it pawed the ground; its head up, ears back and its eyes staring wildly as the metallic stench of freshly spilled blood assailed its nostrils.

Hengist pulled his dagger from Catherine's neck and then prised her dagger from her dead fingers. It was beautifully made with an intricately carved hilt and finely honed blade. "So this is Fire-Sting."

He climbed unsteadily to his feet and stood waveringly as he weighed the two daggers in his hands. He managed a weak smile and threw his own into the mud.

Charley struggled to her feet and ran unsteadily to Catherine and dropped to her side. "No! Please God, I can't be too late." She reached out and grasped Catherine's shoulder. "Don't die, please don't die."

She looked up to see Hengist climbing up the river bank. He looked back at the two women and grinned broadly before he turned and made his way back to his men. "You fucking bastard!" she screamed.

She pulled herself up and knelt beside Catherine; she rammed two fingers into the slit in her neck and pressed down hard. "Do not die on me."

Catherine opened her eyes. "It is my time; my gods are waiting." Her voice was just a whisper.

"No!" wailed Charley. "You cannot leave me. I will save you."

Blood spluttered from Catherine's mouth. "You cannot." She coughed and blood spurted past Charley's fingers. "You must not."

Charley knew that was true, but her instinct to save her priestess's life was too strong. Catherine however pulled Charley's fingers from her wound. "No. Let me join my gods." She was fading fast.

"Catherine..." Charley had no idea what to say. This amazingly courageous woman had become Charley's inspiration. She knew that she wanted her life to change – to mirror Catherine's ideals, generosity of spirit and calmness.

Catherine's eyes flared, but weakly. "I now know who you are," she said, her voice now barely audible.

"What? What are you trying to say?"

"I know who you are."

"Yes I know you do. I'm Charley. I'm your friend from the future, remember?"

"No. I know who you really are." She coughed and blood splattered over Charley's face. Catherine was barely conscious as the last of her blood drained from the wound in her neck."

"I don't understand," Charley cried.

"Your arm."

Charley pulled up her sleeve to reveal her crescent of eczema; the same crescent that Catherine possessed. "This?"

The faintest smile touched Catherine's lips as Charley's tears fell onto Catherine's cheek, creating clean rivulets through the blood, mud and grime on her pale skin. "I don't understand. What do you mean, you know who I am?"

Catherine mouthed something inaudible so Charley pressed her ear to the dying woman's mouth "What are you trying to say? Who am I, Catherine?"

Catherine struggled to form the words she wanted to say, but with her final breath managed the three words that would change Charley's life forever.

"You are…me!"

And with that truth finally spoken, Catherine's eyes closed and she joined Madron, Ailla, Vortiger, Taraghlan and everyone she had ever loved.

Charley buried her face in Catherine's chest and sobbed. The anguish and pain she felt was beyond her imagination. She pushed herself back on her haunches and fell heavily into the mud. Her head was spinning and the matching crescent of eczema on her arm was red raw and stinging. Her friend was gone.

She stared agonisingly at Avertci's queen and priestess lying in the blood-red mud. She didn't understand what Catherine had meant by those three words. "How can I be her?"

As Vortigern and his army galloped furiously across the causeway, Charley pulled herself to her feet, spread out her arms and leant back. She stared skywards at the grey clouds that scudded across the dull sky and, overcome with grief, she let out a long, heart-breaking cry of anguish and as she did so, her eyes flared the brightest blue.

CHAPTER 64
Two years later

Charley surveyed the audience from the small stage and felt a slight pang of sadness that this was the final stop on her universities lecture tour. The history students, who had eagerly awaited her talk, had listened in rapped fascination as she painted vivid, colourful pictures of Britons and Saxons.

In a very short space of time, Charley had become famous for her in-depth knowledge of the Dark Ages and her book, "Catherine, Queen of the Avertci" was a best-seller and required reading on most history courses.

Of course, it was impossible for her to explain the true origins of her knowledge, but as far as the public were concerned, it was down to very extensive and detailed research, combined with educated assumptions and a little dash of fiction and a wonderful flare for bringing it all to life.

Quite naturally she often thought about her adventure with Catherine; after all it had been a huge part of her life and she had been lucky that nothing untoward had happened to her when Catherine died, unlike Rosemary Forrester's grisly end. There had been no duplicate wounds, no blood gushing from severed arteries, nothing. She couldn't explain it, she was just grateful for it.

The police investigations into Forester's death had been closed, as had Richard's, even though Hallam was convinced there was more to their deaths than anyone would admit.

The whole adventure seemed like a dream, although she did have one souvenir to treasure, Catherine's silver brooch. When the police returned it to Antoinette, she slipped it to Charley. "This is rightfully yours, Mon Cher."

378

Charley shook her head. "It belongs to the nation surely."

Antoinette disagreed. Charley, after you told me Catherine's last words, I have no doubt it belongs to you...by birth right."

Charley pushed her thoughts to the back of her mind and snapped her attention back to her audience. "Any questions?" she asked.

Dozens of hands shot up. "What happened to Vortigern? Did he marry Rowena?"

"Indeed he did. The peace treaty lasted for about seven years, until she poisoned his son, Vortimir."

"I bet that pissed him off"

Laughter rippled around the auditorium and Charley laughed too. "Indeed it did. The Britons started to push back at the Saxons again and there were several battles. But in the end, the Saxons won them all.

"So what happened to Vortigern in the end?"

"No one really knows. Some say he was exiled by his own people and died of a broken heart, some say he was burnt to death."

Another hand raised. "I've never been able to find any references to the Avertci tribe and apart from your book, there's no record of Catherine. How do you know so much detail about them?"

"I'm so sorry ladies and gentlemen," said a soft French voice, "but Mrs. Collier has a book signing in Cambridge tomorrow and we need to make tracks." Antoinette Deselle had risen from her seat at the back of the stage and walked over to stand next to Charley. "You can order her book and other resource materials from her website."

Charley grinned. "Thank you Antoinette. It's getting harder to side-step questions like that. Where's Greg?"

Antoinette nodded toward the wings where Charley's new husband stood grinning. "I have a meeting with the faculty so I will see you two lovebirds in the pub later."

Charley skipped into the wings where Greg put his arm around her shoulders and guided her to the stage door. "Mrs. Collier eh? I still can't get used to that. I might call you Ms Chandler-Price instead."

Charley snuggled under his arm. "Don't you dare; I love my new name."

He patted her belly, "Talking of names, we should have that discussion soon. I'm guessing you'll want to call her Catherine?"

Charley put a hand on top of his. "Feel that? She's kicking."

Greg smiled, "Well? Is it going to be Catherine?"

Charley shook her head. "If you have no objections, sweetheart, I'd like to name her...Ailla"

Greg thought about it for a second and nodded. "After your mother? Ailla it is then."

Charley grinned broadly and her eyes flared blue once more.

THE END

HISTORICAL NOTE

Although Catherine, Vortiger and the Avertci tribe are fictitious, King Vortigern and his sons, Vortimer, Pascent, Catigern and Faustus were real. Vortigern is known to be the first king of an almost united Britain.

It is also true that he invited the displaced Saxon hordes to Britain to help rid the southern lands of the Pict's raiding parties. Whether or not the Saxon leaders were Hengist and Horsa is still a matter for debate, but in the, account of Vortigern and the Saxons, written by the historian, Bede in the 8th century, he did name them as Hengist and Horsa.

It is also fact that Vortigern gave them land in Kent but what is not completely clear is whether he also gave them Essex and Suffolk, or whether the Saxons took those lands for themselves. I chose the latter for the purposes of this novel.

Vortigern did indeed marry Hengist's daughter, Rowena which caused Vortimer to rebel against his father. It is believed that Rowena poisoned Vortimer which sent Vortigern slightly mad. From this point on, there are many conflicting accounts of what happened to the king. If all are to be believed, he must have died several times in different ways.

The Saxon Stronghold in this novel was Sturigao, now known as Sturry and is situated three miles north-east of Canterbury just off the A28 and close to what would have been the Wantsum channel between Kent and the Isle of Thanet.